No Road To Khartoum

From Dublin to the Sands of the Desert, to Fight and Die for the British Empire

By

Nigel Seed

The First Book in the Michael McGuire Trilogy

www.nigelseedauthor.com

About the Cover Image

The pistol shown in the cover image is a Mark VI Webley revolver so is not quite accurate for the time period. I apologise for that, but finding the original model proved to be too difficult. The two medals are accurate though. The Egypt medal with its blue and white ribbon was awarded to the men who took part in the Gordon Relief Expedition. The Sudan medal was awarded for service during the later reconquest of the Sudan. Both medals had bars issued to record the battles that the recipient had been involved in.

Uncommon Words

There are a number of words used in this book that are peculiar to the region and may puzzle some readers. I have listed the most relevant below to try and increase your enjoyment.

Mahdi – The Mahdi (The Expected One) was a religious leader who united the disparate tribes of the Sudan and led the revolution against Egyptian rule.

Mahdists – Followers of the Mahdi

Khalifa – The title taken by the man who succeeded the Mahdi after his death

Gharry – A horse drawn carriage. Still in use in parts of Egypt today as a taxi or excursion vehicle.

Wadi – A dry water course or deep gulley.

Zariba – A defensive fence made of thorn bushes used to surround camps or positions when an attack is likely.

Sirdar – The Sirdar was the British Officer who commanded the Egyptian army at this time.

Jibba – The robe worn by many Egyptians and Sudanese. Commonly white in colour the Mahdists sewed coloured patches onto theirs to show they were of the Mahdi's army.

This book is for Pam Fine.
Who badgered me into writing it.

This book is a work of fiction. I have placed my characters into the real events as far as I could to make my story work. There are a few places where my hero has stolen the actions of real people who fought this difficult campaign, in others he has interacted with real people. In the final chapter I have detailed the real events, places and people that actually existed so that you, the reader, can judge whether I have done them justice. If you find this campaign interesting I have also listed some useful books that you may wish to investigate. This book is intended to be the first in a trilogy that takes my hero through an interesting period of history that was the beginning of the end for the British Empire. I hope you enjoy it and the books that follow, if you do, an honest review on Amazon.com, or any other of the good book websites, would be very much appreciated.

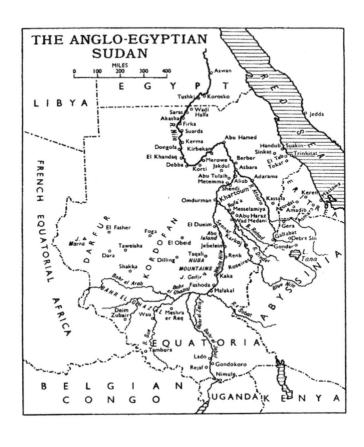

THE ANGLO-EGYPTIAN SUDAN

Chapter 1.
5th November 1883 – The Sudan

The millions of flies did not bother the dark skinned tribesman as he wandered through the mass of bodies scattered around him. The booty to be taken was far more important than mere flies and he was used to them anyway. Any of the wounded he found were despatched with a swift blade to the throat and the gush of bright blood fed yet more flies.

All around him thousands of his brothers were doing the same. Picking up swords, rifles, ammunition, food or any clothes that might be useful, no matter if they were blood stained. Even with God and the Mahdi on their side they were surprised at how complete their victory had been. Truly their enemies had been weak, except for the handful that had fought to the end, around their leader.

The corpses were mostly Egyptians who had been sent into the Sudan to quell the uprising. They had thought their Krupp guns and Nordenfelt multi barrelled machine guns would make them the lords of the battlefield. They had hugely underestimated the blind courage of the warlike tribes who had made this unforgiving land their home for thousands of years.

The man with the long greasy hair walked slowly across to where the battle had ended. He watched as the corpse of the enemy leader was beheaded and the head mounted on the broad blade of a spear. The bloody head bobbed above the crowd as it was taken away.

He turned and looked around him once more. Though he did not know it, close to eleven thousand Egyptian soldiers and their camp followers lay scattered through the thorn scrub. The vultures were circling above in a mighty flock, waiting for the tribesmen to leave, so they could begin their banquet.

That morning the force of Egyptian troops, under the command of Lieutenant General William Hicks had started to advance in three ragged defensive squares with the camp followers inside. The troops were mostly conscripts who had been dragged from their villages, some of them in chains, and forced to join the army. They were dispirited, hungry and racked by thirst. Their officers were commonly corrupt and stole their meagre wages and even their food, while treating them badly.

As they stumbled forward their rifles were slung across their backs or were dragging alongside them through the dust. At around midday they entered the *Shaykan* forest in the west of the Sudan. The stunted trees made keeping their formation even more difficult and concealed their enemies. At a signal, forty thousand warriors rose from the ground and attacked them from left, right and in front. Moments later more had wheeled in behind them and they were totally surrounded by screaming Dervishes who lived by a savage warrior code.

Their modern weapons should have allowed them to master tribesmen armed with swords, spears and even sticks, but their morale was at rock bottom. Leadership was absent and weapons had not been properly maintained or deployed. As the tribesmen executed a wild screaming charge the leading square buckled almost immediately. The men in the flanking squares were so exhausted and dehydrated they could hardly focus and fired their weapons wildly at friend and foe alike.

Dervishes died as the bullets smacked into them, but the rest never even thought of pausing. In a society where bravery and reputation counted for much more than mere wealth, the warrior creed drove them forward. Ancient blades flashed in the sunlight and swung again, now covered in fresh blood. In short order the ground was littered with torn and mangled Egyptian corpses and the battle was over.

Over confidence and disdain for the warriors of the Sudan had been the downfall of the expedition, sent by the Egyptian Colonial government. The Mahdi, a Muslim holy man who claimed to be a direct successor of the prophet, had proved his power. Many of his warriors had joined the rebellion due to ill treatment and excessive taxes levied by the government, but now, in their easy victory, they saw the power of their religion. It was to cost many more lives and untold suffering over the coming years.

Chapter 2.
5th November 1883 – Dublin Assizes

The court bailiff sat on his uncomfortable wooden chair at the bottom of the flight of stone stairs that led up to the back of the dock in the courtroom above. The magistrates had decided to take a break before dealing with the last case of the day. So he had to sit and wait with the final prisoner.

He looked across the corridor at the young man who sat on the bench across from him, with his head down and his elbows resting on his knees. The boy's hair was thick and dark and although he was thin from lack of food, like so many in Ireland in these days, he seemed well made. The boy looked up and the bailiff looked into his clear blue eyes.

"What do you think they'll give me?" The younger man asked.

"Depends what you did and if they have had a good day."

"I stole a loaf of bread for my mother and sister. They hadn't eaten for days."

The bailiff shook his balding head sadly. "Not good. There's a lot of those about and the magistrates don't like to be reminded of what the people are suffering."

"So what will a stale loaf get me?"

The bailiff leaned back in his chair and sighed. "With this magistrate you might get a choice. Stand up straight, look him in the eye and don't lie. Admit what you did and tell him why. Then you might get the choice."

The voice down the stair case echoed in the waiting area as they were called up. The bailiff stood and motioned for the younger man to join him at the bottom of the stairs. As he paused and looked up towards the dock the bailiff rested a hand on his shoulder.

"Remember what I said. It might help. Now, up you go."

The bailiff put the dark blue, pill box cap on his head and the two men climbed the stairs until they stepped into the dock. The younger man moved to the front of the box and took hold of the short, metal spikes sticking up in front of him. The magistrate behind the high imposing bench looked down at him sternly as the clerk of the court shuffled his papers and cleared his throat.

"Michael McGuire you are charged with theft in that you stole foodstuff, to whit a loaf of bread, from Coogan's bakery. How do you plead? Guilty or Not Guilty?"

McGuire swallowed and straightened his back. He looked across the courtroom into the angry eyes of the magistrate. His hands dropped to his sides as he spoke.

"It's true that I stole the bread sir. My widowed mother and my sister were starving. I had to do something."

The magistrate sniffed in irritation. "This court does not care why you stole, just that you did. I shall accept that as a plea of guilty as charged." He turned to the clerk. "Is anything further known?"

"No your Honour. The defendant has never been before the courts before."

"So," the magistrate said, returning his eyes to McGuire. "Does that mean you have never stolen before or just never been caught?"

McGuire held his gaze. "I have never stolen anything before, sir. I was desperate. We have fallen on hard times since my father died."

"Who was your father?"

"Sir, he was the Estate Manager for Lord Kilcraighie. When he died his Lordship had us thrown out of the house to make room for the new manager."

"That seems a little harsh, even for Kilcraighie."

McGuire looked down at his feet remembering the incident then looked back at the magistrate. "That may have been my fault if it please your Honour. I had an argument with him and lost my temper. I may have said some things I should not have."

"So you have a problem controlling your temper do you?"

"I do sir. Tis a weakness of mine."

"You sound more educated than most of the thieves who come before me."

McGuire swallowed. "His Lordship's son was too sickly to be sent away to school so he was educated at home and I took classes with him. Well, I did until he died."

For long seconds the magistrate stared across the courtroom. "For some reason I believe you. Now, do you have any infirmities?"

"Infirmities?"

"Is there anything wrong with you physically?"

"No sir, I am healthy, but just a little hungry."

The magistrate nodded. "I shall give you the choice of making something worthwhile of yourself then and it might help you control your aggression. You may have the choice of going to prison or of enlisting in the Army. What do you say?"

McGuire's mouth dropped open and then snapped shut. He felt his mind racing. In prison he could do nothing for his mother or his sister. They would be left to starve or to go to the workhouse. In the army he might be able to give them some of the small pay that a soldier received. He had no choice.

"I'll take the army if it please you sir:"

"Very well. Bailiff, take him to the barracks and stay with him to see that he enlists. Once the papers are signed your duty is done for the day. McGuire, listen to me, this is more an opportunity to better yourself than a punishment, see that you make your country proud. Take him down."

The bailiff took McGuire by the elbow and steered him around to the stairs behind him. The young man felt he was in a dream as he stumbled back down. He slumped to the wooden bench he had left so recently and looked up at the bailiff.

"What have I done?"

The bailiff smiled down at him. "The right thing, boy. The army will feed you and clothe you as well as giving you a bed to sleep in. It's not a bad life once you get used to it and it's a damn sight better than rotting in a stinking prison cell.

Come on, we've a way to walk yet and I foresee a glass or two of porter in my future, once I have delivered you."

Chapter 3.
Dublin Castle

McGuire and the court bailiff made their way up the cobbled street towards the imposing Dublin Castle. McGuire's thoughts were in a turmoil as he contemplated what he had just agreed to. They came alongside a tavern and the bailiff tapped his arm.

"Your last drink as a civilian. Well for the next six years at least."

"I've no money. That's why I'm here in the first place."

"Never mind son, I'll buy you a glass of porter to see you on your way."

They walked into the dim bar room and stood at the main bar. The barman saw them and hurried along to serve them.

"Good afternoon Bailiff. Delivering another of Victoria's hard bargains are you?"

The bailiff shook his head. "You know better than that. This young man is desirous of serving his Queen and Country and I have the honour of escorting him to the castle for enlistment."

The barman smiled knowingly. "So that will be the usual two porters will it?"

"It will. My young friend here is thirsty after his long day."

"He'll be a damn sight thirstier tomorrow by this time. The new recruit draft starts training in the morning. The last of them arrived about an hour ago."

McGuire said nothing, but lifted the glass to his lips and sipped. It tasted good after sitting in the dusty waiting area, below the court, for hours. He watched as the bailiff drank his glass in one and slapped it back on the bar with a loud appreciative sigh.

"My friend here is a little slow so I'd better have another while I'm waiting."

That too disappeared, as did the third, by the time McGuire had finished his drink. He put the glass carefully down on the bar and turned to look at the now florid faced bailiff. The older man sighed and tossed a few small coins onto the wooden board next to their glasses.

"Come on then, my young friend, let's away to your new life."

They left the tavern and continued up the steep cobbled street with the ancient castle looming larger with every step. The guards either side of the gate in their scarlet tunics grinned slightly as they approached and then the one to the right called back into the castle. As they reached the gate a tall soldier with broad shoulders and the two white arm stripes of a corporal was waiting for them,

"Well then Bailiff, you brought me another hero desperate to serve his Queen have you?"

"Sure and I think he'll make you a fine soldier given a little seasoning."

Ignoring McGuire, the Corporal turned away saying. "Bring him into the guardroom and we'll have him sign the papers there."

He strode away with the swagger stick under his arm and the two men followed him. As he

17

passed the guards McGuire heard one whisper to him.

"By this time next week you'll wish you'd chosen prison."

The Corporal turned around, once he reached the guardroom. "Right you, in here and wait until we get the recruiting sergeant and the surgeon down here, I've sent runners to get them. We need to get you signed in now. The recruit training platoon starts in the morning and you wouldn't want to miss the fun."

The old bailiff held out his hand to McGuire. "Listen boy. The next twelve weeks will be hard, but I promise you it will be worth it. And the guard on the gate is wrong, this is better than prison for you. The Magistrate was right, this is a chance for you to better yourself. Grab that chance with both hands."

McGuire watched as the older man in the dark blue uniform with his pillbox cap walked back down the slope and turned into the tavern they had left only minutes ago. He looked around the other way and saw two men striding towards him alongside the drill square from different directions. Neither looked pleased at being disturbed.

The Corporal slammed to attention and saluted as the first man entered. "Sorry to disturb you sir, but this man has volunteered to join the regiment from the magistrate's court."

The florid faced man looked McGuire up and down. "Right you, get your jacket and shirt off.

We'll do the examination here. No point wasting time."

McGuire did as he had been told and was pulling his ragged shirt over his head as the second man appeared. This one was in a soldier's scarlet tunic, with three gold stripes on his arm. His moustache was large and covered half his face. He too saluted the man that McGuire assumed was the surgeon.

"Right stand up straight let's have a look at you." The surgeon looked him over and tapped his chest. "Turn round." This time he tapped his back between the shoulder blades. "Now drop your trousers and bend over. Don't mess around, I'm late for my dinner."

McGuire bent over as the surgeon peered at him. "Fine he's healthy enough. You can sign the papers Sergeant, but get him a bath first thing, he smells like a midden."

"Thank you sir. I'll bring the form for you to sign in the morning if I may?"

"You may. Don't forget that bath and burn these clothes. I don't want an outbreak of lice in the barracks."

The Sergeant slammed up a salute as the officer left the guardroom, then turned to McGuire. He slid a piece of paper out of a folder and placed it on the guardroom table. Then he borrowed a pen and an ink well from the corporal's desk.

"Right you, sign your name here, make your mark it's all the same to me."

McGuire spoke for the first time since he had come through the tall iron gates. "I'll sign. I can read and write."

"I don't give a tinker's curse, it's not important until you reach the rank of Sergeant and that won't be for a good few years." The Sergeant picked up the paper and blew on it to dry the ink. "Right Corporal detail one of your men to take our new recruit to the bath house, get him scrubbed and burn those rags, like the surgeon said."

"What do I wear then?" McGuire asked.

The large moustache turned slowly towards him. "See these stripes on my arm boy? That means I am a Sergeant and that means you speak to me when spoken to and you call me Sergeant. That's the last time you get told that without punishment. You'll pick up your basic drill uniform on the way to the bath house. Now get outside and wait."

A minute later a young soldier with no stripes on his arm trotted down the steps of the guardroom and walked across to McGuire. "Now then mate, let's get you cleaned up and find you a bed. If we're quick you should be in time to get you something to eat as well. This way."

The soldier set off along the side of the barrack square talking as he went. "That's the barrack square we're walking past. Never ever walk on it unless you are doing drill or a parade. Trust me, never take a short cut across it. That's the headquarters building, you probably won't go in there for a long time, it's for officers and clerks.

Now this is the quartermaster's store, we go in here."

McGuire said nothing, but followed the soldier inside. He came to attention before the counter and spoke to the Sergeant on the other side.

"New recruit Sergeant, just arrived. Sergeant Hillier asked if you could issue him his basic kit so he can join the recruit platoon that starts tomorrow."

The Sergeant looked McGuire up and down. "Another sorry wretch for the regiment to turn into something useful eh? Right then, get your arse over here."

McGuire moved forward and followed the stores sergeant along the counter as an array of clothing and equipment was dumped into his arms. The last item was a pair of heavy boots that were dropped on to the top of the pile. Then a block of brown soap was dropped into one of the boots.

"Now then Miller, get him away and get him scrubbed up before he gets any lice in Her Majesty's uniform."

McGuire followed Miller back out of the building balancing the pile of equipment in his arms. They walked around to the rear of a barrack block and went inside.

"Put your stuff down there and take the soap." Miller said. "Make sure you never leave your uniform or equipment where you can't see it or some thieving bastard will have it away. Now strip and throw your clothes in that box over there. They'll get burned later."

McGuire stripped as he was ordered and took his clothes across to the big hamper against the wall. As he lifted the lid the smell of old and dirty clothes rose up and he dumped his clothes in and slammed the lid back down.

Miller was standing by a bath. There was a steam coming from the water and McGuire climbed in as Miller pointed. He lowered himself down into the water for the first hot bath of his life. The metal tub in front of the small peat fire had been his only way to clean himself before now. The warmth seeped into his bones and he felt sleepy until the block of carbolic soap landed on his chest.

He looked up to see Miller grinning down at him. "There you go, now scrub yourself all over, including your hair. Then we'll see about a bed and food for you. It won't be much, the main meal is in the middle of the day."

"It'll be better than the sunlight I've been eating."

McGuire started to rub the soap across himself, amazed at the change in his own skin colour as the filth of years of poverty floated off him.

Chapter 4.
Training

McGuire stood on the road outside the barracks in the chilly morning with the rest of the recruit platoon. Twenty four shivering and nervous young men stood in the drizzling rain wondering what was to happen to them next. They had been dragged from their straw stuffed mattresses before dawn, by two screaming corporals who seemed to be angry with them already. As they stood, a large man with a narrow waist and broad shoulders strutted along the road towards them. He came to a halt in a crash of studded boots and turned towards them. He looked slowly along the lines of men and boys.

"I do not believe I have ever seen such a sorry apology for recruits in my entire life!" He screamed at them. "But the Colonel and Her Majesty want me to turn you into soldiers and that is what I am going to do. My name is Sergeant Senior and I am your training sergeant. I will be assisted by two corporals that you have already met. They are Corporal Selwood and Corporal Love. Your training platoon officer is 2nd Lieutenant Storr-Lessing, but you won't be seeing much of him. He has other more important things to do than talk to wretches like you. You will obey every order given to you by any of us and you will address us by our rank. Training will last for twelve weeks and you will find there are just two ways to do things, the Army way and the wrong way. You will learn the Army way and the quicker you do that the easier your life will be."

Senior walked slowly to the right hand end of the front row of men. He looked the first man up and down, snorted and moved along the line looking at each of them in turn. Once he had returned to the front of the platoon he looked to his right and called to one of the Corporals.

"Corporal Selwood front and centre!"

The taller of the two corporals marched smartly to the front of the platoon slammed to a halt and then spun to face them with much crashing of boots. Sergeant Senior walked slowly alongside the man standing rigid before them.

"Some of you may believe you know how to stand and how to walk. You are wrong and I will now teach you how to stand. Observe the corporal here. He is standing at attention. The purpose of teaching this drill movement is so that a single soldier or body of men may stand at attention in smart soldier like and uniform manner. Observe the head is up with the eyes to the front. The heels are together with the toes of the boots four inches apart. The arms are straight down by the sides with the thumb in line with the seam of the trousers. All of you adopt this position now!"

It took considerable pushing, pulling and screaming before the corporals were satisfied that the platoon was acceptable. The Sergeant waited and then told them he was going to teach them to turn.

"Corporal Love, front and centre. Next I am going to teach you the right turn. The purpose of teaching this drill movement is so that a single soldier or body of men can turn to the right in a smart soldier like and uniform manner. Watch the corporal demonstrate."

And so it went on. Every drill movement they were taught was preceded by the same mantra and followed by loud screaming and repetition until they got it right. Once they were able to form up as a platoon and march in step, turning right and left when ordered, the route marches began. Five miles, then ten miles, then further. Once they were proficient at that they started over with packs and webbing, each time carrying heavier weights. Then with a full pack and a rifle. They turned out for physical training, known as 'bars and rings', to develop upper body strength. They were taught to care for their uniforms and to pipe clay their web equipment. Brasses gleamed and boots shone until they were finally fit to be issued their scarlet tunics and blue trousers. To his own surprise McGuire found that, despite the constant verbal abuse and tiredness, the order and discipline suited him and he was actually enjoying himself.

They were taught field craft. How to live during war and how to set up tents and equipment. How to move across country without scattering. They were taught patrolling and always the damned route marches.

They pounded into the castle at the end of a long march, with the sweat running down their backs and into their eyes. McGuire looked at the Sergeant who had shouted and screamed at them the whole way. His face was slightly red, but he was not panting and sweating like the recruits. He wondered how long it took before a man became so used to such toil.

As they reached their own barracks they were halted on the road outside and turned to face the parade square. Before the Sergeant could speak Corporal Selwood slammed to attention behind the training platoon.

"Officer approaching, Sergeant."

As the Sergeant turned smartly to the left McGuire risked a glance along the road. A young officer was riding slowly towards them on a large black horse. He reined in and sat looking down at them. Sergeant Senior marched across and came to attention if front of the horse. He saluted crisply.

The officer looked languidly down at him and then at the platoon. "Have someone hold my horse. I shall inspect the men."

Senior turned and paused before selecting a man. "McGuire here, now! Double time!"

McGuire turned from the ranks and trotted across to take the reins of the horse as the officer dismounted. Ignoring him, the young man in the immaculate dress uniform walked slowly to the front of the platoon. He walked slowly along the ranks, one after the other with Sergeant Senior two paces behind him.

At the end of the rear rank he turned and looked the Sergeant up and down. "Well Senior, these men are in an appalling state. You should be ashamed to let them be seen like this. In fact I am not impressed with the turnout I see in you and your junior NCOs either."

McGuire saw the Sergeant flush. "With respect sir, these men are just completing a fifteen mile forced march."

"That's no excuse. I expect my men to be smart at all times. Do something about it and smarten yourself up as well."

The officer spun on his heel and walked across to where McGuire still stood holding the horse. The officer flicked his riding crop across McGuire's chest.

"Out of my way you apology for a soldier."

Before he could stop himself McGuire's hands balled into fists and he stepped forward. The officer flicked his crop across his face and called back to Sergeant Senior.

"Sergeant. This man has committed dumb insolence. Give him punishment drill now."

"Yes sir! McGuire, rifle above your head and double time around the square. Move!"

Holding down his boiling temper, McGuire raised the heavy rifle above his head and started to run around the square. As he ran he saw the officer mount his horse and ride away smiling.

After five circuits of the square McGuire felt that his arms were on fire. His vision was blurring and he could feel his legs about to fail him. Sergeant Senior and Corporal Selwood were waiting for him as he reached the front of the barracks again.

"Alright son, that's far enough. Corporal, take him into the barracks and get him squared away."

McGuire was on the verge of crying with relief as he staggered alongside the tall Corporal. "Who was that officer Corporal?"

Selwood gave a small smile that had no warmth in it. "That was our training platoon officer, Lieutenant Storr-Lessing."

"Does he do that often?"

"No son he's mostly too bloody important to talk to the likes of us. Now get your kit put away and get ready to go for dinner. I guess you might need it."

Chapter 5
The Rifle Range

Then came a week of musketry training. Without knowing quite why, McGuire found that he could hit the targets with ease, time after time, while others were struggling.

As they lay at the side of a rifle range, taking a well-earned break, the Colonel of the regiment, Lieutenant Colonel Simon Latham, rode up on a beautiful bay horse. His uniform was immaculate and his moustache impressive. Sergeant Senior called them to attention and spun to salute their commanding officer.

The Colonel looked them over before he spoke to the Sergeant. "Is Lieutenant Storr-Lessing with you Sergeant Senior?"

"No sir I think he must be busy with other things today."

"I see. Well Sergeant and how is your latest platoon progressing?"

"Coming together nicely thank you sir."

"Any that stand out yet?"

"Not really sir, although McGuire is turning out to be a good shot with the rifle."

"Really? Do you think he can beat me?"

"I doubt it sir, but he can have a go if you have the time."

"Which one's McGuire?"

He sat his horse and contemplated the young man the Sergeant pointed out. Slightly above average height, dark hair and blue eyes, skin darkened from the hours of marching in all weathers that recruits undertook. The boy looked back at him steadily and didn't drop his eyes, that was a good sign.

The Colonel smiled and dismounted, his shiny high boots kicking up the dust as he turned around. "Very well let's see what McGuire can do. Bring me a rifle and twenty rounds Sergeant."

The Colonel strode to the firing point and waited. "McGuire! Draw twenty rounds and double to the firing point. Private Drabble you draw twenty rounds as well and take them and your rifle to the Colonel. Move!"

McGuire ran to the firing point and stood to attention as the Colonel looked him up and down. "So McGuire is it? Fifteen rounds we have at two hundred yards. Five standing, five kneeling, then five lying. The last five rounds at three hundred yards, also lying. Understand?"

"Yes sir, if it please your honour."

"So what has made you a good shot McGuire?"

"Sir, if it please you, the Sergeant is a fine teacher and my father had a small rifle that he let me use to hunt rabbits and birds before I joined.

The Colonel nodded. "Right Sergeant let's have a couple of your men out there to set up the targets."

Sergeant Senior detailed four men to run forward and set up the targets then run back out of harm's way.

The Colonel turned around and looked over his shoulder at the Sergeant. "Right then Sergeant, it's your firing point."

"Very well sir. From the standing position, at your target in front, at two hundred yards, five rounds, in your own time, carry on."

The two men fired their Martini Henry rifles at the target before them. McGuire finished first by a couple of seconds. "Take up the kneeling position and once again at your target in front, five rounds, in your own time, carry on."

This time the Colonel finished first and grinned across at McGuire. Next they took up the prone position and fired their five rounds. The Colonel seemed not to care about his immaculate uniform being soiled, but then he would not be the one to clean it.

Sergeant Senior cleared his throat. "At three hundred yards, at your target in front, five rounds, in your own time, carry on."

McGuire squinted through the sights and tried to ignore the chatter from his platoon who were now spread out behind him. He controlled his breathing and squeezed off the first round as he had been taught. He pulled down the lever below the rifle and the spent casing ejected. He inserted the next round and pushed it fully forward before raising the lever to close the breech. He took aim and fired again until he had expended his last five rounds.

"Weapons down and stand up!"

The Colonel and McGuire lay their rifles down and stood up on the command of the Sergeant. "Walk forward to your targets."

They walked forward in silence to examine the targets and Senior counted the hits. "Twenty

hits for the Colonel. Good shooting, sir, as usual."
He walked across and examined McGuire's targets.
"Also twenty hits."

The Colonel smiled at McGuire. "Well done man. Now I think we need to decide this contest eh? Sergeant, set up two targets at six hundred yards. McGuire and I will wait for you at the firing point."

Sargent Senior waved two men forward who double timed out to the six hundred yard point with the two targets. Once they were in place he strode back and stood alongside the Colonel.

"Ten rounds prone I think, don't you Sergeant?"

"Certainly sir, though McGuire hasn't fired at that range before."

There was a pause as the ammunition was brought forward, then Senior started his orders again. "At six hundred yards, at your target in front, from the prone position, ten rounds, in your own time, carry on."

McGuire made himself comfortable, moving pebbles away from under his elbow so he could concentrate. He pulled the butt of the heavy rifle tightly into his shoulder and paused to look around him. He watched the way the grass bent over in the breeze from his left and then looked at the nearby tree tops. The Colonel took his first shot and McGuire watched the thick white smoke drift away. Then he dropped his eye to the back sight and aimed at the distant target. He made allowances for the breeze and gently squeezed the trigger. The rifle pounded back into his shoulder as the .477 round flew down the range. He reloaded then waited, until his own smoke cleared and he could see the target clearly again, before firing. Once both men had finished they walked forward with the Sergeant to examine the results and count their scores.

"Colonel, eight hits, damned fine shooting at this range sir." Sergeant Senior said, then walked across to McGuire's target. "Well I'm damned. Ten hits out of ten."

"Have my horse brought forward Sergeant."

Once the horse had been trotted forward the Colonel mounted. He looked down at the two men standing there.

"Congratulations Sergeant Senior, that man is a credit to your training. Well done. McGuire, I think I will have to keep an eye on you, how old are you?"

"Seventeen, sir."

"Very good. Sergeant, grade him marksman."

With that he pulled his horses head round and touched him with his spurs. As he cantered away Sergeant Senior turned to McGuire.

"You've done me a good turn there boy. I won't forget it. Now, as we get back to barracks go and get your marksman's badge from the Quartermaster and sew it onto your tunic. That's a rare honour for a recruit."

McGuire came to attention. "Thank you Sergeant."

"And I'll do you a good deed in return. The Sergeant Major is looking for two men to be trained to use the heliograph signalling equipment. I'm putting you and Tom Drabble forward for it."

The training to use the signalling equipment did not excuse the two men the dreaded route marches in fact it made them worse. Tom carried the tripod of the heliograph across the top of his pack while McGuire had the signalling head strapped to his.

As they laboured up yet another hill, Drabble glanced across at his friend. "Does it ever stop raining in this bloody country?"

"Ah Thomas tis a fine soft day right enough. If it wasn't for the rain how do you think we'd have all this good grass and the fine butter from the cows?"

Sergeant Senior yelled from behind them. "Right you two, talking in the ranks! If you've breath enough for that you have breath enough to run. Double time ahead of the column to the top of the hill. Move!"

The two friends ran panting past the rest of the platoon with the awkward heliograph equipment pounding on their backs. They laboured up to the top and waited for the rest of the men to reach them.

Tom looked around as he tried to catch his breath. "And another thing, how come everywhere in this island is bloody uphill?"

Chapter 6.
September 1884 - Dublin Castle Officers' Mess

Colonel Latham strode into the ante room of the Officers' Mess, to find all of his officers waiting for him. They stood as he entered and he waved them back into their brown leather chairs. He walked across to the wide stone fireplace and stood with his back to it. The large portrait of Queen Victoria looked out over his head. He knew he was being a little theatrical, but he was enjoying the moment.

"Gentlemen, thank you for joining me this morning. I have a rather interesting announcement to make, as you have probably guessed." He looked around the room, to wait for the usual witty comments, but there were none. "You will all be aware that General Gordon was sent down to Khartoum to evacuate the civilians before the Dervish army gets there and kills them all. And you will also be aware that has not gone well. No doubt you will have been following the fuss in the newspapers about General Gordon being stranded down in Khartoum. There have been noisy public demonstrations across the country, demanding that he be rescued from the Dervish horde and, as of last night, the government has given way. Mr Gladstone, our beloved Prime Minister, has finally agreed to send a rescue force to extract Gordon from Khartoum and to evacuate all the remaining Egyptians and Europeans before the Mahdi can attack the city and slaughter them."

He paused as one of the mess servants brought him the coffee he had ordered on the way in. He took a sip and looked around at the assembled group. He had expected more of a reaction, but they were waiting expectantly, in silence.

"I think you would agree that is good news. The Gordon Relief Expedition, as it is to be known, is to be commanded by Garnet Wolseley and he has developed a rather interesting idea. Instead of detailing whole battalions to go he wants each, of a number of nominated units, to select their best men who will be formed into a Camel Corps to fight in the desert."

That caused a stir among the assembled officers as they each realised that here was a chance for fame and advancement. Latham smiled to himself as he sipped his coffee again.

"Gentlemen, quiet down if you please. I am sure you all wish to volunteer for this important and high profile task, but, in order to avoid any bad feeling amongst you, I will make the selection of who is to go. Those of you who are not selected should not feel slighted in any way. The number we can take is very small and it has been a difficult choice, since you are all fully capable of undertaking this arduous adventure."

He paused and allowed the muttering from the group to die down before he continued. His eyes ran across the men before him as he considered the choice he had made as soon as the instructions reached him.

"Very well. If I may be allowed to continue? I will command the detachment; Captain Carter will be the adjutant for the Guards' Camel Regiment of which we will be part. Lieutenant Colonel Bone will be the Chief Signalling Officer for the regiment and I shall take two junior Lieutenants with me, The Lieutenants will be Mr Storr-Lessing and Mr Evans. I will brook no arguments about my decision so please do not waste your breath pleading with me."

Latham carefully placed the bone china cup and saucer on the wide stone mantelpiece behind him and then turned back to watch his officers absorb the news. The ones he had selected wore broad smiles while the rest looked downcast. Storr-Lessing stood to one side, he was not smiling, that seemed strange. No doubt he would cheer up shortly when he realised what an opportunity this was for a young officer.

He cleared his throat to get their attention. "Now Gentlemen, we have other decisions to make. I need to select thirty eight soldiers and five NCOs to make up the rest of our detachment. I would like your suggestions on my desk by three o'clock this afternoon. The requirements I have been given are as follows. They must all be marksmen or at least first class shots and at least twenty two years of age. They must all be robust and medically fit and should all be of good character. Do not hold back your best men, we will be under the eye of the whole nation, including Her Majesty, so select me our finest. I suggest you do this now, so off you go gentlemen."

Colonel Latham watched as his officers left, until there was just him and Lieutenant Storr-Lessing in the room. "What is it Stephen? You don't seem overjoyed to have been chosen."

"Ah, no sir. I appreciate the honour you have done me, but I wonder if one of the other Lieutenants might be more suitable."

"Stephen I don't think you understand. This is an important task and will look good on the record of any officer taking part. Your father did me a great service during the Crimean War and this goes a small way to paying my debt to him. If you are ever to reach the dizzy heights in rank, as he has done, you need to be in action, not just mounting guard on Dublin Castle."

The younger man shuffled his feet and looked down, then looked up again. "Sir I would be most grateful if you could see your way clear to removing my name from the list."

"That would be seen as a slur on your character. I cannot do that to you. Your father would never forgive me."

"Then sir, I may have to resign my commission or exchange into another regiment."

Colonel Latham sighed; he had been worried about this officer for some time now, but had thought this expedition could be the making of him. He shook his head slowly.

"No Stephen I can't allow either of those things. You are now officially under orders to deploy overseas on active service. If you were to 'dodge the column' like that, it could be seen as cowardice, and no officer in my regiment is going

to drag our good name through the dirt. You are
going to the Sudan with me and that, sir, is final."

Chapter 7.
September to 7th October 1884

The four officers he had selected to go stood in a row behind Colonel Latham as he faced the battalion, drawn up by companies on the barrack square. Those officers not selected stood behind their men.

"Men we have been honoured by being selected as one of the battalions that will provide soldiers for the Relief Force that is going to Khartoum, in the Sudan, to rescue General Gordon. Your officers have recommended the most suitable men for this undertaking and those chosen have every reason to be proud of themselves. Listen for your names and, as you are called, fall out and form up to the right of the parade."

He began to read the names, starting with the five NCOs who executed a sharp right turn and marched across to the end of the parade. Then he read out the thirty eight names of the soldiers who would be going. McGuire was startled to hear his own name called and hesitated, not believing his ears.

His platoon sergeant spun round. "McGuire I know you're here! Move your idle arse!"

McGuire swallowed, executed a right turn and marched across the square. The last man to join the group, that would soon be riding camels across a desert. He listened as the Colonel praised the rest of the men and then waited as the parade was dismissed, and Colonel Latham and the other four officers walked across to them.

"Now then men. As I told the rest of the battalion this is a great honour for the regiment and for you in particular. We have to make ready to leave at short notice. Special uniforms, suitable for the desert, will be issued first thing in the morning, provided they arrive on time, and we will leave for England as soon after that as possible. Now get your affairs in order since we will be gone for a long time I think."

With that the Colonel handed over the small company to Sergeant Major Lewis who was to go with them. The officers marched away, back to their mess to make their plans and Lewis turned back to the selected men.

"Now men, all of you have been chosen because you are strong, fit and excellent shots. You are all over twenty two years of age. Did you hear me McGuire and Drabble? If anybody asks, you are twenty two. Got it? Now any problems come to me and we'll see what we can do."

The group was marched off the barrack square and dismissed. McGuire marched straight up to Sergeant Major Lewis and came to attention before him.

"What is it McGuire?"

"Sergeant Major, it's my mother and sister."

"What about them?"

"Every payday I take whatever I am paid and give it to them. It's all they have to live on. What will they do when I am away in the Sudan?"

Lewis looked at the young soldier before him. "So that's why you never go out drinking is it? I was beginning to worry that you were a bloody Methodist. Go and see the Regimental Agent, he will have an arrangement with another agent with us on the march. You give your pay to that one and the agent here gives the same amount to your mother, less a commission of course."

"Can that really work?"

"The married men will be doing the same. It's not difficult. Just know that if you die the money stops and they need to put a bit by, in case of that."

McGuire smiled. "Thank you Sergeant Major. I'll do that now."

"And another thing. You make sure the agent knows that you intend to come back and see him if there's any funny stuff."

McGuire was puzzled. "Funny stuff?"

"Any short payments or trying to get your mother and sister to do things they don't want to. Get my meaning?"

"I do Sergeant Major, thank you. Can I ask another question?"

"Go ahead."

"What the hell is a camel?"

McGuire marched straight to the Agent's office at the back of the Headquarters building. He knocked and walked in to find a fat civilian in a grey suit sitting behind a wide wooden desk. The man looked him up and down then leaned back in his chair.

"I take it you are one of the draft going to get 'Chinese' Gordon back?"

"Yes sir and the Sergeant Major says I need to talk to you about getting my pay given to my family while I am away."

"You're quick off the mark. You're the first one to come and see me. Right then we need to fill out the agreement and it can start right now."

"The Sergeant Major tells me I should also tell you that I am coming back. If there's any funny stuff with my mother or my sister, we'll be having words."

The fat man leaned forward. "You're right to tell me that, but I'm not that kind of man. They'll be treated fair I promise you. Now, one other thing. I don't know what it's like in the Sudan, but if you come across any booty you can give it to the agent in country and collect the price of it here when you get back."

"Booty? What do you mean?"

"A lot of these natives carry their wealth with them. If you was to come into possession of some of it, after a battle say, then you could do yourself some good."

The new uniforms arrived later than expected and were issued three days later. Leather bandoliers for fifty rounds of ammunition, yellow-ochre breeches and long dark blue puttees to wind around the lower leg. A grey and a red tunic jacket were also issued along with a white pith helmet to protect them from the desert sun. There was also a range of equipment to carry that may or may not be useful in the desert as well as the normal rifle and sword bayonet.

The new uniforms caused quite a lot of merriment for the troops who were not to go, but they were more comfortable for campaign use than the uniforms suitable for Dublin Castle.

As usual with most urgent tasks in the army, they rushed around and got everything ready and then waited for four days with nothing to do, before the ship arrived that was to carry them from Dublin to Holyhead on Anglesey Island. A special train carriage had been added to the train that was waiting for them and the men and equipment were loaded into it. Naturally the officers travelled in the first class coach.

As the train arrived in Portsmouth Harbour station they could see the P&O liner, Deccan, moored close by. The railway company provided carts and their baggage and equipment were trundled across to the ship before being loaded aboard. Most of the rest of what was to be the Camel Corps were already aboard. The last detachment, from the 18th Hussars, arrived as McGuire made it out onto the deck of the ship. Within the hour they cast off from the quay and were on the way to Egypt.

To start with, the troops treated the whole trip as a spree, but once discipline was re-imposed they settled down. The seasickness was a problem for the first three days, but that too settled down as well. McGuire was pleased to find that he did not suffer from the affliction and could enjoy a shorter wait in the ship's mess, at least until the rest of the men got their sea legs.

The government had decided that each man should be given sixty rounds of rifle ammunition to practice with on the journey and naturally the officers decided to make a game of it. After each man had been given a chance to fire at various items floating in the ship's wake, the detachments were allowed to select their champion to represent them. The officers made themselves comfortable on an upper deck, with champagne on ice, and made bets on their favourites.

McGuire found that he had been chosen to shoot on behalf of the 1st Grenadier Guards. He hung back to watch how the more experienced soldiers handled the task and watched the movement of the ship and the targets bobbing in the wake. When his turn came he stepped up to the rail and lifted the nine pound Martini Henry rifle to his shoulder. He took his time and waited until the ship was on the top of a roll and the target was raised on a wave before firing. That way he hit everything he aimed at.

He and two other men were judged to be the best on the ship and Colonel Latham decided they should decide the winner by shooting at beer bottles with a cork in the neck to ensure they floated. The three bottles were to be thrown over, one after the other, with each man having five rounds to hit the receding target. The first shooter started firing as soon as the bottle bobbed to the surface. He took all five rounds, but hit his mark to the loud cheers of the troops clustering at the rails of the upper decks. The second shooter stepped up to the rail and nodded for the bottle to be dropped in. He too started to fire as soon as the target reappeared. He fired rapidly, but the bottle sailed away unharmed.

McGuire stepped to the rail, he felt the movement of the ship and looked down at the waves for a moment before he nodded. He raised the rifle to the firing position and waited for his moment. The raucous cheering faded away as he stood there swaying with the motion of the ship. There was silence now, as the bottle moved away behind them. He squeezed the trigger and the bottle shattered and vanished in a cloud of spray. The silence continued for a long moment and then the men of the 1st Grenadiers started to yell for their man when they realised what he had done.

The Colonel of the Light Camel Regiment walked across to stand beside McGuire. "Young man if I ever need my life saving I hope you are standing by my side. That was a remarkable shot. You've done your battalion proud."

He handed across the bottle of whiskey that had been put up as the prize for the best shot and patted McGuire on the shoulder. The men on the upper decks were still yelling as the other two finalists came and shook his hand.

As he walked towards the armoury to clean his weapon he was stopped by Sergeant Major Lewis. "McGuire, come with me. Colonel Latham wants to see you. Your mate Drabble can clean your weapon for you."

Following the big Sergeant Major, McGuire walked along the deck towards the bow of the ship. They reached the forward area the officers had selected as their deck, away from the smoke and cinders of the funnel. Colonel Latham turned as they approached.

Both men came to attention and the Sergeant Major saluted. "McGuire reporting as ordered sir."

"Thank you Sergeant Major. Now then McGuire that was a remarkable shot. Tell me though, why did you wait so long?"

"Begging your pardon sir, I wanted to be sure of a hit so I waited until the ship was at the top of a roll and the bottle was at the top of a wave. That way, for just a second or two, the ship is still before it rolls down again."

Latham shook his head slowly. "Remarkable. Well done. You've won me a case of rather fine champagne from my fellow officers. I shall think of you while I am enjoying it. Now back to your mess mates. I'm sure they would like to help you celebrate your prize."

McGuire saluted and turned smartly before leaving. Latham watched him go and then turned back to the Sergeant Major. "Well Mr Lewis what do you think of him?"

"Damned fine shot sir."

"What else?" Latham asked.

"He's sober. Keeps his kit in good order. Absorbs training well and doesn't talk back. Gives all his pay to his widowed mother and his sister, through the agent."

"Why did he join?"

"One of Her Majesty's 'hard bargains', sir. Stole a loaf of bread for his mother. Seems she

47

hadn't eaten in some days. The Magistrate gave him the choice."

"Do you think he has the makings of a good soldier?"

"If he carries on the way he is, I think he could be a credit to the regiment, sir."

"Thank you Sergeant Major. I think so too. Keep a close eye on him will you, we need to encourage good men even in a special draft like this one. We'll be in Egypt tomorrow morning, by the way, so make sure our men are ready to go with all their equipment in good order. There will no doubt be the usual confusion as we disembark."

Chapter 8.
Arrival in Egypt

McGuire stood by the rail of the ship as it manoeuvred slowly into the docks at Alexandria with his friend Tom Drabble by his side. "What the hell is that smell Tom? If the whole country smells like this, I may need a new nose when we finish.

Tom looked over the side of the ship then pointed at the end of the dock. "Could be something to do with the dead goats on the mud down there. All cities stink, even Dublin on a warm day and it's damned hot here. I guess we'll be out in the countryside soon enough."

"Countryside? Did you see all that sand as we came in? There's no grass, no bushes, nothing. It looks like it never rains here."

"Michael, there may be less rain than in Ireland, but there has to be something. All these people wandering about on the docks must eat something." Tom said, pointing at the crowd of natives in their long flowing robes.

"Suppose so, they're noisy bleeders though ain't they? Wonder what all the shouting is about."

Tom looked along the docks. "By the look of things they are trying to sell us something. Maybe all sorts of somethings?"

Michael shrugged. "Well they're wasting their time with me. I've got no money."

Tom nodded and turned to his friend with his elbows resting on the rail. "Do you have to send all your money to your family? Couldn't you keep some back?"

Michael sighed. "Not really. Since my father died my mother has nothing coming into the house, and I don't want my sister to end up walking the streets just to buy bread and with my bit of money they don't have to eat rats any more either."

Tom nodded. "I see your problem. Never mind the army feeds you and clothes you and pays for a nice sea cruise. What more could you need eh?"

"You two enjoying the sights then?"

They spun round to find Sergeant Major Lewis standing behind them with his magnificent moustache teased out into two waxed points. Both men came to attention and kept silent.

"Is your kit all ready for disembarkation?"

"Yes Sergeant Major." McGuire answered for both of them. "Just waiting for the word to move."

"Stay alert then. The officers are taking a walk in the town to stretch their legs and to try and find out where we are supposed to go next. No point us all going down onto that dock. That bunch of scruffy beggars would have half of you robbed blind in five minutes."

McGuire grinned. "Yes Sergeant Major."

"And McGuire, back in Dublin, you asked me what a camel was. Well unless I am mistaken, if you look over to the left there's one coming along the dock making a god awful groaning noise."

The three men turned and watched the strange creature being driven along by the warehouses. It was heavily laden with an array of bags across its back and the groaning seemed to be a protest at the cruelty of overloading.

As it came alongside them McGuire turned his head towards Lewis. "Don't like the look of those big, yellow teeth and all that drool hanging out of its mouth, Sergeant Major. You reckon that's what we are going to be riding then?"

"Seems like it. Now get your kit and get down that gangplank, the Colonel is down there waving for us to come to him. Tell him I'm getting the rest of our detachment moving. Go!"

With the detachments all lined up along the dock the British troops were marched through the town to the Red Barracks. Egyptian soldiers moved in front to clear the swarms of insistent hawkers out of the way. At 6 am the next morning they were all loaded onto a train in the ramshackle station and then sat there until 8:15, sweating, until it finally started off. At one point they were shunted into a siding for a faster train and watched the other half of the regiment pass them by. In the end, the train dawdled along and took some twelve hours to travel the 120 hot, dusty miles to Cairo.

Initially the Guards' Camel Regiment were supposed to be quartered in the *Kasr en Nil* palace, but were then marched out onto the flat plain by the pyramids to live under canvas for a week. Here they explored the pyramids or hid from the sun in the sweltering tents and learned more about the incessant flies that are the scourge of that part of Egypt.

On the third day the Camel Corps were paraded on the flat area in front of the Sphinx. As they stood in the blazing sun McGuire could feel the sweat soaking through his jacket. Unable to move they stood as the flies crawled over any exposed skin and tried to drink from the corner of their eyes.

Tom Drabble was the first to spot the group of officers riding slowly across the sand towards them. "Officers approaching, Sergeant Major."

Sergeant Major Lewis turned and looked at the approaching group. "Right lads that's the Sirdar approaching. He'll be a while at that speed, but listen for the words of command."

"Permission to speak sir?"

"What is it McGuire?"

"What the devil is a Sirdar sir?"

"The Sirdar is the British officer who commands the Egyptian army. Seems like their own officers have problems, so British ones hold key positions."

"So how come they don't send the Egyptian army down to evacuate Khartoum then sir?"

"Because they're not as good as we are. Now shut up and pay attention."

At the end of the week they were then marched back to the railway for another extremely hot, dusty and uncomfortable journey to Assiut where they detrained and were marched to the river Nile. They found there a small steamer which was to take the officers and two barges for the men that were to be towed along behind it.

Chapter 9.
Up the Nile

Michael McGuire sat at the back end of the barge, idly staring at the landscape that passed by on either side of the wide river. Beyond the greenery of the area that was watered by the Nile he could see the pale golden sands of the Sahara desert. Arabs in their flowing white robes drove emaciated donkeys around in circles to turn the wheels that lifted water out of the river and into the irrigation channels that supported their crops. Small boats with one or two men in them were floating near the reed beds casting nets into the water. All this had been fascinating as they started out, but that was days ago.

Out of sheer boredom McGuire made a point of sitting next to the Arab helmsman who steered the ungainly barge. Initially they had difficulty communicating, but over the days the Irishman found he was rapidly learning the other man's language. The helmsman for his part was delighted to have someone to talk to and helped McGuire as much as he could.

Around them, bored men sweated and dozed, as best they could, lying on the nests they had made of their equipment and swatting the flies away. Even Sergeant Major Lewis had given in to the torpor and the tedium. Each night they moored up, as the Egyptian captain would not run the risk of hitting rocks in the dark. They were allowed ashore to stretch their cramped legs and to try and buy fresh food from the inevitable traders. Once they learned the Egyptian way of bargaining, buying the eggs, chickens and vegetables became almost a game, with each side enjoying it as much as the other.

As they reached Assouan the officers decided it was time to give the men a proper chance to clean themselves and they were all allowed to strip and dive into the river. Sergeant Major Lewis watched as they took their sweaty uniforms off.

"Drabble! McGuire! Not you two. I want somebody on here to make sure those thieving Arabs don't steal our weapons or equipment. You two are the first guard detail."

Tom Drabble stated to protest, but was shut up by a sharp elbow in the ribs from his friend. "Shut it. We'll get our turn later when the rest are out of the way."

The two men collected their rifles and bandoliers and sat on the roof of the barge to watch the men wading into the water. They were careful to put on their solar helmets to guard against the sun. Even in the winter they had been told that men could die of sunstroke.

The horseplay started, with water splashing everywhere and the men shouting to each other. McGuire smiled; it had been a long eleven days to get here on these boats. Maybe the officers had been more comfortable on their steamer? Then he saw the Colonel and the other officers climbing down the river bank to take their own dip in the cooling water. Naturally they were in front of the steamer and away from the men and their antics.

McGuire stood and took a walk around the narrow deck. As far as he could see none of the 'thieving Arabs' were paying them any attention. He continued his slow walk with the Martini Henry held in the crook of his arm. He completed the circuit and came back to sit beside Tom.

"What do you reckon that is Michael?" Tom asked, pointing out into the river.

McGuire shaded his eyes with his hand and looked to where Drabble was pointing. With the lowering sun glinting off the water all he could see was ripples moving towards the front of the steamer. A small cloud passed across the sun and he saw what was making those ripples.

"Holy Mother of God!"

McGuire jumped to his feet and brought the rifle to his shoulder. He heaved the lever down below the trigger and opened the breech. He rapidly withdrew one of the heavy rounds from his bandolier and slipped it into the weapon before pulling the cocking lever back up. He lowered his eye to the rear sight and aimed at the approaching ripples. He controlled his breathing and waited for his moment before firing.

The loud explosion from the rifle barrel brought all the heads of the men in the river snapping around to look at him as he reloaded, as quickly as he was able. He aimed and fired again and seconds later he did it again. The crocodile that had been heading into the group of officers rolled onto its back and lay still in the water.

Before the carcase could float away, one of the native crewmen on the steamer snagged it with a boat hook and pulled it in towards the shore. It took a number of men to heave it up onto the muddy beach. The officers walked along from the front of the steamer with towels wrapped around their middles for modesty's sake.

Colonel Latham stood staring down at the beast while one of the men paced alongside it from nose to tail. "Thirteen feet, sir. Has to be the biggest one we've seen so far, it's a bloody monster."

Latham looked up at McGuire who stood on the bow of the barge still holding his smoking rifle. "McGuire! Who gave you permission to fire that weapon?"

McGuire came to attention and stared straight ahead. "Nobody sir. Sorry sir."

"In my regiment, nobody fires a rifle unless they have orders from at least an NCO and certainly not a private soldier without authority. Is that clear to you?"

"Yes sir. Won't happen again sir."

"Sergeant Major Lewis!"

Lewis drew himself up, worried that there was going to be some capricious officer nonsense. Did they not know McGuire had saved at least one life and that an officer as well?

"McGuire is improperly dressed. Make sure he has a Lance Corporal's stripe on his sleeve the next time I see him."

Lewis smiled. "Yes sir."

Chapter 10.
Wadi Haifa and Dongola

McGuire and Drabble walked across the precarious gangplank into the base that was in the process of being set up at Wadi Haifa. Just south of the formal border between Egypt and the Sudan, it had been the Egyptian Army's forward location for some time. Now it was being expanded as a supply base and forward jumping off point for the Relief Column.

The guide who was pointing out where they should go stood at the end of the gangplank. "Welcome to 'Bloody Halfway'", he said, as McGuire reached him.

"Not good then?"

The soldier shook his head. "It's a shithole. The Gyppos have been dumping their stinking rubbish around the place and in this heat the bloody flies love it. Try and get a mouthful of food into you without half a dozen flies going in as well. It's a challenge I can tell you."

McGuire grinned at Drabble. "A proper home from home then eh?"

They walked across to where the rest of the Guards Camel Regiment were setting themselves up in the shade of makeshift shelters The guide had not been lying about the flies, even at this early hour of the morning the creatures were swarming around them, trying to drink the sweat off their faces.

Sergeant Major Lewis turned as they came towards him. "Stow your kit in that shed then get back here in five minutes. We are going to meet our transport."

They were back in the required time and the detachment marched across towards a low ridge. As they came to the top of it they could see a large herd of camels of all colours lying on the desert floor. The stench from the animals was a trial and the drool hanging from their mouths was disgusting. Some of the other detachments were already there. The Arab handlers were sitting beside the herd under small canvas shelters, sipping coffee from tiny cups.

Each man was issued with a saddle and shown how to fit it to a camel. Then they were taken into the herd and allocated an animal. As soon as the saddle was thrown up onto their backs the camels started the loud groans of protest that they were soon to become used to. Naturally, the army issued saddles didn't fit, since each camel was that little bit different in shape. The Arab handlers showed the soldiers how to adjust and fit the saddles then retired to a short distance to watch.

A loud voiced Sergeant Major from the Scots Guards gave the command. "Guards Camel Regiment! Mount!"

Soldiers flung their legs across the beast that was laid by them. Unfamiliar with camels they tried to mount in a way the camels were not expecting and the animals reacted. Lumbering to their feet they set off in any direction they felt like. Some men fell to the ground, others ended up draped across the camel's neck and others clung to the saddle in all sorts of strange postures. The Arab handlers sat in their huddles and hooted with delight at the performance.

Eventually the Arabs were persuaded to come forward and instruct the troops. Once the soldiers had been shown the correct method of mounting and controlling the camel they started to enjoy themselves, riding all around the wide, flat ground. After two hours of this mayhem the men had got the idea of how to ride and the drill started. It was to go on for two days until the mob began to act as a unit.

McGuire named his camel Kathleen after his sister and took pains to ensure the animal was properly fed and watered. Two other men were less careful of their mounts and took nasty bites to the leg from irritated animals.

On the 12th of November the regiment received orders to move forward to Dongola. Skin bags for water were issued and almost every one leaked. McGuire and Drabble sat together in the shade of Kathleen and did their best to stitch up the holes. Even then, they still leaked.

The column formed in the cool of the early morning along with a Field Hospital section and others from the Commissariat and Transport troops. They moved off at the stately two miles an hour that the camels decided. With two hundred and thirty five miles to go, they did not wish to wear out the animals. Each day the target was to make twenty miles. Some days it was less and some days more, as the desert allowed. The sand desert they had expected vanished as they moved forward, until they were passing through an area of low, rocky black hills and hard gravel with sparse tufts of long grass and everywhere the inevitable thorn bushes.

A day out from Wadi Haifa Colonel Latham found that a young black boy had joined the column, having escaped from his master. As is common with British soldiers, they shared their food with him and let him ride on one of the pack camels. Four days into the journey an irate Arab merchant caught up with them, demanding the return of his slave.

Latham sat his camel quietly while the man ranted at him and then turned his head slowly to the watching soldiers. "McGuire, ride over here!"

McGuire kicked his camel into motion and rode over to reign in beside the Colonel. "Now then McGuire, how does your camel react to rifle fire close by?"

"Never takes any notice of it sir. We tried it at Wadi Haifa and she never even looked up."

"Good. Good. Now you see that lonely rock out there about two hundred yards away?"

"Yes sir."

"Shoot it from camelback."

"Yes sir. Shall I ask this Arab here to move out of the way first?"

Latham smiled. "No, He's fine where he is."

McGuire pulled the Martini Henry out of the saddle boot and loaded it. Then taking aim he fired over the Arab's head and hit the rock the Colonel had indicated. As the bullet whined off into the desert the Arab started yelling again.

Latham turned around. "You've learned some of the language, haven't you? Tell him there is no slavery under the British flag and the boy is staying with us. If I see him again he will take the place of that rock."

McGuire passed on the message and despite his patchy Arabic the merchant got the message and visibly paled before he rushed back to his camel and rode off.

"Thank you McGuire, re-join your section."

They camped each night by the side of the Nile so that the camels could be watered and the water skins refilled. Two days rest were granted at Akasheh and Abu Fatmeh. In all this travel they saw not one of the Dervishes, although they had expected to see their scouts.

On the 26th of November the column arrived opposite the mud brick town of Dongola. They had to ride a further twenty miles along the river to find a place where the camels and men could be ferried across the river by the native *nuggers,* a boat that has been used on the Nile since antiquity.

Here the whole of the Camel Corps was brought together. The Guards Camel Regiment, The Heavies made up of detachments from heavy cavalry regiments and the Mounted Infantry regiment made up of detachments from many line regiments. Completing the set was the Light Camel Regiment made up of men from the light cavalry. There was also a detachment of the 19th Hussars mounted on Egyptian ponies and intended to carry out normal scouting and screening duties ahead of the column.

McGuire sat on his camel and looked around at the force. More than 2000 well armed and trained men looked impressive until he raised his eyes to the wide expanse of rocky desert around them. They had heard that the Mahdi had tens of thousands of fighting men under his hand and they lived in this place, knew its secrets and wanted to defend their own homes.

"With all this we can't lose eh Michael?" Drabble called across from his own camel.

McGuire smiled slightly and nodded. "From your mouth to God's ears, Tom. It's an awful terrible place to fight a war."

Chapter 11.
Advance to Contact

Lieutenant Colonel Latham stood on the small ridge looking out across the desert. The silver light of the moon cast deep shadows in the wadis and gulleys, but showed the desert floor in stark relief. Behind him he could hear the camels grumbling as they were settled down, by their owners, with the occasional swear word as one of the beasts swung round and tried to bite its rider. They really were bad tempered animals, yet so placid on the march. Strange creatures.

He turned as he heard the soft footsteps behind him. "Ah Sergeant Major Lewis, a fine night don't you think'"

"Indeed sir, nice and calm."

Latham nodded. "And that's what I wanted to talk to you about. How are the men feeling? Are they in good heart do you think?"

"They're doing well sir. Still grumbling, but they wouldn't be British soldiers if they didn't have a moan now and then."

"Good for them. Now then, tomorrow we head south again, as you know. Up to now we have seen nothing of the enemy and I fear the men and some of the officers have started to relax a little. From tomorrow on I think we are moving into their playground. I want the men to be alert, night sentries on their mettle. That sort of thing."

"I'll see to that, sir, never fear."

"My worry is that they will look down on our enemies. They have seen the Arabs in these mud towns and think the Dervishes are the same quality. That can't be true. These are the people that wiped out Billy Hicks and his column. He had modern weapons and they had sticks and swords. That speaks to a rare sort of courage and determination."

"I'll make sure they understand that, sir."

"You might want to have a word with the senior NCOs of the other detachments as well. If we do get attacked we can't afford a weak spot anywhere."

"That's true, sir, we've been speaking about that already, but I will pass on your thoughts again."

The two men stood silently for a moment or two looking out over the harsh silver desert. The camp behind them was silent now until a single voice started to sing.

"I'll take you home again Kathleen across the ocean wild and wide."

"A fine voice," said Latham. "Who is that?"

"Corporal McGuire, sir, he's christened his camel Kathleen. He sings to settle the damned thing down."

As they listened, other voices around the camp picked up the song and soon the desert air was filled with the sounds of Irish lament and longing. The song finished and the silence returned.

"A good man that McGuire. Don't you think?"

"I do, sir. He's turning out to be a fine soldier even if he is a bit young."

"Thank you Sergeant Major. I'll see you in the morning."

Lewis drew himself up to attention, saluted and walked back down into the camp. Latham watched him go and found himself humming the song again. He smiled and made his way back to where his blanket was laid out on the ground.

The march south continued as the column started out in the early hours of the morning. Moving at the stately pace dictated by their mounts, the Camel Corps headed towards Khartoum and the rescue of General Gordon. Ahead of them the men of the 19th Hussars fanned out on their hardy ponies, scouting for the Dervish army.

As they moved on, they passed between the harsh black rocks of the low hills and mountains that made up the desert in this area. After days of walking, feeling the almost hypnotic movement of the camels, a larger peak came into view. Lieutenant Colonel Latham rode forward and consulted the column commander, and then he pulled his camel to one side of the march and waited for his men to reach him. He spotted Lieutenant Storr-Lessing and then Sergeant Major Lewis. He waved them both out of the column to join him.

"Gentlemen, I have spoken with the commander and he agrees with me that despite the best efforts of the Hussars a little extra precaution would not go amiss. Stephen I want you to go to the top of that peak over there and keep watch around us as we move forward."

Storr-Lessing paled under his suntan. "On my own, sir?"

"No, that would not be dreadfully useful. Sergeant Major Lewis will give you two men to go with you. One will be a heliograph operator and the other an escort. If you see any sign of the Dervishes signal immediately and then get back to the column."

"Very good sir. When do I leave?"

"As soon as your men are detailed off. Who will you send Sergeant Major?"

Lewis looked across at the column. "Lance Corporal McGuire with the heliograph and Private Tinker as the escort. Both good men on damn good camels. They'll see you right sir."

Lewis kicked his camel into motion and rode up alongside the column. As he came alongside the detachment for the 1st Grenadiers, he called the two selected men out of line.

"You two are going with Lieutenant Storr-Lessing, on a reconnaissance task for the Colonel. Keep your wits about you and act quickly when you have to."

The three men angled away from the slow moving column and rode their camels away up the slope of the hill. The animals groaned and complained as they mounted the slope, but never slackened their pace. Their soft feet gripped the uneven ground and pushed the loose rocks to the side.

As they neared the peak they found a shallow gulley and dismounted. With the camels secured they walked up to the peak and stared around them.

The harsh desert stretched away from them in all directions. The column continued to trudge their way along the faint track towards the wells they were seeking and in the distance they could see the scattered riders of the 19th Hussars.

The Lieutenant scanned all around with his binoculars, he saw nothing untoward. "Now then you two, set up a camp in the gulley. No fires and keep your heads down, I don't want anyone seeing us moving around."

"Should I get the heliograph set up now sir?" McGuire asked.

"No. I don't want anything to delay us if we have to vacate this hillside in a hurry."

"With respect, sir, the manual says the equipment should be set up and tested as soon as we are in position."

Storr-Lessing turned and looked at McGuire with undisguised contempt. "No doubt that is what your training sergeant told you? Well, he is not here seeing what I see and he is not an officer. You leave that heliograph packed on your camel. Is that clear?"

McGuire thought about protesting but looked at the officer's face and thought better of it. "Yes sir. Sorry sir."

Chapter 12.
A Rude Awakening

Dawn broke over the rocky hills around them as Michael McGuire sat and looked across the valleys below them. The light had not reached down into the deep, dry watercourses that scarred the desert floor, but the sky was alive with the colours that came in the early mornings. He lifted the binoculars he had been loaned by the Lieutenant and scanned the camp below him. Inside the improvised fence of thorn bushes they called a *zariba* he could see the troops were at the ready as they were at every dawn while in the field.

As he watched, the men started to drift away from the perimeter leaving only the pickets on guard. He saw the small fires start up and he could almost taste the tea they would be brewing down there. He looked over his shoulder and saw that in the small gulley behind him Private David Tinker was sitting up and throwing his blanket to one side The Lieutenant slept on, until he heard Tinker open one of the cans of bully beef that was to be their breakfast.

McGuire turned back and scanned around with the binoculars again. He paused. There was movement in one of the wadis. The rising sun was casting just enough light into the deep cleft to show him that something was moving. He swung the powerful glasses around and peered into the other gouges in the earth. He could hardly believe what he was seeing.

He slithered back down from his position then stood and ran down to the gulley. "Sir, Dervishes! Bloody thousands of them. They've crept up during the night and they're nearly all around the column."

The Lieutenant's eyes opened wide and McGuire could have sworn he saw panic in them. "Show me! And give me those damned binoculars!"

The two men ran back up the slope to the observation point they had made, with Tinker following close behind. They threw themselves down on the stones and wormed their way forward to the edge of the small drop.

Michael pointed. "Over there, sir, to the right and then right below us and across the valley. There's so many I can't count them. Then look on the hillsides, they've got marksmen with rifles behind the rocks. The column won't be able to see them until they open fire."

The Lieutenant's face had gone pale as he swept the binoculars around to where McGuire was pointing. "Holy God! We have to get out of here or we'll be trapped. Get the camels untied we're leaving. We should be able to get clear out to the north."

Storr-Lessing jumped to his feet and ran down to where the camels lay tethered. McGuire looked across at Tinker whose mouth was hanging open in surprise. He rose and ran down the slope after the officer. As he reached his camel he fumbled with the leather straps that held the heliograph equipment.

"What the hell are you doing man? Get on your camel and ride!"

McGuire stopped and looked at the officer. "Sir we have to warn the column. They'll be slaughtered."

Storr-Lessing had his camel freed now and flung himself into the saddle. As the animal stood up he looked down at McGuire.

"Don't be a damned fool. Do you know what those bloody people do to any of us they capture? We need to go and fast! Mount up we're leaving!"

Michael McGuire stood with his hands hanging at his side. He was torn between obeying the order and sending the warning. The punishment for disobeying an officer was severe, but he couldn't do it. He turned back to his camel and continued to release the straps.

Without another word the Lieutenant hauled his camel's head around and kicked it into a trot down the hillside. McGuire looked around to find Tinker standing, still open mouthed, behind him watching the officer recede into the distance.

"David! Help me with this. We have to get it set up at the top there."

Tinker shook himself out of his surprise and stepped forward to wrestle with the stiff straps. Together they dragged the tripod and the signalling head out of the pouches and set off back up the slope to where they could see the column and, more importantly, where the column could see them.

As the two men were assembling the equipment, down below them on the desert floor,

Sergeant Major Lewis was reporting to Colonel Latham for his morning orders. "Good morning Sergeant Major. A good quiet night eh? The men sleep well?"

"All quiet sir. Nothing to report. The men are making breakfast now and will be ready to move as soon as the General gives the word."

Latham nodded. "According to the guides we are only about three miles from the wells so we are having a later start today. Give the men a bit of a break."

Lewis looked up at the hill; a movement had attracted his attention. "Rider on the hillside sir."

Latham flipped open the brown leather case that hung on his chest and pulled out his binoculars. He raised them to his eyes and looked towards the rider that Lewis had pointed at. He twirled the focus wheel until the image became clear.

"It's one of ours. Going at quite a speed. A bit risky whipping the camel along on that slope I would have thought. It's Lieutenant Storr-Lessing. Now where are his two men?"

There was a flash of light from the hill top. "Heliograph sir, up there."

"What are they saying Sergeant Major?" Latham smiled. "I suppose you still recall your own heliograph training after all these years."

Lewis did not reply. He shaded his eyes and stared at the flashing light coming from the mirror of the heliograph. The message ended and started to repeat.

Lewis spun round away from his colonel and yelled across the column in a voice that had controlled wide parade grounds for years. "Form square! Form square!"

The men dropped their breakfast and grabbed their rifles before running to take position behind the thorn *zariba*. Lewis turned back to the colonel.

"Begging your pardon sir, but the message reports we have large enemy forces closing in on three sides."

Latham nodded. "Quite right Sergeant Major, not a second to lose. See to your men, I'll report to the General."

As Lewis strode away to the defence lines, where the Grenadiers stood in two close packed ranks, Latham raised his binoculars again. It took him a second or two to find the camel rider that was now clearly heading away from the square to the north. He put his binoculars away and sadly shook his head as he turned and walked towards the General's command area.

Chapter 13.
Abu Klea

On the hill top, McGuire and Tinker heard the bugles blow below them and saw the men running for the edge of the *zariba* surrounded compound. They could also see that the surrounding Dervishes had spotted them and some were firing at them. At this range they should be safe, but the odd round was passing close by.

Tinker looked across at McGuire nervously. "What do we do now Corporal?"

McGuire smiled to reassure his first independent command. "We pack the heliograph away and then we ride like madmen back to the column."

Tinker nodded and started to help to dismantle the signalling equipment. "What about the Dervishes between us and the column?"

McGuire thought for a moment before he answered. Tinker was right he realised, this was going to be devilish risky.

"We'll be riding from behind them, so with luck they won't notice us until we are past. We'll sling blankets round us to try and look like their robes and then we just pray like you've never done before."

"That's your plan?"

McGuire grinned. "That's the plan unless you've got a better one?"

"How about we ride back down the other side of the hill until it's all over?"

McGuire shook his head. "Not a good idea. Out in the desert, just the two of us, with thousands of Dervishes wandering about? No thank you. We'll take our chances on the mad dash."

They trotted back to their camels and strapped the heliograph back into its pouches on the saddle. With the camels released they mounted and slung the blankets around them like cloaks. McGuire remembered to take off the distinctive solar helmet and hung it from the front of his saddle.

"Ready David?"

"Not really."

McGuire grinned again. "Nor me, let's go."

They kicked the camels into motion down the rocky slope careful to keep them at a safe speed. They could not afford to lose an animal now and they needed to conserve their energy for the run into the column, through the attacking Dervish army.

Behind the two lines of soldiers Sergeant Major Lewis walked slowly backwards and forwards. "Steady lads, remember your training. Listen for the orders and if you feel like spewing up make sure you miss my boots."

The reassuring and familiar voice behind them and the small jokes calmed the men and some even smiled a little. Their eyes were wide as they looked left and right, searching for the invisible enemy. Most of them checked their rifles and then checked them again. Ammunition pouches on the bandoliers were unbuttoned to save the extra second that might take once the firing started.

"Sights set for two hundred yards. Stand still and watch your front. Drabble, you need a haircut. You must have trouble shitting with it that length."

The men chuckled at the parade ground joke and checked their weapons again. Lieutenant Evans joined Lewis and stood watching him prowl the ranks. As he came nearer the Lieutenant whispered to the big man.

"What do I do Sergeant Major?"

"Good morning sir. Lovely day for it don't you think?" Then the old soldier dropped his voice. "Walk up and down slowly, don't rush. Talk to them. Make a joke if you can, just make sure you look confident."

The young officer nodded and whispered back. "Sergeant Major I'm bloody scared."

"Of course you are sir. Every man here is scared and so am I. The secret is to convince the men that you aren't. Off you go."

Evans swallowed and then nodded before hitching his Sam Browne belt to a more comfortable position where he could reach the heavy revolver quickly. He walked as casually as he could along the line of men. He reached one man who was wearing only his vest and trousers.

"This really won't do you know. I can't have the Grenadiers meeting the enemy improperly dressed. Fall out and get your jacket, hurry now."

The man in question turned and ran to where his jacket lay. Once he had it on he ran back into the line.

Evans nodded. "Far better. We have to maintain certain standards or people will think we're the bloody artillery."

There was a nervous chuckle from the men nearest to him and Lewis smiled to himself. This young man had the makings he decided.

Captain Carter the adjutant strolled up to the Sergeant Major who turned and saluted him. "Good morning Sergeant Major," he said just a little too loudly. "In all this excitement I nearly didn't get to finish my breakfast. Now that would never do would it?"

Lewis smiled and nodded. "Quite right sir."

He was about to continue the charade when he heard the cry from the Scots Guards to their right. "Enemy front! Prepare to fire."

He turned to see hundreds and then thousands of Dervishes rising out of the deep wadi to their front. Their long straight swords reflected the sun as did the broad blades of their spears. The started to run towards the British with almost inhuman screams.

"Hold your fire. Aim low. I don't want anybody shooting vultures today. Front rank kneel." Lewis kept walking and talking even though it felt like his guts had turned to water. "At your target in front, at two hundred yards, volley fire present."

The rifles along the line came up into the aim. "Steady, wait for the order you're not at a Dublin fair sideshow now."

Lewis turned to Captain Carter. "With your permission sir?"

Carter nodded. "Oh, please do carry on Sergeant Major."

Lewis looked along the line to where all the other senior non-commissioned officers stood waiting for the signal from the left hand company. He saw the flag go down and bellowed to his men.

"Fire! Reload!" A pause of two or three seconds then, "Front rank fire! Reload! Rear rank fire! Reload! Front rank fire! Reload"

The rigid rifle drill of the British infantryman had been their most potent weapon since the wars against Napoleon. Now it was the turn of the Dervishes to feel the impact of those heavy lead Martini Henry bullets. By now any European army would have staggered and might even have stopped. The Dervishes never paused, but ran forward screaming their war cries and trying to get within killing distance of the steady lines of men before them.

Behind the screaming mass McGuire and Tinker rode forward. As they reached the last of the crowd they whipped their two camels up to their fastest trot and rode into the melee. The camels groaned and roared at being made to work so hard, but that noise alerted the Dervishes before them who opened the way to allow, what they assumed were their own people, to charge through.

Lieutenant Colonel Latham stood on the slightly raised ground beside the General watching the battle on three sides of the square. The men were holding steady and firing rapidly. The Dervishes were being cut down by the disciplined fire, but not a man turned away. Their courage was truly remarkable he decided.

He raised his binoculars to follow the progress of his errant Lieutenant. He could see Storr-Lessing just about to disappear from view to the north, when he suddenly reined his camel to a halt, turned its head and started back towards the square. Had the man come to his senses? Then the reason became obvious. As Storr-Lessing approached, a strong force of camel mounted Dervish cavalry appeared behind him, charging in towards the last side of the square to be attacked.

The Lieutenant rode as fast as he was able towards the two ranks of rifle men, screaming at the top of his voice that he was British. The ranks parted and a section of the *zariba* hedge was pulled back to let him in. As soon as he was inside the square the *zariba* was repaired and the ranks closed up to await this latest attack from the Dervishes.

Storr- Lessing leapt from his camel and stood looking around in an obvious panic. Latham walked through the rows of tethered camels in the centre of the square and approached his officer.

"Young man, your soldiers are on that side of the square. Report to Captain Carter."

"But sir I think I should report what I have seen to the General." He said pointing to the rise in the middle of the square.

"Lieutenant, look around you. It is blindingly obvious what you have seen. Now report to Captain Carter and then come and see me after the battle."

Storr-Lessing paused looking around him. He looked at Latham with pleading in his eyes then, seeing no hope there, he slowly walked on stiff legs towards his detachment. He reached Carter who was standing calmly smoking the last of his cigars.

Carter turned and looked him up and down. "Ah young Stephen. Nice of you to join us at last. We've saved a few for you, as you can see. Off you go, the Sergeant Major will position you."

The young man stumbled towards the ranks of men who were loading and firing like machines. The Dervishes were slower now, but only because they were struggling to climb over the bodies of their dead.

Lewis turned and waved him forward. "Right then sir. Just like Mr Evans walk up and down the line. Talk to the men if any look scared rest your hand on his shoulder. Keep them working."

As he spoke a large battle axe came spinning out of the crowd of Dervish warriors. It dipped down and the razor sharp blade sliced through the helmet of a man in the rear rank and carved into his brain, killing him instantly.

"Now's your chance sir. Pick up his rifle and step into the firing line. Quickly sir."

Storr-Lessing stared at the Sergeant Major. "You can't be serious?"

Lewis lowered his face to just in front of the Lieutenant's. "Listen to me sir. The men saw your little ride out to the north. God only knows what they think you were doing, but they'll work it out. You get into that line and stand shoulder to

79

shoulder with them and you might just rescue your reputation."

With that he took the younger man by the shoulder and turned him towards the gap in the line. A firm push between the shoulder blades put him into the line and then Lewis slapped the heavy rifle into his hands. A second later Lewis dropped the bandolier of ammunition, from the fallen man, over his shoulder. Uncertainly, the young officer began to load and fire at the screaming mass before him.

McGuire's heart was in his mouth as he and Tinker rode through the swirling mass of attackers. Through the clouds of smoke from the rifles they could see the British lines getting closer. Then Michael saw one of the Emirs who was leading the attack turn round and look at him. There was a second or two of puzzlement on the man's face and then realisation dawned. He pointed at the two men and started to roar loudly in his own language. All around them heads turned in their direction. A spear flew past McGuire's head, then another. A long shining sword was swung at the camel's legs in an attempt to hock it and bring it down.

Two hundred yards to go now and they were still moving. McGuire let the blanket slip from his shoulders and slapped his helmet on his head, in the hopes that his comrades would recognise the uniform, even through the smoke of the rifle fire. He heard the shout of triumph and turned his head in time to see Tinker falling from his camel with a broad headed spear embedded in his chest. The huge gout of blood pouring from the wound told the story, there was no saving him. As he fell to the stony ground, he was surrounded by Dervishes and the mass of blades rose and fell, hacking the soldier to pieces.

McGuire rode on. He could see now there was no way he would be recognised through the drifting cloud of gunpowder smoke. His mind raced and he smiled a little to himself.

Ahead in the square with the screaming and rifle fire the noise was intense. Through it all Lewis heard a voice coming from the Dervish army. It was incredible. Someone was singing. "*I'll take you home again Kathleen* ...".

"Cease fire! Cease fire! Prepare to open the *zariba*!"

Through the smoke the camel emerged with McGuire, singing as loudly as he knew how, on its back. The *zariba* was pulled to one side and a narrow gap opened in the line of rifle men to let him through. As the camel passed the Sergeant Major, McGuire withdrew his rifle from its saddle boot and lifted his leg over the saddle.

McGuire hit the ground directly in front of the Sergeant Major and came to attention. "Sorry I'm late Sergeant Major. Permission to join the line?"

Lewis shook his head in wonder. "Fall in you mad paddy. Quick as you like now."

McGuire grinned and ran to take his place in the rear rank. The Dervishes had paused and regrouped. They showed no sign of turning away.

Captain Carter dropped his cigar to the ground and stepped forward. "Fix bayonets!"

Along the line the command was repeated as others saw what was about to happen. With an incredible renewed fury the Dervishes threw themselves at the British line. Their mad charge brought them to the edge of the *zariba*. Some stabbed with their long spears or their huge straight swords while others tore at the savage thorn bushes with their bare hands.

The front rank rose to their feet and stabbed forward with their bayonets. Blood spurted from the wicked wounds that the long blades on the end of the rifles inflicted. The second rank continued firing at point blank range into the mob. When a man in the front rank fell McGuire stepped forward and thrust his bayonet into the throat of one of the more richly dressed emirs. The man collapsed onto the thorn hedge and the men around him recoiled. They backed away and then turned to walk in the direction they had come. Their warrior code would not allow them to run and the Martini Henry rifles continued to drop men left and right.

As the Dervishes dropped back down into their wadi the order was given to cease fire. All around the square the attack was petering out and the enemy retreated out of range. The soldiers stood still, panting with the exertion and relief. McGuire looked up as a single warrior mounted on a jet black horse executed a lone charge directly towards him. Regretting it even as he did it McGuire lifted his rifle, took careful aim and fired a round into the man's chest. The heavy lead round lifted the man off his horse a smashed him to the ground, never to move again.

Chapter 14.

The Aftermath

Once it was clear that the enemy had withdrawn, double pickets were set and the sorry task of dealing with the casualties began. The 19th Hussars re-joined the column and were set to following the retiring army to ensure they did not regroup and return for another try. British casualties were surprisingly light but the modern rifles and the Gardner guns manned by Navy Blue Jackets had done terrible damage to the attackers.

Men were sent forward to try and find enemy wounded. As the soldiers moved forward one of the Dervishes, who had been shaming, rolled over and drove his broad bladed spear into the belly of one of the medical staff who were trying to help the enemy casualties. The attacker died in a hail of bullets from the soldiers around him and the search parties were called back. They carried their disembowelled comrade with them.

The dead were buried as quickly as possible and the wounded were loaded on to the *cacolets* that were strapped to the camels for just such a purpose. Lieutenant Colonel Latham walked slowly through the debris of war until he came to Captain Carter.

"That's a nasty gash you've got there Carter. Shouldn't you let the doctors have a look at it?"

The Captain smiled at his commanding officer. "I will sir, but there are men with far worse than this who need to be seen to first. I'll get along there directly."

"Can I do anything for you?"

"Well sir if you have a spare jacket I would appreciate it. This one seems to be completely ruined."

Latham laughed. He was glad to see his officers maintaining the *sang froid* so prized by the army. He turned and looked around his men. They were dog tired he could see, but they were still working. Repairing the *zariba*, cleaning weapons and recharging their bandoliers of ammunition.

He turned again to find Lieutenant Storr-Lessing standing a little way off. He seemed to be nervous of approaching his Colonel.

Latham walked past him and spoke as he came alongside him. "Follow me, young man, we need to talk."

The two men walked into the camel lines, where the beasts were still lying, apparently unconcerned by all the mayhem that had occurred around them. Latham looked around to see that they could not be overheard and then turned back to his junior officer.

He looked him in the eye. "What in the name of all that's holy did you think you were doing? You left your post without warning the column of the enemy's approach and then instead of coming back here you rode away."

"No sir, you don't understand I was coming to warn you, but I had to circle wide to get around the Dervish contingent between my position and you."

Latham looked at him with disgust. "Do you think I have no eyes? I watched you come down the hill and I watched you ride away. The only reason you came back at all was to escape the Dervish cavalry. So don't you bloody lie to me."

The younger man was trembling now and a tear rolled down his pale cheek. "I'm sorry sir. I don't know what came over me. I ..."

"Enough. Don't snivel. I told you back in Dublin that I owe your father a great debt from our time in the Crimea. If he heard about this, it would break his heart and I can't do that to him. Re-join your men and for God's sake try to act like an officer. When you get there, send Sergeant Major Lewis to me."

Latham watched the younger man stumble away through the camel lines, then turned away and looked around the square. The medical staff were everywhere and the men were carrying casualties in to them on stretchers. On the side of the column away from his own men, at least part of the square had been driven back from the *zariba*, but their lines had held and eventually they had succeeded in pushing the enemy out again.

He heard the footsteps behind him and turned to return the salute from his Sergeant Major. "How are the men? Did we lose any?"

"They're tired sir, but they'll be fine after a rest. Casualties are lighter than I expected in our detachment. Three men dead and four injured, but the surgeon says they are going to make it."

"What about the two men we sent up to the hill top?"

"Private Tinker is one of the dead sir. The Dervishes caught him charging through their force and cut him to pieces. We are going to look for his body shortly. McGuire made it through without a scratch."

Latham nodded slowly then looked into the tired eyes of the man before him. "How long have we served together Sergeant Major?"

"That'll be sixteen years now sir. You were my first platoon commander when I joined the regiment in Chelsea barracks."

Latham smiled at the memory. "Indeed I was. We were both wet behind the ears in those days eh?"

"And now here we are, sir. Times do change."

"They do Sergeant Major, they do. Now we have a problem and I need your help."

"Anything, sir, you know that."

Latham looked up at the sky and saw the vultures gathering and circling over the battlefield. He looked back at Lewis, who waited patiently.

"You remember that day in the Crimea when Storr-Lessing's father came forward and saved us?"

Lewis nodded and drew a breath in through his teeth. "Not a day I like to remember. We'd have been cut up for fish bait except for him. A bloody brave man that one and a fine officer."

Latham sighed. "Indeed he is. I take it you saw what happened with his son?"

"I did sir, and so did all the men. Even the units to either side of us were watching."

Latham looked down at his dusty boots and spoke quietly. "I can't have him labelled a coward.

Not just for his father's sake, but for the honour of the regiment. I can concoct some story about him carrying out a reconnaissance to the north to confirm what was out there, but will the men believe it?"

"He took his place in the firing line when Private Martins was cut down. I can make sure they remember that. They won't have seen me push him in there."

Latham looked up. "That's good, please do that. Now what about McGuire? He was the one who stayed on the hill and warned us. Without him I think we might have been over run and slaughtered. If there was any justice I should put him forward for a medal. That new Distinguished Conduct Medal perhaps? But, if I do that, it highlights what one of my officers did."

"So what do you want to do then sir?"

Latham shook his head slowly. "Right now, I don't bloody know. I can't have McGuire talking to the rest of the men and letting them know what really happened. It would destroy my cover story and would certainly get back to the General before long. I think we need to get him away from here, but I don't know how the hell to do it."

"Could he be sent back with despatches to headquarters?"

"I wish he could, but with all the Dervishes around that would be a death sentence and he does not deserve that. Let me think about it and, for the time being, I want you to make sure he keeps his mouth firmly shut."

Lewis returned to the detachment. The casualties had been cleared away to the surgeons' area or to the area chosen for the burials. The men were sitting around, some still cleaning their rifles, others brewing the inevitable tea.

"McGuire, to me."

McGuire trotted across and came to attention.

"McGuire pick a detail and then go and find Tinker's body. Be careful, you know how those clever beggars play dead and then come at you."

"Yes Sergeant Major. How many men should I take?"

"Make it six. Four to carry him and two to watch for any shamming warriors."

McGuire picked his men and the seven of them walked out through a gap in the thorn hedge. Three other men took up position by the hedge, with their rifles at the ready in case the group should be attacked. They picked their way through the tangled and mangled corpses of their enemies. The pools of blood caused by the massive injuries a Martini Henry bullet inflicted were soaking into the sand and gravel of the desert, but their boots were soon caked in it.

They found Tinker. His body had been hacked apart and badly mutilated by the bladed weapons of the Dervishes. McGuire looked down in pity and said nothing as one of the men vomited at the sight. They picked up all the parts of him they could find and carried him back to the column. As they went, they came upon the man who had charged alone and been shot down by McGuire.

McGuire sent the men on and knelt down beside the man he had killed. He had a handsome face and his eyes were still open, seeming to stare at the vultures above him. McGuire closed his eyes for him and whispered an apology. As he did so the man's turban rolled from his head and there was a glint of metal. Reaching forward McGuire picked up the wound cloth and opened it up. Seven gold coins fell to the ground as he did so. He remembered the words of the agent, back in Dublin, and scooped them up.

As he stood up, he saw the curved dagger in the man's waist band and picked that up as well. The jewels in the hilt caught the light and sparkled red and green. He tucked it inside his jacket and returned to the detachment.

Chapter 15.
A Visitor

"Riders coming in, sir."

Lieutenant Evans turned to look where the sentry was pointing out into the desert. On the ridge he could see a group of Arabs, in their flowing robes, mounted on camels. Closer in was a single Arab walking his camel forward with three men from the 19th Hussars on their ponies flanking him.

Evans called out the rest of the guard detail and walked forward to the edge of the thorn hedge to wait. One of the Hussars spurred forward and came to a halt in front of him.

The rider saluted. "Good morning sir. Major Kitchener, the intelligence officer, coming in sir."

Kitchener was rapidly making a name for himself in this army. A Royal Engineer officer who was skilled at surveying and map making he had been selected to carry out forward intelligence sweeps into the desert. His only protection was the band of Arabs who had travelled across the Sinai desert with him to get here and who had sworn a blood oath of loyalty to him. His command of Arabic from long years of working in Palestine stood him in good stead when working with these men and others from Egypt.

The man on the camel reached the *zariba* and reined in his mount. To Evans he looked exactly like the men they had been fighting the day before, with his beard, dark skin and wearing the patched robes that signified he was one of the Mahdi's followers. His blue eyes stood out in the dark face, but luckily blue eyes were not unknown in the Arab world.

Evans saluted. "How can I help you sir?"

"First you can open up this damned thorn hedge and then you can point me at the General. I need to report to him and ask him a favour."

The hedge was dragged back and Kitchener entered. Evans escorted him across the compound with their feet crunching the discarded brass cartridge cases into the earth.

Kitchener looked down. "The Hussars tell me you had a stiff fight here yesterday. Was it bad? Many casualties?"

Evans looked back at the man striding beside him. "It got a little dicey for a while sir. Nine officers dead all told. Eighty six men as well. Plus of course a lot of injuries."

"I see you still have a lot of Dervish casualties outside the square."

"That's right sir. We are forming fatigue parties now to go out and do what we can with them. We have to be careful as their wounded are dangerous. I suspect we'll be burning or destroying their weapons so they can't be recovered once we move on."

As Evans finished speaking they arrived outside the General's tent and a staff officer took Kitchener inside. Evans walked across to where Lieutenant Colonel Latham sat, under the shade of a palm tree grove.

He saluted as he reached him. "Major Kitchener has arrived sir. He's reporting to the General now."

Latham looked up and shaded his eyes with his hand. "Indeed? Did he give you any news of Khartoum?"

"Never said anything about it, sir. Just asked what we had been doing."

As they were speaking a young staff officer trotted across to them and saluted. "Colonel Latham sir. The General's compliments and could you join him immediately please."

Latham walked briskly across and ducked into the shaded interior of the tent. The General looked up from the map he was studying with the man in the Arab robes.

"Ah Latham, thank you for coming so promptly. Major Kitchener here needs a favour, he needs a heliograph operator. He is going to try and get close enough to Khartoum to signal General Gordon. We need to know Gordon's situation and he needs to know we are coming."

"Yes sir." Latham smiled. "I have just the man. A good signaller and a remarkable shot with a rifle. He has also picked up quite a bit of Arabic since we arrived, through talking to the boatmen and the camel drivers. Shall I send for him?"

Kitchener straightened up from the map table. "He sounds ideal. If you could tell him to get ready I'll pick him up as I leave."

Latham nodded and left the tent. He was smiling as he walked towards his own men.

Chapter 16.
Major Kitchener

Michael McGuire stood next to his camel outside the thorn hedge and waited for the officer he had been attached to. He saw the tall Arab striding through the camp towards him, but thought nothing of it until the man spoke.

"I take it you are McGuire? I am Major Kitchener and you are coming with me as my heliograph signaller, do you understand that?"

McGuire came to attention and saluted the officer. "I do sir. Sergeant Major Lewis told me."

Kitchener looked him up and down. The man before him was of slightly above average height and build. His uniform was patched and dirty, but no worse than the rest of the troops around him. His rifle was in his hand and looked well cared for. He looked into the young Irishman's eyes and liked the confidence he saw there.

"A couple of things you need to know. You will be travelling mostly with my Arab tribesmen. They have sworn an oath to me and are totally loyal. They are also brave and remarkably fearless. Treat them with respect and they will look after you in the desert. That is the last time you will salute me or anybody else during your time with me. If the enemy scouts saw that they would know I was a target for them."

He turned away and dug into the bag that hung from the back of his camel. Pulling out a white robe with coloured patches sewn to it he tossed it to McGuire.

"That is called a *jibba* and the patches show that you are a follower of the Mahdi, "The Expected One". From now until you re-join the army, that is what you will wear. My tribesmen will teach you the customs of the Arabs so you do not give yourself away. Now you need to understand that, if you are caught by the Mahdi's troops, your death will be long and painful, so be careful and keep your rifle close by at all times."

McGuire looked down at the robe in his hands. "I didn't expect to be wearing a dress to go to war, but if you say so, sir, then I'll do it."

"Good, now get yourself a second bandolier of ammunition and mount up then we'll get back to my men. The first thing I'll have them do is sort out that bloody awful saddle you've been issued. You need to look after that camel if you want to survive. Oh and lose that damned silly helmet."

McGuire ran back to the *zariba* and got one of his comrades to throw him a second full bandolier of ammunition for the Martini Henry. He re-joined the Major with the two leather bandoliers across his chest. They mounted and were led away from the column by two escorts from the Hussars. Once they were out of rifle shot, the cavalrymen left them and they continued their progress into the desert at the stately pace the camels preferred.

As they rode side by side McGuire looked across at the man who was taking him into the unknown. He was tall and wiry, with a full beard. He had startlingly clear blue eyes although there was a squint in one of them. His manner was brusque, but McGuire was used to that from his own officers so saw nothing wrong with it.

They rode in silence for an hour or more and then the Major turned in his saddle and looked at McGuire. "You haven't asked why I want a heliograph. Don't you care?"

"I thought you'd tell me when you were good and ready sir."

Kitchener snorted. "Fair enough. Well I'm ready now. You know of course that Chinese Gordon is trapped in Khartoum. His own damned fault really, he refused to leave when the government ordered him to. Now the Mahdi's men have cut the telegraph wires and closed the Nile to the steamers that could have brought people out. I believe the city will be surrounded or at least heavily patrolled. What I want you to do is to get within heliograph range of the city and find out what Gordon's situation is. You will also tell him about the progress of the relief column."

"On my own sir?"

"No. I am going to send two of my best with you. They will try and keep you safe and get you back in one piece."

"And if they fail sir?"

"If they fail, keep one of those bullets back to the last. Don't let the Mahdi's people capture you, unless you want a slow, painful death and your head on a spear outside their tents."

"One thing sir. Does General Gordon have a signaller to read the message I send him?"

Kitchener smiled grimly. "We don't know what he has or doesn't have left. I do know he is a

Royal Engineer, as I am, so he has a lot of technical ability. He may be able to read it himself. I certainly could. He also has a Colonel Stewart with him as his aide; he is a cavalryman so again he may be able to understand a heliograph message."

McGuire rode on for a few paces before he spoke. "So really I could be flashing away at Khartoum with nobody able to read the message or to send one back? And for that I could end up getting my head removed?"

Kitchener nodded. "That's about the size of it. Then again you could get the message in and get one back and that could be very valuable to Gordon and to Lord Wolseley."

Chapter 17.
Off Into the Blue

The two men rode towards the small campfire. They stopped before they reached it and dismounted, then walked forward leading their camels. McGuire could see nobody near the flickering flames. In fact he had not seen the fire until they were almost on top of it. It had been built in a narrow gulley and then it had been dug into a hole in the sand.

Kitchener came to a halt and stood quietly before giving a low whistle. McGuire did not recognise the tune, but clearly the Arabs who appeared from nowhere did. From out of the darkness men came towards them from all directions. They too were dressed in the *jibbas* of the Mahdi, with wicked looking curved daggers in their waist bands and each man carried a rifle.

There was no great show of affection for Kitchener as they all made their way back to sit around the fire. They sat down quietly and waited for their leader to speak. Although he had learned a lot over the last few months McGuire had to concentrate hard to keep up with Kitchener's rapid Arabic.

He pointed at McGuire. "This one is one of us. He needs to learn the ways of the desert and he is the one we spoke of, who will speak with Gordon Pasha through the flashing light. He is to be a brother to you and you will be brothers to him."

The Arabs sat silently and looked carefully at McGuire. Kitchener waited a moment or two before he turned to the young Irish soldier.

"As I told you." He said, still speaking in Arabic. "These men are to be trusted. They have honour and are due respect. They are not the *fellahin* of Egypt who are terrified of the desert, these men are Bedouin. They are a warrior people who know the ways of the deep desert. Most of all they have courage."

McGuire looked around at the men who sat and watched him keenly. He nodded slowly to Kitchener and then turned back to the group before he spoke.

"I will try to be worthy of your trust and I will learn from you. If the time comes then I will die with you."

There was muttering and then smiles from the men of the desert. Kitchener slapped him on the shoulder.

"Well said young man. Make sure you keep those promises. Now then, your first lesson in Arabic culture. We will eat from a common bowl placed between us. Make sure to only use your right hand, never the left."

"Why not the left, sir?"

"The left hand is used for bodily functions so it is unclean. The Arabs are very particular about that. At the end of the meal ensure you belch to show appreciation. It is an odd custom to us, but it is their way. Never drink deeply of your water if a brother has none, by sharing we all survive."

They sat cross legged on the sand while the meal was prepared. Kitchener waved two of the men to come and sit by him. They walked across without a word and sank to the sand.

Kitchener turned to McGuire. "These two are the ones who will take you to Khartoum. This one is Haroun, he is the older of the two and so is the wisest. Then this one, with the one eye, is Asif. He lost the eye to a hawk years ago, but he can still shoot better than any man I have ever seen. Is that not true Asif?"

"It is true if Kitchener says it is true." Asif said, spreading his hands, palm upwards.

Kitchener gave one of his rare smiles. "Kitchener does say it." He turned to McGuire. "They carry no map or navigation equipment, but they will take you there without an error. They make take what seems to be a strange direction, but that will be to avoid the Mahdi and his army. Listen to what Haroun tells you and you may even come back alive."

Haroun sat looking at McGuire appraisingly, and then he turned to Kitchener. "Is he ready for the desert, this one?"

Kitchener shook his head. "No my friend, he needs your wisdom before he leaves. His saddle is wrong and his water bags leak. He rides his camel like an Englishman. Though he has the skills we need. He speaks your tongue, but not well. You must teach him all things that a man needs in this country."

"It will be as you say. How long before we must go?"

"One day only. You must be looking at Khartoum as soon as a man of your skill is able."

"Shall we go into the city and find Gordon Pasha?"

Kitchener put out a hand and rested it on the man's shoulder. "Haroun, your life is precious to me. If you can speak to Gordon Pasha and come safe back to me then do. If it puts your life in too much danger then use the flashing light only."

Haroun nodded. "It will be as you say. Now the food is ready and we must eat together as friends."

McGuire spent the next day being taught how to live in the desert away from a commissariat. Haroun laughed at his saddle and the way he sat on it, but once the saddle was adjusted to his liking then it seemed obvious to sit the beast Arab style. He spent time telling the Irishman about the ways of the camel and how to ensure it stayed healthy.

Asif was quieter, but as they took a break for thick black coffee from tiny cups, he showed McGuire his Remington rifle. McGuire took the hint and walked across to his camel to bring back the Martini Henry and handed it to Asif. The Arab ran his hands across the woodwork and admired the weapon. He sat entranced as McGuire took the rifle back and showed him how to load it with the heavy calibre bullet. His face lit up when the loaded rifle was handed back to him and he turned to fire at a rock some distance away. He was unhappy when his shot fell short and McGuire showed him how to adjust the sight for distance.

His second shot struck the target full in the centre and Michael had to admit Kitchener had been right about the one eyed man's ability.

By the middle of the afternoon Haroun declared that McGuire now knew enough that he would not be a burden on their journey and they returned to the camp where Kitchener was in deep discussion with three more of the Bedouin. He looked up as McGuire walked towards him after hobbling his camel. He nodded to the young soldier then turned to Haroun.

"Is he ready, my wise friend?"

Haroun sat down with his back against a rock wall and nodded. "He will survive the desert. He learns quickly this one. When he has learned to speak the language of our people properly he will be a force in the desert."

Kitchener smiled slightly and turned to McGuire. "That is the highest praise a man can get from Haroun. I will have to keep an eye on you, even when this is over."

McGuire smiled. "Haroun is a fine teacher. He tells me we are leaving before dawn to get to Khartoum so do you have the messages you want me to send sir?"

Kitchener reached inside his patched *jibba* and brought out a small leather bound notebook. "The messages you need to send are on the first three pages. If he has a heliograph and can reply, there are questions that I need you to ask him on the next few pages. They are mostly about conditions inside the city and the readiness of the Egyptian troops he has there."

McGuire flipped through the pages reading the messages and the questions. "I have no problem with any of those, sir."

"Good, now if it all goes wrong and it looks like you are about to be captured or overrun destroy that book. The Mahdi has people who can read English and it would not do to let him know what is in there. He is no fool and the information would be of use to him."

McGuire slipped the book into the empty pouch on his ammunition bandolier. "Anything else I should know, sir?"

Kitchener looked at him steadily, the cast in his eye more obvious, now that he was tired. "I have told you to trust Haroun and Asif. I should also tell you that the Mahdi's people should not be underestimated. Your column beat them off this time, but they are brave warriors and, although their tactical ability is lacking, they are not stupid. Be wary of them and be ready to run if they spot you."

Chapter 18.
Action at Abu Kru

With the dead buried and the wounded made as comfortable as possible the relief column's need for water was now becoming more urgent. The casualties were loaded on to the stretchers slung on either side of camels and the remainder were formed into a loose defensive square as they moved on. They marched along the barely discernible tracks with no sign of the promised water until a Hussar patrol found the wells off to the left. The square wheeled around and moved forward.

The wells consisted of a series of pits dug into the desert floor with muddy brown water in them. The wounded were given the water first and then each man and animal was given a ration. The water disappeared in a disappointingly short time and it would need more of the time they did not have for the wells to fill again.

Early the next morning the column moved on again across a vast gravelly slope covered in scrub and tussocks towards the Nile. They hoped to reach the river, unseen by the enemy, somewhere below Metemma so as to allow the men to rest and replenish their water before any further action.

As the column moved forward the Hussar screen reported Dervish patrols in the area, just as the green belt of cultivation came into view. The sniping started from the areas of scrub, but gave the British nothing to shoot at, except puffs of white smoke. Initially the fire from seven or eight hundred yards away was no more than an annoyance. Then at around nine in the morning the commanding general, Sir Herbert Stewart, received a bullet in the groin. The wound was felt to be mortal and so command was passed to Sir Charles Wilson who was not accustomed to a combat command.

Orders were given to take a position on a nearby low ridge and the column moved rapidly to occupy it. A low wall of saddles and biscuit boxes reinforced by stones was constructed and the men lay down to take cover behind it, but not before some of the builders were knocked over by the increasingly effective sniper fire.

Colonel Latham was speaking to Captain Carter when he spun round and fell to the ground. He was untouched, but a bullet had passed through his beard. Lieutenant Evans was struck in the stomach and fell down gasping for breath. He was carried into the camel lines and examined. There was no puncture wound only a massive bruise and it was found that a ricochet bullet had struck one of the brass buttons of his jacket and saved his life. The special correspondent of The Standard newspaper was less lucky and was found dead moments later.

As the casualties mounted, Sir Charles Wilson realised he could not fight his way to the river encumbered by the wounded and the baggage train. He decided to split the force in half. The wounded to be left in the small redoubt while the remainder of those who were capable of fighting moved forward to clear the Dervishes away.

The Heavy Camel Regiment and the Blue Jackets with their heavy Nordenfelt guns were left behind, to protect the wounded, while the rest formed up into a marching square and moved out. The sniping continued and men fell, slowing the pace of the advance even more as the medical team dealt with them within the square.

At length the Arabs began to form into large bodies and Latham smiled as he turned to his men. "Thank God! They are going to charge. At least we will be able to come to grips with them."

Sergeant Major Lewis and all the other senior NCOs prepared their men and waited. Several thousand of the enemy massed on the slope to the left front of the square and then executed a screaming charge. The banners waved above them as they came on and the British troops stood silently waiting.

At four hundred yards the order was given and volley fire commenced. Still they came on and the volley fire became a continuous roar of musketry. Hundreds fell before the disciplined rifle fire, but still they advanced. The British stood and fired as if they were on a parade square and the attack started to falter. Not a man got within eighty yards of the square without being cut down.

The Dervishes held in reserve saw what had happened to their comrades and they dispersed and ran. The battle was over and the way to the river was open. The square marched forward into the sunset and by the feeble light of a crescent moon they reached the river. The wounded were given water first. Despite their raging thirst the men stood in position until their turn came. Not a man left his place in the ranks.

The tom-tom drums were sounding around them, but the exhausted troops lay down to sleep with just the sentries to guard them. Tomorrow they would return to the redoubt and collect the wounded and their stores, but tonight they would rest.

Chapter 19.
By Camel to Khartoum

The same feeble moonlight lit the way across the desert for the three men on camels. Asif took the lead and McGuire followed him, with Haroun behind him. In the clear, cold night the stars seemed close enough to touch and the Irishman found he was enjoying the stately swaying ride through the darkness.

After riding for three hours the horizon brightened with the yellow and ochre colours of the dawn. As the light swept across the rocky gravel plain they could see for miles, before the heat haze started to hide things from them. Nothing moved in any direction and the black hills were bare of any enemy.

As they rode Haroun came up alongside McGuire and looked across at him. "You are well this morning?"

"I am well. The desert seems empty, will it stay that way?"

Haroun nodded off to one side. "Your eyes are not used to the desert yet it seems. There are gazelle over to that side. Our meal would be better for fresh meat I think. Do you bring your rifle and take one down for us?"

"It shall be as you say, if Asif does not want the chance to show his skill again?"

"Asif will watch around us while we hunt. It is not safe to think there is no enemy here."

The two men turned their camels and approached the small group of gazelle. Too few to be called a herd. As they got closer McGuire slipped down from his mount and walked silently forward. The animals did not see him or maybe did not recognise him as a threat and he was able to get within easy rifle range. He picked his target and aimed carefully. The loud report of his rifle rolled across the empty desert and his quarry dropped.

He walked forwards as the rest of the gazelle ran. Haroun rode forward, leading Kathleen by the halter rope and McGuire lifted the small animal and passed it up to the now smiling Bedouin.

"A fine weapon for hunting. I think I must ask Kitchener for one when this is over."

They rode back to Asif who admired the gazelle across Haroun's saddle. "But I think I will hunt for us from this day. The hole your bullet makes wastes too much meat."

McGuire looked across at the gaping exit hole in the gazelle's shoulder. "You are right. For a small animal it is too much, but for the crazy Dervishes it needs something like this to stop them."

Haroun shook his head slowly. "No they are not crazy. This is their land and for many years the Egyptians have robbed them and called it taxes. They have attacked them and violated their women. Their crops and livestock have been taken and villages left to starve. They have good reason for what they do. All they needed was a leader and now they have the Mahdi who says he is the Expected One. Maybe not all of them believe, but that does not matter, he is still a leader."

McGuire was quiet as he contemplated Haroun's words. The scant briefings he and the other troops had been given had said nothing about this. He looked at the older man and saw only truth in his eyes.

"It sounds a little like the way my people have been treated by the English, but worse. Why do you not fight with them? Why do you help us?"

Haroun sniffed and spat into the dry ground. "This is not my land. Nobody taxes the Bedouin. We live in our own way in our own desert. If we had trouble these would not come to aid us. Why do you fight for the English?"

McGuire smiled at the Arab beside him. "It is better than starving in a dirty hovel in my home land and while I live my family can eat."

Haroun snorted. "You are right. English gold shines brightly and feeds many mouths. When we go back to our land there will be many goats and fine camels."

Asif reined his camel to a halt and pointed. "A village over there. I see no smoke from cooking fires and it is the time of a meal."

Haroun shaded his eyes and looked where his friend pointed. "We shall see. There may be water and we could shelter there for the night. It would be warmer than the desert floor."

As they rode slowly towards the village nothing moved. The mud brick huts were silent and no dogs or chickens roamed between them. McGuire pulled his rifle out of the carrying boot of his saddle and made sure it was loaded. His companions did the same as they approached. They paused on the edge of the small jumble of huts and looked around warily. There was nothing.

Asif dismounted while the other two watched over him. He walked quickly to the first hut and looked inside. There were signs that people had left in a hurry with household items in disarray. He went from hut to hut and each told the same story. There was nobody left in the village and no sign of why they had left their homes. Perhaps they feared the advance of the British or perhaps they fled the Dervishes. They would never know.

Night was approaching so they moved into one of the surprisingly clean huts and hobbled their camels just outside. Asif found the small village well and McGuire helped him to bring water for the animals and then to fill their water skins. They made a fire in the hut, confident that the light would not be seen and attract the enemy.

The gazelle was butchered and cooked with half being dried to make a jerky for the next day. They ate in a friendly silence then rolled themselves in their blankets and slept. Haroun had promised that in only two days they would see Khartoum and needed to start early in the morning.

Chapter 20.
Khartoum

Haroun was proved right as they breasted a low rise after two days of hard riding. Before them they could see the walls of the city with the Blue and the White Niles either side of it. McGuire stared hard, but could not make out what the flag was that flew above the walls.

"Asif of the keen eye. What flag is that above the tower? Is that the banner of the Mahdi?"

Asif turned and looked at the brown walled town. "It is not the Mahdi's banner. I can see his men across the river in that camp. The flag you see is the same one your column carries and another that flies is that for the Egyptians."

McGuire stroked his ear. "So the city has not fallen yet. We are in time. Will you watch while I send the messages with the flashing light?"

"This is not a good time." Haroun said as he pointed off to the right. "There rides a patrol of the Mahdi's soldiers and they have seen us. They come this way. Stay silent if you value your head. I will speak for us. Cover your light machine and the rifle of the English. If they see them we are lost."

McGuire rearranged his saddle blanket and the three men sat their camels as the patrol rode up to them. The leader of the six riders came forward when the others stopped.

"Who are you brother? We did not expect to see any others here."

Haroun looked at the patches on their *jibbas* and took a guess. "We are of the Green Banner regiment. We have been sent to look at the city to see if there is a weakness we can use when the Expected One gives the command to attack."

"We of the Black Banner have been given that task. Why would you come here as well?"

"We come because out Emir would have it so. We do not question. Maybe more eyes will see what has been missed by others?"

"You think we have not looked though keen eyes? We have been here for days we know this place and we know the city. The spies of the Black Banner walk in the streets and tell us much."

Haroun nodded and smiled with a flash of gold at his mouth. "That is a good thing brother. Perhaps we are on a fool's errand, but it is the will of the Emir."

The leader of the patrol looked at Haroun and made his decision. "It is ever the way with Emirs. They trust no one, but their own. It is foolish, but it is the way of such men."

"It is as you say, brother." Haroun agreed.

"We will continue. You may enjoy your wasted journey. Perhaps we will meet in the city over the bodies of the infidels."

With that he turned the head of his horse and rode down the ridge with his men following him. McGuire breathed a huge sigh of relief, his heart had been in his mouth and he had been convinced his time had come.

"Haroun are you sure you're not Irish? I would swear you've kissed the Blarney Stone."

Haroun looked puzzled. "I do not know what that means, but we have been lucky this day. When those men of the Black Banner are out of sight you may send your message, but be quick, there will be more of them and if those come back they will not be fooled again."

McGuire got his camel to kneel below the top of the ridge and hobbled it in place. He slung his rifle across his back and then stumbled back up the slope carrying the ungainly heliograph. He checked that the Black Banner patrol was gone before he opened up the tripod and started to set up his equipment. Once satisfied he was ready, he looked up to find his two companions watching him curiously.

"I am ready to try now Haroun, if you say it is safe."

Haroun pointed out towards the left. "Asif you will go there and keep a watch. I will go the other way. Waste no time with your flashing lights. We will be seen by the Dervishes around the city."

McGuire nodded and withdrew the leather notebook from inside his *jibba*. He opened the book and placed it next to the signalling head. He read through the first message again and then started to send. With the message finished he straightened up and watched for a reply. There was nothing. He repeated the message again and again, but still without a reaction. He considered the options. Maybe they had seen the signal, but could not reply? Maybe nobody could read the message? Maybe they were bringing somebody forward who could read the message? Without a response he could not know what was happening inside Khartoum.

He sent the second message and then the third. He started from the beginning and repeated all three messages again and again. He stopped as Asif rode towards him.

"We are seen. The patrol is coming back and they hurry. We must go."

McGuire started to take the heliograph to pieces as Haroun rode up. "There is no time for that. If we live through this day we will come back for this thing of light."

McGuire looked up at the man on the camel. Kitchener had told him to trust this one and so far he had not failed. He collapsed the tripod and laid the equipment on the ground then hurriedly covered it over with sand. He ran down the slope followed by his two companions and released Kathleen. Once he was mounted the three of them trotted back the way they had come.

They had been riding for only ten minutes when they heard the shouts from behind them as the patrol arrived at the top of the ridge. Haroun turned in the saddle and considered the problem. Being mounted on horses the patrol would be faster than the camels and they would be soon caught.

"Asif! We must find a place to fight."

Asif pointed away to his left and rode his camel towards the shallow rocky gulley. They stopped the camels in the centre of the gulley and made them kneel to be hobbled. All three men returned to the lip of the gulley with their rifles at the ready. They could hear the drumbeat of the chasing hooves and seconds later the six pursuers appeared over the edge of the slight slope.

The blades they had in their hands reflected the sunlight and the jangling of the horses' harness gained volume. They spotted the gulley and rode directly towards it breaking into a full gallop as they did so.

Haroun pushed his rifle forward between two rocks on the lip of the depression. "All must die or we are lost. None can return to tell his story."

Asif took his first shot and lifted the right hand rider out of his saddle and down to the unforgiving desert. His head smashed against a rock and if the bullet had not killed him then the impact had. Haroun fired next and he too took a man down.

McGuire waited for his moment. Then fired and reloaded, he fired again and then again. Each time he fired an enemy fell. The last man was almost upon them when he fired a fourth time. The blast just before his face made the pony slide to a stop and the rider with the splash of bright blood across his chest flew over the horse's head and landed face down in the gravel.

Haroun and Asif were up and moving before the last man hit the ground. They went to the five men in front of them and, as they reached them, they slashed their wicked curved daggers across the throats of their enemies. They walked back to where McGuire was standing, stunned at such casual violence.

"Is that one dead?" Asif asked.

"I haven't looked." McGuire said.

Asif stepped forward, rolled the man over and again the shining blade flickered across the Arab's throat. He wiped the blade on the dead man's robe and straightened up.

"Your rifle fires fast my friend. With one like that I could do much."

"I will ask Kitchener to get one for you when he gets one for Haroun."

"Good. That is good. Now we must see what kind providence has brought for us. You should see the four you killed. We will see ours."

McGuire stood and watched as the two Bedouin walked back to their victims and started to search through their clothing. He remembered the words of the agent back in Dublin and realised here was another opportunity to help his mother. He stooped and searched the man who lay at his feet, then walked out of the gulley and searched the other three. He found only *piasters* until he reached the one who had been the leader. This one had another jewelled dagger in his sash and had gold pieces in a small leather bag around his neck. He counted them out and slipped them back into the pouch that he then put under his *jibba*.

Haroun called to him. "Now we must go. Others will have heard the noise of our rifles. They will come to see what has happened. We must be far away before they come here."

The three men mounted and rode away, behind them the six ponies stood and waited for riders who would never rise again. Before nightfall they had found a wadi to rest in though they could not risk a fire this close to the enemy. They sat and chewed on the dried gazelle meat as they cleaned their weapons

McGuire drew the leather pouch out and emptied it onto the blanket he was sitting on. Without a word he counted the gold and then split the pieces into three equal piles as the two Arabs watched him. He rose from the blanket and handed a small pile of gold coins to each man, then returned and sat down again.

Haroun and Asif looked at each other before the older man spoke. "What is this? This came from the one you killed, it is yours. We have what ours carried."

McGuire returned his small cache of coins to the leather pouch and looked up. "We are brothers in the desert are we not? Since we left Kitchener we have shared everything. The water, the meat and the danger. All these we have shared. Now we share our good fortune. Is this not right?"

Haroun looked at the man before him for a moment before he spoke. "It is not our way, but it is good to share with a brother."

McGuire laid the jewelled dagger on the ground. He looked at the two men who waited for him to speak.

"This we cannot share. There is only one. It would look best in the sash of a wise man. Is that not true Asif?"

Asif gave McGuire a toothy grin. "It is the dagger of an old man who will pass it on to his friend one day."

"It is as you say." McGuire said, as he passed the beautifully worked weapon to Haroun.

Chapter 21.

Into Danger

"Haroun, I need your wisdom."

The older man looked up from the water skin he was repairing. "What is your need?

McGuire paused, he knew he was about to ask a lot of these two men. "My friend I have been tasked to deliver messages to Gordon and to bring answers back to Kitchener. I do not know if my messages were seen and I have no answers."

"And what does this have to do with my wisdom?"

"Haroun, is it possible for three men of the desert to go through the Dervish patrols into the city and come out again alive? I would go to the house of Gordon Pasha and speak my messages to him. He must know that the column is coming and he must hold on for only a few days more."

Haroun put the water skin to one side and thought. "It was my wish to see old age, to sit in my tent and tell my grandchildren stories of the things we have done."

"If it cannot be done we can leave and you can still tell your stories."

"You speak the truth, but if we can do it what a story that would make for the long nights by the fire. None will believe an old man until my friend Asif sits with me and says it is true."

McGuire nodded. "Asif will you help us?"

"The English are truly mad. This is not a thing that is wise to do. But if Haroun will go then

I must go with my friend and try to bring him home alive."

"You are right that it is a mad thing to do, but I am not English and the Irish are madder still."

Haroun pulled his blanket around him and eased himself down. "I must think on this. In the morning we will try. A city of this size must have a gate for three weary travellers."

McGuire woke with the dawn to see Asif walking back into their small camp. He sat down and dropped a few dry sticks on the fire to make the morning tea. Haroun threw back his blanket and sat up. He looked at Asif in silence and the other man nodded.

McGuire sat up and waited but neither of his companions spoke. "What has happened?"

Haroun looked across the small fire at him and the gold flashed in his mouth as he smiled. "Asif, of the one eye that sees more than many with two eyes, has been to the city in the night. He has found a way in."

"Tell me Asif. How can it be done?"

Asif said nothing until he had poured the tea into three small cups and passed them around. "When the rains come to the country far in the south, the Nile rises. The water is allowed into the city and fills the great cisterns they have built within the walls. Now is the time when the Nile falls and the waterway into the city is dry. Once, long ago, there was a barred gate across it, but it has rotted in the years and has fallen. It is not guarded and a man can crawl through into the city."

"How do you know there are no guards inside the walls by the cisterns?"

Asif grinned. "I have been in the city and walked its streets."

"How is it in the city?"

"The people walk slowly and have dull eyes for want of food. They eat rats when they can catch them. The food stores are empty and the soldiers give out small rations. The Dervish army stops any food getting in. This is not a city that can fight against the might of the Mahdi. If you wish to see Gordon alive it must be tonight."

McGuire nodded slowly then sipped his tea. "Then tonight it must be, if you will help me my friends?"

"We will help you." Haroun said. "We will need the patched *jibbas* of the Mahdi to approach the wall, but must wear other clothes inside or we shall be killed by the Egyptian soldiers."

"What news of the Mahdi? Does anyone know when he will attack?"

Asif nodded. "The tom-tom drums are beating all night to make the people of the city fear. A fleet of boats lies on the sand of the river by the Mahdi's camp. Every day more followers join him. I do not think it will be long before he prays in the grand mosque of Khartoum as he has foretold."

"When do we move Haroun?"

"You are eager English. You must use the patience of the desert. We leave here an hour before night. We arrive at the wall when the sun is down and then we change our robes to crawl into the city like the rats."

"It shall be as you say." McGuire said, before reaching for his rifle and starting to clean it.

Haroun shook his head. "This is not a thing for rifles. If they are seen there will be questions. For tonight we have daggers only."

Chapter 22.
Into the City

The three men hobbled their camels across the river from the city on the side away from the Mahdi's camp. They rolled their patched *jibbas* and changed into plain ones before they waded into the water. At this season the Nile was low and they forced their way across with the water only coming up to their chests. They climbed up the rocky bank and stood before the city wall. There was no challenge and they heard no sound from any patrolling sentries.

Silently Asif led the way along the narrow bank between the wall and the river until he came to a shallow gulley. The pale moonlight showed a round opening to their left that cut through beneath the wall. The remains of an iron gate lay scattered around it, where the bars had fallen as they rusted through.

With Asif leading the way they dropped to their knees and crawled into the stone lined tunnel. After fifty uncomfortable feet Asif dropped out of sight at the end of the water course. McGuire stopped as he reached the opening and looked around. The cistern was deep and stone lined, with a set of stone stairs curling around the side wall and down to the water below them.

Asif was already walking up the staircase to check for any danger outside the cistern when McGuire dropped down, Haroun followed quickly and they mounted the stairs. Asif turned around at the top of the cistern and waved them forward. As they joined him, McGuire looked around the city square that surrounded the cistern. Nothing moved and there were no lights from any of the windows of the houses.

"Now then Asif, do you know the way to the big house where Gordon Pasha lives?"

Asif pointed down one of the lanes that entered the square. "It is that way, English. There are iron gates and walls with soldiers around the gardens. We must find a way in that does not cause them to shoot us."

McGuire straightened up behind the low wall that surrounded the cistern. He walked out into the square and marvelled at the silence. It was never this quiet in Dublin city no matter what time of night it was. The three men walked across the square, unconsciously trying to be as silent as the rest. They entered the narrow street that Asif had pointed out and walked along it close to the walls of the houses.

Five minutes of walking brought them in sight of the tall wrought iron gates that were the entrance to Government House. Through the bars they could see two sentries in their white uniforms with the red fez of the Egyptian army. McGuire could see from the way they held themselves that these men were nervous His original plan, of walking to the gate and announcing himself, seemed too risky to attempt now.

McGuire pointed to a narrow alleyway they had passed as they walked. It led them between rows of squalid houses towards the next decent sized street that led towards the residence. Half way along the alley they found their first dead body. The man had been there for a day of so in the heat and the stench was almost intolerable in the small space. They pushed their way through the cloud of flies, which rose up as they passed, and reached the wider street.

They turned to the right, back towards the residence and found themselves looking at a high white wall topped with sharp iron spikes. The wall stretched away into the darkness to the left and to the right it led back to the iron gate. With sentries probably patrolling the grounds, attempting to climb the wall would almost certainly be fatal. They were left with only the direct approach.

McGuire motioned his companions back out of sight of the gate guards. "If you two stay back out of sight I will walk up to the gate and show them I am alone. I will tell them who I am and ask to be allowed in to see Gordon Pasha."

Haroun looked at the Irishman with sad eyes. "The Egyptians at the gate are frightened men. They will shoot at anything they see move in the night. Your plan is not a good one."

"Then my friend what do we do? We have come a long dark way just to turn around and leave."

Haroun walked a few steps until he could see the gate again, and then turned back to the other two men who waited. "We must find a place to rest until morning. With the light much of the fear will go and you can walk to the gate. It is not long until the dawn. We must wait."

McGuire looked at the older man for a moment or two. "Alright then. Kitchener told me that I should trust your wisdom and it will be so. We can walk back and wait by the cistern wall, until the morning comes."

Chapter 23.
The Mahdi Comes

The soft light of dawn woke the three men who dozed by the cistern wall. Asif stood and looked around him. Nobody was stirring in the houses and the square was silent. He came fully awake at the sound of a massive explosion from the direction of the main city gate. The screaming battle cries of the Mahdists mixed with the sound of rifle fire and harsh trumpets.

He grabbed Haroun and McGuire by the shoulders and shook them fully awake. "We must leave, the Mahdi has come. The city will fall and we will fall with it if we are found."

Both men staggered up and listened to the insane sounds of pitched battle. The people of Khartoum appeared from the street that led into the square, running from the fury of the Expected One. McGuire watched in amazement as the crowds streamed past. Where were they going? How did they think they could escape? He knew that the Mahdi would have all the gates into and out of the city attacked together.

Asif grabbed the Irishman's arm. "We must go, English. We have missed our chance. Now we must save our lives and take the news to Kitchener."

McGuire turned slowly to his two companions. "You two should go. I must try and get to Gordon. Maybe I can get him to the cistern and we can get him away?"

Haroun shook his head slowly. "You said that your people were madder than the English. You spoke the truth, but we have shared everything so far and must share this too. The story for my grandchildren would not be good if I had to tell them I left a friend behind."

McGuire nodded and gripped the older man's forearm. "So how do we do this?"

Asif spat into the cistern. "This is foolish. We are to die for a children's story?"

Haroun looked at both men and the gold teeth from his slow smile caught the light of the sun. "But what a story we will tell, if we live my brother. Our people will remember the tale long after we join the sand of the desert. Will you let a soldier of the English be braver than a warrior of the Bedouin?"

Asif looked at his friend for a long moment. "I must be mad, but I cannot leave you, to do this thing that cannot be done, alone."

Haroun patted Asif's shoulder. "Come then. In a short time these streets will be filled with the Dervish warriors in their patched *jibbas*. They will be mad for blood and booty. If we look like them they will pass us by without a glance. Put on the *jibba* of the Mahdi and we will walk to the house of Gordon Pasha."

Standing in the square they pulled off the robes they had on and slipped the patched white *jibbas* over their heads. They tied the sashes around their waists and slipped the wicked curved daggers into place.

129

"I just wish I had my rifle with me. A knife is not much in the middle of a battle." McGuire said.

Haroun looked him up and down to ensure he looked like an Arab of the Dervish army. "Be at peace my young friend, there will be weapons enough to pick up as we go. Let us go and make the story for the long nights around our cooking fires."

They walked back towards the Governor's Residence down the dusty street. As they reached the halfway point, the mob of screaming tribesmen appeared running towards the gate. The two Egyptian soldiers fired once and then ran. The mob of sword and spear waving Dervishes wrenched the gates open and poured through. McGuire and the two Arabs ran forward and joined the crush to get through into the gardens.

The tribesmen spread out, with some going left and right, chasing the soldiers who had been camped within the walls. Any they caught were butchered in a sea of flashing blades and screams. The majority ran towards the Residence itself and battered on the high wooden double doors. McGuire stayed with them and then noticed he was alone. His two companions had been swept away from him in the mob.

The doors gave way and flew open with a splintering crash. The screaming war cries got louder as the Dervishes felt the triumph and ran forward into the courtyard. McGuire managed to reach the edge of the crowd and sheltered in an alcove by the wall to watch the tragedy unfold.

Across the courtyard a set of stone steps led up to a wide balcony and the remaining Egyptian soldiers had retreated behind the stone balustrade and were firing down into the crowd as fast as they could. The leading edge of the mob started up the stairs and then stopped. There was Gordon, dressed in a dark blue dress uniform with a single scarlet stripe down the seam of the trousers. In his left hand he held a heavy revolver and in his right a curved cavalry sabre. McGuire could not believe how calm he looked as he stood and regarded the men below him.

The Dervishes stopped and fell silent. They stared at the man who had defied them for so long. As Gordon took a step forward the men who were half way up the stairs recoiled a step. It seemed as if Gordon was going to speak to them and McGuire waited with the rest. Then in front of him there was a movement, an arm came back and a spear flew. The broad blade of the spear sank into Gordon's chest and for a second he stood and stared down at it in wonder. The revolver fell from his hand and then the sword drooped and fell too.

The spell was broken and the mob howled its rage and pounded up the stairs as Gordon fell. Long blades flashed and Gordon's head was slashed from his neck. It was lifted and forced down onto the blade of the spear that had killed him. The bloody trophy danced above the jubilant crowd as they ran through the building slaughtering the remainder of its defenders.

McGuire stayed in his alcove watching the drama unfold and listening to the death screams of

131

the Egyptian soldiers. He watched silently as the Dervishes came back out of the building with Gordon's head above them. His sword had been picked up and was being waved around the head in a grotesque victory dance as the attackers left the courtyard.

The noise of the warrior's cries grew less as they left the residence grounds and McGuire pushed himself forward towards the staircase. Gordon's headless and bloodied corpse had been thrown from the top of the stairs and lay in an untidy heap in the dust of the courtyard. The young soldier knelt down next to the remains of the General and wondered what he could do next. He turned the body over and went through the pockets searching for some token that he could take back to the column as proof of what he had seen. He found nothing but a handful of pistol bullets in a trouser pocket and he slipped them beneath his now blood stained *jibba*.

As he stood he looked back down at the remains of the man they had all come so far to save. He saw the black barrel of the pistol just to his side. The rest had been covered in sand and dust and forgotten. He picked it up and shook what sand he could off it before slipping it into his waist sash next to the dagger.

As he walked slowly out of the courtyard he saw Haroun and Asif running towards him. They slid to a stop and looked behind McGuire into the courtyard.

"That is Gordon Pasha?" Haroun asked.

"It is. We came too late. I watched him die the death of a hero facing his enemies."

Haroun patted the younger man on the arm. "Then that is the story we shall tell. A story of a brave man's death is worthy. But now we must get back to the cistern and get out of the city before we are noticed."

McGuire nodded sadly. "And we have to get the news of this back to Kitchener and the Relief Column."

Chapter 24.
A Rest by the Well

The crawl back through the water pipe went unnoticed by the army that was sacking the city. Khartoum was a place of screams and blood as they left it. As the Mahdi had promised, all those who were left in the city as he captured it were slaughtered, except for a few of the more attractive women who were taken as slaves after first being raped multiple times.

Night was falling as they waded back through the river and found their camels calmly lying where they had been left. In the darkness they walked the animals to the river and let them drink their fill, before they mounted and rode back the way they had come. They rode until the heat of midday found them close to one of the wells and Haroun decreed that this was the place to rest, before setting out across the worst of the desert.

They set up their rudimentary camp in the rocks to one side of the well where a small fire would not be seen. The pool was filled with green and unpleasant water so McGuire climbed through the rocks to try and find the source of the stream that fed it. He followed a narrow path that had been beaten flat by the hooves of gazelle and came across a smaller pool with clear, clean water. He made his way to the waterside and scooped up a handful of the sweetest water he had tasted in a long time.

He made his way back to the camp and showed the two Arabs what he had found. They drank and then filled the water skins. McGuire decided he would use the water and wash the filth of the last few weeks off himself. He stripped and walked into the pool. It was surprisingly cool and he wallowed in it. He then sat on a rock and washed his filthy clothes. As they dried, he went back into the water and washed his body again.

He looked up to find Asif standing on the bank. "English, you have found the water and now we will find the meat. The gazelle tracks will lead us to them."

With that, the one eyed Arab turned and walked back into the rocks. McGuire reluctantly climbed out of the water and let the sun dry him. He put the now dry clothes back on and waked back to the camp. He settled down on a blanket where he could see out across the desert and began to clean his rifle. Once that was done to his satisfaction he drew Gordon's heavy revolver out of his sash and started to clean the sand and grit out of it. He hefted it in his hand. The big, heavy pistol did not feel as natural as the Martini Henry when he held that. Satisfied it was clean he worked the action a few times to make sure before he reloaded it with the large pistol bullets.

He slipped the weapon into his waist sash and then started to gather the brushwood they would need for the cooking fire. The curved dagger served as a useful tool for cutting down the scrub bushes and then slicing them into the smaller pieces for the fire. Once he had a decent store assembled he sat himself down to watch across the wide plain in case of any enemies coming for the water of the well.

His eyes were beginning to droop, after missing a night's sleep, when he saw the three figures moving through the heat haze. At first he could not see what they were and wondered if the gazelle were coming back to drink. Then he saw that they were too big and were horses. As they drew nearer still, he could see that they had riders and then he could see the patched jibba that signified Dervishes.

He pulled his rifle closer to him and checked that it was loaded. Then he unbuttoned the pouches on his ammunition bandolier ready to grab his reloads quickly. Maybe if he lay still and the camels stayed quiet they would drink their fill and move on? He looked at the sun that was rapidly dropping towards the horizon and realised these men were probably going to camp for the night and move on the next day.

He kept watching them approach and running through his limited options. Then he saw that the man to the left had a rope in his hand and was dragging a captive along behind him. As they came nearer he saw that the captive had long hair, a woman. Then he saw that the hair was blond, a European woman. How the devil had she got out here to be captured by a Dervish?

The woman was stumbling and clearly on the edge of collapse. He realised his options had come down to one. There was no sign of his two companions so he was on his own. The odds were not brilliant at three to one, but he had no choice.

Picking up his weapon he slipped through the rocks down to ground level and then crawled behind a low ridge of gravel that had been thrown up by the scouring wind of the desert.

He checked his rifle one more time and waited until they were well within range. He stood up and walked out with the rifle held across his chest at the ready. The three horsemen reined in and stopped, looking at him.

The one dragging the captive was obviously the leader as he spoke for them. "And who is this who stands between us and the water?"

McGuire kept silent hoping they would come closer. He knew the sun had burnt his skin to a dark colour and his beard was full after so many weeks with no water to shave in. He knew the patched jibba would confuse then as well.

"I ask again, who is this who stands before me with a gun? Do you think this is your well?"

"It is my well. Would you pay to drink my water?" McGuire replied.

"This well is for all who follow the Mahdi. But your speech is strange in my ear. I hear your words, but they do not seem to be of our people. Who are you and what are you?"

McGuire decided his time had come and the play acting had to end. "My name is McGuire and I come from a city many miles to the north that we call Dublin."

"And how came you here from this city that I do not know?"

"I came with the army that is to take Khartoum from the Mahdi." McGuire smiled, now he was for it.

"An Infidel! Kill him!"

The leader dropped the rope and his captive collapsed to her knees behind him. The three horsemen spurred forward, drawing their swords as they came on screaming their war cries.

McGuire dropped to one knee raised the rifle to his shoulder and aimed at the closest man. He fired and the powerful lead bullet smashed into the centre of the rider's chest. The sword fell from his nerveless fingers and he slid sideways from his racing horse to plough a furrow in the desert.

Without pausing the soldier jacked the cocking arm of the Martini Henry down, slid in a cartridge and heaved the lever back up. He aimed at the next man and fired again. The heavy round flew straight and true and ripped into the man's throat, severing his artery and ripping out his windpipe. He rolled over the rump of his horse in a cartwheel of spouting blood and crashed to the ground.

The third man was uncomfortably close as McGuire reloaded. He raised the rifle, aimed and pulled the trigger. He heard the click of the firing pin going forward but the weapon did not go off. Misfire! He could almost feel the hot breath of the charging horse as he grabbed the stock of the rifle and swung the butt straight into the animal's face. The horse screamed and stopped stiff legged, flinging the rider over its head to land in a crumpled heap beyond the Irishman.

McGuire spun around trying to work the action of the rifle to let him load another round. The cocking lever moved half way and jammed on the damaged cartridge. The Arab was on his feet and moving towards him still gripping the wicked looking sword. If he had his bayonet with him he could have made a fight of it, but that was somewhere to the north in Kitchener's camp. The Arab made his mind up and raised the sword above his head as he charged. With a small prayer McGuire dragged Gordon's Webley revolver out of his waist sash and fired. The large calibre bullet flew as the weapon bucked in his hand. The round caught the Arab in the stomach and knocked him backwards, but it did not put him down. As he came on again McGuire fired twice more in rapid succession and the Arab fell to his knees. He swayed there for a second or two and then pitched forward on his face.

As he straightened up McGuire scanned the area all around. The young girl was still on her knees with her head sunk onto her chest. Other than that he could see no signs of life anywhere. Remembering the Dervish habit of shamming after a battle, he walked up to the nearest man. With two pistol bullets in him he was going nowhere. The remaining two were equally no threat with the remarkable damage that the Martini Henry had done to them.

He walked across to where the girl knelt and squatted down next to her. "It's all over miss, you're safe now."

Her head came up and she stared at him in wide eyed wonder. "But you're English. I saw you wearing the *jibba* of the Mahdi. Who are you? How did you get here?"

"As a matter of fact I'm as Irish as the shamrock. I'm Michael McGuire from fair Dublin city, at present a member of the Relief Force coming to rescue General Gordon."

"I hope you are going to hurry. The Mahdi was ready to attack as we left Khartoum."

McGuire shook his head sadly. "It's too late for that. I was in the city and I saw Gordon killed. We're too late, but I have to get back and tell them that."

Her head fell and he could see she was quietly sobbing. He started to gently untie the blood stained rope from around her wrists, as he did so he could see the skin was raw and torn. Her bare feet were had been ripped by the harsh gravel desert she had been dragged across and there was a raw scrape down one side of her face.

He stood up then bent down and scooped her up in his arms. He walked slowly back towards the camp site as she leaned her head against his chest still sobbing. He lay her down on his blanket and fetched her a water skin. She drank the cool sweet water greedily then lay down and rolled away from him.

Chapter 25.
A Bargain in the Wilderness.

Having decided that what the girl needed now was rest McGuire walked back out to the three men he had so recently killed. Their horses were standing about with their reins dangling to the ground. He walked to the furthest body, the one he had shot first. He was lying face down and the exit hole the heavy lead bullet had torn through him was already crawling with flies. McGuire rolled him over and searched him. In his waist sash he found an embroidered canvas pouch and when he opened it the gold coins tumbled out in a sparkling stream.

The coins were rapidly retrieved and pushed back into the bag while the search continued. The curved scimitar the man had been waving was unusual so he took that as a gift for his friends. The dagger at the man's waist was nothing special so he left it where it was. As he stood he took the nearby horse by the reins and led it across to stand next to its stable mate.

He knelt down next to the second corpse. This one had been almost beheaded by the bullet tearing through his neck. McGuire did his best to avoid looking at the mangled mess as he searched the body. He found another pouch. This one too was stuffed with gold coins and a ring with a large ruby mounted in it. He pocketed that and then led both horses across to the third man. The third horse whinnied as he came close and he spoke softly to it to calm it. Perhaps it remembered the pain he had given it with his rifle butt? He stroked its muzzle gently and checked that there was no serious damage before he turned to the last man who lay on the ground before him.

The man lay staring at the vultures just starting to appear above them. Flies crawled across his open eyes and into his gaping mouth. As McGuire searched him he found two pouches of gold coins and slipped them under his robe. Then he solved the mystery of why the first bullet to the stomach had not put this man down. Around his neck was a leather strap that held a small, brown leather satchel. The first bullet he had fired had punched through the leather and was embedded in the papers he found within.

McGuire sat back on his heels and looked at the sheaf of letters. The first was addressed to Lord Wolseley, the commander of the Relief Force. The next was addressed to the Prime Minster, Mr Gladstone and was marked as personal. Then there was another addressed to the Duke of Cambridge at Horse Guards and finally he found the most amazing one of all. It was addressed to Queen Victoria and was marked as urgent and personal. He turned the letters over and on the back of the cream envelope he found General Gordon's name. These must be dispatches that had been smuggled out of the city. He had to get these back to Kitchener urgently.

Leading the horses he walked back to the camp site. He could see that the girl was asleep and decided to leave her while he watered the horses at the lower well, before hobbling them near the camels. As he returned to the girl, he could see that flies were crawling on her bloody wounds. The wounds needed to be attended to before they started to rot. Her dress was tattered and ripped. She would need something else for the cold desert nights.

He walked back to the man he had killed with the revolver and struggled to remove his *jibba*. It was filthy, but had a lot less blood on it than the other two. He looked down at the man's feet and pulled off his sandals as well. He returned to the girl and gently touched her shoulder to wake her. She screamed and recoiled at his touch.

"Hush now miss. You're safe, they can't hurt you anymore."

She looked into his eyes and calmed a little although she was still trembling. "We need to get your wounds seen to before they go bad. There's a pool of clear water a little up the slope here, but I don't think you should walk with your feet in that state, so I'm going to carry you."

She nodded nervously and he scooped her from the ground and stood up. He walked slowly up the narrow path through the rocks until he reached the crystal clear pool of cool water. Then he sat her down on a flat rock while he waded into the water and washed the *jibba* and sandals. He laid them out in the sun to dry and turned back to the young girl who was watching him wide eyed.

"I think it's time you told me your name now lass."

She paused and then spoke in a small frightened voice. "It's Emma. I'm Emma Drover."

"A pleasure to meet you Miss Drover." He said as he stood up to his knees in the water and made an exaggerated bow.

"Now then we need to wash your injuries to get the dirt out of them and then we need to cover them to keep the flies off. If I help you can you step into the water?"

He held out his hands and she took hold of them to stand up. She winced as the weight came on her torn feet, but took the two steps into the shallow edge of the pool. She sighed as the cool water eased the pain in her feet and ankles. McGuire knelt down in the water and gently washed the dirt from her wounds as she rested her hands on his shoulders to keep her balance.

"It will be easier if you come deeper in to the water so I can do your hands and wrists next."

She moved forward, with him helping her and stopped as the water reached her waist. Again he washed the raw and torn skin slowly and gently.

"There's a nasty gash down your cheek. Do you want to wash that or should I?"

"Can you do it?" Emma said. "You're very gentle and you can see it better than I can."

With infinite care he cupped water in his hands and poured it down the side of her face. Then he gently picked the small pieces of gravel out of the skin where they were embedded.

"I fell and they just dragged me." She said. "That's what caused that. It hurt a lot but the water helps."

McGuire nodded. "We've got a problem now. I need to bandage the wounds but I don't have anything to do it with."

"Could you tear my petticoat? Would that do?"

"It would, now there is another thing. This dress of yours is in rags so I've got you a *jibba* to wear. It should be dry soon and it will keep you warmer at night and if we are seen you will look like one of the Mahdi's followers. So how would it be if you took your clothes off and have a bath here while I make the bandages? I won't look I promise."

She nodded shyly and waited until he turned his back then she slipped her clothes over her head and threw them to the bank. McGuire heard her sigh as she immersed herself and he stepped forward to pick up the petticoat. The curved dagger he now wore at his waist sliced through the fabric and made adequate bandages. He walked carefully backwards into the water, careful not to turn and break his promise. He washed the improvised bandages and draped them over his shoulder.

"Are you ready to come out?"

"I am. Are you sure you won't look?"

"Miss Drover a good catholic boy never breaks a promise. You walk up behind me and I'll hand you the jibba for you to put on. Then I can dress your wounds."

She did as she was told and then walked painfully back to the flat rock and sat down. Being as careful as he knew how, he wound the bandages around her wrists and then around her feet and ankles. Next he slipped the sandals onto her feet. They would have been too big, but with the extra cloth wound around them her feet fitted well enough.

"I still don't think you ought to walk, so I'll carry you back down again."

She smiled a little. "That would be nice."

He lifted her up and walked back down the rocky path. Once back at his blanket he laid her down and sat across from her. She looked a little lost in the robe, that was too big for her, but from a distance it might do, he decided.

"I know your name is Emma, but how did you get out here and how did you come to be captured by those Arabs?"

"My father is, or was, a merchant. His business is in Cairo, but deals with the Sudan. Since I am his only child he wanted me to understand the business, so we came down the Nile and managed to get trapped in Khartoum. When the last steamer left, with the other Europeans on it, my father and three of his friends decided that it was too risky to go on it with the Dervishes controlling the river at Berber. We would escape across the desert on camels. We had a guide and the best camels available. It turned out that our trusted guide was a Dervish spy and he led us into a trap."

"What happened?"

"We stopped last night and at dawn this morning they attacked. There were five of them, two were killed, but the other three slaughtered all the men and took me prisoner. I speak Arabic so

146

heard them talking and after we got to these wells I was to be the evening's entertainment."

"I don't understand."

Emma wiped a small tear away. "Don't you know what Dervishes do to their captives? I was to be raped by all three of them and then probably sold into slavery later. You saved me from that and I can't thank you enough."

McGuire nodded. "I found a satchel of letters around the neck of one of them."

"Those were the despatches from General Gordon. He had sent the same with Colonel Stewart, his aide, on the steamer. These were copies just in case. We were there when he gave Colonel Stewart his ruby ring as a keepsake. It was very moving."

Michael delved into one of the pouches he had about him and pulled out the ring. "Was this the ring?"

Her hand flew to her mouth. "Oh God, yes. That's the one."

"So it looks like the steamer didn't make it through. Your father was right about that."

He thought for a moment and then asked. "And what about the gold?"

"Gold? Oh yes each of the men had their gold with them. The Dervishes took it off their bodies."

McGuire extracted the four pouches from under his robe. "Which one is your father's?"

She pointed with a trembling finger. "That one. I made that embroidered one for him when I was younger. He said it brought him luck."

Michael picked up the embroidered pouch and handed it to her. "Put that on a string around your neck and keep it safe. The others need to be shared to keep us both safe."

"Shared with who?"

"By the sound of it, you are about to meet my two traveling companions. Don't panic they are on our side, despite wearing the robes of the Mahdi."

As he finished speaking Asif appeared around a rock with a gazelle draped around his shoulders. He stopped as he saw Emma and then looked out across the desert to where the vultures were feeding.

"It seems you have been as busy as I have my friend. This should be a good story while the meat is cooking."

McGuire nodded. "I promise it will be Asif. Is Haroun not with you?"

"I have seen Haroun as I came here. He will be back before we have the fire burning."

Asif sat and immediately started to butcher the gazelle. He had hardly made two cuts before Haroun walked into the camp. He too stopped and looked at Emma who was looking at both Arabs nervously.

"I rode through three bodies on my way here. Are they your kills English?"

"They are and I have promised Asif a story while the meat cooks."

Haroun nodded. "That is good, it has been a long ride. I went back to Khartoum. From the ridge I could see the fires burning and the smoke rising.

Never in my life have I seen so many vultures in one place. I think it is now a city of the dead."

"And the Dervishes?"

"They are returning to their tents near Omdurman, across the river."

"Can we go back to the city?"

Haroun shook his head. "There is nothing there for us now. Even your machine with the flashing lights is here. I dug it up and brought it to you. While I was digging, a steamer came up the river. I could see the soldiers in their red coats on the deck. There was much firing from the Dervishes. The steamer turned around and went down river again."

McGuire absorbed this news. "I would guess they saw the city as you did. No flags on the walls and nothing but destruction."

Later as they sat and waited for the meat to cook, McGuire told them of his fight with the three men and how he had saved Emma. As his story ended he put down the rifle he had been cleaning, while he spoke. He withdrew the glittering scimitar from under his blanket and placed it before Asif.

"It does not have the jewels of the dagger I gave to Haroun, but it will sit well at your waist."

Asif picked the blade up and examined it with a broad smile before McGuire continued. "There is more."

He poured out the contents of the three remaining money pouches and the gold coins made a pretty pile. As before, he divided the money into three equal piles in front of him. As the two men watched him he lifted four coins from the centre pile and put two on each of the other piles.

He looked at the two men and pointed at Emma. "I take this one as part of my share so you should have more of the gold."

Emma leaned past him and took two more coins from his pile. She put one on each of the other piles.

"If I am to be bought then let it be for the right price."

The two Arabs looked at her in surprise then burst into howls of laughter. Any tension about the girl was gone and they turned to the meat.

Chapter 26.
A Sad Return

Before dawn they mounted their camels and started the long ride back to Major Kitchener. They had filled all the water skins so as to be able to keep the horses alive. The camels and the horses had drunk their fill before they a left, but it was still a risk for horses to travel that far through the desert.

Asif had taken the best of the horses and rode a little way ahead, to seek out any Dervish patrols that might be a threat. Emma rode his camel, alongside McGuire, with practised ease.

As dawn broke across the black stone hills that surrounded them, Haroun turned in his saddle. "English, I have thought long about the steamer that turned around and left."

McGuire looked at him. "And what does your thinking tell you wise one?"

"It tells me that your war on the Nile is finished. The Major Kitchener told me you came to rescue Gordon Pasha. Now he is dead there is no reason for your war and men will die for nothing. I think you will now go to your home and leave this place."

The Irishman rode on and thought about Haroun's words. "I think you should be right, but what of vengeance? Do you not think we will punish the Dervishes?"

Haroun shook his head. "You are too few. You saw the tents of the Dervish army around Omdurman. They are as the sands of the desert.

Even with your guns and cannons you cannot beat so many. It is time for you to leave."

"You may be right, but I think there will be a vengeance one day though you and I may not see it. Maybe when they have made a road to Khartoum for the Queen's soldiers to march down?"

Haroun chuckled. "There is no road to Khartoum. The Dervishes will not make one and they will not let the Egyptians do it."

McGuire nodded. "Your words may be true, but the world changes."

They rode on north in silence, into the desert. They rode for the whole day and even Haroun was tired by the time they came to the empty village. There was still no living thing there, but the water in the well was still sweet and the animals and people were glad of it.

As they settled down for the night they did not light a fire. Asif had seen Dervish patrols and the smell of the smoke would carry a long way across the open plain they were now on.

Emma came and sat close beside her rescuer. "Do you think the army will help me to get back to Cairo? I need to get there before news of my father's death, so I can take over the business before the workers rob me blind."

McGuire looked at her. "Really? I thought you would be going back to England."

She shook her head. "Egypt is my home. I've lived here for the last nine years, since I was eight years old. My father's business is my only income so why would I leave it? I don't want to have to

152

throw myself on the mercy of parts of my family and have to rely on their charity."

He looked at her, impressed. She had a strength he had not seen up till now. He smiled at her and patted her arm.

"A damsel in distress in a foreign land, how could English officers resist that? I think they will move heaven and earth to get you home, so they can say that something good came out of all this."

She gave him a happy smile and leaned against the back wall of the hut. "Maybe they will let you come with me to Cairo?"

He shook his head. "No, I don't think so. Once we are back with the column I'll be back doing work for Sergeant Major Lewis. There won't be any trip down the Nile for me."

"Not even if a damsel in distress asks for you?"

McGuire laughed. "Not even then Emma. The Army doesn't work like that."

They rode on the next morning and the next until they came to the place Kitchener had been camped. It was deserted and had been for some days by the look of it. Asif rode in a circle around the site until he found the tracks leading away from it.

"Kitchener has ridden towards the Nile. We must follow."

Once again they filled the water skins and watered their mounts before setting off to find the intelligence officer. A day's ride brought them in sight of the British encampment and McGuire threw off his robe and rode forward. As he came nearer four of the hussars rode out to meet him. They reined in and looked him over. As he looked down at the filthy remains of his uniform he realised he must look quite a sight.

"Afternoon lads. I'm Lance Corporal McGuire, Grenadier Guards. I've been on detachment to Major Kitchener and now I'm back home."

"The hussar to his right stroked his magnificent moustache. "That's Corporal of Horse when you talk to me. Now what are those three hanging about back there?"

McGuire smiled slightly; he was back in the army for sure. "Sorry Corporal of Horse. Those are my friends. Two are Arabs who are part of Major Kitchener's scouts and the other one is a young lady we rescued as she came out of Khartoum."

"You've been down near Khartoum?"

"I've been in Khartoum and I need to report in as soon as possible."

The senior man snorted derisively. "You've been in Khartoum? What now, did the Mahdi invite you in for tea and crumpets? Don't make me laugh."

McGuire decided not to argue. "In any case I need to report back. Can I bring my companions forward?"

"Bring them forward, but no funny stuff. We'll be watching and if they touch a weapon they'll be hacked down, I promise you."

McGuire rode back and brought the other three forward to where the hussars waited. They wheeled their horses round and rode alongside as the party rode slowly towards the camp. As they rode through the gap in the surrounding *zariba* they saw Kitchener striding towards them. He looked strange now that he was back in uniform. He reached them and reached up to take Haroun's hand.

"You have returned safely my friend. I am glad." He turned to the escorting cavalry men and said. "Thank you gentlemen I will take these people forward from here."

The horsemen saluted then turned their mounts and rode away. Kitchener watched them go and looked up at the weary travellers.

"Asif you are safe, that is good. And McGuire you too. Did you get the messages into Khartoum? Then who is this other one'"

The girl threw back the hood of her patched robe. "Hello. I am Emma Drover and Michael saved me when I had been captured by Dervishes. The other two helped him bring me here."

"An English woman out here? My goodness. Would you all come to my tent? I have good Arabic coffee and we can speak of what you have seen."

Kitchener led the way to a tent that was pitched under the shade of palm trees. He helped Emma down from her camel and then asked them to sit on the rugs that were laid inside. Observing the courtesy of the Arabs he waited until they had their coffee before he started to question them.

"Well McGuire did you contact General Gordon?"

155

"Sorry sir, but no we didn't. There was no reply to the heliograph so Asif found us a way into the city and …"

"You were inside Khartoum?"

"Yes sir. We tried to reach the General, but then the Dervish army attacked. They swarmed all over the city. We were wearing the patched *jibbas* and tried to go unnoticed. I made it into the Governor's Residence and I'm sorry sir but General Gordon is dead."

Kitchener nodded sadly. "Yes we thought that must be the case. We sent a steamer up to him, but it was too late."

"I saw him die, sir. He came out and faced a huge mob of the enemy and they backed down. Then he took a spear to the chest and fell. Sir, they took his head. I couldn't do anything about it."

"It sounds typical of Gordon to try and face down an army."

McGuire nodded. "Yes sir. He was wearing his full dress uniform and had a sword and pistol. He stood at the top of the stairs alone. He was a brave man."

Kitchener looked at McGuire. "He was always that. Thank you for telling me. You will have to tell this tale again to General Wilson and then probably to Lord Wolseley. Wolseley will be glad to hear Gordon died well, he was quite an admirer of his."

McGuire reached in to the satchel he had lying next to him. He pulled out the heavy revolver and laid it on the rug before him.

156

"This is General Gordon's pistol sir and, in here, I have the despatches he asked Miss Drover's father to carry for him. They are the same as the ones he gave Colonel Stewart to bring down river, but we think he fell into Dervish hands because we have Gordon's ring as well."

Kitchener touched the revolver and then reached for the satchel. He withdrew the letters and looked at who they were addressed to.

"Have you opened these?"

"No sir they are as I found them. Sorry about the bullet hole, but the man carrying them didn't want to give them up."

Kitchener put the letters back into the satchel and laid it aside. "Now then miss Drover I think you have a story to tell me as well. Would you like another coffee before we begin?"

Emma told the story of her father's death and her capture. She told about the despatches and the ring that Gordon had given to Colonel Stewart. Then she told of being dragged across the desert and being rescued by McGuire. As she finished she handed Gordon's ring to Kitchener who sat and stared at it in the palm of his hand.

He shook his head sadly. "We knew that Stewart's steamer had been wrecked and now we know what happened to him. You must all be tired. McGuire I should send you back to your unit, but I need you all to stay here. I must report to General Wilson and he will want to hear what you have told me first hand."

Chapter 27.
Lord Wolseley and Beyond

McGuire and Emma walked across from Kitchener's tent towards the larger tent they could see on the slight rise before them. Soldiers straightened up from their tasks and watched them walk by. Then McGuire saw Lieutenant Colonel Latham walking towards him. He stopped came to attention and was about to salute when he remembered he had no hat on.

"McGuire, good to see you made it back. I had a message from the General that he wanted me there when you were talking to him."

"Thank you, sir. May I introduce Miss Drover, sir. Emma this is Colonel Latham, he commands my battalion back in Dublin."

Latham gave Emma small bow. "Your servant ma'am. May I ask how you came to be here with McGuire?"

A young lieutenant ran up to them and saluted the Colonel. "Sorry to interrupt, sir, but the General has sent me to hurry these two along. He wants to hear their report urgently."

Latham suppressed his irritation. "Of course. Lead on Lieutenant. We can't keep the General waiting."

As they reached the tent the General was standing outside waiting for them. He looked McGuire up and down then gave Emma a small bow and waved all three of them into his command tent. Folding chairs were brought forward and they all sat.

"Colonel Latham, I asked you here to vouch for your man. Major Kitchener informs me he has an amazing tale to tell. He didn't want to tell me it himself so that I can judge McGuire's veracity. I take it you know him well?"

"I do sir. He saved my life from a crocodile as we were moving south and he is the only man in the regiment who has ever outshot me."

"Very well then. McGuire let's hear your report. Then I am told the young lady has a story to tell as well."

The two young people told their tale again just as they had to Major Kitchener. When McGuire produced the heavy Webley revolver General Wilson held it and turned it over in his hands.

"I was with Gordon when he bought this. Its twin sits in my own holster. Take it back McGuire you will be taking this report to Lord Wolseley in the morning."

He handed the weapon back and listened as the story continued to unfold. He looked at the despatches, but since none were addressed to him he did not open them. He sat silently as Emma told of her tragedy. When they were finished he looked at Latham.

"Colonel, I don't think we need to doubt your soldier with the proof he has brought with him, do you?"

"No sir I don't, but I can tell you that Lance Corporal McGuire has my confidence."

General Wilson paused then smiled. "I can't have a mere Lance Corporal taking these despatches to his Lordship can I? Sergeant McGuire I want you to find yourself a decent uniform and make sure there are three stripes on the sleeve. You will be embarking on the steamer that is leaving shortly. You will escort Miss Drover to Lord Wolseley and you will give him the same report you gave me. Do you understand?"

"Yes sir. Thank you sir."

"Miss Drover you have my condolences on the loss of your father and my congratulations on your narrow escape. I will give you a letter to take to Lord Wolseley in which I will ask him to expedite your return to Cairo. Colonel Latham I think you could usefully escort these two and carry my despatches to our commander if you will?"

Latham agreed and McGuire was sent to find more or less decent items of uniform, to make himself look presentable when speaking to the commander of the Relief Expedition. Emma was found a clean jibba, without the patches of the Mahdi since no women's clothing was available.

McGuire walked around the camp area scrounging whatever pieces of uniform he could find to replace his rags. Then he went to find Kitchener's tribesmen. As he arrived they were packing their belongings and loading their camels.

"Haroun, Asif. Were you going to leave without a word?"

Haroun looked at the young man in his borrowed clothes. "English, our time here is done. Your Army is going back north as I have foretold. They have no need of us now. We will return to our tents in the northern sand deserts."

McGuire looked in his eyes. "Wise one, you have been my brother in the desert and you as well Asif of the one keen eye. Without you I would not have survived I think. We have done something special together and you have my gratitude."

Asif grinned. "And you English have shared your gold with us. It will make a better story when we are back in our own tents."

"I do not know if I will ever see you or your deserts again my brothers. I do not know what the Army will do with me now, but if I can ever do you a service you only need to say the words."

Haroun held out his hand and McGuire took it firmly. "And you, English, are ever welcome in the tents of Haroun and Asif. Your fame among the tents of the Bedouin will grow each time I tell my stories and you will become a greater hero with each telling."

McGuire nodded and released the older man's hand. He stepped across to Asif and took his hand. "Use the scimitar well and do not let Haroun's story become too wild or he will have us flying across the desert on the backs of eagles."

The two men mounted their camels and rode to join the rest of their small band. McGuire watched them until they faded into the heat haze and then turned back to his own life.

They embarked on the steamer for the short journey downstream to Lord Wolseley's headquarters. McGuire ate with the crew while Emma was invited to eat with the officers. She found him later, standing at the stern rail watching the stars reflected in their wake.

"What's the matter Michael?"

He turned and gazed at her. He had thought she was pretty, but now she had been able to have a proper bath and to wash her golden hair she was beautiful.

"Nothing much. I'd forgotten what it was like in the Army. While we were out in the desert I felt free. I felt like I could do anything. I felt truly alive. Now here I am back in the old routine. I can't eat in the same room as you. I go where I am told and I stand to attention while officers peer at me and talk down to me."

Emma laid a hand on his arm. "Can't you leave the army? Could you stay here in Egypt?"

"Even if I could, what would I do? Where would I live?"

Her voice fell to just more than a whisper. "You could stay with me. We could run my father's business together. You speak Arabic well enough now and the workers would respect you."

"What do you mean stay with you?"

She raised her head and took the small step between them. Her arms went around him and she raised her face to his. He leaned down and kissed her gently. Then more urgently. He could feel her returning the kiss. He pulled her close to him and he imagined he could feel the beating of her heart. They stood holding each other until he broke the embrace.

"It's no use Emma, the Army will never let me go. I have to finish my six years and by the end of that you will have found somebody better.

Maybe one of the young Lieutenants would suit you?"

He saw the tear in her eye and regretted what he had said. She turned and walked away from him and he felt terrible. She stopped and turned back at the door into her cabin.

"I don't know what sort of person you think I am, but I know you Michael McGuire and there is nobody better."

She closed the door behind her and he turned back to the rail. The twinkling starlight had lost its appeal and he stood thinking what a fool he had just been.

They arrived at Lord Wolseley's headquarters in the early hours of the morning and McGuire was waiting by the gangplank, as Colonel Latham and Emma came towards him. He saluted the Colonel, but did not speak to her.

"Good morning McGuire, or should I say Sergeant McGuire? I think you have achieved the fastest promotion my regiment has ever seen."

Latham led the way onto the shore and they walked through the camp to where they had been told they could find Lord Wolseley. McGuire and Emma waited outside the large tent while Latham went in to announce their arrival.

"Emma, I'm sorry I shouldn't have said what I did last night."

She looked at him. "Then why did you?"

"Because I was unhappy. There could be nothing better for me than to be with you, but I can't and that hurts."

She smiled at him. "I knew that and I forgive you. How much more of your six years do you have to serve? I can wait you know."

Before he could answer they were called inside the tent to meet a tall austere looking man who turned out to be the famous Lord Garnet Wolseley. He sat down in his camp chair and indicated that they should do the same. As they sat in front of the force commander other senior officers came and stood behind them to listen to the report.

McGuire told his story again from the beginning and Emma told hers. They handed over the revolver, the despatches and the ruby ring which Wolseley placed on a table beside him. Throughout their telling Wolseley never spoke, but kept his eyes fixed on whichever of them was speaking.

As they finished the General cleared his throat. "Sergeant McGuire wait outside. You, Miss Drover, may wait here in the shade while I consider what you have both told me."

"Thank you sir," she said, "but I will wait with Michael. We have something to discuss."

The two young people stood up and McGuire saluted his general before turning to leave. They made their way through the silent crowd of officers and then stood in the shade of a palm tree. They could hear discussions going on inside the tent, but could not make out any words. Emma didn't mind, she was just happy to be holding Michael's hand.

After around a quarter of an hour the two young people were called back inside the tent.

Wolseley looked marginally less fearsome this time and he may have even smiled at Emma a little.

"I have made my decision about you two and these despatches. You may not know your history, but for hundreds of years, at the conclusion of a campaign, commanding generals have sent a despatch to the Monarch in the hands of a trusted officer. I am entrusting my despatch, and the ones you brought from Gordon, to Colonel Latham. He will take the next steamer down the Nile and will then travel by the fastest means possible to the palace. Miss Drover you may accompany him as far as Cairo, as you have requested."

He paused and took a drink from the glass that stood beside him on the table with the dusty leather satchel. He turned back and looked at McGuire for a long moment before he spoke.

"Now you, McGuire. You may not know, but Gordon was a good friend of mine. I admired him greatly. Having you tell me that he died a soldier's death in the face of his enemies has been a comfort to me and will be to the British people, who also love 'Chinese' Gordon. Her Majesty also took a personal interest in Gordon and, in fact, she insisted he should be sent to Khartoum in the first place. You should go with Colonel Latham, so that Her Majesty can hear the same story you told me. However, your uniform is a disgrace and those stripes, poorly sewn on your arm are an embarrassment, rip them off at once."

McGuire reached around and tore the Sergeant's stripes from his arm. He found that he did not care about losing the rank, but he did care about losing Emma. Wolseley stood up and walked towards him. McGuire looked stiffly to his front as Wolseley stopped in front of him.

"McGuire, for what you have done and the honour you have brought to this expedition I am exercising my rights as a commander. I am giving you a battlefield commission. Here take these."

McGuire looked down in amazement at the General's open hand where lay the gleaming rank badges of a Second Lieutenant.

"Put them on as you leave the tent. You will be on the steamer this afternoon with your Colonel. I have charged him with the task of instructing you how to be an officer as you float down the Nile. I have also given him money to buy you a properly tailored uniform when you reach Cairo. You will have to find a regiment to join as well. You can't stay with the Guards. Apart from anything else the officers' mess bills would be beyond you."

Chapter 28.
To Cairo and Beyond

Second Lieutenant Michael McGuire stood on the upper deck of the steamer as it sailed down the broad river. To his right he could see the temples of Luxor and, with his binoculars, off to his left in the desert he could see the massive temple of Queen Hatshepsut carved into the sandstone cliffs. Emma stood next to him explaining what he was seeing. Having lived in Egypt for so long she knew its history, while Michael had never dreamed of such things in the narrow back streets of Dublin.

They would have liked to stop and wander through the tall pillars of the temples, but Lord Wolseley had given clear orders, they were to travel back to Britain as quickly as possible. The captain of the steamer had complained, but had agreed to push his craft on at maximum speed the whole way. The only stops were to take on wood at the fuelling stations and none of the passengers were permitted to disembark.

For Michael and Emma this was a dream cruise. They spent much of the day and most of the evening together talking and just being close. Two hours a day were set aside for Colonel Latham to instruct Michael how to conduct himself as an officer. His lessons wandered far and near. They covered his day to day duties, how to treat his soldiers, table manners, history, politics and ethics.

By the time they docked in Cairo, McGuire was beginning to feel that he could adapt to the new station in life that had been thrust upon him.

He had little time to see the city as Latham took him straight into the winding streets to a tailor's shop. The small bent backed Jewish tailor measured him and promised to have the uniform ready in a week. Latham insisted it was needed immediately and after some hard bargaining on price the tailor agreed to have it ready by the end of the next day.

Latham did not want McGuire to appear in the Headquarters of the British Garrison until he was properly dressed as an officer, so Michael was given time to explore the city. His first action was to hire a horse drawn gharry, to take him to the warehouse down on the docks that Emma now owned. He walked into the building and was amazed at the huge stacks of material being dealt with by what looked like an army of workers.

He asked about Emma and was pointed to an office at the back of the building. As he approached he could hear raised voices and as he opened the door he saw a man towering over Emma who sat in a chair behind the big desk.

The man turned as McGuire entered. "And what the hell do you want soldier?"

McGuire smiled a little. "Right now I want to beat you to a pulp and, if you yell at Emma just once more, that is exactly what I'm going to do."

The red faced man sized up the soldier who stood before him. He noted the officer's rank badges and sneered.

"This isn't your fancy club in Pall Mall. We don't have gentlemanly duels with pistols at dawn round here. Be on your way, before you get hurt."

"I've never been to Pall Mall and where I come from we don't have gentlemanly duels."

The man sneered again. "Get out before I throw you out."

Michael McGuire realised this was not the behaviour expected of a junior army officer, but he didn't care.

"Why don't you try?" He said quietly.

"Thank you Michael but this is my business and I can handle it." She turned to the red faced man. "And as for you Mr Brown, your employment with this company is terminated. Leave my premises at once and never return."

"What about my wages?"

"I think we both know you have taken far more than your wages while my father was away. Just leave."

The man stamped out of the office muttering threats under his breath. Michael and Emma followed him to see him off the premises. He stopped by a pile of small boxes and reached to take one.

"You leave that where it lies Brown. You heard what Miss Drover said."

The man swung his leather riding crop at McGuire who rocked back out of the way and then stepped forward to deliver a short sharp jab to the man's stomach. It had little effect except to enrage the angry man even further. He roared and rushed at McGuire swinging a massive roundhouse punch as he did so. Michael ducked and came up inside the swing of the punch. He delivered two rapid punches to the man's stomach and, as he bent over winded, he smashed his knee into the man's face.

The attacker collapsed to the floor with blood pouring from his newly broken nose. McGuire stepped in and delivered a hard kick to his back before Emma dashed forward and stopped him.

"Michael! No more, please."

McGuire looked down at the man on the floor who now lay still, trying to catch his breath. "What was the shouting about?"

"He was my father's foreman and he was upset because I just caught him out. He has been stealing from the warehouse for weeks and the books showed it."

"So what do you want to do with him now?"

Emma looked down at the man on the floor. "I think I am going to have him thrown in the street right now."

"Good. Do you mind if I help?"

"What are you going to do?"

"I'm going to stamp your authority on this place. We're going to march this jackass to the door so all your workers can see and then throw him out of the door. Then you need to choose a new foreman."

Emma considered this for a moment or two. "I suppose that is the way to deal with this thief. I'm not sure how to find a new foreman at such short notice, unless you want the job?"

"Well for a change why not choose an Arab? This one has proved that not all Europeans can be trusted. Maybe a Bedouin? We know their worth."

Emma nodded and McGuire reached down and dragged the thieving foreman to his feet. He took him by the collar of his jacket and frog marched him through the warehouse. All around, the workers stopped and watched the performance. There was a small cheer as McGuire propelled the ex-foreman through the door and into the street.

As the man lay in the dust McGuire stood over him. "I didn't learn that in Pall Mall. The back streets of Dublin are a better teacher. Now you listen carefully. I know you think you are going to come back here for revenge, but it's not in your best interests I promise you. If anything happens to Miss Drover, or anything she owns, I will take it personally and I will blame you. Do you take my meaning?"

McGuire walked back into the warehouse where Emma stood, waiting for him. "Thank you for that. It was becoming a little difficult. I have sent for the only Bedouin who works here. His name is Abdullah, he came here when he lost his leg and could no longer ride with his people. You have a special connection with the Bedouin, will you talk to him for me?"

McGuire nodded and turned as an Arab limped across the warehouse towards him. His left leg had been replaced by a crude wooden one that thumped loudly as he walked.

The man stopped in front of them and gave a small bow. "You sent for me?"

McGuire glanced at Emma and waited until she nodded before he spoke. "You are Abdullah of the Bedouin?"

"I am."

"I have ridden across the deserts of the Sudan with two of your brothers. They are as my blood. We have fought and thirsted together. We have a bond that will not break. Are you another of the Bedouin that I can trust?"

The man looked McGuire in the eyes. "If you have fought alongside my people then command me and I will do your bidding faithfully."

"The father of Miss Drover is dead in the Sudan. She now rules here and she is my friend. The one I have thrown in the street was a thief. Will you take his place and serve Miss Drover as faithfully as you would me?"

"It shall be as you say."

"Good. Now do two things for me. Tell your men that you are now the overseer and then tell a wood worker to make you a better leg. A man in authority should have a better one. I have gold that I shared with my Bedouin brothers and I will pay for it."

They watched him walk away. His back now straighter with his new authority. Emma took Michael's hand and led him back to the office.

She closed the door. "I thought I was more than your friend?"

"You are and we'll work on that. Colonel Latham has told me that we are sailing very soon to go to Italy and then on by train to England. We don't have a lot of time."

"I have an idea about that. Lord Wolseley said you still had to choose a regiment. Why not ask for the Royal Irish Fusiliers? They are part of the garrison here in Cairo."

Chapter 29.
Osborne House

The fast steamer from Alexandria took them to Italy then they travelled by rail to the north coast of France and on to England. Now they were on the steam ferry from Portsmouth Harbour railway station to the Isle of Wight. As the ferry docked they could see a coach and horses waiting for them with the liveried footman standing by the door. Latham led the way to the coach as they disembarked and then it was a short drive across the Isle of Wight to Osborne House.

McGuire swallowed nervously as they drove through the imposing gates of the royal estate. He straightened his khaki drill uniform and adjusted the brown leather Sam Browne belt as he climbed down from the carriage. They were met by a tall, thin Major from one of the fashionable Household Cavalry regiments. He saluted Latham and then looked them both up and down.

He sniffed slightly before speaking. "Are you sure that this uniform is appropriate for meeting Her Majesty'"

Latham looked the supercilious officer in the eye. "These are the uniforms worn by real soldiers Major. We don't have dress uniforms like yours with us."

The Major sniffed again. "Very well follow me."

He led them into the Queen's impressive summer residence and to an ante room. "You may not enter the Queen's presence carrying weapons. You will have to leave your revolvers here."

Latham drew his pistol from its polished leather holster and laid it on a side table. "Lieutenant McGuire will be taking that revolver in for the Queen to see. He will unload it though."

McGuire nodded and opened up the break back revolver. The six rounds were automatically ejected by the mechanism and he picked them off the carpet then placed them next to Latham's weapon.

"I suppose that will do. No insult intended gentlemen but there have been a number of attempts on Her Majesty's life and we need to be careful."

They were led through into a reception room to find Queen Victoria with two of her ladies in waiting already seated at the other end of the room. Both men stopped and bowed before walking forward. McGuire was glad Latham had made him rehearse his bow on the way across the English Channel. He was surprised at quite how small this powerful woman was, she seemed lost in the black clothes she always wore, since her husband, Prince Albert, had died.

They stopped again and the Major introduced them. The Queen looked at them for a while before she spoke.

"You have come directly from the Sudan? You have despatches from Lord Wolseley and a story to tell us about the death of General Gordon I believe?"

Latham nodded. "We have your Majesty. Lieutenant McGuire here was the only British soldier to get into Khartoum and he witnessed the end of General Gordon."

Victoria turned to the Major. "Have two chairs brought forward for our guests. Let us all be comfortable for the telling of tales."

Latham handed over the despatches and the Queen handed them to one of the ladies and looked at McGuire. "We will read those later. I want you to tell us how you came to be in Khartoum and how our General died."

McGuire started to tell of his actions a little nervously, but then he saw the Queen's rapt attention the nervousness left him. Once he had described everything he had done, and how he had saved Emma, he withdrew the heavy Webley revolver from his holster and handed it to the Major who took it to the Queen. She laid it across her hands and gazed at it before she looked up. McGuire could have sworn he saw a small tear in her eye.

"So he died a brave Christian gentleman, as he lived?"

McGuire nodded. "He did ma'am. I have never seen anything quite so brave as the way he faced down the mob of armed Dervishes."

She looked down again at the pistol and then back up to the two men before her. "We must read the despatches now. Perhaps you would care to inspect the gardens? Prince Albert designed them and he was very proud of them, they really are very beautiful. We will see you again before you leave."

As they walked between the manicured flower beds McGuire turned his head and looked at the Colonel. "What happens now, sir? Where do I go?"

"What do you mean?"

"The General said I had to choose a regiment to join and then see if they will take me. Until then I am just a nobody with nowhere to go."

"Which regiment would you like to go to?"

"The Royal Irish Fusiliers are stationed in Egypt and I want to get back to Emma. I am going to ask her to marry me."

Latham stopped and turned. "The Fusiliers are a good choice, they are a fine regiment, but marriage is not possible. Officers are not usually permitted to marry before the age of twenty five so you have some years to wait, I'm afraid."

McGuire was absorbing the implications of Latham's statement when the aristocratic cavalry Major came to summon them back to the reception room. They bowed again as they entered and were summoned forward. They stood silently waiting for the Queen to speak.

"Colonel Latham, the despatches tell me that you and your men distinguished themselves during the campaign so in accordance with ancient tradition we are minded to honour you."

As she spoke, a red velvet stool was brought forward and placed in front of her. "Kneel if you please Colonel."

Latham took two steps forward and knelt on the stool. The Queen took a sword from the hands of the equerry who stood beside her them tapped the Colonel on both shoulders.

"Arise, Sir Simon, with our grateful thanks."

The newly knighted Latham stood, bowed and stepped back.

The Queen turned next to McGuire. "Now, young man. You have brought us news that was not in the Despatches. Is there anything we can do for you?"

McGuire was taken by surprise and floundered, so Latham answered for him. "If I may your Majesty? Second Lieutenant McGuire would like to be posted to the Royal Irish Fusiliers in Egypt so that he can marry the young lady he rescued. Unfortunately he has no influence with the Colonel of the Regiment and at the age of just turned twenty he is too young to be allowed to marry."

One of the ladies in waiting sighed and whispered. "Young love, how romantic."

The Queen looked at her and gave a slight nod. "We have some slight influence with the Colonel of the Fusiliers we are sure. Would a letter from us to the Colonel asking him to accept Lieutenant McGuire, and to allow him to marry, suffice?"

McGuire stuttered his thanks. "Your Majesty I would be eternally grateful."

"You may both go. Wait in the ante room while we have the letter prepared then you may take it with you."

McGuire was summoned back into the reception room alone some half an hour later. He bowed and was called forward. On the table beside the Queen was a letter in a heavy cream envelope and a rolled parchment tied with a red ribbon.

The equerry handed the envelope to McGuire at a nod from the Queen. "That is your letter to the Colonel." She said. "You were given a battlefield commission for your actions, but we feel that is not enough. This parchment is your commission as full Lieutenant in our Army, signed by your monarch. Also we thank you for the gift of General Gordon's revolver, but if we keep it the dust in the museum will spoil it. We should like you to carry it with the same honour that General Gordon did, for the rest of your military career. We shall watch your progress with interest."

Chapter 30.
Dublin 1885

Before he returned to Egypt, Lieutenant Michael McGuire took the chance to visit his small family in Dublin. From the docks he walked through the dirty streets to the hovel his mother and sister called home. The street urchins danced around him, mocking his uniform but he smiled and ignored them. At his mother's door he knocked and waited. His sister Kathleen was the one who opened it for him. For a moment she did not recognise the healthy suntanned man who stood before her as the scrawny youth her brother had been when he left for Egypt.

"Is there tea on the fire for your brother, Kathleen McGuire?"

"Michael? Is it you?"

"It's me. Is mother well?"

"Away and come inside. Mother is sitting by the fire to keep warm and she will be well when she sees you."

McGuire walked quietly into the small parlour where the peat fire sputtered in the grate. He couldn't help but compare the place his family lived with the splendour of Osborne House. His mother cried and held his hands for a long time, overjoyed as she was to see him alive. The three of them sat by the fire and Michael told them of his adventures. Then he and Kathleen went along the road to the small market and bought more food than the two women had seen for a long time.

There was no bed for Michael and he refused to let them give him one of theirs. He slept on the floor in front of the small fire wrapped in a thin blanket and thought about Emma and what she would make of this.

With the morning, Lieutenant McGuire took himself to the court house and sought out the old bailiff. He shook the older man's hand and repaid a kindness with a glass or two of best porter before walking into one of the better parts of Dublin city to find a lawyer.

With the help of the lawyer he found a small neat terraced house overlooking a small park and not far from the river. It was the work of just a day to buy the house and then to buy the furniture to fill it. He hired a carriage and drove back to his mother's hovel. The two women were stunned when they saw the carriage at their door with Michael helping them into it. They drove out of the filthy slum area with the urchins running beside them cat calling as they went.

They stopped outside the small neat house and Michael climbed down and held out a hand to his mother. "What is this Michael?"

"This is where you live. The days of you living in that filth are over."

"How can I live here dressed in these rags? This is no place for us."

"The dressmaker will be here within the hour and then you can burn those rags."

"But how can we pay for this?"

"Never a worry mother. Tis all paid for and there will be money each month for food and the like."

His mother walked up the short flight of stairs with Kathleen just behind her. Michael turned the key and flung the door wide. As she looked inside the bright and airy hallway and then walked into the sitting room she burst into tears and fell to her knees. Kathleen leaned against the door post and she too cried for joy.

Chapter 31.
Egypt Again

Lieutenant Michael McGuire walked down the gangplank on to the Alexandria dockside. The last time he had done this he was a naïve private in the Grenadier Guards. Now he was an officer going to see the Colonel of the Irish Fusiliers with a letter signed by the Queen, in his pocket. Now he was also able to deal with the hawkers and shysters in their own language.

He hired a horse drawn *gharry* and had it take him to the railway station once his baggage had been loaded. From there he took the train to Cairo. This time in a first class compartment. He thought back to how his life had changed over just a few months. His visit to his mother and sister in a wet and cold Dublin had convinced him that his life lay with the army. The gold he had picked up in the desert had bought them a small neat house in a pleasant area of the city and he had deposited much of the rest in a bank that would pay enough interest each month to keep them comfortably. Now he could think about his own happiness.

Another *gharry* took him to the barracks in Cairo and he returned the salute of the sentry on the gate as he entered. He walked into the headquarters building and asked to see Lieutenant Colonel O'Brian. He waited for a half hour while the Colonel finished with whatever he had been dealing with, and was then ushered into his office by a clerk.

McGuire came to attention and saluted the Colonel. The Colonel looked up from his paper covered desk and then waved McGuire to a wooden chair.

"What can I do for you Lieutenant?"

"Sir, I have a letter for you that will explain everything." McGuire said, as he handed the cream envelope across the desk.

O'Brian looked at him a little quizzically then opened the letter. As he drew out the contents he sat up straighter in his chair when he saw the letter head. He looked at McGuire again and then started to read. He finished the letter and laid it gently down on his desk.

"Well Lieutenant it seems you have friends in very high places. I never expected to receive a letter from Her Majesty this morning. I am requested to grant you two favours as you probably know. First, I am to admit you to my regiment and then I am to give you permission to marry, despite your age. Is that what you want?"

"If it please you, sir, yes."

O'Brian leaned back and contemplated the young man opposite him. "I don't have a vacancy in the battalion at the moment, but I suppose I could carry you as a supernumerary. I have been contemplating having a Reconnaissance and Intelligence officer. Would you be able to fill that role?"

"I think so sir. I speak Arabic and I was working for Major Kitchener during the Relief Expedition."

"That's Lieutenant Colonel Kitchener now. His brevet was published last week. Can't say I like the man, but he seems to be effective."

McGuire decided not to comment on Kitchener. He waited while O'Brian read the letter again.

"Very well I'll take you as my Reconnaissance officer. I can only give you a few men and if I know my officers you'll end up with the trouble makers that they want to be rid of. Still want the job?"

"Very much, sir."

"Fine that's settled then. Send the Chief Clerk in as you leave and I'll get you put on the rolls. Then off to the quartermaster for you to get proper badges for your uniform. Speaking of uniforms, now that you are one of us, the regimental tailor will run you up the required dress uniforms. You'll find he is reasonably priced. I will have the RSM allocate you an office and your men. Whatever equipment you need is up to you to acquire. Anything else?"

McGuire stood up and paused. "Just one thing, sir. Would you mind if I take some time to arrange my personal affairs before I start work?"

O'Brian nodded. "You will find there is little urgency for us in Egypt most of the time. I suppose these personal affairs are to do with this marriage? I would prefer my younger officers to be single, but Her Majesty disagrees in your case. Take whatever time you need."

Later that day, now wearing the proper embellishments of an officer of Fusiliers McGuire walked slowly along the Cairo dockside towards Emma's warehouse. He had no idea whether she would be there, but it was the only place he knew that she might be. He pushed open the small door and stepped into the shaded interior. It took a moment for his eyes to adjust after the brilliant sunshine outside and then he saw Abdullah limping towards him.

"Greetings Abdullah. The new leg suits you well."

"Greetings sir. It is a good leg. It does not rub my skin to bleed as the old one did."

McGuire smiled. "It is good to hear that and how are the workers now that they have an honourable man to lead them."

Abdullah bowed slightly at the compliment. "They are happier now that Brown is gone. His riding crop has scarred many of them for no good reason."

"Brown? Is that his name? I never asked. Has he been back? Has there been any trouble?"

"He has been seen around the docks and he has said bad things about the Miss Drover, but the people along the dock know him and take no notice."

McGuire nodded and smiled. "That is good. Is Miss Drover here today?"

"Not today. She is at her mother's house by the river."

"Can you send someone to show me where that is? I would see her soon."

"It is not needed. I will send for a *gharry* and tell the driver where to take you. It is not far."

The *gharry* stopped outside a neat white villa that overlooked the Nile. The lateen sailed boats cruised up and down and in the shallows he could see fishermen spinning their nets out across the water from small rowing boats. He opened the gate and walked along a path between neat flower beds. The path led him around to a wide terrace on the river side of the building. As he reached the steps up to the terrace a servant in a snow white *jibba* appeared.

"Yes sir? Is there something I can do for you?"

"Please could you tell Miss Drover she has a visitor?"

"Do you have a card sir?"

"No I don't have a card, but you may tell her it is a friend."

The man bowed and turned away on silent sandals to vanish into the house. Michael stood looking out across the wide blue river. So different from the muddy brown Liffey that runs through Dublin and carries away the waste of the city. He heard the sound of footsteps behind him and turned as Emma appeared through the doorway. She stopped and her hand flew to her mouth before she ran towards him.

"Michael! You're back."

She flung herself into his arms and he held her close while trying not to topple over the low wall of the terrace. Her hair smelled of jasmine and he could hardly speak.

"Yes, I'm back."

She wiped the tears from her eyes and pulled back a little. "Mother is asleep right now, but I know she wants to meet you. What shall we do until she wakes?"

"We could just sit and talk."

"Oh no! I'm too excited for that. I know, let me get Bassem to hitch the horses to the *gharry* and we can talk as we drive along beside the river."

"You have your own *gharry*?"

"Of course, some of the ones around the city are a bit dirty and the drivers spit a lot."

They drove for an hour along the, riverside speaking of what had happened while they were apart. Eventually the white villa came back into view and, as they reached it, Bassem climbed down from the driver's seat to open the gate.

A figure appeared from behind a bush and ran towards them. McGuire just had time to recognise the angry face of the man Brown before he registered the pistol in the man's hand. Brown raised the weapon and fired. Michael felt the passage of the bullet between Emma and him. He drew the heavy Webley from his holster and fired. The bullet missed and punched a hole in the whitewashed wall. The enraged man fired again and the round struck the side of the *gharry* sending wood chips flying. McGuire took his time and fired again. Brown never had the chance of a third shot as the large calibre bullet from Michaels's weapon took him full in the chest. He crashed to the ground and lay still.

As Bassem stood open mouthed, Michael climbed down from the carriage and walked across to the body on the ground. There was no doubt that he was never going to cause trouble again. He turned back to make sure Emma was alright and found her sitting in the carriage quite composed.

He walked to her and took her hand. "What do we do now?"

She gave him a small smile. "This is Cairo. We have our own way of dealing with dirt like that one. Bassem! Bring one of the others and clear that up."

She took Michael's hand and climbed down from the *gharry*. Without another word she led him around to the terrace and had him sit in one of the white wicker chairs. She sat opposite him and looked at him steadily.

"You didn't seem surprised by that?"

She shook her head and he admired the way her hair shone as it swung. She reached into her purse and drew out a small pistol.

"In fact I have been waiting for him to try something, but you were just too fast for me. Don't worry about it, his carcase will vanish like the morning mist. It will probably end up in one of the crocodiles."

He shook his head in wonder. "You really are a remarkable woman Emma Drover, but now it's time for what I really came here for."

She watched wide eyed as he stood from his chair and then dropped to one knee. Before he could say a word she took his hands and said just one word.

"Yes."

Chapter 32.
A First Command

McGuire reported back to the Colonel in the cool hours of the morning. He was ushered straight in to see him and came to attention and gave his sharpest salute.

O'Brian looked him over as he stood there. "Well you look like a Fusilier officer at least. Now what can I do for you?"

"It's more what I can do for you sir. You said you had been contemplating creating this post in the Regiment. My question is, what do you want me to achieve?"

O'Brian rocked back in his chair. "Sit down. Now, when we are out on operations the cavalry provide a screen in front of us. They should warn us about enemy movements. However, I have read the accounts of the battle at Abu Klea. The Hussars missed the movement of tens of thousands of Dervish tribesmen. The column was saved by the actions of a heliograph operator on a hill top. I want you and your people to be out gaining me intelligence and spotting whatever the cavalry might miss. Is that clear enough?"

"Yes sir. Do I have any constraints about training my men? And how many men do I get?"

O'Brian stayed still and looked across the desk at him before speaking. "No constraints, but also not much in the way of support either. My major headache in this job is keeping the regiment up to a fighting standard with a parsimonious War Office starving me of the means to do it. As to men, you will get just six and I venture to guess the Regimental Sergeant Major will give you whoever is the most trouble or the most useless."

McGuire nodded slowly as he thought. "Very well sir. I'll do my best."

"The RSM will also allocate you quarters for your unit. I doubt if he will be giving you the best for that either."

"Yes sir. I'll make do." McGuire saluted and turned to leave.

"One or two more things, Lieutenant, before you go. I know it was you on that hilltop and yet you didn't claim the credit. I also know about Storr-Lessing. You should know I like a modest officer. There's one more thing you should be ready for. You may well find that some of my officers resent having an ex-ranker in their midst. You may experience some rudeness. There will also be some envy; a junior officer who has the favour of the Queen herself is a threat to their promotion chances. You should just be aware of those problems. Away you go and meet your men now."

McGuire left the Colonel's office and asked for directions to the Regimental Sergeant Major. He was directed to the end of a long corridor still in the headquarters building and he walked along to knock on the door. A stern voice bade him enter and he walked in. The RSM behind the desk stood to attention as he came in.

"Good morning sir. You'd be Lieutenant McGuire I take it. Welcome to the regiment."

McGuire nodded. "Good morning RSM. Thank you for the welcome. I think you have some men and accommodation waiting for me?"

"I do sir, if you would care to follow me I'll introduce you to both."

The RSM picked up his hat then stepped to the mirror to adjust it. He pulled his jacket down straight then picked up his swagger cane. Without a backward glance he strode to the door, obviously expecting the new Lieutenant to follow on. As they walked through the barracks McGuire was mildly amused to notice soldiers scuttling away as soon as they caught sight of the RSM marching towards them.

They rounded the end of one of the barrack blocks and a stable block came into view. With one of the doors hanging off its hinges it had obviously not been used for some time. They walked in though the damaged double door and McGuire looked around. There was rubbish all over the place and he could swear he saw a rat dash into a hole in the wall.

"Not much sir, but it's all I have spare I'm afraid. Since they moved the Artillery in with us we've been short of space."

"Never mind RSM, I'm sure it will clean up nicely."

"There's an office at the end there sir and there are tack rooms on the floor above."

McGuire nodded as he looked slowly round at the slum he had been given. "And the men?"

"Waiting in the office sir. At least that's where I told them to be."

"I see and just what kind of reprobates have you landed me with?"

The RSM turned to protest, but decided against it. "Well sir the other officers were unwilling to give up their good men as you might understand, but I'm sure they'll do you proud."

McGuire paused then looked the RSM in the eye. "RSM, I'm new here, but you and I need to get along. I understand how important you are in the regiment and I understand I'm just a Lieutenant. So from this day on, how about you and I talk to each other openly and honestly. I will take your valuable advice and you will not come the old soldier with me. Do we agree?"

The RSM looked back at McGuire then nodded slowly. "You may just do for the regiment sir. Right what have you got? Let's see. Two thieves, a forger, one drunkard, a thug and a cry baby. Not very promising."

McGuire sighed. "Just about what I expected. Tell me about the cry baby."

"He was forced into the army by a magistrate same as the others. He doesn't respond well to army discipline after an hour on the drill square the shouting gets too much for him and the tears roll down his face. He's an embarrassment to real soldiers."

"Wonderful. Shall we meet them?"

The RSM strode off again, this time to the door at the end of the stable area. He flung it open and the six men inside shot to attention. He walked in slowly and looked each man up and down.

"Disgusting! I have never seen such a shower of useless scum. Stand still!"

McGuire entered the room and looked around as the RSM continued. "Right you lot. From today, this is your officer, Lieutenant McGuire, and you are going to become the Intelligence and Reconnaissance detachment for this regiment." He looked around the room again. "Intelligence? Pah!"

McGuire stepped forward. "Thank you RSM, I'll take it from here."

The RSM saluted and left McGuire with his six regimental rejects. "Which of you is the senior man?"

"That would be me sir."

"And who are you?"

"Private Jones sir."

"And what sort of crook are you Jones? What got you allocated to this duty?"

The man shuffled his feet then looked at McGuire. "Bit of a problem with the drink sir."

"I see. Very well Jones you are in charge of this work detail. All of you, clean up this pig sty. I'm going to go to see the Quartermaster about equipment for our new task."

One man sniggered. "Good luck with that sir."

"Who are you and what did you mean by that?"

"O'Leary sir. And I just meant good luck with the Quartermaster sir. Captain Early is one who believes that 'Stores is for storing, if they was for issuing they'd be called issues' sir."

"And why are you here?"

"Bit of a misunderstanding about property sir. I was going to put it back, honest."

"I don't care. The rest of you, we'll talk later, now get to the cleaning. Jones, keep them at it."

McGuire left the stable block and walked to the Quartermaster's stores with a list of requirements forming in his head. He met the Captain and found that O'Leary had been sadly correct. The Reconnaissance unit was not on the regimental rolls and so was entitled to nothing. No amount of argument had any effect on a man completely hidebound in regulations, so McGuire returned to the stables.

The cleaning work was being done in desultory manner as he expected. He stood in the doorway and decided it was time to meet his men.

"Jones! Form them in one rank now!"

They formed up and McGuire walked along the line until he got to Jones. "I told you to clean this sty up, not push the dirt around a bit. What the hell are you playing at?"

"Sorry sir, the men were a bit tired sir."

"All of you listen. This building is ours. It's where you work and where you sleep. You will not stand down until it is clean enough for you to live in. You will not break for meals and you will not stop working until it's done. So, unless you want to spend the whole night on your feet, shift your lazy arses and get it cleaned. Now move! Jones come here!"

The men returned to the cleaning and Jones marched across to McGuire. "Yes sir."

"Jones, I put you in charge of this task and you have failed me. Every man is allowed just one failure before he finds out what a miserable shit I can be. I learned my trade in the Guards so I know how to inflict misery. Get those bloody men working and keep them at it."

He watched as Jones marched away and started yelling at the men. There was a noticeable increase in tempo as the dust and dirt started to fly. McGuire smiled to himself, that was a start, but now he had to work out what to do about equipment and training.

Chapter 33.
A New Beginning

In the cool of the morning, Lieutenant McGuire sat in his newly cleaned office reading the files of each of his men. Above him he could hear the tack rooms being cleaned. As he put down the last one there was a light knock at his door. The door opened and a soldier looked in.

"Lieutenant McGuire sir?"

"That's me come in."

The man walked in slowly and saluted. Although a private, he looked older than most soldiers. He moved stiffly and his cheeks were sunken and pale.

"Private Fine sir. The RSM has sent me along to be your personal servant."

"That's nice of him, but I didn't ask for a servant."

"Every officer has a servant sir and I'm not much use for anything else since the fever last year."

McGuire looked the man up and down. His uniform was immaculate with knife edge creases in all the right places. His boots shone like mirrors. His deep set eyes had the look of an intelligent man.

"Fine, I don't need a servant, but I do have a need for something a little different. I take it you are unfit for field service is that right?"

"That's right, sir, but the Colonel doesn't want to throw me on the scrapheap until I've served enough time for my pension."

"Sit down and let me tell you what I need and you tell me if you're willing. First you should know I've been allocated a bunch of ne'er do wells to be my soldiers. Every time they walk round the barracks they are screamed at for the state of their uniforms. I need someone to bring their uniforms and mine up to the standard of yours. The same person will keep this place looking good when we are out in the desert, training. I need someone here to tell, anybody that asks, that we are not available and to make up a plausible story about where we are. Can you do those things?"

Fine nodded stiffly. "I'd be happy to sir."

McGuire opened the drawer in his desk and drew out a small package. He tossed it onto the scarred wood in front of him. He then stood and took off his jacket before handing it to Fine.

He pointed at the packet. "I had those made yesterday in the town, I want one sewn on the right sleeve of all the men. You'll find their jackets hanging in the stable outside here and put one on your jacket as well, since you are now one of us."

Fine picked up the packet and shook out the contents. He picked up one of the small red cloth diamonds with a yellow R embroidered in the middle. He gave McGuire a puzzled look.

"It stands for Reconnaissance and it makes our small detachment different. Maybe in time it will make the men feel special and give them a bit of the pride they lack now."

Fine took the packet of badges and McGuire's jacket and started to leave the office. McGuire stopped him.

"You can work in here. Do my jacket first if you will. I need to leave the barracks for a while."

As Fine sat down and started to work with the needle and thread, that were also in the packet, McGuire walked out into the stable. As he turned towards the stairs he saw rats running away from him and scuttling into their holes. He mounted the stairs and found that the two long tack rooms were now clean.

He called his men to him and sat down on a rickety chair. "All of you sit down and take a breather while I tell you what I want from you."

He waited until they had settled before he spoke. "I've read all your files and now I know why you were sent to me. The regiment doesn't want you. So what do we do about that? I don't need an answer, I'm going to tell you. During the fighting down in the Sudan the Dervishes nearly destroyed a British Square and that's never happened before. They did it by sneaking past the cavalry screen. So our job, once we are ready, is to see what the cavalry doesn't. That way we protect the army when it's on the move."

He looked around at his men and saw that he had their attention. "Strangely enough the reasons that the regiment doesn't want you are the reasons that I do. Let's start, O'Leary and Macklin they've got you down as thieves. I'm going to use you as the people who find me the equipment I need. Connolly you were a forger, now you are going to be our map maker. Donnelly you keep getting into fights and last time you pulled a knife on an Arab. You won all those fights, so you are going to teach the rest of us, especially how to use a knife. Jones, you're a drunkard, I think that's because you are bored. Where we are going there won't be any drink and I promise you won't be bored. Last but not least Parks. You are a farm boy who should never have joined up since you hate drill, especially the shouting and stamping. You are going to look after the camels we are going to get. Since those animals are going to save our lives out in the deep desert you may be our most valuable asset."

As he looked around the men again, he saw smiles and they were sitting up and taking notice. "One more member of our little band is downstairs. Private Fine is sewing a new badge on your uniform jackets. I expect you to be made fun of to start with, but you will not react. Got that Donnelly? Very soon that badge will be a mark of honour and others will covet it, I promise you. Fine is going to be helping us though he may not be able to deploy with us."

He paused. "Any questions? Yes O'Leary?"

"Two questions sir. if I may? What do you want us to acquire and when do we start training?"

"I have a list down in my office for you and we start as soon as I have found our camels. Before that, find me a couple of big nasty cats. I want those damned rats dealt with. Parks you're coming with me to buy some bigger animals. I want the best we can get and you are going to help choose them."

Chapter 34.
Training

Buying the camels took the last of the gold McGuire had picked up in the Sudan, but he hoped it would be worth it. Parks had proven to be good with the camels and he had an eye for animal problems. The bargaining had been hard, but both sides had enjoyed it. The Arab trader had been delighted to find that McGuire could speak his language and knew the courtesies of the Arabs. The sale had taken a long time, but both sides were satisfied and the trader loaned McGuire two of his men to lead the camels back to barracks.

The Sergeant of the guard had stood in the barrack gate as they approached. "You can't bring those smelly creatures in here sir. Colonel's orders."

"These are the transport for the Reconnaissance section Sergeant. They have to come in."

"I don't mean the camels, sir. The camels are welcome. I mean those two scruffy creatures leading them."

"You can't be serious?"

"Sorry sir. I've got strict orders not to allow street Arabs in to the barracks."

McGuire decided not to argue, with more people assembling to watch what was happening. He walked to the two men and gave them his thanks and a handful of piasters, rather than have them embarrassed.

"Right Sergeant I want two of your men out here now to help me lead these animals in to the stables."

The sergeant thought better of arguing with an angry officer, and two men were dragged out to lead two camels each. They reached the stables and led the eight animals inside into the shade. The rest of the unit gathered round to look at their new mounts and McGuire was pleased to see that they were all wearing the red diamond.

He and Parks closed the double door of the stable and the soldier looked at him. "No wonder the Arabs hate us eh sir?"

"No wonder at all Parks. Now let's get these beasts in to their stalls and watered. From now on, looking after the camels comes first. Once we get into the desert you'll all find out why."

McGuire walked across, to where O'Leary and Macklin were standing by a tarpaulin covered mound. Both men were wearing broad grins as they whipped the cover back to reveal eight camel saddles and eight saddle blankets.

"That's a nice pile. I suppose I shouldn't ask where they came from?"

"They're not stolen sir. We traded for them."

"And what did you trade?"

O'Leary grinned again. "Ah now then, that would be the question you shouldn't ask sir."

McGuire nodded and tried to suppress a grin of his own. "Well done, now are you ready for a difficult one?"

"Always ready to help sir." Macklin said.

"Good. I want a thousand rounds of rifle ammunition. Sixteen water skins and field rations for a week for seven men. Can you do that?"

Macklin shook his head as he looked at O'Leary. "The skins and the food are no problem sir, but the ammunition might take a couple of days. That's a bit tricky and if we're found with it, well you understand."

"I understand well enough now can you do it?"

O'Leary nodded with a look of concentration on his face. "I think we can, but as yer man says it could take a couple of days, maybe more."

McGuire smiled. "Good. All the rest of you, work with Parks and get the camels settled. We start riding lessons in the morning, but this afternoon we need to fix the saddles so they don't rub their humps."

He walked away to his office where Fine was standing in the doorway. "What's the matter Fine?"

"Nothing sir. Just wondering why you need eight camels for seven men and why so much ammunition? We usually only get thirty rounds a year to keep our hands in."

"The eighth camel is for carrying extra stores if we need to, but tomorrow you are going to be riding it."

"Me sir? Why sir?"

McGuire leaned forward and tapped the red diamond badge of Fine's sleeve. "Because you're one of us and one day I may need you. So you are doing some of the training with us. That includes the musketry. Every man in this unit is going to be a crack shot by the time I'm finished."

"We're already qualified shots sir and I am already desert trained."

"And in the firing line when the volleys are roaring that's good enough. We won't be shoulder to shoulder in the square, we will be off on our own and every round has to count if we get found by the enemy. That way we might just survive. That's also why Donnelly is going to teach us to fight with knives, you don't need to do that until you're stronger, but come and watch the lessons anyway. Your desert training is good enough when you are with the regiment, but not for what we are doing."

The riding lesson was far less chaotic than the Camel Corps one had been at the start of the Gordon Relief Expedition. Within an hour all of his men were riding confidently around the stable yard. McGuire suspected that had a lot to do with the quality of the animals he had procured and maybe something to do with Parks keeping them calm. In any event the misfits he had been given were proving that they were worth the effort.

The lessons in street fighting from Donnelly were McGuire's best chance to see what sort of men he had been given. They sat in a circle as the big man showed them how to hold the curved dagger low and thrust upwards into an enemy's stomach. Then he stood and looked around.

"Now then, who wants to be the first to try me?"

There was a silence as the men glanced at each other. "I think I'll go first."

"You sir? I can't hit you sir."

McGuire stood up and removed his jacket. He handed it to Fine and then loosened his shirt around the neck.

He stepped towards Donnelly. "Well if you don't stop me I'm going to have to knock you on your arse Donnelly. So let's see what you've got."

Donnelly nodded and smiled. He picked up the second dagger and handed it to McGuire. Both weapons were still sheathed to prevent injury. He dropped into a crouch and began to circle his officer. McGuire turned slowly watching Donnelly's eyes. The thrust when it came was lightning fast but McGuire was faster and slipped to one side. The big man was off balance when he felt the butt of the knife tap him behind the ear.

"Very good sir. A lucky move."

"Where are you from Donnelly? Your accent sounds like the north of Ireland."

"Belfast sir. I come from the Shankhill Road. That's where I learned to fight."

The second he finished speaking he lunged forward again slashing across McGuire's stomach. Again his officer was ready for him and leapt backwards to avoid the blow. This time he stepped forward and with his foot swept Donnelly's legs from under him. As he fell to the ground Michael dropped with him and pinned him to the ground with the dagger across the throat.

"A lesson for you all here. Donnelly is fast and vicious in the attack, but never underestimate your enemy. After all he could have learned to fight in the back streets of Dublin or Cairo."

A couple of weeks later as he was watching his men ride around the yard he became aware of someone standing behind him. He spun round to find Colonel O'Brian standing in the shade and watching quietly. McGuire came to attention and saluted.

The Colonel walked over and stood beside him. "Your men seem to be getting on with the camels rather well McGuire. What else have you been teaching them?"

"All the things they might need to survive in the desert, sir. Their musketry is improving, they are learning hand to hand fighting, navigation and Arabic."

The Colonel nodded. "What's next?"

"Next I intend to take them out into the desert to live like the Bedouin. They need to look and act like real Arabs, rather than British soldiers, if we are to be able to move around without attracting too much attention."

O'Brian nodded again, then tapped McGuire's red diamond badge with his swagger cane. "It seems your little badge is paying off. These men already don't look like the reprobates you were given. It seems I was right to give you all this leeway. However, there have been complaints of some unusual thefts around the garrison. None from this regiment luckily. I don't suppose you know anything about that do you?"

"Thefts sir? That's a shame. I wonder who it might be."

The Colonel chuckled. "Tell me where you are going in the desert I might come out and visit you."

Chapter 35.
The Desert

The eight camels strode across the sandy desert beyond the pyramids with Abdullah riding the leader. His wooden leg made sitting the camel awkward, but he was managing and seemed to be enjoying riding over the dunes once more. Behind him the Reconnaissance group was dressed in the *jibba* of the Arabs with a *Shemagh* scarf on their heads, secured with the rope *Agai*. From a distance they might have passed for Bedouin if only they could ride in the casual way of the desert dwellers.

They crested another rise and McGuire found himself looking down at a small group of tents spread around a small oasis. They rode forward and slowly approached. McGuire brought his men to a halt just short of the tents and then rode the last few yard alongside Abdullah. As they reined in a man came out of the nearest tent and stood waiting for them. They made their camels kneel and then dismounted.

McGuire strode forward and gripped the man's hand. "Asif of the keen eye. It is good to see you my friend."

"It is good to see you as well English and good to see my brother Abdullah of the wooden leg."

"It was a joy to me when Abdullah told me you were near here. I am in your debt yet again for offering to teach my men the way of your people."

Asif made a small bow. "It is nothing, I am glad to help my friend. Bring your men forward they are welcome here."

McGuire waved his men forward and waited while they dismounted and then walked to him. "All of you, this is Asif. His one eye is keener than any man with two. He is the finest man with a rifle in all of Egypt. He is also one of the two bravest men I know. He was the one who showed me the way into Khartoum."

Jones looked at Asif and then at McGuire. "You were in Khartoum? We heard a British soldier had gone in alone, but we didn't know it was you."

"It was me, but I was not alone. If it was not for my friend here and another brave man I would never have been able to do it."

A voice from behind made McGuire turn. "And it has given me a fine story, as I promised it would."

"Haroun! My day is complete. Men, this is Haroun, a man wise in the ways of the desert. He was the other brave man who helped me into Khartoum."

Haroun nodded with pleasure. "You and your men must be tired. Come, a meal is waiting for you by the water. Have you taught them yet how to eat?"

"I have not Haroun. Lead the way and we will tell them stories of our travels in the deserts of the Sudan."

They sat around the communal pots of food on a wide carpet and listened to the stories as they ate. The men missed some of the tale as their Arabic was not yet fluent. McGuire translated for them. As the meal ended they all tried to belch in appreciation as Haroun and Asif had done, while the women cleared the plates away.

McGuire waited until things started to quiet down before he fished under his robe and brought out a small package that he laid on the carpet before him. "Haroun, Asif I have something to tell you. When British soldiers fight a war the Queen sometimes gives them a medal to wear on their jackets with pride. This she has done for all the soldiers who fought in the Sudan. I told her of your bravery, when I took Gordon's revolver to her, and she has said that you must have the medal as well."

He opened the packet and took out the two small blue medal boxes. He opened one, to show the silver medal with the head of the Queen on it and the blue and white striped ribbon of the Egypt medal.

"When you tell your stories around the camp fire you have a gift from my Queen to show that you do not lie."

Asif and Haroun sat quietly looking down at their medals. They tucked them away in their robes and said nothing.

In the early morning the teaching began. The men were shown how to wear their robes. How to adjust the *Shemagh,* when the wind picked up and the sand blew around them, how to ride Arab style and how to cook the food of the desert. Then McGuire and Asif took them out to the top of a dune and they practiced with their rifles at longer and longer ranges. All the time they were learning and their Arabic was improving without them noticing. The relaxed discipline appropriate to this kind of training worked wonders for their confidence and McGuire began to believe they could be successful.

The day before they were due to return to barracks two horsemen were spotted riding towards the oasis. Their uniforms marked them out as British officers and as they came closer McGuire could see that one of them was Colonel O'Brian. They rode into the camp and dismounted by the first tent.

McGuire walked across to them and greeted his commanding officer. "Good afternoon sir. Nice of you to come for a visit."

"Don't you usually salute a superior officer Lieutenant?"

"Not out here sir. Colonel Kitchener taught me that. If I salute you it marks you out as a valuable target to anyone watching with a rifle."

The other officer laughed. "Quite right too. I'll have to make sure my other men know about that."

O'Brian nodded at his companion. "Our laughing friend here is Major Reginald Wingate. He's the chief of intelligence at headquarters. I was telling him about you at dinner last week and he wanted to see how you are doing."

"Nice to meet you sir. Perhaps you would both care to join us for the evening meal. It should be ready by now, and then I can tell you what progress we have made."

They walked across to the tent by the waterside and sat down cross legged on the carpet that was spread there. The women brought out the food and then withdrew as was customary.

O'Brian looked around at the tribesmen who were sitting around him eating their food. "Where are your men eating McGuire? I'd like to say hello to them."

"We all eat together sir."

"Then shouldn't we wait for them? These Arabs will have everything finished if we don't."

McGuire smiled slightly. "Sir to your left, may I present Private Donnelly. He is our expert with that curved dagger you see at his waist. To his left is Private Parks, our camel expert and the rest of the men are all here as well."

O'Brian looked around at the swarthy faces half wrapped in the *shemagh*, he had not recognised them as his own men. "My Lord. What have you done to them?"

"Made them into people who can hide in plain sight I hope, sir."

Wingate was delighted. "Brilliant! You were right Colonel, these are just the sort of men I need. When will training be complete Lieutenant?"

"Not long sir. We ride back to barracks in the morning and then I have heliograph training scheduled for all of them. After that we are ready."

"Why train all of them on the heliograph. Surely just one or two would do?"

McGuire shook his head. "All of us have done all the training. Even our sick man Private Fine has done as much as he could. That means I

212

know I can send any man to do any job. It gives me flexibility when we are off in the wilderness."

Wingate shook his head in admiration. "Sound thinking young man. I may have to borrow you from the regiment very shortly. We have some rumblings coming out of the Sudan that need looking into."

The next morning they rode back into the barracks, still in desert dress, with the Colonel on his horse in the lead. As they reached the gate, the Guard sergeant came out and started to yell at the dirty Arabs trying to enter his domain.

Colonel O'Brian turned in his saddle. "Open the gate Sergeant, my elite Reconnaissance unit is coming home."

Chapter 36.
First Task

Lieutenant McGuire walked through the cool halls of the garrison headquarters building to Major Wingate's office. It was his first time in the building and he had to admit it was far more impressive than his stable block. He reached the office and knocked on the white painted door.

The door swung open and Major Wingate ushered him inside. "Welcome young McGuire. Thank you for coming."

"Colonel O'Brian said you needed my help sir. What can I do for you?"

Wingate settled himself behind his desk and looked at McGuire over the piles of paperwork. "You know. I joined the artillery to fire the big guns. I never imagined ending up behind mountains of reports and paperwork. Still, we do what needs doing eh?"

McGuire nodded slowly, not sure where this was going. "Indeed, sir, I'm sure you're right."

"I'm sure you don't need to hear all my woes so let's get to the business in hand. We have heard rumours from the Sudan that the Mahdi is dead and one of his people has taken over. I need to confirm that and to know whether that poses a threat to Egypt."

McGuire said nothing and waited. "So, what I would like you to do is, to go down to the Sudan as quickly as possible and find out which of all the rumours we hear are accurate. Let me explain why. All the British troops are concentrated up here in the north to safeguard the Suez Canal. So we have to rely on the Egyptian army. You will be aware that the last time they ran up against the Dervishes they proved to be sadly lacking?"

"Yes sir the disaster of Hicks' column and the Baker expedition."

"Indeed yes. Now the Egyptians are reforming their army rapidly. The corrupt officers are being weeded out and the men are starting to be treated decently for a change. They are being properly trained and equipped. There's nothing wrong with the Egyptians if they are properly led, but they need time to correct the abuses of the past."

"Surely that's all to the good, sir?"

"It is, but if the Dervish army comes north, before they are ready, all that good work could be lost. We may need to send British units south to bolster them up if that happens. It will take time to get them down there so we need to know what to expect."

McGuire could feel the excitement of action building within him. "So what are my orders?"

"Take your detachment into the Sudan. Look for any sign of a military build-up. Talk to the people and find out what the Dervish leaders are intending. We have been told that Abdallahi wad Torshayn has taken over. He has taken the title of Khalifa. As far as we know he was a simple nomad from Dafur, but he was the Mahdi's right hand man. I'd like that confirmed. Now that the Mahdi is gone, we hope there may be some dissent since the unifying force of "The Expected One" might not continue. After that use your initiative and gather any information you think may be useful if we have to take an army down there. Any other questions?"

"Just one, sir, when do we leave?"

"Can you be ready by the end of this week? I will have papers prepared that will allow you to commandeer whatever transport you need. The transport officer will also make you an itinerary and put in place as much as he can to ease your passage south. You will also be issued gold coins to use while in the Sudan. Does that satisfy you?"

"Just one point sir, could the Transport Officer make provision for us to take our own camels. They're in far better condition that the ones we picked up down south for the Relief Expedition."

"Not a problem and your Colonel will ensure that you get anything you need issued to you without the customary red tape. Anything else?"

McGuire stood and saluted. "No sir, but now I have to break it to my intended that all her careful wedding plans are going to be disrupted. I'm more nervous of that than the Sudan."

McGuire hailed one of the horse drawn gharries that always waited outside the headquarters and had himself driven back to the barracks. Instructing the driver to wait at the gate he walked to the stable block. As he walked in he found the men sitting around a long table, field stripping and cleaning their rifles.

He didn't wait for the salutes, but called for their attention. "All of you listen. If you have anything that you need to do get it done now. We are being deployed on an Intelligence gathering task at the end of this week. We will be moving out on Sunday morning. Get all your kit packed and ready for a long ride in the desert. Any questions?"

Jones raised a hand. "If you please sir. Where are we going?"

"You'll find that out after we set off. We need to keep this quiet. No more? Right, finish the rifles then take the rest of the day to start getting ready. I will see you here first thing in the morning."

Without waiting for any further questions he left the stable block and went back to the gharry. Twenty minutes later he stepped down outside the whitewashed villa by the Nile. He paid the driver and went in. As he walked around the house and onto the terrace he saw Emma siting with her mother, both sipping tea from bone china cups.

Emma jumped up from the small table and ran as soon as she saw him. She flung her arms round his neck and kissed him, ignoring the intake of breath from her mother. She took his hand a led him back to the table.

"Mother is feeling much better today. She thinks she will be completely ready for the wedding next month. Isn't that wonderful?"

McGuire cleared his throat and looked down at his feet, he looked up into Emma's concerned eyes. "What's the matter? What's gone wrong?"

He looked at her and then her mother. "I'm really sorry about this, but I have been issued orders and I have to go away for a while. I don't know how long, but certainly longer than a month."

Emma's mother gave a grim smile. She didn't think McGuire was good enough for her daughter and had made that very clear. She stood up from the table and walked back into the house without a word.

"What are we going to do?" Emma asked.

"There is one thing we could do if you are willing."

"Tell me."

"We could get married before I go. I have to leave on Sunday morning, but maybe we can swing it?"

"My dress isn't ready, the food isn't ordered yet. The church is booked for next month not this week. The guests won't be able to come at such short notice and Mother will be furious."

"I know all that, but I don't want to go and leave you in the lurch."

"I think it would be very romantic to get married this week, all in a rush. I know the pastor and he will do it for me if I ask him nicely. We don't need guests and the cook here can make lunch. Instead of a church, shall we marry here, overlooking the Nile?"

Emma was right, her mother was furious and the pastor was willing. The guest list was very small. Colonel O'Brian gave the bride away and eight soldiers made a guard of honour with their uniforms specially pressed and polished by Private Fine. A few of Emma's friends made it and seemed very interested in the smart soldiers who made a point of keeping Jones away from the beer table.

As the service ended and before the lunch started the gate opened and two Bedouin tribesmen walked in. "Haroun, Asif, you made it. I am so glad to have you here." Emma told them.

McGuire was delighted to see them and turned to Emma quizzically. "We couldn't get married without your two best friends in Egypt now could we? I had Abdullah get a message to them."

McGuire turned to the two men. "I am glad to share this day with you. It may be some time before I see you again."

Asif shook his head. "Not so English, for I am coming south with you."

"How do you know where I am going?"

Asif and Haroun both smiled. "English, this is Egypt and the sands of the desert speak to us. We know where you go and why. You will need Asif if you are to return alive. I am sad that I cannot go as well."

McGuire nodded and took Asif's hand again. "I will be proud to have you with me Asif of the keen eye."

The reception in the garden ended and the guests left, shouting their congratulations as they did so. Even Emma's mother had the good grace to go and stay with friends in the city, leaving the young couple alone in the villa by the Nile. They sat on the terrace together and watched the sun go down, then Emma stood up and kissed McGuire on the forehead.

"I'll be getting ready" she said, as she turned and walked slowly into the house.

McGuire sat alone watching the lights across the river flicker into life. He finished the tea that had now gone cold in his cup and stood up from his chair. The house was silent as he walked through the doors into the neat sitting room. He walked across to the door into the corridor and then along to the main bedroom.

He swung the door open to find two candles throwing a warm glow across the room. Emma stood between him and the bed wearing an ivory silk night gown that reached down to the floor. He took the three steps towards her and took her by the shoulders then leaned down and kissed her gently. She returned his kiss and it became more urgent. He ran his hands gently across her back and felt her tremble at his touch. He lifted his hands and slipped the nightdress off her shoulders and let it fall to the floor around her ankles. She stood absolutely still as he took a half step backwards and looked at her.

"My God" he whispered. "You are the most beautiful creature I have ever seen."

She smiled and took his hands, pulling him gently to the bed. She sank down and lay back as he lay down beside her.

His fingertips trailed slowly across her smooth skin that seemed to glow in the candlelight, as she unbuttoned his shirt. He sat up to slip the shirt from his shoulders and returned to stroking her as she unbuttoned his trousers.

"I'm going to miss you while I'm in the south."

"And I'll miss you too, but we have tonight and all day tomorrow."

Chapter 37.
South Again

The journey south was long and trying, alternating between the railway and river boats. At every railway halt Parks dashed to the cattle cars to check on the camels he was really starting to think of as his. At every dock there was an argument with the ship's captain that was settled by the authority papers and the change of ownership of some of the gold coins. The camels seemed to enjoy the water borne parts of the journey as much as the men, though other passengers were less than enthused at having some of their promenade deck given over to the beasts.

They reached Wadi Haifa on the Egyptian border to find the Egyptian army in place and training its new men. The camp was neat and well-ordered with properly equipped and alert sentries. McGuire was impressed with the change from the slovenly Egyptian troops he had seen in the past. Proper leadership and decent treatment had started to work wonders.

After watering their camels in the Nile and drawing rations they set off south into the Sudan. They had patched their *jibbas* during the journey and now looked like a Dervish patrol, at least from a distance. If they ran into any inquisitive enemy troops it might be a different story. McGuire's Arabic was good enough to pass for a native from the north and Donnelly had proved to be a very fast learner, the rest were still learning and obviously so.

McGuire decided they should ride up the Nile on the east bank as far as Kerma. From here they would cut out the bend in the river and cross the desert to Abu Hamed. That would keep them clear of the major town of Dongola and its probable garrison, but allow them to find local people to talk to about the situation further south and along the great river.

They rode in the early morning before the sun had crested the horizon and found secluded camp sites once the heat of the day had built up. They saw occasional Dervish patrols in the distance and avoided them until they came in sight of the mud walls of Kerma. Asif and McGuire rode forward alone to find the street market being set up. They sat at a stall in the corner of a small square, drinking the strong black coffee and watching the merchants go about their business.

Once the market was busy enough that they would not be noticed, the two men walked slowly into the crowd and past the stalls. They needed vegetables to supplement the field rations and dried meat they had been living on, but more than that they needed information.

Asif walked to a stall and examined the produce. "Some poor offerings here today my brother. Have you nothing better for a traveller?"

The merchant looked at him keenly. "You must indeed be a traveller if you do not know of our troubles. The Khalifa has sent his Baggara soldiers out through the villages. They take all the best of our crops and give us nothing, but savage blows if we object. This is the best I have left."

Asif gave a small bow. "My apologies brother, I spoke without thinking. The Baggara have always been troublesome."

"Now more than ever. With the Expected One gone, there is no curb on them and the Khalifa uses them to impose his will on those, like us, who just want to make a small living."

Asif nodded as sympathetically as he could. "It is as you say my friend, but I need some of your food for the journey."

The stall holder brightened and the two men began to bargain as McGuire looked around him. The market was a poor shadow of the markets of Egypt just a little way to the north. The people seemed downcast and the bargaining, that was usually so enjoyable to both parties, was almost desultory. He turned back as Asif completed the transaction and they walked back to where the camels waited carrying the four small sacks.

"Did you learn what you needed, English?"

"I think so Asif. The new ruler is imposing his will where the Mahdi inspired loyalty. This is a good thing for us. Let us go now and see if it is true further up the river."

At dawn the next day the group were already riding across the flat plain towards Abu Hamed. Out here, away from the Nile, they did not expect to run into any of the Dervish forces, still they were wary. They found a place to rest near to a small well, set among an area of tumbled rocks.

McGuire climbed to the top of the rocky outcrop and scanned the empty desert before he went back to his men. "Set up camp here, Jones, detail a man to watch from up there. Connolly, mark this well down on that map of yours. It could be useful one of these days."

They sat around as the evening drew on, while Asif cooked the beans with the meat of a gazelle he had shot during the day. McGuire looked up at a whistle from the man on watch. Above him he could see Macklin pointing to the east and then holding up three fingers.

"Parks you look after dinner, don't let it burn. Asif you are with me. The rest of you take cover in the rocks and keep quiet."

Asif and McGuire walked to the edge of the rocky area, where they could see three mules being ridden slowly towards them. They sat down and waited, not wanting to alarm the people coming closer. They stood when they could see the faces of the riders. The mules stopped and the lead rider watched them warily.

"Asif. Go you forward and tell them we are friends. Ask them to come and share the water."

Asif nodded and walked out alone. He spoke with the lead rider and waved his hand towards McGuire. The man nodded and the three rode forward with Asif leading the way. As they came closer McGuire could see that the lead person was an old man and with him he had two women with their faces covered as was the tradition in this area.

He stepped forward as the old man dismounted. "Welcome grandfather. The water is sweet and cool here and you are in time to share our food if you will."

The old man stood and regarded McGuire carefully. "I am glad of the water and it is generous to share your food. We have not eaten since yesterday."

McGuire nodded. "Since we are here first you are our guests. Do not be alarmed, but I have men in the rocks. We did not know if you might be enemies."

The old man looked around, but saw nobody. "Are we safe here?"

"You are safe here. A guest is always safe. Is that not so?"

"It is as you say. We will spread our small camp over there by the rock wall."

"And then all three of you are welcome at our fire. The food is yours as it is ours."

"My wife and daughter are safe?"

"They are safe grandfather, as if they were my own."

They sat around the cooking fire later that evening. The men helped themselves from the communal pot and the two women sat behind waiting for their turn to eat from what was left. McGuire would have liked to bring them forward or to give them a bowl each, but he knew the old man would have been offended at this breach of custom.

"Tell me grandfather. What news from the south?"

The old man belched his appreciation and then looked at McGuire. "It is not good. The Baggara horsemen came to Berber which is our town. They read out the proclamation of the

226

Khalifa and then took our land, our cattle and the best of our crops. Women are dragged off the streets and raped yet we can do nothing. It is not good."

McGuire paused and looked at the old man. "So where do you go grandfather?"

"I go north to my brother in Tushki. It is beyond the border where the rule of the Khalifa does not run."

"Do all your people suffer in this way?"

The old man nodded sadly. "It is so. Not many are prepared to brave the desert to escape or have somewhere to go if they do. As long as we avoid the patrols we will be safe, we will stay away from the river."

"To stay away from the river a man must know the wells."

"I know the wells across this land."

McGuire handed the old man a cup of the strong coffee Asif had made. "My friend draws a picture of this land and where a man can find water. Will you show him so he can mark these places?"

"A guest should always help his host. I will show you."

"Tell me truly grandfather, are there those who would welcome the Egyptians back here?"

The old man sipped from the small coffee bowl. "It is as you say. The people of Metemma are of the Ja'aliyyin people and hate the Baggara nomads. I have heard it told that the sheikh, Abdallah wad Sa'ad, would rise against the Khalifa, if he had support from the north. Alone he cannot do this and his people would be slaughtered."

"My friend it is late and your women should eat before they sleep. We will leave here before the dawn. Will you do the same to avoid the Dervish patrols?"

"I will do this."

"We will speak in the morning before you go. My friend who draws the picture is this one. Will you show him the wells now, before sleep?"

In the morning the two parties prepared to leave, McGuire and his men to the east and the old man to the north. The men mounted the camels and waited while McGuire walked across to the old man carrying a water skin and a sack.

"My friend, I see you have no food and little water. Take these small things as a gift and be safe on your travels."

The old man thanked his benefactor profusely and then they set off towards Egypt and safety. McGuire mounted and followed Asif out on to the desert followed by his men. The ride was long and tiring, but after three days they came in sight of Abu Hamed. The mud brick walls around the town were in poor state and many of the houses seemed deserted. As they rested on a ridge looking down at the town and considering their options, O'Leary spotted movement to their left.

"Sir! Horsemen moving in from the left. Looks like ten of them."

McGuire turned in his saddle and looked to where O'Leary was pointing. He raised his binoculars and studied the group, before turning to Asif.

"They are riding hard and they have their swords in their hands."

Asif squinted at the approaching group. "They are Baggara, they will not stop to talk, but will attack. The chance to convince them we are friends is gone, English. It is time to fight."

McGuire took another look at the rapidly approaching horsemen. "All of you listen. Stay in your saddles until I give the word. When I give the order grab your rifles and drop to the ground. Pick a target and drop them. Do not wait for an order to fire. None of them can be allowed to get away or we are finished. Now spread out a little, stay steady and wait for my word."

McGuire turned his camel and walked slowly in the direction of the Baggara as they mounted the slope at the end of the ridge. Behind him and equally slowly his soldiers spread out and waited.

The Baggara reached the top of the ridge and showed no sign of slowing. The leader screamed and then the rest joined in with their battle cries. McGuire waited for his moment, he could not afford to give them chance to ride away and raise the rest of the tribesmen against them.

"Now! Drop them all!"

All eight men drew the rifles from the saddle pouches that held them and dropped from their camel's backs without getting the animal to kneel first. Connolly was the first to fire, and the second man in the approaching pack was lifted from his saddle in a mist of blood, as the heavy round

229

passed through him. The others were less than a second behind him and the saddles emptied rapidly.

The last man in the attacking group saw what was happening and reined his horse in hard. The animal slid to a stiff legged stop and then turned away. With the tribesman beating hard at its rump the horse set off down the slope towards the town.

The last tribesman who had decided to continue the attack selected McGuire as his target and charged at him. His sword arm raised and then swung the large sword down towards the young officer's head. A rifle to the left roared and the man's head virtually vanished as the large lead round ripped into and through it. The body stayed in the saddle for another ten paces and then fell to the left in a tumble of limbs.

McGuire stood and looked at the fleeing man. "Bring that one down all of you."

There was a single shot and the man fell from his mount. His hand still clasped the reins and the horse was dragged to a stop as the body dragged alongside it. Asif stood and smiled at McGuire.

"As ever Asif, my keen eyed friend, you save us all."

McGuire turned round to see who had fired the shot that saved him, to find that the only man out to the left was the inoffensive Private Parks. "Parks, was it you who shot this one?"

"Yes sir, sorry sir."

"Why sorry?"

"I thought maybe you wanted him for yourself sir."

"Nice shooting Parks. Not bad at all for the man the RSM said should never be a soldier."

McGuire looked around at the men who waited for his next command. "All of you, search the bodies. Bring everything you find back here. If there's anything of any worth we share it."

They moved quickly to obey his instructions and Asif and McGuire rode down to the man, who had nearly got away to raise the alarm.

"McGuire looked down at him and then turned to Asif. "That was a truly fine shot my friend. You should search this one and keep what you find."

Asif dropped to the ground and rapidly went through the man's clothing. He picked up the curved dagger from his sash and his sword then went to the horse and went through the saddle pouches. Satisfied he remounted and then rode with McGuire back up to the ridge.

"Connolly, do you think we can find the wells from the information the old man gave you?"

"If he told me the truth then yes sir, with help from Asif"

McGuire nodded. "Good work all of you, but after this we'd better get away from here. Going into the town would be too much of a risk now. We ride north west back to Wadi Haifa."

They mounted and turned their camels to the north. They rode all through the blazing heat of afternoon and came to the first well as the sun was setting. With two guards set, they made no fire that night and ate only the dried gazelle meat. Before dawn they were on their way to the next well and reached it before noon. They had seen no sign of pursuit so risked a fire to cook their evening meal. It seemed the old man had told them the truth and the well water was clear and clean.

On the third day they rode on until they saw the vultures circling ahead of them. They spread out and rode forward carefully. The three corpses were almost unrecognizable after the vultures had eaten. The damage had not just been done by the birds. The Baggara had made sure the old man and his two women had died hard and slowly. McGuire said nothing, but wished he could vomit the way that Donnelly did.

"Ride on. We can't risk staying to bury them."

Donnelly rode close alongside him. "Sir we can't leave them. They deserve a decent burial."

"You're right of course, but now we know the Baggara are around here and, if we get caught in the open, we might not be as lucky as last time."

"You're a hard man sir."

"It's a hard country Donnelly and never you forget that."

Chapter 38.
Back to Egypt

They rode hard and the camels were almost worn out by the time they reached Wadi Haifa. The Egyptian army officers were surprised to see them. They had thought they would not survive below the border. They found the tents they had been allocated and unsaddled before walking the camels down to the Nile to drink their fill. They settled down outside the tents with the camels hobbled alongside them and started to cook their evening meal. McGuire had been invited to the officers' mess, but had declined.

As they sat around waiting for the food to cook, Macklin was the first to bring out the things he had taken from the body he searched. McGuire was pleased that one of his two thieves was the first. They all laid whatever they had picked up in the middle of the group.

Jones looked at McGuire. "Will you divide it up sir?"

McGuire slid forward and started to sort the coins and trinkets into eight equal piles. There was little gold, but there were quite a few Egyptian piasters. There were curved daggers and two good swords as well as jewellery.

Asif sat quietly to one side and watched the sorting. As McGuire finished he leaned forward and tapped him on his arm.

"I have some for your sorting as well. First I must make a gift."

"A gift?"

"Yes English. The quiet one saved the life of my brother and I have a gift for him."

From under his robe he drew out the jewelled dagger he had picked up from the escaping man he had shot. "I do not know why that man had such a weapon, but it should be at the side of a brave man."

He rose to his feet and walked across the small circle to where Parks sat. "This pays a small part of the debt I owe you for the life of my friend. Wear it when you go to battle and may it save your life as you saved his."

Parks sat open mouthed as Asif walked back to his place and sat down. He smiled and nodded at the young Englishman, then reached under his robe again. He drew out a leather purse and tossed it to where McGuire sat cross legged.

"This should be shared as well. The spoils of a kill are shared. It is the way McGuire taught me that last time we fought in the Sudan."

McGuire opened the pouch and upended it. A shower of gold coins fell to the ground and lay between his knees. He looked up at Asif.

"Truly, my generous friend, you are a man of honour."

"It is easy to be a man of honour in such company as this, English."

McGuire wrote a report for Wingate and sent it by telegraph the next morning. With that duty done he set about getting his men and animals back to Cairo. They were arranging passage when the telegraphed reply arrived. McGuire was ordered to make his way back as quickly as possible using any and all means he deemed fit.

With the added urgency he reached Cairo in the August of 1886. He sent his men back to the barracks while he and Asif made their way to the headquarters of the British garrison. They had orders to give a briefing to a newly arrived officer and McGuire was also keen to ensure that Asif received the pay he was due.

They were met at the gate by a fresh faced subaltern who saluted McGuire, but looked down his nose at Asif in his native robes.

Controlling his anger, McGuire tapped the young man on the arm. "If you want to lose that rather fine nose of yours, I suggest you look down it at my friend Asif one more time. This is a man who could kill you where you stand for an insult like that and I would hold his coat while he did it."

The blood drained from the young officer's face as did his arrogance. He led them quickly along the passage ways of the large building to a meeting room. The highly polished table was surrounded by chairs, but they were alone. The end wall was decorated with a large map of Egypt and the Sudan. No more than five minutes passed before the door swung open and Wingate walked in, he was followed by a tall officer with striking blue eyes.

Asif leapt to his feet. "It is the Kitchener. My heart is glad to see you again."

Kitchener smiled. "My old comrade and friend Asif. Is your eye still as keen as the desert hawk?"

Asif laughed and gripped Kitchener's hand. "It is and it has been in your service these past months."

Wingate cleared his throat. "Perhaps we could sit down and let Lieutenant McGuire tell us what he knows?"

They sat around the table and McGuire noticed Kitchener was staring at him. "McGuire? I had a signaller with me in the Sudan, but he was a Lance Corporal."

McGuire smiled. "Nice to see you again sir."

"Well I'll be damned. I didn't know you had obtained a commission."

"Lord Wolseley seemed to think I had been of use to him so gave me a field commission then sent me with the despatches to Her Majesty. She was kind enough to give me a formal commission as a Lieutenant, sir."

Kitchener shook his head. "And you are still roaming the deserts of the Sudan eh?"

Wingate leaned forward. "McGuire, you should know that, while he was passing through Suez, Colonel Kitchener received a new appointment from London. Along with his promotion he has been appointed Governor General of East Sudan."

McGuire looked at Kitchener. "Congratulations sir. I think you will have problems with the Dervishes even there. Osman Digna has left the main Mahdist force in the Nile valley and has gone home to the east. He still has command of his men and still hates us and the Egyptians."

Kitchener nodded. "I expected as much, but I will have a decent sized force under me to control the region. Now though, tell me what you found out in the Northern Sudan. I have read your despatch to Wingate, but I want to hear your thoughts about the situation there."

"As Asif will confirm, we spoke to a few people and found that they are unhappy. When they joined the Mahdi they mainly did it because of the rotten treatment they got from their Egyptian overlords. Once they threw them out they thought things would get better and for a while they did. Now the Mahdi is dead the Baggara nomads have been sent out to enforce obedience and they are far worse than the Egyptians ever were."

Wingate rested his elbows on the table. "Your report mentioned Metemma in particular. Is there something there we could exploit?"

"The sheik of Metemma is aggrieved at the treatment of his people and he might rise, if he had arms and support, but we would have to send our people a long way into the Sudan to help him. In my opinion the time for that is not right for us."

Wingate nodded and looked at Kitchener. "We'll keep that one in our back pocket for another time then. Now carry on, talk us through everything you saw."

The briefing carried on for another hour with both senior officers asking pointed and relevant questions. McGuire gained the distinct impression that both men had an invasion of the Sudan in mind, when the time was ripe. Once they had every fact and opinion wrung out of them, Asif and

McGuire were thanked and sent on their way with instructions to the subaltern to take Asif to the paymaster on the way out. Wingate handed him a chit to present, to get Asif paid.

Outside the headquarters the two friends parted and went their separate ways. Asif headed for the bazaar to buy trinkets for his family, while McGuire made his way back to his barracks. He walked from the gate around to the stable block to check on his men. As he came in through the doors he found the camels in their stalls with the feed and water containers full. Private Fine was standing in the door of his office.

"Nice to see you back sir. I've got your spare uniform ready for you."

McGuire was surprised. "Why would I want that?"

"Sir, the Colonel wants to see you and I couldn't let you go in that uniform. Heaven knows what kind of creatures might be crawling around in it."

McGuire smiled. "Thank you Fine. You are quite right of course. Where are the men?"

"I sent them off to the bath house. They'll be back soon."

"I'd better go and see the Colonel. Tell them to take it easy for the rest of the day and I'll see them in the morning."

McGuire's interview with Lieutenant Colonel O'Brian was short and to the point. After this he headed back to the white villa by the Nile as fast as the *gharry* could carry him. He walked through the gate and round on to the terrace to find

Emma sitting there sewing. She struggled out of the chair as soon as she saw him and as soon as he saw her he realised why.

She patted her stomach. "Yes Michael, you're going to be a father. You've arrived in good time to meet the new arrival."

Chapter 39.
Preparation

With his uniform pressed to knife edge creases and his brasses gleaming McGuire waited at the stable door for the arrival of his commanding officer. O'Brian had informed him the day before that his small unit was overdue an inspection and today was to be the day. The men had worked hard and long to make sure there was nothing that would let them down and Private Fine had made sure their uniforms were perfect. McGuire supposed this was one of the joys of barrack life that working in the Sudan had allowed him to avoid.

McGuire stiffened as the Colonel appeared around the corner of the building. He had the Regimental Sergeant Major with him, so this was to be an intensive inspection. As the two men drew near McGuire saluted the Colonel.

"Good morning sir and good morning RSM."

"Are your men ready Lieutenant?" The Colonel asked.

"Yes sir perfectly ready."

The RSM almost growled. "We'll see about that."

The three men walked into the shade of the stable where each of the Reconnaissance section stood rigidly to attention by the stall of his own camel. The camels themselves were lying contentedly in their stalls chewing slowly on the fodder that had been laid out for them. O'Brian walked slowly along the line looking each man up and down while the RSM followed and did the same. McGuire followed on behind, expecting some harsh comment from the Sergeant Major at any moment, but there was nothing.

Private Fine stood by the door to the office staring rigidly ahead as the two inspecting officers approached him. The Colonel stopped and looked him up and down.

"Good morning, Fine. How's your health?"

"Improving every day sir."

"Good. How long before you are due for discharge from the army?"

"Just a few months sir. Unless I sign on again."

O'Brian smiled. "I'd like to have you, but with what the fever did to you I don't think that's possible. You'll be off back to England I'm afraid."

"Yes sir."

O'Brian turned to McGuire. "You have some rooms on the upper floor?"

"Yes sir accommodation for the men and a tack room for all the equipment."

"We'll go there next then shall we?"

McGuire led them up the staircase, to the accommodation, and noticed the RSM wiping his finger along every horizontal surface looking for dust. The tack room held saddles, blankets, water skins, weapons and everything else they needed to survive in the desert. All of it was neatly placed and clean.

O'Brian nodded at the RSM who nodded back. "A good turn out Lieutenant. Your men have done you proud. Now we need to sit down and discuss your future, shall we go to your office?"

As they entered the office McGuire dismissed the men and asked Fine to bring coffee. When it arrived he saw the RSM grimace a little at the strong Arab style drink in the small cups.

The Colonel put down his cup and sat back in his chair. "First of all, my compliments on what you have done with these men. The RSM gave you the worst the regiment had to offer and I have to confess that was because you had been imposed on us. Since you took command of them, not one of them has broken a rule and they are starting to be envied by the rest of the battalion."

"Thank you sir."

"But now they are going to face a stern test and I need to know if you think your small unit is up to it."

"I think we are as ready as we'll ever be. What do you need sir?"

"Not me, headquarters want to borrow you again. Kitchener and Wingate have hatched a plan and they need you to help them with it. You seem to have made quite an impression on Kitchener."

McGuire waited, saying nothing while the Colonel gathered his thoughts. "This is a secret and must not be discussed outside your unit. Only the RSM and I, within the regiment, know about it. Is that clear?"

"Crystal clear sir."

"It is the firm belief among the senior commanders at headquarters that one day we will be sent back into the Sudan to deal with the

Dervishes. They think it will be some years before we do it, but that it is almost inevitable if we are to protect southern Egypt. Kitchener and Wingate, without the knowledge of the Sirdar, are starting to prepare for that invasion. They believe that the key to success is the supply line and, after the debacle in the Crimea, I think they are right."

He paused and sipped at his coffee. "The Nile is unreliable and at low water the cataracts make it difficult to get supplies through in any quantity. They believe that we should build a railway into the Sudan to move troops quickly and to supply them with all their wants."

McGuire smiled. "Across that desert? Really?"

"Don't smile McGuire, they are quite serious and you are going to see if it is possible, or at least you are going to help the man who does. Kitchener has found a Royal Engineer Lieutenant called Edward Cator and he has agreed to fully survey the two hundred or more miles of the route. Your job is to get him there and keep him alive to do it. Now, is there anything you need to make sure this is a success?"

McGuire put down the coffee cup he had been cradling. "I have the equipment I need and the men are trained for it. Some of them can even pass for Arabs now that their language skills have improved. Can I take Asif with me as a guide?"

"Sadly no. The security around this is intense and he might speak of it. We don't want the Dervishes to have wind of this until the track starts to be laid, if that is at all possible."

"Then I do have a request sir. It is unconventional but it will motivate the men a lot and I think I need that."

"Go on, I'm listening."

"I would like to promote all of them to Lance Corporal except Private Fine. Him I would like to promote to full Corporal."

O'Brian's eyebrows lifted. "A whole unit of NCOs? I've never heard of such a thing. RSM what is your opinion?"

The RSM turned to McGuire and looked him in the eye. "I've never heard of it either, but I'd like to hear your reasoning, sir, before I state my opinion."

"Thank you RSM. Fine is the easy one. He has served this regiment for years and would still be doing so if the fever hadn't crippled him. I checked and the pension he will get for his service is pathetic. He will struggle to live on it and especially so as he probably can't work. A Corporal's pension would make his life easier and be a reward for his service."

O'Brian smiled and the RSM nodded. "I would have done it months ago, but I can't be seen to play favourites in the regiment. Fine has served with me for years. So that one is agreed. RSM please ensure the order goes out tonight."

"The rest are a little more difficult." McGuire said. "For this task they are going to be off on their own in small groups acting independently. Private soldiers can't do that. They will be at risk every hour of every day. Their soldiering skills are at a high standard and they have all worked hard without complaint. I think they need some reward."

"RSM your opinion?"

"Lieutenant McGuire makes some good points sir. They used to be the scum of the regiment, now they are envied and they carry themselves like soldiers. I think it might be a good example to the rest of the regiment, sir."

"Very well, I agree. Issue the orders tonight with the one for Fine if you please RSM. And as for you Lieutenant you need to get across to the headquarters to meet Lieutenant Cator and find out what he needs from you. Remember, at all costs he must come back alive with his survey information."

Chapter 40.
Water for the Railway

McGuire sat in the shade of a tree next to the river at Wadi Haifa, watching Lieutenant Cator practice riding a camel under the instructions of Lance Corporal Parks. He had quickly understood that this was no horse and the animal had its own way of doing things. He was an intelligent man and treated the soldiers of the Reconnaissance detachment with respect once he had been told of their past exploits for Wingate.

Cator dismounted and walked across to flop down in the camp chair by McGuire. "Your man Parks is very definite about how I am to treat his camel."

"He's a farm boy from way back and he loves animals. More than that he knows that those smelly, noisy beasts are what is going to keep us going through some bloody awful desert."

"You've been this way before. Is it as bad as people have been telling me?"

"For an army it's bloody awful. The lack of water feels like your throat has been ripped. Then as the sun gets up the heat is pretty grim until you get used to it. You start to long for the cold of the nights until you are trying to sleep with your teeth chattering. For a small group like us, who know the ways of this area, it's not too bad. The early mornings can be quite beautiful as the sun paints the sky."

"You sound like an artist."

"I'm Irish; it's much the same thing. Now though I want you to get to know another of my men."

McGuire waved and Donnelly lumbered to his feet from under the tree he had been leaning against. He walked across and stood by their chairs.

"Yes sir?"

Cator looked at McGuire. "Don't your men salute you?"

"Not from now on. Unless you want to be marked out as a useful target to any watching Dervishes?"

"Are they watching?"

"We work on the assumption that they are always watching. We eat like Arabs, we ride like them and we dress like them. Blending in to the background as much as we can might just save our lives. Any time you do anything that makes you look English we'll tell you about it."

Cator nodded, he was an intelligent officer and he could see that McGuire and his men knew their business. He looked up at Donnelly who was standing patiently.

"Now then Edward, this is Lance Corporal Donnelly. He was given to me because he was nothing but trouble. Always getting into fights. The good thing about him is that he wins those fights. Down here, away from civilised society, Donnelly is a major asset and, from the minute we leave Wadi Haifa, he is going to be your shadow. He is not going to be your servant, but he is going to be your bodyguard. He is a fine shot with a rifle, his fists and boots are weapons and you don't want to know what he can do up close with a knife."

Cator looked at the man in front of him. "I'm sure we'll get on well. Nice to meet you Donnelly."

"Nice to meet you as well sir. Anything else sir?"

McGuire smiled. "No thank you, go and get your evening meal now and tell the men we'll be leaving before dawn."

As the dawn broke the next morning, Cator rode alongside McGuire as the remarkable colours of a desert dawn painted the sky. "I can see why you like the dawn Michael. Do we always start off this early?"

"We do. We avoid the heat of the day and it's more difficult for any watchers to see where we came from."

"You seem to worry about watchers a lot."

McGuire pointed of to the right. "Take a look at that ridge over there. See anything?"

Cator turned in his saddle. "No nothing, should I?"

"There are three men watching us. I saw them as they topped the ridge just now. They've dropped down into the shadow of a wadi, but they're there. With luck they are more intent on taking a look at the army in Wadi Haifa and they'll ignore us."

"You think they are Dervishes?"

"I'd be very surprised if they aren't. You should remember the Dervish army is not as advanced as ours, or the Egyptians, in weapons or tactics, but they are far from stupid. They keep an eye on their enemies just as we do."

Later in the day Cator set up his theodolite and started to take measurements. Connolly assisted him by taking down the readings and improving the maps they had with them. Donnelly stayed close by and watched all around.

The men were fascinated when they found that Cator was also a skilled water diviner and they were excited when the bent sticks in his hands moved and detected water beneath the desert. They marked the spots on the map for others to dig at a later date. As the days passed they found a well, set into a jumbled mountain ridge, and decided to rest for a day to let the camels recover.

Jones and Macklin were sent out hunting and returned with an Ibex slung across the saddle of their spare camel. The fresh meat made a welcome change from the army field rations they had been eating and the men relaxed around the small camp fire.

With O'Leary taking the first watch they settled down around the remains of the fire to sleep. The night was clear and silent, McGuire felt he could reach up and touch the stars that hung above him. He wondered if Emma and the twins were watching the same sky far to the north. He sighed and pulled the blanket around him to sleep.

The tiny sound of a pebble falling brought Donnelly awake. He did not move, but just opened his eyes and looked around. There was nothing to worry him and he was about to settle down again, when he saw the slight movement behind

Lieutenant Cator. It took him a second or two to recognise what he was seeing. There was a man moving towards the sleeping officer. The starlight glinted off the blade in his hand. Donnelley shifted position slowly to free his hand below the thin blanket.

He watched as the man slid open the bag that lay beside Cator. He found nothing to interest him, just a sheaf of papers. He reached over the sleeping man and started to reach for the purse that lay temptingly in front of him. Cator sensed something and stirred. His eyes flew open to see the Arab leaning over him. Realising the officer was about to raise the alarm the Arab thrust down with his curved dagger. It stopped an inch or so from Cator's neck and then dropped as the assailant clawed at his own throat.

As the man fell back against the rock behind him, with a strangled croak, Cator felt the warm liquid soaking into his blanket. Then he saw the hilt of a knife protruding from his assailant's throat. The man struggled to pull it clear then sagged down to die on the sand. Cator was stunned and looked around to see Donnelly approaching.

"Sorry about all the blood sir. A throwing knife to the throat makes a bit of a mess."

Donnelly pulled the knife free and wiped the blade on the dead man's robe. Satisfied it was clean he tucked it back into the hidden sheath he wore on his forearm. He stood up and looked around as McGuire reached him.

"Nice throw Donnelly. You all right Edward?"

"I'm fine. I think he was trying to rob me when I woke up and startled him. Is he dead'"

McGuire looked down at the Arab. "Very dead. How the hell did he get this close? Donnelly, go and see if O'Leary is asleep. I'll skin him if he is."

Donnelly went up into the rocks to find O'Leary. He was back in a couple of minutes and took McGuire to one side.

"I think you should come and look at this sir."

Together they climbed back to the sentry position. O'Leary sat with his back against a boulder. He looked peaceful, but the blood soaking his clothes from his slashed throat was black in the starlight. McGuire knelt next to the dead soldier and then looked around he could feel the anger rising inside himself. He felt the pounding behind his eyes and forced it back down, the coldness filled his stomach.

"His rifle and bandolier are gone. Our friend down there didn't have them, so there must be more of them. Wake the others quietly."

Donnelly left and McGuire got to his feet and looked around. To the west he heard a jingle of harness and a voice. They were there and had to be stopped before they raised the alarm. He ran back down the short slope to his men.

"Jones, Macklin mount up and head that way. Connolly and Parks further north over that way. I'll go straight for them. Whichever way they go I want them dead. We can't let them get away. Now move!"

251

Cator was about to move for his camel when Donnelly put a hand on his arm. "We'll stay here sir. They'll be wanting breakfast when they get back."

"But we can help."

"Lieutenant McGuire can handle it sir. This is our bread and butter and we can't afford to risk you."

McGuire rode hard in the direction he had heard the noise. As the sky paled, he could see his men spreading out to either side of him, intent on avenging their friend. Ahead of him he saw two men on camels silhouetted against the morning light. He reined his camel to a halt and drew the rifle from its saddle pouch. He jacked the first round into the chamber and took aim. The camel beneath him stood stock still, as it had been trained, and he fired.

Two hundred yards away the left hand saddle was emptied, as the man was lifted clear by the heavy lead round and dumped to the desert floor. The second man spun round and saw that there was just one attacker. He hauled hard on the camels head and turned it as he drew his long sword. Kicking the camel into a trot he charged at McGuire with the sword raised high.

McGuire sat his mount and calmly reloaded. He waited for the man to get closer, to be certain of his shot. He raised the rifle and took aim, just in time to see the man's head blow apart in a fountain of blood and brain matter. He was puzzled by the loud report of the rifle until he realised that all four of his men had fired simultaneously. He rode slowly forward and looked down at the revolting mess on the sand. He dismounted and walked to the carcase on the ground. Bending down he took O'Leary's bandolier off the body then walked across to the camel and retrieved the rifle.

The five men rode sadly back into the camp in the rocks. "Jones, I need you to bury O'Leary's body and then cover it in stones to make it look like part of the ridge."

"No marker sir?"

"No marker. I'm sorry we can't risk that. Connolly mark this spot on the map will you and call it O'Leary's well."

Cator looked up at the circling vultures. "What about the three Dervishes? Where are we going to bury them?"

McGuire turned and looked at his companion. "We're not going to bury them. When a tribesman is killed out here he is left for the vultures and the hyenas. If we bury them, any Dervish patrol will know it was not the locals who killed them, and your mission will be exposed."

Cator's mouth dropped open a little. "That seems pretty cold."

McGuire nodded. "It is and it has to be that way. Your job is the survey and my job is to get you back with the information. So whatever that takes is what we will do, no matter how distasteful."

With O'Leary decently covered over they set out for the next area that needed to be surveyed. Donnelly rode up alongside Cator and held out a curved dagger to him.

"There you go sir. Stick that in your belt sash. You can regale the ladies with how close that came to opening you up."

Cator took the weapon and looked down at it as he rode. He shivered at the memory of how close that wicked blade had been to his throat. He looked at the rough and ready soldier riding beside him and nodded his thanks.

In the end, the survey showed that the railway would be two hundred and thirty miles long with few, if any, resources to help with the building. The train would have to carry everything forward to the end of the track, to allow the next section to be laid and to feed the work gangs that were laying it.

Cator sat looking down at his notes and maps as McGuire sat down beside him. "Well Edward, can it be done?"

The Engineer looked at McGuire. "It can, but it is going to be damned difficult and it would be very easy for the Dervish patrols to slow the work by raiding. I'll have to explain all that to Wingate and make him understand this is not like laying track in England."

"Then tomorrow we ride north back to Wadi Haifa and you can send an initial telegraph to Wingate. He'll want all your detailed work when we get back to Cairo, but you can tidy that up as we steam down the Nile."

Chapter 41.
January 1888, East Sudan

"Sir, we've found him."

Kitchener looked up from the papers spread across his desk. "A little more clarity if you please Captain. Who have you found?"

The Captain pulled himself together. "Sorry sir, got a little over excited. We've found Osman Digna sir. Our scouts report that he has moved into Hardub village with his warriors."

Kitchener stood and walked to the large wall map of the Eastern Sudan. "Osman Digna," he said almost to himself. "The most effective of the Dervish commanders. It would be useful to have him out of the way if we ever go after the Dervish main army."

He turned and strode across the room back to his desk. Sitting down he wrote a note and then handed it to the Captain.

"Get that sent to the Sirdar in Cairo immediately. It requests permission to engage."

Kitchener waited impatiently for the reply, eventually taking a brisk walk around the gardens of his residence to calm himself. He saw the Captain approaching with a telegraph note in his hand and forced himself to appear unperturbed.

"Ah Captain, the flowers are doing well this year. Remind me to commend the gardeners."

"Yes sir. Your reply from the Sirdar has arrived."

"Indeed? Give me the gist of it will you?"

The Captain paused as he read the note again. "You are given permission to attack at your discretion sir, but you may not use regular British or Egyptian troops. You are permitted to use irregular forces and the Egyptian police."

"That rather ties one arm behind my back. Never mind, this is an opportunity. Call out the Turkish irregulars, the *bashibazouks*, then the police and see if any of the local tribesmen will join in. Try and keep this low key, we don't want to alarm our enemies."

By the end of the day the force of around four hundred men had been assembled. Kitchener and his second in command, Hickman, rode out to join them. As they looked them over they couldn't help but notice a number of the Black Sudanese regular troops had turned out dressed in shirts and drawers and were pretending to be local volunteers.

"Should I send them back to barracks?" Hickman asked.

"No, I think not, our Sudanese soldiers hate the Mahdists and a little stiffening from these men will do the force good. Turn a blind eye."

They marched through the night and took the Mahdists by surprise. They were closing in on Osman Digna when some of his men counter attacked from the rear. The tribesmen and the *bashibazouks* broke and ran leaving the Egyptian police and the black soldiers to fight on with much reduced numbers. They rallied on a small hillock and Kitchener rode forward, ready to lead his people in a charge that should win the day. As he turned along the line of soldiers a bullet struck below the lobe of his right ear, it splintered a piece of his jaw and that lodged close to his throat. He dare not dismount as his troops might waver. The medical officer rode up and dressed the wound with him still in the saddle.

Without Kitchener the troops did not charge. He handed command over to Hickman who conducted a skilful fighting retreat under heavy fire. By this time Kitchener could hardly speak and was in great pain. When he reached Government House it was found that the splinter of bone had very nearly pierced his windpipe and he had just had a very narrow escape. The medical officer was unable to find the bullet and in later years Kitchener claimed it had subsequently moved and nearly choked him, until he swallowed it.

Osman Digna escaped and moved further into the interior. The defeat at Hardub did not damage Kitchener's reputation; in fact the main reaction was sympathy and worry about his wound. The scarring gave his face a cruel look and further damaged his eyesight. He was happy to exploit his harsh appearance to keep unwanted people at a distance, but the harshness vanished when he smiled.

Kitchener's wound refused to heal and he was obliged to take leave in England where the doctors managed to help him. He was promoted again and appointed as Adjutant General of the Egyptian army and, as such, was second in command to the Sirdar, Grenfell.

Chapter 42.
A Gathering Storm

Corporal Fine walked out to the exercise area where McGuire and his small troop were training a new pair of pack camels. He waited until they had finished then, as the camels were walked back into the shade, he approached his commander.

"Sir, the Colonel has just sent a message, he would like to see you in his office."

"Thank you Corporal, did he say when?"

"No sir, so my guess would be now."

McGuire nodded and walked away towards the Headquarters building at the edge of the barrack square. He walked through the cool corridor until he reached the Colonel's outer office. The clerk stood as he entered and told him to go straight in. McGuire knocked and then opened the door to the inner office.

"McGuire, good of you to come. Sit down I have some news for you."

McGuire sat opposite the Colonel and waited. "Right then, I guess you know Kitchener is back with yet another promotion under his belt?"

"I had heard, sir, yes."

"Yes, well, it seems there are rumours that the Dervishes down in the Sudan are getting ready to move against us. Wingate is heading south in three days' time and Kitchener wants you and your men to go with him as his eyes and ears."

"I see, sir, and are you prepared to let us go?"

O'Brian smiled. "Nice of you to ask, but when the Adjutant General asks for something it is

258

not a request. There's something else. He wants you and your men to work with Wingate full time, he feels your talents are wasted in the regiment."

McGuire sat forward in the chair. "Not sure I understand what that means, sir."

"It means that you will no longer be under my command, but will report to Major Wingate who in turn reports direct to Kitchener. It could be good career move for you, since I have a number of Lieutenants who are senior to you and will take any Captain's vacancies that arise."

"Is there any way to object, sir? You and the Regiment have been good to me and I would not want to seem disloyal."

O'Brian shook his head almost sadly. "Not possible when the word comes down from on high. You can keep your stable and I will help you when I can, but, from tomorrow, you and your men are not formally part of the regiment, but on long term detachment. You are of course welcome to remain a member of my officers' mess. Any questions?"

McGuire shook his head. "No sir. Though I would like to remain an Irish Fusilier as would my men, I'm sure, even though we are working for headquarters."

"I'm glad you feel that way. And I would like to think that a least a part of my regiment is at the forefront of any coming engagements. Then you'd better cut along to see Major Wingate and find out where he wants you and when."

McGuire left the Colonel's office in a slight daze. It was unusual for things to happen so quickly, but then Kitchener had a reputation for making things move to his timetable. He hailed one of the gharries that hung around by the barrack gate and had himself taken to the Headquarters of the Egyptian army.

Once at Wingate's office he knocked and entered. Wingate and Kitchener were standing by the large wall map at the end of the room. They turned as he opened the door and Wingate waved him in.

"Your timing is good McGuire. We were just discussing where to deploy you."

"I see sir and where were you thinking of?"

Kitchener pointed at the map. "My guess is that the Dervishes will mass their troops here at Dongola before they move north to attack us. I want you and your people to go down there and take a look around. I need to know how many they are, when they might move and whether their weapons have improved since our last meeting with them."

McGuire looked at the map. "Dongola is a long way into their territory if they are starting to move down the Nile."

Kitchener looked again at the map and then turned to McGuire. "It is. You are quite correct and it will be damned risky, but you and your people are the ones for the job. Moving by night and laying up during the day, you should be able to avoid any encounters with the patrols."

"From your mouth to God's ears, sir."

"That's the spirit! You will move with Major Wingate on Friday morning. Can you be ready?"

"We're ready now sir. We travel light, as you know. Is there any chance I could take Asif with me this time? He's a valuable man. I'd like Haroun as well, but I think he is feeling his age."

"Wingate, what do you think?"

Wingate paused and looked at McGuire before turning to Kitchener. "I know you both think highly of him. So, if you two vouch for him, then I have no objection."

McGuire smiled. "Thank you, sir. Now all I have to do is find him and persuade him to come."

Kitchener walked to the head of the long table and sat down. He waved to indicate that the other two should join him. They sat and waited.

"McGuire I believe you are married?"

"Yes sir with two children, twins."

"You may be away for some time and this is risky. How will your wife react?"

"She'll be unhappy, but she will cope. She is rather an exceptional woman sir."

Kitchener smiled and his whole demeanour changed. "Yes I remember when you brought her out of the desert. No weeping and wailing, she was very steady. I have to say I do not approve of junior officers being married, it is a distraction when they should be concentrating on learning their duties."

"Yes sir."

"So to avoid my disapproval I am making you a Brevet Captain, as of tomorrow morning. See that you turn up here with the proper badges of rank on your uniform. You will be working out details with Major Wingate. Now you'd better go home and tell your wife as well as getting your men ready to move."

McGuire arrived back at the stable block as his men returned from their meal. He briefed them about their new task and their new commander before calling Corporal Fine into the office.

"Two things to deal with today. First I'd like you to sew Captain's stars on my uniforms ready for tomorrow morning."

"Congratulations sir."

"Thank you. Now the other thing is you. Your enlistment is going to run out while we are away. So I want to thank you for all you have done for me and wish you well once you get back to England."

Fine looked down at his feet and then up at McGuire. "I'm not looking forward to it sir. I've got nobody in England now that my mother has died. My brother went to America and I don't know where he is. I'll miss the regiment and I'm dreading the cold and wet."

"So what are you going to do? With the damage the fever did to you, the army won't let you sign on again."

"I know that sir. I was thinking I might see about staying in Egypt. At least I won't be cold."

"Well good luck in whatever you decide to do. I've got to go home now and tell my wife she is being abandoned again. Could you bring the jackets around to me this evening?"

"Certainly, sir, it will be nice to see Mrs McGuire again, a very nice lady you have there."

McGuire found he was right. Emma was unhappy that he was going away again, but he was also right that she would cope and did not make a fuss that would be difficult for him. He played with the children and they ate a subdued evening meal with his mother in law being disapproving as usual.

Corporal Fine arrived as the sun was dipping down to turn the surface of the Nile to beaten gold. They stood on the wide terrace to watch as the white sails of the native boats slid along through the golden water. McGuire took the two jackets and Emma admired the new shiny star on his shoulder.

She turned to the Corporal. "Will you join us for a drink Mr Fine? I need to ask you something."

"If the Captain doesn't mind ma'am."

McGuire smiled at him. "He doesn't and in fact the Captain will go and get the drinks while you two talk."

When he came back carrying the small tray of drinks he found that Emma and Fine were both smiling. "I take it that means you have accepted Mr Fine?"

"Yes sir. It seems I am to be a warehouse manager, after you go south, with Abdullah as my foreman."

McGuire passed the glasses around. "Thank you for accepting. It's good for me to know that Emma has someone else she can trust as well as Abdullah." He raised the glass. "Your very good health."

Chapter 43.
Summer 1889

Through the binoculars McGuire could see that the Dervish army was getting ready to move. They had been camped outside Dongola, alongside the Nile, for some time now and each day more warriors came to join them. From the ridge on which he lay he estimated their strength to be about four thousand fighting men with the usual complement of camp followers.

He rolled to one side and passed the glasses to Asif who lay on his belly beside him. "Tell me what you see old friend."

Asif adjusted his position and looked through the powerful lenses. "From the way they are moving I think they are a soon to move. Tents are being folded. Tonight they will sleep beneath the stars and before the dawn they will start."

McGuire took the glasses back. "I think so as well. Now we need to tell Kitchener and the Sirdar to expect them soon. Where do you think the attack will be?"

Asif leaned on one elbow to look at McGuire. "It is not certain in my mind. The camp that is nearest is Wadi Haifa, but the Egyptians are many there and the place is ready for an attack. Was I in command of those Dervishes I would want more men to attack that place. I think we must wait and see where they walk."

"I agree, but we must be certain or the army could be caught off guard. I will send a message to the army and then we will stay and keep watch."

Asif nodded as he rolled back onto his stomach and continued to watch the Dervish encampment. "Perhaps we will have time to try your new rifles? We will see if the smaller bullet will stop a charging Dervish as well as the one from the Martini Henry."

McGuire smiled. "You want to feed your friends, the vultures, again? The new bullets are smaller but they fly further and faster. If they hit a man they will strike him hard."

"We will see, English, very soon I think."

McGuire slid back from the top of the ridge and then dropped down to where the rest of his men waited, by their camels. He took the message pad from his saddle pouch and wrote out the message to Wingate and Kitchener twice, before tearing the two sheets out of the book.

"Jones, Parks I have a job for both of you."

The two men walked across and sat down next to him. He handed each man a copy of the message he had just written.

"You need to get back to the army and find Major Wingate or Colonel Kitchener. Make sure they get that message. Now listen carefully. If one of you falls behind, for any reason, the other carries on. That message must get through. Is that absolutely clear?"

Jones nodded. "Yes, sir, we've got that."

"If anything goes wrong you can come back to find your mate, but the message must be delivered first."

Parks looked a little worried then looked at Jones and smiled. "We'll be fine sir."

"Make sure you are. Now get some sleep, you leave at nightfall. Send Macklin over will you."

The two men walked away and returned to the area where their animals were hobbled. Macklin joined McGuire soon after.

"Your turn to cook today isn't it?"

"That's right sir, just going to start the fire now."

"Keep the fire small and dig it deep into the sand. If I was the Dervish commander I would be sending out advance patrols soon and we don't want extra guests for dinner. How much of that jerky have you got left?"

"A fair amount sir. These new Lee Metford rifles make it a lot easier to take down game when we find it and they don't waste so much meat with the .303 bullets."

"Good. Make up rations for Jones and Parks they've got a long hard ride ahead. We'll be staying here a while longer."

They sat and ate their evening meal before the two men were sent on their way, back to the army. McGuire stood and watched them ride away until the vanished into the gathering darkness, before he returned to the crest of the ridge. As he lay down beside Donnelly he could hear the beat of the tom toms drumming from the camp down by the river. They seemed louder than last night.

As dawn broke McGuire was back on the ridge watching the large camp. They were still there. The smoke from the cooking fires climbed up to the sky in straight columns in the still morning air. He smiled to himself, it seemed his messengers would have another day's start and the army would have another day's warning.

The day passed with the usual routine of a hidden camp in the desert. The men took turns to stand watch on the ridge and the rest stayed out of sight. McGuire fretted in case he had sent the message too early. If the Dervishes withdrew to the south he would look a fool. Then three hours before dawn he was shaken awake by Asif.

"Come, English, something is stirring in the camp." They both returned to the ridge and Connolly handed McGuire the binoculars.

"Fair bit of noise coming from our friends sir. Camels bellowing and men shouting as far as I can make out."

McGuire sat cross legged looking though the glasses. In the darkness he could not see any detail of the enemy force. He drank from the water skin before he spoke.

"From what you've heard what do you think?"

"I think they are on the move. If I was a betting man I might wager a day's pay on it."

McGuire grinned. "That's a fair bet."

As he spoke, the moon came from behind a thick bank of cloud and flooded the plain with a silvery light. Through the lenses McGuire could now see that Connolly had guessed correctly. The Dervishes were on the move, taking advantage of the cool air before dawn. The jingling of harnesses came across the desert and the mass of moving men was plain to see.

"Four thousand men, camels and horses should be easy to follow across the desert. We will hang back behind them until they tell us where they are going."

Asif tapped McGuire's elbow and pointed. "See there, the patrols are riding out ahead. None are to the sides I think. They are too sure of themselves."

"We must still be careful. These men are not fools and we are few."

With the dawn the Dervish army was out of sight and the small group of scouts mounted to follow them. As McGuire had predicted, the tracks, even across the rough ground, were easy to follow and they moved beside the river, to stay near the water.

After days of marching the Dervishes turned and moved away from the Nile. McGuire looked down at the tracks and compared it to the map that Connolly had drawn as they travelled south to find the enemy.

"It seems you were right Asif. They are moving away from Wadi Haifa. This we must tell Kitchener."

He turned and walked across to where his two men were waiting. Again he wrote two messages and handed one to each of them.

"You need to leave now. Stay well clear of the Dervishes and get those messages back to the army. Go as quickly as you can, but get there whatever happens. The Dervishes will stop to rest at night, you must carry on and get ahead of them."

"When do we leave sir?"

"Right now. The army needs as much warning as possible. Maybe they will have enough time to get British troops down here to stiffen the Egyptians?"

"What happens if they don't?"

"Then we find out if the new Egyptian army is better than the old one. Now go."

Chapter 44.
The Battle of Toski

McGuire stood beside Kitchener and Wingate watching the Dervish force assemble. Behind them were the staff officers who were to support Kitchener and then behind them and to the left stood the five men of the Reconnaissance unit and Asif.

Kitchener lowered his field glasses and turned to McGuire. "Your information seems to have been accurate Captain. I would estimate four thousand or so warriors even after they had their run in with the gunboats on the river."

"Thank you sir. Do you have any orders for us now though?"

Kitchener looked at Wingate then shook his head. "I think not. Your task is done and done well. Now it's up to the Egyptian army to show what they are worth."

"Will they stand sir?"

Kitchener gave McGuire one of his rare smiles. "Unless I am very much mistaken I think they will. The Sudanese battalions are all veterans and have the same warrior ethic as the Dervishes. The Fellaheen have been well trained and well treated since the army reforms. Their officers are properly trained as well, but in this battle it will come down to the soldiers themselves and their own pride."

"A shame the British units could not reach here in time to give them a little stiffening though."

"Captain McGuire I think we may surprise you. In any event the Sirdar will control the battle and I shall take the cavalry. I have a single squadron of the 20th Hussars with me, but the majority are Egyptian. Now if you wish to stay here and observe please do so. If you wish to take a more active part, I suggest your new rifles might be useful at picking off the Emirs and standard bearers. Don't get in the way of the troops though."

McGuire saluted and walked briskly across to his men. "We have a job to do. Hobble your camels then take yourselves down to the firing line and find a useful position, this side of the *zariba*. Firing prone so you don't obstruct the volley fire I want you to pick off anybody who looks like a leader. Emirs, flag bearers, anybody out the front waving people on. Take your time, but the longer range you can hit them at the better. It might discourage them a little."

The men grinned and ran to hobble the camels. Then they took themselves down to where the battalions were standing in line waiting for the attack. They wormed their way through the close packed lines and took up position lying on the ground. McGuire could hear the good natured comments, from the standing troops, about his men needing a sleep. He smiled to himself, at least that showed the Egyptian forces were confident and not cowed by the approaching Dervishes.

He turned to Asif. "Will you come and shoot with me my friend? A skill such as yours should not be wasted."

"I will come. I wish to be with a Sudanese regiment. Then they can see how an Arab can shoot."

"Come then. Choose a place and we will work together."

Asif chose a battalion and McGuire reported to the commander, who stood directly behind the rear rank of his men. "Good morning sir. With your permission the Adjutant General has asked that we use our longer range rifles to start discouraging the Dervishes a little."

"You carry the Lee Metford I see. How effective is it?"

"We have an effective range of 800 yards. Maximum range is 1800 yards. So with a mob like that we can start hitting them very soon and then get selective as they advance."

"Enjoy yourselves, but once we start firing keep your heads down, my soldiers can be very enthusiastic once I let them loose."

"Will they stand sir?"

"Stand? I'll have trouble stopping them charging. These men are the 9th Sudanese battalion, all from the South Sudan and the Nuba Hills. Bloody fine soldiers with just a little discipline imposed by their officers. You'll see and so will the Dervishes."

"Thank you sir. We'll go and see what we can do."

Together the two men made their way in front of the two ranks of soldiers who watched them with interest. They lay down and adjusted their sights to maximum range. McGuire took his binoculars out and scanned the approaching enemy. At this range it was impossible to identify the leaders. That would come later.

"Asif, you start and I will see if I can see any that fall."

The Bedouin made himself more comfortable and aimed at the centre of the approaching army. He fired and the Sudanese behind him jeered at his wasting ammunition at this range. McGuire smiled as he saw the horse in the distance stumble as the rider fell from its back. He rolled to one side and looked up at the grinning Sudanese. He held up one finger to indicate a hit and they stopped grinning for a moment. Then the excitement of being able to reach out and touch an enemy at this distance caught them and they grinned for a different reason.

Along the line the six Lee Metfords fired slowly picking men off at maximum range. The commander of the 9th Battalion walked up alongside McGuire and watched the approaching Dervishes through his own field glasses. He took a knee next to them and tapped McGuire on the shoulder.

"Yes sir?"

"That's a damned fine rifle you have there. Would you mind if I tried it?"

McGuire handed over his rifle and stood back. "Be my guest sir. You'll find she kicks less than the Martini Henry and with the new smokeless powder you don't have to wait for the cloud to clear."

The Colonel took aim while McGuire watched through his binoculars. The weapon fired and in the distance he saw a tribesman spin round and fall.

"A hit sir, with your first shot. Damned fine shooting."

The colonel stood up and handed the rifle back to McGuire. He turned to his men and spoke to them in their own language. As he finished speaking they cheered and waved their rifles over their heads.

"What did you say to them sir'"

"I promised I would try and get them rifles like this as soon as possible. I told them the finest battalion in the Egyptian army deserved them."

"That should motivate them."

The Colonel shook his head. "That wasn't for motivation. I meant it. With rifles like that my people would be unstoppable. Now, by the look of things, our Dervish friends are - inside your effective range. Dropping a few of their leaders might help, if you wouldn't mind?"

As the Dervish army approached the Lee Metfords hit a number of standard bearers and those who looked as though they were important. The tribesmen never faltered but continued to advance, screaming their war cries. At three hundred yards the first volleys from the Sudanese regiments cut swaths in their ranks, but still they came on. Firing became ragged as the soldiers became excited, but a few commands from their officers and NCOs steadied them and the firing continued like a well-oiled machine.

McGuire looked around. The Fellaheen regiments were drawn up in reserve behind the Sudanese. Not a man moved. Their officers and their NCOs paced along the ranks chatting to the men. Here and there they smiled. McGuire remembered from his days in the firing line of the Grenadier Guards, the highest praise for a regiment in the British army was to call them 'steady'. He looked along the ranks of the Sudanese and the Fellaheen, these were steady soldiers, Kitchener had been right.

The impact of the fast accurate fire from the ranks of the Egyptians had an effect. The Dervishes slowed and then started slowly to retreat, even before their customary screaming charge. Then, from out of the desert, the Egyptian cavalry arrived. Horsemen and Camel Corps had outflanked the Dervishes and were sweeping in behind them. McGuire could see the flashing blades of the Hussars, but they were just a small part of the tide that was sweeping towards the demoralised enemy.

The Dervishes retired to hill tops and took up defensive positions. The Sudanese 9th, 10th and 13th battalions moved forward and drove them out. The years of suppression of the south Sudan by the Mahdists were paid back in full, at the point of many bayonets. The remnants of the Dervish force straggled back towards the Sudan harassed along the way by the Egyptian cavalry. The victory had been complete and had proved the worth of the Egyptian army.

McGuire assembled his small unit and returned to Major Wingate for orders. "What price the Egyptians now young McGuire?"

"They were impressive sir. A far cry from what they used to be."

Wingate gave a satisfied nod. "They are aren't they? Bloody fine soldiers, very steady under fire, but you watch, there'll be nothing in the British newspapers about this. Only British victories get reported and this one belongs to Egypt."

Chapter 45.
Years of Peace

After the Battle of Toski, McGuire and his small unit were returned to Cairo to settle back into the quiet routine of barracks life. They carried on training and improving their skills by making long rides out into the desert. They camped alongside the Bedouin and shared their food with them. The children of the Bedouin seemed to develop a great fondness for the sweets and candies that McGuire's men brought for them on every visit.

The simple ordered life of the desert people was a huge contrast to the life of a British officer in barracks. The stifling formality and the jockeying for influence and advancement repelled McGuire and he gave thanks that, as long as he worked for Wingate, he avoided most of that. The periodic formal dinners in the Officers' Mess were a trial to him, but the occasional Ladies' Nights were an exception. With the wives of the officers in their best gowns, the silver on the polished tables illuminated by candlelight these evenings were a joy to Emma. She loved the ceremony and the dancing afterwards. McGuire always allowed himself a secret smile at these events, convinced as he was that his wife was the most beautiful and certainly the most accomplished. While the rest of the wives attended coffee mornings, or visited the dress shops, his wife was running her own successful business.

The business grew as the months went by. John Fine and Abdullah had formed a good working bond and the warehouse ran like a well-oiled machine. Emma expanded the business and started exporting dates and cotton to England on the faster cargo ships that were now appearing.

McGuire took leave for the first time in a long time now that the frontier was so settled. He and Emma, with the twins, took passage to England. From there they travelled by train to Holyhead and then across the Irish Sea to Dublin. Kathleen was waiting on the dockside as they arrived and they took a carriage to the house where his mother waited. The visit was not a success. The cold and rain of Dublin did not sit well with Emma or the children. All of them came down with snivelling colds and coughs. McGuire's mother did not take to Emma and there was an unpleasant atmosphere in the house. She and Kathleen seemed to resent their restricted lives in Dublin while others could live in the sunshine. Kathleen in particular was unhappy in being trapped in the house looking after her ailing mother.

As soon as they decently could McGuire and Emma took the twins back to England to visit some of her relations. The cold and rain did not let up and they yearned to be back among the smells and noise of Cairo. The children had never been happier than when they were told they were going home at last. Back in the sunshine of Egypt the pinched feeling they had all felt in England vanished, as the warmth seeped back into their bones.

In January of 1892 the Sirdar, Grenfell, was recalled to England and there was speculation about who would replace him. It was known that there was political wrangling going on between the Army at Horse Guards and the Foreign Office. The Prime Minister and the British Envoy to Egypt had their own opinions. Eventually the decision was made and the new Sirdar was announced to be Brigadier General Herbert Kitchener. The army was delighted. Although not a warm or hugely popular officer he was known to be professional and was greatly respected. One of his first actions was to request that Horse Guards confirmed Captain McGuire in his rank.

McGuire was summoned to the Sirdar's office some weeks later. As he entered he found the newly promoted Lieutenant Colonel Wingate already there. The extremely stern expression on Kitchener's face, caused by his wound, was always worrying, but it vanished as he smiled at McGuire.

"Come in Captain, sit down. We've been discussing your little band of desert dwellers. How are they doing nowadays?"

"They're all well sir. Maybe even a little bored."

"Good then I have some work for them. I want you to expand your unit. I want to be able to send scouting parties out ahead of the army when we move south."

"Are we moving south sir?"

"No we are not, at least not yet. The government has determined from London that the frontier is settled and the Dervishes are contained. Reports I send from here are apparently alarmist and there is nothing to be concerned about. As you will appreciate, I disagree. I am firmly convinced that sooner or later the Mahdist threat will have to be dealt with. That is why Wingate here and, through him, you are so important. We need to be prepared for when the day comes. Intelligence gathering is just one of the areas we need to be ready in. The others don't concern you just yet."

"Very well sir. How large would you like my unit to become?"

"Wingate and I will take your advice on that. I need you to be able to send out a number of scouting parties in various directions at any one time. How many men would you need to do that?"

McGuire leaned back in his chair and thought the problem through while the two senior officers waited. "If I form small groups based around my present men that will give you five teams, plus me. I think each team, or maybe I should call them patrols, should be of four men, so that would mean a unit strength of twenty one. I need to find fifteen new men."

Kitchener nodded and turned to Wingate. "Does that align with your thinking?"

"It does. McGuire I would like you to spend more time back away from the desert, to coordinate the reports coming in from your men and to make assessments of their significance."

"I'm not sure I'm the best one to do that sir. I would prefer to be out doing the scouting for you."

"I'm sure you would, but that's not what I need. Now how about your Bedouin friends? Could you use some of them?"

"If you need people to go into the towns and villages to speak to the people then yes that would be wise. I can pass for an Arab, and so can one or two of my men, but true Arabs would be safer."

"Agreed. So start finding those extra people. They don't need to know what we are preparing for, but you should have some Arabs chosen that you can use when the time comes as it surely will."

McGuire started to recruit suitable men from the British garrison and then to train them to meet his needs. He did not select the excellent soldiers that were available, but went looking for the ones with a talent for trouble. Not all of them worked out and some had to be sent back to their regiments, but slowly he created a useful reconnaissance troop to go where the cavalry would not and to see what they might miss.

In the summer of 1894 Kitchener took leave in England and while there urged the government to authorise an advance into the Dongola province of the Sudan as a prelude to reconquering the country. He was rebuffed, but not discouraged. He knew the day would come and he knew he would be ready.

Chapter 46.
The Officers' Mess

Captain McGuire walked into the officers' mess with Emma on his arm. She had spent hours getting ready for this ladies night and it showed. He was confident she was the most elegant and beautiful woman in the room. He stood a little taller with his pride in her.

After the customary aperitifs in the ante room the officers and their ladies walked in pairs into the dining room. The tables gleamed with the regimental silver reflecting the candle light. McGuire lead Emma to her allocated seat and then went around to the other side of the long table to sit opposite her. He gazed across at her. In the light of the candles if anything she was even more beautiful. She felt his gaze and smiled back at him before turning to speak with the Quartermaster who was sitting next to her.

McGuire turned and spoke to the Quartermaster's wife, a slightly overweight but happy and pleasant woman. To his other side he had the wife of an artillery officer, who had made it very plain she had no wish to speak to him or to Emma.

The mess servants in their white uniforms moved silently around the room serving the excellent food and ensuring that wine glasses never emptied. The meal was pleasant and McGuire relaxed and started to enjoy himself. The only real irritant was the three unmarried Lieutenants, at the junior end of the table, who had clearly had too much wine and were sniggering when they looked at him. He was feeling too mellow to take real offence.

The meal ended with the customary toast to the Queen and then the whole company retired to the ballroom where the regimental band was playing. Never one for dancing, McGuire sat by the wall and watched his wife whirl around the room with a succession of partners. At the end of each dance the partner would bow and there would be another to whisk her into the next. Her smile was beaming. She loved these occasions.

McGuire leaned back in his chair and watched as one of the young Lieutenants asked Emma to dance. It was a waltz and he seemed to be an accomplished partner. They whirled past him and Emma smiled at him each time they did. As the waltz ended the Lieutenant seemed to be asking in Emma would like a drink and led her outside onto the terrace that looked out over the manicured gardens.

McGuire decided he would join them and stood up from his chair before walking around the dance floor towards the French doors that led to the terrace. As he walked forward the other two irritating Lieutenants met him.

"Ah, Captain McGuire. We haven't been formally introduced. I'm Forbes and this is Gentry."

"Nice to meet you." McGuire said and started to move off.

The larger of the two, Forbes, put a hand on his chest. "Don't go. We wanted to ask about conditions in the Sudan, as you seem to be something of an expert."

McGuire nodded. "Happy to help. Come round to my office in the morning and I'll tell you whatever you need to know."

As he stepped forward Gentry took his arm. "Surely you could spare us a few moments of your valuable time now?"

McGuire shook Gentry's hand free and went to move forward again. "Not now gentlemen. Hardly the right place and time to discuss things like that eh?"

Once again Forbes put his hand on McGuire's chest. "Don't be like that. We only want a chat about you and your love for those smelly camels of yours."

"Get out of my way gentlemen, you are beginning to annoy me."

Gentry grinned. "Oh, we wouldn't want to do that now, would we Forbes old boy?"

McGuire pushed his way between them and walked towards the French doors. The mellow feeling was gone and he needed some cooler air. As he reached the entrance to the terrace the penny dropped and he realised what that little play had been about. Emma was pressed back against the railing and the third Lieutenant was trying to kiss her. His hands were running over her and she was obviously angry.

She pushed him back and as he came forward again she raised her hand. The young man grinned, expecting a ladylike slap. He was mistaken. Emma's hand balled into a fist and she punched him as hard as she was able. The officer staggered back and tripped on an uneven paving slab. He fell to the ground and hissed his displeasure.

"You bitch!"

McGuire took two steps forward and pushed down on his shoulder as he tried to get up. "That was a little rude Lieutenant."

The Lieutenant looked up then dabbed the blood from his nose. "Go to hell!"

McGuire was about to grab the man when a quiet voice behind him caused him to pause. "I agree with the Captain, Lieutenant Donovan. I think you owe Mrs McGuire an apology."

McGuire turned to find Colonel O'Brian standing calmly by the French door smoking a large cigar and holding a brandy glass. As he stood there, the regimental doctor and the Quartermaster joined him. Behind them McGuire could see Forbes and Gentry craning their necks to watch what was going on, both were grinning from ear to ear.

Turning back to the man on the ground McGuire looked down and said, "I think the Colonel is correct don't you?"

Donovan struggled to his feet and faced the Colonel. Even in the dim light from the windows McGuire could see that his face had flushed a deep red.

"Sir, I would of course apologise to a lady, but not to some jumped up ranker's whore."

The Colonel nodded slowly. "I see. Well Captain McGuire, it appears that some of my junior officers need a lesson in manners. Do carry on."

The Colonel turned to go back into the ballroom then stopped and looked over his shoulder. "One thing though Captain."

"Yes sir?"

"Don't kill him will you? The paperwork is just too tiresome."

As the Colonel walked back inside the doctor and the Quartermaster settled themselves on two of the wicker chairs by the wall. McGuire turned to face Donovan.

"Well Mr Donovan, shall we discuss that apology?"

Donovan spat out some of the blood that had run into his mouth then put up his fists in a boxing stance, the way he had been taught. "Come on then. Let's see what you learned in your filthy barrack room."

McGuire controlled the anger that had boiled inside him as Emma was insulted. The coldness of a killing fury spread through him. He paused to bring that too under control.

Donovan stared to bob around in front of him. "Well come on then. Come and get your thrashing from a gentleman."

"A gentleman? Is that what you are?"

McGuire watched the man in front of him then stepped rapidly forward and delivered a jab straight to his forehead. Donovan staggered back. Nobody hits the forehead so his defence was too low. He recovered and rushed forward swinging a wild punch. McGuire took a pace forward inside the swinging arm and smashed his fist into Donovan's stomach. Winded, the younger man bent forward at the waist and McGuire smashed his knee into the already bleeding nose. He heard the satisfying crack as Donovan's nose broke.

Donovan fell to his knees and vomited onto the flagstones of the terrace. McGuire bent down and took a firm grip of the waistband of his trousers and the neck of his jacket. Wrenching him up from the floor he propelled him forward and over the ornamental balustrade.

McGuire walked to Emma and took her hand. Together they looked over the balustrade to where Donovan lay still on his back in the ruins of one of the flower beds.

"Are you alright? He didn't hurt you?"

"I'm fine. He just took me by surprise."

McGuire nodded and turned around to where Forbes and Gentry were standing open mouthed. "And now you two. I may be scum to you gentlemen, but I'm not totally stupid. I realise quite clearly what that little scene in the ballroom was about. You'd been plotting this all through dinner."

Gentry was the first to speak. "So what do you think you're going to do about it?"

"Surely two such fine gentlemen as yourselves can handle a gutter rat like me? Why don't you give me that thrashing I so richly deserve? That should put me back in my place."

The two men grinned at each other and started forward. Had they been sober they might have learned from Donovan's experience. Side by side they advanced on McGuire. They too had been taught boxing and their fists went up in front of them.

McGuire stood very still with his hands by his sides. Forbes was the first to try and strike him. As he made his move. McGuire dropped to the ground and swung his leg, sweeping Forbes off his feet and sending him crashing to the stone floor. Without rising McGuire rolled and punched into Gentry between the legs. As expected Gentry screamed and folded over. As his face came down it met McGuire's fist coming up. His head snapped back and he collapsed to the ground unconscious.

McGuire jumped to his feet and turned to deal with the expected second attack from Forbes. There was going to be no second attack. The man lay on the ground moaning and cradling his shoulder.

There was a sigh from the wicker chairs as the doctor heaved himself upwards and walked across to look at the two men laying on the terrace. "This one is out for the count and that one seems to have broken a bone or two as he landed. I'll go and see about Donovan."

The Quartermaster wandered across to join McGuire as he walked back to Emma. "Mrs McGuire, may I suggest you deal with your gloves quickly or that blood will stain. Get one of the mess servants to soak it in white wine and then have it washed as soon as you get home. Now with your permission may I borrow your husband for a moment?"

Emma smiled as she was peeling off the stained glove. "Of course, Captain Early, but then I think he can take me home. I've had enough excitement for one evening."

The two men walked as short way from Emma and looked down at the doctor who was kneeling in the flowerbed checking on Donovan. "You made a nice job of those three young men, a shame you couldn't make it last a little longer. The doctor and I were quite looking forward to it."

"I suppose I should apologise to the Colonel?"

"What for? Those three have been overdue a lesson since they joined the regiment and the Colonel knows it full well. No I think you will find he is quite pleased. You, on the other hand, may have gained some respect, but no affection. The members of this mess will like you even less I think."

McGuire chuckled. "Well, since they loath me already I think I can live with that."

"Indeed. However, those three arrogant young men will be your sworn enemies I suspect. So watch your back."

"Thank you, I will."

Early smiled. "And another thing. If you need any further equipment you don't need to send your thieves out scrounging. Come to me and I'll help you."

Chapter 47.
March 1896

Lieutenant Colonel Wingate walked into the stable block unannounced; he strolled past the camels and equipment casting an expert eye over everything. As he reached the door to the office at the end of the stable area he knocked and opened the door. McGuire looked up from the orders he was reading and then came to his feet.

"Good morning, sir, this is a pleasant surprise."

"More than you know Michael. Where are your men?"

"Round behind the back of the building sir. I've got them drying meat to be ready for a field training day I've got planned."

"Well training is over. How soon can you deploy?"

"I could probably have everything ready in a day sir. What's happened?"

Wingate leaned back in his chair. "Late last night, the twelfth, a coded cable came in from London. By the time it was decoded it was after midnight and it was taken round to the Sirdar at his residence. I am told that when he read it Kitchener danced a little jig, with Captain Watson of the 60th, he was so pleased, but you don't need to tell your men that part. The Italians have been soundly beaten by the Ethiopians at a place called Adowa in Eritrea. They are concerned that this might encourage the Mahdist army to attack their garrison just over the border from the Sudan at

Kassala. Their ambassador in London approached the British government to ask for some action from us, in the Nile valley, to distract the Dervishes,"

McGuire leaned forward and rested his elbows on the desk. "I thought the Sirdar had been forbidden to enter the Sudan?"

"He was, but the situation has changed and the Prime Minister, Lord Salisbury, has given orders that we are to support the Italians by an advance into Dongola province, just as Kitchener proposed."

"So do we have a plan yet'?"

"We've had a plan drawn up for over a year and the first part involves you. I want your scouting patrols over the Sudanese border and spreading out across the desert to ascertain the detailed situation. We have good intelligence gathered by the Egyptians down at Wadi Haifa, but now I want you to go deeper into the Sudan. The Egyptians will be on the move very shortly, they will have orders to move forward and form a fortified base at Akasha. You can establish yourself there initially."

"Very well sir, do we know how long we will be gone?"

Wingate looked at the younger man. "Worried about Emma? Well, I'm afraid this is going to be a full campaign, it could last well over a year or more depending how quickly we get the railway built."

"So we're going to build the railway?"

"That's right. The Sirdar's plan is for men and supplies to be moved rapidly by rail as well as in boats on the Nile. This is where that survey Lieutenant Cator carried out with you pays off. Just a shame that young man can't be here to see it."

McGuire nodded. "He was a good man. My soldiers thought a lot of him. They were all sad when the Typhoid fever took him."

Wingate sighed. "Disease always takes more of our people than the enemy on these campaigns. Maybe we'll be luckier this time eh? Now make your preparations and get your unit heading south. The transport officers will have your orders and authorities ready for you this afternoon."

The Egyptian army from Wadi Haifa moved into the Sudan on the 16th March. Four days later they had taken Akasha, eighty seven miles up the Nile, and begun to fortify it. McGuire and his men travelled fast and light to join them and, within six hours of arriving, all five of the four man teams were riding out into the desert with two of the patrols heading for Firka, sixteen miles further on.

McGuire, Asif, and his son Yussuf, rode with Corporal Donnelly's group with the Nile beside them, gleaming in the moonlight. As the sun rose they were in position on a small hill overlooking the village of Firka. McGuire and Asif lay at the top of the hill with Donnelly alongside them. Through their field glasses they could see that the village had been fortified and that the Mahdist army had concentrated a good number of troops there.

Donnelly nudged McGuire's arm. "Out to the left sir. They've got horsemen patrolling."

McGuire swung the binoculars around and studied the five horsemen. "They seem to be carrying rifles as well as swords. Probably still the ones they picked up after the Hicks massacre. You keep an eye on them while we try and work out how many of the Dervishes are in the village."

Asif lowered his glasses and turned to look over his shoulder. "If you want to know about the village then we must go into it and see what can be seen. From here we see nothing, but a few men walking about or building the walls higher."

"It is as you say. Shall you and I walk in there tonight old friend?"

Asif shook his head. "I think the men in that village will be on their guard with the army moving south behind us. Your disguise may not be safe. This is a task for me and for Yussuf. We will go there and be back before the dawn."

"You want to risk your son?"

"My son is fifteen summers old. He is a man and deserves the chance to tell his own stories by the evening fire."

McGuire nodded. "He is a fine young man and he shoots nearly as well as his father. You should be proud of him."

"I would not have brought him to the Sudan if I did not trust him."

"It shall be as you say. We will stay out of the village, but while you are inside I will take Donnelly and we will circle around to see what their defences may be."

Asif smiled. "As the night comes we will go into the village. The food will be better than the cold rations you will eat tonight."

McGuire grinned back at him. "There will be enough hot food when we take our report back to the army."

Asif and Yussuf rode into the village wearing their patched jibbas. The sentry at the gate hardly looked at them as they passed. The streets were busy with a small market and they tied their camels, before walking through the back alleys to find a place to eat. In a small square they found a stall that was selling places around a communal platter of food. They sat and helped themselves from the large bowl and the plates of flat bread. They sat quietly eating and listening to the others around them bragging, about what they would do to the cowardly Egyptians, should they ever dare to come this far south.

Well-fed they wandered on through the village until the Dervishes started to bed down for the night and the streets grew gradually quieter. Now was the time to leave before they were noticed. They collected their camels and walked them slowly back towards the gate they had entered.

The sentry was awake this time and looked at them as they approached. "Where are you going brothers? It is time to close the gate for the night."

Asif carried on walking slowly towards the man. "We have been sent to look at the Egyptians to see if they are daring to move against us. We ride through the night and will be at Akasha by morning."

The man looked puzzled. "The patrol to look at the Egyptians has already gone. Why would they send another?"

"Who can tell the minds of our leaders? We go where we are sent."

The sentry shook his head. "This is not right. You must wait until I speak with the Emir who holds this gate. We will speak of what should be done. Perhaps you will get a night in a bed instead of riding."

Asif nodded and half turned. "It shall be as you say." He spun back to the sentry with the wicked blade of his curved dagger catching the light of the moon. One hand clamped across the startled man's mouth as the blade plunged up into his stomach. Asif felt the warm blood spurt across his hand as he withdrew the knife and then slashed through the man's throat. As the man crumpled to the ground Asif caught hold of his rifle so that it did not fall and make a noise that might attract attention.

"Yussuf, help me."

Together they lifted the corpse of the sentry and dragged him into a dark shadow against the mud wall. They pulled the half closed gate open wide and led the camels through, before mounting and riding out into the desert.

"Did he have to die, father?"

Asif turned in his saddle and looked at the son riding beside him. "If he had cried out then my head, and yours, would have been on a spear point above the gate to greet the morning sun. This is how war is my son."

They were back in the hollow behind the small hill as McGuire and Donnelly returned. "We should ride north, English. They will be searching for us soon."

"Why? Nobody saw us." McGuire said.

"My father had to kill the gate guard for us to get away. They will find him soon."

McGuire stood up and quietly gave his orders. "Everybody mount. We leave now. Asif ride with me and tell me what you saw."

The small party rode across the desert at the stately walking pace of the camel. Once they were well clear, McGuire turned to Asif.

"And what did your keen eye learn my friend?"

"There are three or four thousand soldiers with many emirs. They are confident and have contempt for the Egyptians. They remember the Hicks massacre and think they are cowards. I saw their rifles. They are not good and the bullets they have made themselves. I saw no big guns and the walls of the village are of mud."

McGuire wrote this down in his small notebook. "We saw nothing prepared outside the walls. They seem to think that the mud walls and their rifles will be enough against our army. We will see what the Sirdar thinks when we get back to Akasha."

Chapter 48.
Firka

Kitchener stood by the map table, lost in thought, while his senior officers stood around him and waited. Captain McGuire was the most junior officer there and they had all listened intently as he described what he had discovered at Firka. Now he waited with the rest for the Sirdar to make his decision.

Kitchener looked up from the map. "From what our reconnaissance has found I think we should approach under cover of darkness and attack at dawn. I want two columns. The infantry can follow the Nile while the mounted troops cut across the desert and come at the village from the other side. Captain McGuire will provide guides since the maps are not as accurate as we might wish. Any questions?"

Colonel Wingate cleared his throat. "Not a question sir, but may I suggest we put a couple of Captain McGuire's patrols out to keep an eye on the village, to see that nothing changes as we prepare."

"Indeed. McGuire can you do that?"

"Certainly sir. They can be on the move this afternoon."

"Good. Archie, I want you to command the attack, so start making your detailed plans and then you and I will go over them."

Colonel Archie Hamilton nodded. "Very good, sir. When do you think we should make our move?"

Kitchener returned to one of the papers on his table. "According to my latest information we should have enough troops deployed here to form a garrison and an attacking force by early June. Shall we say 7th June for your attack?"

Hamilton nodded slowly and stroked his ear. "Firka is sixteen miles away according to McGuire and the map agrees for once. So we should be able to cover that comfortably in a single night march, with the troops still fit to fight on arrival."

Kitchener looked around at his officers. "Thank you gentlemen that will be all, please make yourself available to Colonel Hamilton for his planning. Captain McGuire thank you and well done."

The officers filed out of the large tent and McGuire was about to go to his men, to detail the parties to carry out the watching task, when Hamilton called to him. "McGuire. We haven't met properly. You seem to be doing a good job with your irregular unit."

"Thank you sir. They're a good bunch of men."

"They seem to be. Wingate was telling me you went looking for rogues and scoundrels when you were detailed to expand the unit."

McGuire smiled. "Not quite rogues, sir. I did go looking for the sort of men who don't fit into the usual British army mould. Men with an independent mind set maybe."

Hamilton nodded. "I see. Well let's keep them occupied. I would like regular reports back from your watchers. I don't want any surprises when we get to Firka. If your report is as accurate as we hope it is then the battle should go our way."

"I think you're right, sir, and I will ensure you know of any changes at Firka."

"Try not to let your men get seen Captain. I would like the Dervishes to feel secure in their garrison. Then maybe they won't improve the defences much."

"I'll pass that on to the men, sir."

In the late afternoon of the 6th June the attack force was paraded for an inspection by Kitchener. The men were well rested and well fed. They knew what was expected of them and they were keen to move off and get on with it. McGuire and the men he had selected to guide the columns stood off to one side watching.

"They look good sir, and from walking around talking to them they seem ready for a fight." Jones said.

"They do look ready. If we can achieve surprise it's going to help." He turned round to the rest of the men waiting behind him. "Now listen. I know I've said this before, but bear with me. Guides, keep them on track and keep them moving. Those of you out in front as a screen keep clear unless there is something the column really has to know. I don't want you riding in and being shot by a nervous rifleman. Corporal Macklin and his team are watching the village and they should let you know if there is anything untoward."

"Have you decided which column you are going with sir?"

"Yes, or rather, it has been decided for me. Colonel Hamilton wants me with him in the infantry column. Corporal Parks and his men will be with me as will Asif and Yussuf. We may be deployed forward as we approach so check before you open fire on anyone you see on the desert."

"Inspection's over sir." Jones said. "Looks like we'll be off any minute."

"Thank you Corporal Jones. Now all of you. Good luck and make sure you don't get killed. You know I hate the paperwork that goes with that."

His men grinned at the old joke and moved to mount their camels. The parade broke up and the columns started to move out. McGuire sat his camel and watched his men move to their allocated positions. Then he turned the head of his beast and rode to join the commander.

In the early hours of the morning the infantry arrived before Firka. The village was silent as the troops spread out to deploy into their battle formations. As the last units were moving into place the alarm was raised inside the mud wall and the tom toms started to beat out their throbbing rhythm. The first Dervish troops spilled out through the main gate and, without waiting to form up, charged at the deploying Egyptians. The maxim guns and the disciplined volley fire tore them to pieces. There were two more ill coordinated attacks that suffered the same fate and then the gates were closed. The three batteries of horse artillery wheeled into position and opened fire on the village. The gates were ripped off their hinges and great holes were punched through the mud walls.

Unbeknown to the attacking troops the Emir in command of Firka, Hammuda, was killed in the artillery barrage. Most of his disheartened men turned and fled, leaving their dead and wounded behind. These soldiers should have been cut off by the cavalry column but the terrain allowed them to escape detection and make good their escape along the Nile.

Other Dervishes remained in the village and began to fire at the troops lined up outside the walls. Hamilton sat his horse and chewed his bottom lip while he considered his next course of action. He rode forward until he was between a Sudanese and a Fellaheen battalion. In a loud voice, he gave the command to fix bayonets and was greeted with a roar of approval from along the ranks of both battalions.

He waited calmly as the long bayonets were dropped onto the rifle barrels and locked in place. Then rising in his stirrups he pointed forward with his sword and gave the command to advance. The Fellaheen advanced at a regular pace, as they had been trained, keeping step and maintaining alignment with the men on either side of them. The Sudanese surged forward and had to be restrained by their officers.

The troops arrived at the wall together and swept into the village, some through the gates and some through the holes blasted by the artillery. Then the slaughter began as they went from hut to hut, winkling out the defenders at bayonet point.

The screaming showed the progress of the individual battles across the village until at last it was quiet.

McGuire looked at his watch it had been less than three hours since the first shots were fired and it was only just time for breakfast. The men that Dervishes thought of as cowards had proved that a lie and had achieved the start of their revenge. As he rode through the village he was amazed at the number of Mahdist dead lying around the narrow streets, yet there were so few Egyptians. The Fellaheen had rounded up prisoners and were herding them out of the village with a hedge of bayonets behind them. They were carrying their wounded and seemed bemused by the reversal in fortunes in such a short space of time. Despite the best efforts of their officers the Sudanese battalions took very few prisoners.

Once the village was emptied of all the remaining Dervishes, McGuire and his men walked through the streets to try and get an estimate of the number of dead. They counted well over eight hundred and among them were more than forty emirs with their jewelled daggers and plumed turbans.

As he walked along Yussuf ran up behind him and tugged at his sleeve. "My father says I should come and find you, English. He wants you to come with me."

McGuire followed the young Arab until they came to a hut that looked a little larger than the others. He ducked into the shady interior to find Asif sitting cross legged on an ornate rug.

"Welcome, English, to the home of the Emir Hammuda. He who commanded here for the Khalifa. One of his women still lives and I have sent her to make coffee and sweetmeats for the three of us."

McGuire looked around at the wall hangings and cushions scattered about. It seemed that Hammuda had been fond of his home comforts. The curtain at the back of the room was pushed aside and a woman, wearing the full Burka insisted on by the Khalifa, came in carrying the coffee pot and three small cups on a beaten brass tray. She laid the tray down on the low table and backed out of the room in silence.

McGuire waited until he was handed the small cup of intense black coffee and sipped it. "Well my friend you seem to have found a comfortable place for your rest after the battle."

"I have found more than that English."

Asif reached behind him and flipped one of the cushions out of the way. He picked up a small chest and placed it on the table next to the tray.

"What have you found my keen eyed friend?"

"I have found the treasure of Hammuda."

He flipped the two catches that held the chest closed and opened the lid. Inside there was an array of gold coins and jewels. Asif cleared the coffee cups away and up ended the small chest, spilling the contents on to the brass tray.

"Yussuf my son. I have told you about the wars in the Sudan where my friend, English, shared the gold he found on the men he killed. It is

303

a custom between us. Even though we did not kill for this, I wish this custom to continue between friends."

Yussuf nodded and waited for his father to continue. "Now my son, carefully make three piles of equal value on the tray and we will share our good fortune."

Yussuf did as he was told and soon the three piles were stacked before them. He cupped one pile in both hands and handed it to McGuire. He handed the second pile to his father and then sat back and waited.

"Take your share my son. You have earned it this day alongside your father."

"Father. What of the woman?"

"What of her?"

"She will know of this treasure and if she speaks of it others will try and take it from us."

Asif looked at McGuire. "He thinks ahead. This is a good thing in a son." He turned back to Yussuf. "But do not worry my son I have looked upon this woman and she is fair. I have promised I will take her as my fourth wife and will protect her from the Sudanese soldiers that she fears so much."

McGuire nodded at both men. "Again I am in your debt. Now though we must re-join the army and see where this war will take us next."

Chapter 49.
The Soldier's Scourge

The Reconnaissance Troop, as they had now been christened, carried out wide sweeps around the desert to ensure the Dervishes were not allowed to sneak up to the garrison. The 20th Hussars who had now joined the army were engaged in the same work, but closer in to the camp.

As was his custom, McGuire rode with all his men behind him to find a Hussar patrol to guide him back into the camp. That way there was less chance of a jumpy sentry opening fire on them as they approached. They came upon a group of four Hussars under a Corporal who were brewing their morning tea behind a dune.

As they rode up the Corporal stood and held up his hand. "Don't come any closer sir."

McGuire reined his camel to a halt. "Why not?"

"We've got dysentery and cholera in the army and we might have been exposed. You don't want to catch it off us."

"You look healthy enough to me Corporal."

"From your mouth to God's ears sir, but that's the way it works. A man is fine at morning parade and by the time the night sentries are set he's dead."

"How bad is it in the camp?"

"Bad. There's dozens down here and back at Akasha the North Staffordshires are dropping like flies. They only arrived a few days ago and they're losing men hand over fist."

"Are you going back into the camp?"

The Corporal nodded. "We have to sir, but I think you have a choice."

McGuire sat his camel and thought for a moment. "Very well then. Find Colonel Wingate when you get back and tell him we will stay out in the desert. He can send a messenger when the disease has run its course."

With that McGuire wheeled his camel back to his troop and led them out into the desert again. They lived on what meat they could hunt and the food they could buy from the few farms along the river banks. The farmers were wary at first, until they realised that these men were not like the Baggara and would pay for food rather than just steal it. They continued patrolling and found no sign that the Dervishes were coming back north after their defeat at Firka.

They were sitting in their camp in the shadow of a cliff when one of Park's men called down from his sentry position. "Riders coming in."

Without a word every man grabbed his rifle and dispersed around the rocks. McGuire retrieved his field glasses from his saddle bag and scanned across the flat gravel plain. The five riders rose out of the wadi they had been crossing and walked their horses forward. Seeing who it was McGuire smiled and rose to his feet.

"Stand down men. They're ours."

He walked out of the rocks and stood waiting as the horsemen rode up to him. "Good afternoon Colonel Wingate. Would you and your escort care to dine with us?"

Wingate climbed down from his saddle and eased his back. "That depends what you are having. If it's better than tinned bully beef and hard tack biscuits then I think you can count us in."

McGuire smiled. "I think we can do better that that sir. We're having a goat stew and unleavened bread that Asif's new wife is making for us."

"She's still with you?"

"Of course. She's a damned fine cook and Asif has grown very fond of her."

Wingate shook his head. "You do run your part of this war in your own sweet way don't you?"

McGuire smiled and waved for the escort to come forward. "That's the joy of being in an irregular unit sir."

"Well you carry on doing it your way as long as it works. Now then, I have a new task for you. The epidemic in the camps has burned itself out, but it cost us dear. More than three hundred men dead of disease, but now the Sirdar wants us to push on with the railway again. The construction crews are rested and ready and the rolling stock has arrived."

"That's good. What is our part in this?"

"The work crews will be vulnerable to attack while they are out in the desert and the completed lengths of track might be sabotaged. We can't afford the troops to guard the whole length so I need your troop to put out patrols to supplement those of the cavalry. They will be fairly close in and I want yours further out to the front and the sides."

"Who else is guarding the railway?"

"The Egyptian Railway Battalion, under the guidance of Lieutenant Stevenson, is armed with Remingtons. They are protected further by pickets of the 7th Egyptian Battalion. Then the Hussar patrols and then you further out still. You may need to use your heliographs to keep in contact."

"And you think the Dervishes might sabotage the track?"

"We do. The track, the sleepers even the pins to nail them together all have to be shipped in on the railway itself as it moves forward. Food and water for the men comes that way as well. If the enemy manages to disrupt the track, we could have men dying of thirst in the desert next to our own damned railway. On the other hand if we manage to protect the track our speed of movement of troops on the finished railway will allow us to chase the Dervishes to hell and back."

And so began the drudgery of patrolling the deep desert. For days on end they saw no sign of the enemy and then maybe a small party of men in the patched *jibbas* would be seen briefly as they rode away. In the cool of the morning McGuire would sit on the highest point he could find and scan the horizon for the Dervish patrols. Asif and Yusuf would go into the villages to speak to any of the villagers who had not fled from the Baggara horsemen already. It seemed that the Mahdist commanders had not appreciated just what the railway would mean to them when completed.

As the railway moved forward the volume of water it needed to move increased, as much of it had to be poured into the steam boiler of the engine itself. This cut down the amount of other stores that could be carried and the distance laid each day started to decrease. It was Macklin's team that discovered the well that was not marked on any map. They recovered a bottle of water from the new well and took it back to the railhead. Kitchener arrived later that day and his officers offered him a whisky and soda. He tried it and spat it out, but was well pleased when he discovered that the 'soda' had come from a new well, far along the rail route.

The Desert Railroad moved forward at a full half mile a day as the Railway Battalion learned its trade. Only once was there a serious threat to the railway when the patrol led by Jones encountered a group of twenty Dervish Camel troops. After a short fire fight one of the soldiers was cut down and Jones took the rest back to report what had happened. Major Burns-Murdoch was dispatched with three squadrons of cavalry to deal with the threat. Burns-Murdoch rode ahead with Jones to a high point to see if the enemy were in view and was surprised to encounter a mixed force of Dervishes over fifteen hundred strong.

The two men wheeled back to warn the following squadrons, but it was too late. Baggara cavalry crested the ridge and charged the unprepared troopers. To their credit the Egyptian cavalry recovered rapidly and counter charged. The charge was stopped by concentrated rifle fire from the Dervish infantry and the troopers dismounted and took cover in the rocks. The Dervishes began to skirmish forward, but the accurate fire from the superior rifles of the Egyptians drove them back.

The 11th Sudanese battalion came up in support and the Dervishes withdrew leaving their dead behind. The vastly outnumbered Egyptian cavalry had driven off the far superior force for the loss of one man killed and just eight wounded.

From then on the Dervishes made no further attempts to attack the rail line. They contented themselves with cutting the telegraph wires, which suited Kitchener well. The main line had been buried along the banks of the Nile and as long as the Dervishes kept cutting the wire strung beside the railway they did not find the main telegraph line.

Construction of the Desert Railway continued throughout the summer in the baking heat and even when the torrential rains washed out twelve miles of track. The work never stopped and by September the Sirdar was ready to start offensive operations once more.

Chapter 50.
Kerma and Hafir

Wingate sat with Kitchener in the glow of a setting sun. Both men sipping a welcome whisky and soda at the end of a long day. Kitchener placed his glass down carefully on the corner of his map and traced the Nile with his finger.

"Your sources are sure they are concentrated at Kerma?"

"That's what the intelligence says. Shall I send McGuire's people out to confirm?"

Kitchener nodded thoughtfully. "Yes, do. If your information is correct, this could be the perfect time to use Colville's gunboats as mobile artillery. With them on the river and the horse artillery inland we should be able to drive them out rapidly. We'll bring the men up and concentrate at Abu Fatma, according to this map, that's only three miles from Kerma. From there we can take Hafir and then we control that cataract."

"I'll get McGuire moving before dawn."

"We seem to be pressing that troop quite hard. How is McGuire holding up?"

"He seems to revel in it. He loves the desert and his men would move heaven and earth for him. I wish I could give him some leave though. I don't want him burned out."

"Not yet. Not as things are heating up again. I need that information and I can always rely on what he tells me."

Wingate nodded. "He's a valuable officer, no doubt of that."

Kitchener nodded and picked up his whisky again. "Wolseley did us a favour when he gave him that battlefield commission. Still, read that, it should cheer him up somewhat."

Wingate picked up the paper that Kitchener had tossed to him. "So his promotion to Captain has finally been confirmed, that's good. About time Horse Guards got something right."

Kitchener retrieved another piece of paper from the confusion around him; he smiled as he handed it over. "And you, my friend, are now confirmed as a Lieutenant Colonel so score two for Horse Guards."

Wingate nodded. "I suppose that is something I owe you?"

"Not at all. You have been invaluable to this enterprise, as has McGuire. Advance knowledge of the enemy's movements is always vital."

Wingate stood up from the map table. "Well thank you anyway. I'd better go and tell McGuire he's off out into the blue again."

McGuire was standing down by the river watching his camels be watered when Wingate found him. "How are your men holding up Captain?"

"Good evening sir. Very well as it happens. They've had two days solid rest now and the camels are back on top form as well."

"Good to hear. I'm afraid I have another task for you. I need you to take a close look at Kerma. The Dervishes are reputed to have a concentration there and I want the details, before we make our next move forward."

"Very good sir. When would you like us to move?"

"Before dawn if possible."

"What do we know about Kerma?"

"Not much. According to my information it sits where the rocky defiles of the Danagla region stop and the fertile flood plains begin. Long ago it was the capital of ancient Nubia. We don't know what defences are there or what numbers of troops. That's your job. Any questions?"

"How urgent is this?"

"Kitchener is issuing orders tonight to bring men forward to concentrate at Delgo. Using steamers and the railway he expects that to take two days, three at the most. From there we will move forward to the village of Abu Fatma. That should take around eight days. So in ten days from now we will be ready to attack. I need your information well before that."

McGuire nodded. "I think I will only take part of my troop for this. The others can rest a while longer. I'll just take one patrol group of four with Asif and Yussuf. We'll be on the move before dawn."

Wingate smiled. "Good. Oh and one more thing. Kitchener thought you might like to read this." He handed over the paper. "Congratulations."

The night was absolutely silent as they stood outside the mud wall of Kerma. The two soldiers and their two Arab companions stood stock still and listened for any sound before they walked carefully to the gate. McGuire flattened himself against the wall then carefully peered round the edge of the wall where the wooden gate hung open. The streets were pitch black with no sound and no smell of cooking or of a sentry's fire.

He waved his men forward and they walked in together, two at each side of the narrow street. Donnelly hissed from the other side and pointed to a door on McGuire's left. The big Corporal stepped across the street and pushed the door open, before entering. The room inside was empty with cooking pots lying around on the floor and a tattered blanket tossed into a corner.

McGuire waved Asif and Yussuf forward before whispering to them. "We will carry on along this street. You two take the road to the right, towards the river. Be careful my friends, they could be in hiding and waiting for us."

Yussuf nodded and turned to go, but Asif paused. "You should not be here, English. If they take you, your death will be long in coming."

Asif saw McGuire's teeth shine in the pale starlight as he smiled. "My brother you must let me share some of the fun, but I thank you for your caution."

The Arab nodded and with his son he faded into the night. Donnelly stood waiting for his commander and together they moved forward slowly and carefully. Everywhere they looked was empty and deserted. There were signs that the people had moved out in haste, with forgotten items left in the huts and in the street.

After a long twenty minutes McGuire straightened up and looked around the dim street.

"Well Corporal I think it's safe to say we are alone."

"Could be sir, but where the hell have they gone and why?"

"Where I don't know, but as for the why, my guess would be they have either found a better position to defend, or they have fallen back towards their main force."

Donnelly took another look around. "And they didn't leave us anything worth picking up."

McGuire chuckled. "Damned inconsiderate of them. Now let's head back to the gate and wait for Asif."

The two men started to walk back to the gate, more quickly now they knew the enemy was gone. As McGuire passed a doorway to his right there was a blur of movement as a man in the *jibba* of the Dervishes burst out of the hut. His shoulder slammed into the young officer and knocked him to the ground. Before McGuire could react he saw the curved blade of a scimitar raised high and then swinging down towards him. He raised his arm to shield his head but the terrible blow never landed. When McGuire moved his arm he saw that Donnelly had dived forward and flung one arm around the neck of the attacker while the other hand gripped his wrist and stopped the sword from swinging down.

The man gargled deep in his throat as he struggled for breath and then dropped his sword to try and force Donnelley's arm from around his neck. He had no chance of breaking the grip of the street fighter from the filthy back lanes of Belfast.

His feet kicked up as he was lifted clear of the ground and then he went limp and his arms fell to his sides. The soldier waited another fifteen seconds or more before he was convinced his opponent was no longer a threat and then dropped him to the dusty street.

McGuire climbed to his feet and dusted himself down. "That was nice work Sergeant. Drag him back into the hut and we'll get moving."

Donnelly grabbed the man's feet and dragged him inside the hut. As he came back out he was carrying the gleaming curved scimitar and the scabbard that went with it. He handed it to McGuire.

"Don't you want it?"

"I think the other officers would object to a Corporal carrying a sword sir."

McGuire smiled. "A couple of things wrong with that. We spend most of our time in disguise so that sword would help you to look like a Dervish. If I give you permission to wear it then the rest of the column can go hang and I'm pretty sure Colonel Wingate will back me. And last of all you're not a Corporal anymore Sergeant."

"Sergeant, sir? Me?"

"You've just saved my life and you also saved the life of Lieutenant Cator. Did you think I'd forgotten?"

"No sir, but I was just doing my job."

McGuire smiled again. "Don't argue Donnelly, you're a damned Sergeant so get used to it."

Outside the gate they waited for the two Bedouin to arrive. Asif came through the gate closely followed by Yussuf. They dropped down next to the two soldiers and Asif nodded.

"You know where they've gone?" McGuire asked.

"There is another gate towards the river. Across the river I can see boats tied to the shore and I hear the sound of digging. There is much movement across there and nothing this side."

"If I remember my map correctly there is another village just over there, maybe half a mile away. I think it's called Hafir. We need to go now and get this information back to the Sirdar, it will change his plans a little. No point him mounting an attack on an empty town."

Chapter 51.
The Battle of Hafir

Just at daybreak on the 19th September Kitchener rode into Kerma at the head of an Egyptian cavalry troop, Ahead of him he saw Captain McGuire, unusually wearing his uniform, with one of his patrols behind him. McGuire led the Sirdar through the deserted town to a point where the entrenchments at Hafir could be seen. Kitchener studied the Dervish position, half a mile upstream and on the opposite bank, though his field glasses.

McGuire pointed out all the salient points to his commander. He could see the thirty boats and a small steamer moored against the bank. These had clearly been used to ferry the Dervishes across the river. Beyond them, he could see the trenches and gun pits that stretched for around a thousand yards alongside the Nile. Among the mud brick houses he saw scores of enemy tribesmen and beyond that he could see the Baggara cavalry moving into position with the early morning sunlight flashing off their swords and broad bladed spears. In the river to his left was the island of Artgasha and to his right the island of Badin.

Kitchener considered his options and then issued orders for the cavalry to take to the relevant units. The horse artillery was instructed to take their Krupp guns to the south opposite the Dervish positions and to give covering fire for the gun boats. His intention was to run the boats past the position and on towards Dongola. The idea was that the enemy would see that they were about to be outflanked and would pull back out of their prepared entrenchments. It was a good plan, but risky for the boats as they had to sail past the five Krupp breech loading guns that the Dervishes had in position.

The horse artillery opened fire at half past six in the morning and slammed their shells into the enemy positions on the far bank. The Dervish riflemen returned fire, but their Remington rifles were ineffective at that range and none of the artillery gunners were hit. The three gun boats followed by two steamers carrying men of the Staffordshire Regiment made their move up stream. McGuire scanned the river and could see that this was going to be risky. One of the channels through the area was too shallow to allow them to pass and they would be forced to take the western channel, well within range of the enemy guns and riflemen.

The five vessels made their attempt at the western channel. The marine gunners blasted away at the emplacements on the bank and were supported by continuous fire from the maxim guns. On board the steamers the men of the Staffordshire Regiment fired controlled volleys. Despite the fire storm being unleashed on them the Dervishes held their nerve and returned fire, Remington bullets patterned the steel sides of the ships, but initially did no damage. A shell from one of the five Krupp guns smashed into the side of one gunboat, but luckily did not explode. The next gunboat was hit by three shells in rapid succession. Against the third boat the riflemen had more luck, Commander

Colville's wrist was shattered by a Remington bullet and a maxim gunner was shot dead.

Colville turned his boat around and moved it downstream to request more intensive fire from the artillery to give him cover. He was back in minutes to try to force the passage again. Despite the increased fire from the opposite bank the Dervishes could not be silenced and the gun boats were forced to retire down river. Kitchener seethed as he stood in his vantage point in Kerma and heard the Dervish jeers.

After a two and a half hour battle it was clear to Kitchener that a new tactic was needed if he was not to lose his gunboats. He sent his despatch riders out again to order that two field batteries and one horse battery accompanied by a battery of maxims were to ford the shallows of the eastern channel and take up a position on Artgasha Island. Once here, they were within four thousand yards of the Dervish position and could provide more effective fire. Three battalions of infantry were moved up to the bank of the river directly opposite the enemy and they were to be supported by a rocket troop. Then the flotilla was ordered to make a full speed run at the western channel.

At precisely nine o'clock in the morning McGuire and his patrol watched as the artillery opened up an intense barrage from the island. They saw three of the five Dervish Krupp guns knocked out of the fight and shrapnel shells impacting the trenches. At the same moment the rocket troop and the infantry opened fire. In minutes, the palm trees were on fire and the snipers who had hidden there were dropping to the ground with their robes burning. The Steamer that the Dervishes had moored to the bank was hit and quickly sank. The gunboats rushed up the river and as they passed the Dervish emplacements they fired one broadside then sailed on towards Dongola.

The Dervishes did not give up, but carried on firing for the rest of the day without doing any great damage. After dark the shooting stopped and the tribesmen pulled out of Hafir and started south towards Dongola. They left behind over two hundred dead and, possibly more importantly, three wrecked guns.

With Dongola only thirty six miles to the south Kitchener made his preparations. His army was ferried across the Nile in the enemy's boats and the gun boats were sent to shell the Dongola garrison. They returned having captured a fleet of native *nuggars*. Once his force was ready to march, Kitchener sent the gunboat 'Abu Klea', commanded by Lieutenant David Beatty RN, the future First Lord of the Admiralty, to attack the Dervish guns and prevent them being properly deployed.

Chapter 52.
Dongola and Beyond

"You sent for me sir?"

Colonel Wingate looked up from his papers. "Ah yes I did. Come in Captain I have a task for you."

McGuire sat down in the camp chair across from his commander and waited. He looked at the maps spread in front of the Colonel and wondered where he would be sent this time.

Wingate sat back and looked at him steadily. "Now then, you must have guessed that our next objective is Dongola."

"Yes sir. I hear we have a gun boat up the river giving the enemy problems, in preparation for our move."

"That's right we are trying to keep them on edge and unable to prepare a good defence. We are sending the cavalry forward tonight to reconnoitre their positions and hopefully to interfere with their preparations from the landward side."

McGuire nodded. "And you want my troop to go with them?"

Wingate paused. "Yes and no. I want most of your people to support the cavalry, but we also need something considerably more dangerous. You recall that some time ago you reported that the tribes in and around Metemma were seriously unhappy at their treatment under the Khalifa?"

"I remember, yes."

"I want you to send a small patrol deep into Dervish territory to see what the situation is in

Metemma now. A rising behind enemy lines would be of considerable use to us as you can imagine. At the same time I need a report on what the Dervish army are doing. Where are they concentrating? Have they prepared defence positions? What are their numbers? How is their morale? In fact everything you can find that would be of use in planning the next steps."

McGuire leaned back in his chair and looked across the table at Wingate. "Forgive me sir, but I was under the impression that our orders were only to advance into Dongola province to relieve pressure on the Italians."

Wingate nodded and leaned forward with his elbows on the map table. "You're quite right of course. However Kitchener believes that we and Egypt will never be safe until the Dervishes are soundly beaten. To that end he is seeking London's agreement to expanding the war and taking on the main Mahdist army. If we are to do that, we need information from further south and we need it badly."

McGuire nodded slowly, already planning his options. "Very well sir I'll set out as soon as I can."

"You'll go yourself?"

"I can't send my men on a task like this. I'll take my two Bedouins and my Sergeant. The rest will be at your disposal if you can give me an officer they can report to for direction."

Wingate smiled. "I was hoping you'd agree to do it. I need the accuracy I have come to expect from you. I'll sort out an officer to watch over your men, but there is one thing I must ask you to do for me."

"What's that sir?"

"Come back alive. You are far too useful to me to lose."

"I'll do my best sir."

Donnelly stood with the camels watching the army make its last preparations before moving towards Dongola. The gunboats were on the river waiting for their time to move and the Sudanese and Fellaheen battalions were forming up.

"What do you think Sergeant?" McGuire asked as he walked up behind his man.

"They look in good shape sir. They tell me it's about thirty five or six miles to Dongola and these lads look ready for that."

"Do you wish you were going with them?"

"Standing in ranks while the Dervishes charge, waiting for the order to fire? No thank you sir, I'll take my chances in the desert if you please."

McGuire nodded. "Me too. Now where are Asif and his son?"

Donnelly pointed across the rough ground away from the Nile. "Out there, waiting for us to join them."

McGuire looked where the Sergeant had pointed and saw the two camels lying down, with his two Bedouins sitting in front of them. The two soldiers mounted and their camels rose to their feet, groaning and complaining as usual. They padded out to join the two Arabs and then together the four of them headed due south, while the army marched alongside the river.

Once past Debba they turned their course to the south east and rode across the harsh land towards Metemma. Always wary of Dervish patrols despite their disguises they rode mostly at night and rested during the day, in whatever cover they could find.

Out on the river Beatty's gunboat carried on firing at any position he could find around Dongola while the army marched ever southwards. They rested at the village of Sowarat some six miles from Dongola before the final advance on their target. At three o'clock in the morning they began their march forward. As dawn broke Kitchener was delighted to see his best gun boat steam into view. The army fanned out into extended order.

The three brigades formed into line with the artillery in the centre along with British soldiers from the North Staffordshires and the Connaught Rangers. Out to the right, away from the river the cavalry and the camel corps waited for their moment. The whole army advanced across the open flat plain towards the small town.

As they closed in on their objective a body of Baggara horsemen rode out of the town and towards the approaching Egyptian army. They rode with their banners unfurled and with their broad bladed spears and swords catching the sunlight. The charge by so few men against such an army was suicidal and that suddenly seemed to dawn on them as they wheeled back towards the gate they had just come from.

The Cavalry were ordered to pursue the horsemen, but they never managed to catch up with them. The demonstration by the Baggara had been a distraction, designed to divert attention from the main Dervish force that was streaming south, away from the town and towards the Bayuda desert. All of the Bagarra cavalry made it across the desert to Metemma. The Egyptians captured around eight hundred prisoners mostly from the Jihadiyya tribe. Kitchener had now completed his mission to take the whole of the Dongola province of northern Sudan from the Khalifa's tyranny.

With the battle over, the senior officers gathered around Kitchener, to discuss their next moves. The task they had been given from London was now completed, with a remarkably low number of casualties. The Egyptian army had proved itself in battle against a courageous enemy and now they needed to decide on the way forward.

Kitchener sipped on his whisky and soda then turned to his second in command. "Hunter, I need you to consolidate our position here and I need Wingate's people to continue gathering intelligence for the advance south."

"South? I was under the impression we had done as we were asked?"

Kitchener nodded. "Of course you are correct, but if we sit here it is a matter of time before the Khalifa gathers his forces and comes to take back his territory. With a full muster he outnumbers us hugely and, even with our excellent troops, we could not stand."

"So what are your intentions?"

"I am going to leave you here while I go to London to convince our Lords and Masters that it is foolish to leave a job half done. We must continue south and defeat the Mahdists once and for all."

"They still outnumber us and our supply lines are getting rather long."

"Quite true, so I aim to convince London to release the British garrison in Cairo to me and to pay for the railway to be extended. I may even get some further British troops allocated to us."

Hunter turned his glass and admired the evening sunlight sparkling through the amber liquid. He raised it to Kitchener in a toast.

"Your good health sir and I wish you every good fortune in London."

Many miles to the south, even before Kitchener left to try and gain permission to advance, the Khalifa realised that the fall of Dongola would lead to the invasion of the rest of the Sudan and soon he would have to face the onslaught. He sent instructions to his emirs to bring their scattered forces to Omdurman to prepare for the attack he knew would come.

Chapter 53.
Metemma

Yussuf emerged from the dark and sat down next to his father. McGuire passed him a piece of the flat bread he had been cooking and waited for the boy to speak.

"It is well, English. There are Baggara in the town, but a man can walk to avoid them. The sheikh is called Abdallah wad Sa'ad. I have found the way to his house and there are no guards. A man can walk to the door and ask for entry."

McGuire nodded and turned to Asif. "You have taught your son well my friend. He brings you great credit."

Asif nodded and Yussuf smiled at the compliment. They ate their meal in silence making sure they left a share for Donnelly who watched from the top of the dune they sheltered behind.

McGuire belched to show his appreciation and then turned to Asif again. "It would be best if we could meet the sheikh this night and be away before the patrols pass here in the daylight."

"It shall be as you say, English. Do we four go or does the big one stay here with the camels?"

"This time we four shall go together. The big one will guard the door while we speak with the sheikh. Will you speak first and tell him where I come from?"

"That is best." Asif said. "A great man should have his friend speak for him before he speaks himself."

McGuire grinned, his teeth reflecting the moonlight. "I am no great man my friend."

"It is important that the sheikh thinks you are. Let me sing your praises before you speak and he will listen more closely."

McGuire nodded. "I will take your council. Now Donnelly must eat and then we go."

The four men walked through the dark streets of the town, taking the smaller streets and alleys whenever possible. The cooking fires filled the air with the smell of food for the evening meal. They stopped when they heard a woman scream, but she was soon silenced and they moved on. Yussuf led them to a small compound and they entered through the gap in the mud brick wall. The house, set at the back of the compound was larger than those in the rest of the town and had a large wooden double door.

Three of them waited just inside the wall as Asif walked forward to the door. McGuire could hear a whispered conversation and then he saw Asif wave them forward. They entered the house and Donnelly took up a position inside the door to watch the area outside through a small barred window. The other three were led into a room with silk cushions scattered around a wide wooden bench seat where the sheikh sat to await them.

Asif gave him greetings and complimented his house in the Arab custom. The sheikh accepted the courtesy and called for sweetmeats to be brought. McGuire controlled his impatience and waited for the pleasantries to be completed.

Eventually the sheikh looked at McGuire then Yussuf and back to Asif. "So my friends why have you come to see me?"

Asif indicated McGuire. "Not me. It is this one who has come to speak with you."

"Then why does he not speak for himself?"

Asif smiled. "My friend, this is a great one in the army of the Egyptians. He has the ear of the Sirdar. In their councils of war no decision is made until this one has spoken and his wisdom is much valued. When he is in his own land he speaks with the Queen of the English and has her favour. It is because of all this he has been sent to speak with the Sheikh of the Ja'aliyyin."

Sheikh Abdallah sat still and looked at McGuire for long moments before he spoke. "I have heard of this Queen. It is said she has many soldiers in many places in the world. Perhaps she is even greater than the Queen Hatshepsut of Egypt in the far off days? So tell me friend of a Queen, what does the Sirdar want of me?"

McGuire leaned forward in a bow. "The Sirdar has heard of the treatment your people have had from the Baggara nomads of the *goz*. He knows that your people are proud and noble and the over lordship of the nomads is unseemly. He grieves for your pain and so asks me to speak to you."

"The Sirdar knows of all this?"

"The eyes and ears of the Sirdar are everywhere in this land, even as far as Omdurman where the army of the Khalifa is being assembled."

"And what would the far seeing Sirdar have me do?"

McGuire paused and considered his words; he picked up a sweetmeat and nibbled it before he spoke. "Many years ago I was in this country. Then I heard that if the Ja'aliyyin had weapons they would rise against the Baggara and their land would be their own again."

"That was said in those days."

"And in these days'"

"The Baggara are strong. Though there are only thirty of them here, but they can call on many other men if we rose. There would need to be many weapons before we rose and many troops. If British soldiers join us we would surely rise."

McGuire looked calmly at the sheikh. "I will tell you no lie. I do not think the Sirdar will send soldiers. I think he will send weapons and the bullets for them. I will bring my own soldiers to teach your people how to use them well."

Sheikh Abdallah turned to Asif. "Does he speak the truth?"

"Always."

The sheikh examined his finger nails before he looked up at McGuire. "And what would the Sirdar have from me for these weapons? What is his price?"

McGuire spread his hands palm upwards. "He asks only your friendship."

"That is all?"

"In the eyes of the Sirdar the friendship of the Ja'aliyyin is no small thing."

"And what must I do to show my friendship?"

"A letter from you to the Sirdar asking for the weapons to fight the Baggara will be enough."

"I have a man who writes for me. I will have him brought here and you may leave with the letter tonight. Will you carry it to the Sirdar for me?"

"I will carry it as fast as my camel will travel and I will ask the Sirdar for all speed to get the weapons brought to you here."

"Then it shall be as you say."

The scribe took time to write in a fair hand on parchment and then the rolled letter was handed to McGuire. In the early hours of the morning the four men made their way back to where their camels were hobbled and rode back into the deserts. They rode as hard as their camels could tolerate and arrived back at the army as quickly as possible.

McGuire handed the letter to the Sirdar's Chief of Staff, Major General Leslie Rundle, who had it read to him by an interpreter. He realised he had to act quickly and assembled a caravan of rifles and ammunition. As McGuire had predicted he decided against sending troops. With McGuire and his whole troop as an escort the caravan set off to the south as rapidly as possible.

They were too late. After McGuire had left him and in what must have been a moment of madness Sheikh 'Abdallah wad Sa'ad wrote to the

Khalifa renouncing his allegiance. On the first day of July the Emir Mahmud arrived at Metemma at the head of twelve thousand Baggara horsemen. His orders from the Khalifa were to wipe out the Ja'aliyyin. The townspeople resisted as well as they could, but they were swamped by the vicious tribesmen. More than two thousand men women and children were massacred as the Baggara swept through the town spearing and slashing with their long straight swords. Younger women were captured, raped and then forced to become sex slaves to the nomads.

The body of 'Abdallah wad Sa'ad was found and beheaded. He had died fighting bravely to defend his people, but his head was sent to Omdurman to please the Khalifa. What the Baggara did in Metemma, on the orders of the Khalifa, was savage, but it turned the whole province of the Ja'aliyyin against the Khalifa and filled them with a thirst for vengeance.

When McGuire and Asif rode ahead to Metemma they saw the circling vultures from a distance. As they came closer they could hear the screams of the women and see the thousands of horses tethered outside the town. They sat their camels in silence for a minute or two watching the town and feeling the heaviness in their stomachs at what had been done here. They turned their camel's heads away and rode north to stop the caravan and turn it around.

Chapter 54.
The Sudan Military Railway

Through all this time the railway had been pressed forwards. The building gangs were now experienced and hardened to the work. They could now lay two miles of track every day and the supplies they needed were brought forward on the track they had just laid.

Despite a shortage of money Kitchener had managed to find locomotives and rolling stock by borrowing them from Cecil Rhodes who had earmarked them for use in South Africa. He had also ordered fifteen other engines and two hundred wagons that would one day replace the ones he had on loan.

The workers were protected by half a battalion of soldiers at all times and a screen of cavalry rode ahead of the railway to protect against any Dervish raiders. Despite all of this the risks were still great, if the line had been disrupted for two days or more the workers would have started to die from lack of water.

Many miles to the south, the Khalifa sat in the councils of war in Omdurman. He knew the railway was being built. It did not occur to him to attack the railway with small groups to sabotage the construction. In his culture, courage and honour demanded that men fought in open battle not in hit and run raids, so the rail lines moved forward without hindrance from the Dervishes.

The Dervish leaders were also hindered by their lack of understanding of who they now faced.

They still believed that the Egyptian army were cowards who could not withstand the power of the Dervish army. They still thought of them as the demoralised and abused troops they had massacred in the Hicks column all those years before. The Khalifa's strategy was to allow Kitchener to penetrate into the desert further and further until his lines of communication were overstretched. He would lure them to a place of his choosing where the tribesmen could charge without restraint. Then Kitchener's tired, starving and fearful Egyptians would be smashed by the massed charge of the Dervish warriors.

Kitchener knew that, as he moved south, his railway and his troops would become vulnerable to attacks from the garrison at Abu Hamed. He also knew that this was the ideal place for the rail line to re-join the Nile and to run beside it down to Berber. The town must be taken.

Chapter 55.
Abu Hamed and Berber

The troop, under McGuire, was detailed to join with the one hundred and fifty men of the Abada irregulars to carry out a reconnaissance in force towards Abu Hamed. The men were spread out in twos and threes across the desert so as not to attract attention and they then converged on the village of Abtayn, some six or seven miles from Abu Hamed. Anyone they met in the desert was taken prisoner and forced to accompany them to the village which they surrounded.

McGuire and the leader of the Abada, Abd al-Azim Bey Hussain, went in to the village and found the local sheikh. They questioned him in detail for hours and gained as much information as possible about the garrison of Abu Hamed. All through the village others were questioned to ensure that their stories tallied.

Once they had all the information they needed the Abada watered their camels in the Nile then rounded up every man woman and child from the village and forced them to walk into the desert. Once they were six miles from the village the people were released to walk home, ensuring that the alarm could not be raised at Abu Hamed until the reconnaissance party were well clear.

The report to Kitchener told him that the garrison of Abu Hamed was small. Only four hundred and fifty Jihadiyya riflemen, fifty Baggara horsemen and around six hundred tribesmen armed only with swords and spears. Kitchener knew that speed was important as, once they heard of the reconnaissance, reinforcements would be sent from Berber. The sheikh had also told them that the garrison expected an attack by steamers on the river and their defences had been constructed to take account of this. An attack from the landward side could expect to encounter less well prepared defences.

Kitchener assembled his flying column, under the command of Brigadier General Hunter, to move as rapidly as possible across the one hundred and thirty miles of desert to make the attack. McGuire and his men were to act as guides to the two wells along the way while the Abada sent out a screen to protect the column as they laboured across the difficult desert.

Although less rocky than the famous "Belly of Stones" the route was desolate with large areas of soft sand that allowed the wheels of the artillery to sink and dragged at the men's boots. There was no shade and no villages to provide respite. Although they marched at night the daytime temperatures soared above forty degrees so few could sleep. Men started to fall asleep on their feet as they marched. Three men died of exhaustion and fifty eight had to be left behind to catch up when they could.

McGuire and one of his patrols rode forward and then crawled to where they could see Abu Hamed, set in the low crater below them. As they lay on the lip of the depression they could see that the defenders were aware of the approaching force and were preparing trenches on the landward side of the town. Yussuf and Asif went into the town and spoke to some of the men digging.

They came back and dropped down next to McGuire. "It is as we feared English. They know the army is coming and they have sent to Berber for help. Many men are expected here soon."

"Do we know how many are coming?"

"Not the numbers, but we know they are a strong force or so the diggers have been told."

McGuire nodded. "It is what we expected, but Hunter must know of this before he makes his plan." He turned to Connolly who lay beside him with his sketch pad. "How long before you finish your plan of this place?"

"Give me another fifteen minutes, sir. I can tidy it up as we travel."

"Good. No longer than that though, we need to move quickly."

They met up with the flying column in the thick palm groves of Ginnifab where the army lay in the shade and rested, only two miles from Abu Hamed. McGuire made his way to Hunter and handed over Connolly's drawing of the position.

"You've made good time sir. I didn't expect you to be this close yet."

Hunter looked up from the paper in his hands. "The soldiers have been magnificent. We've marched thirty six miles across that bloody sand in thirty five hours and they're still ready for a fight. If anyone ever tells you the Egyptian army is no good you tell them that."

"I will sir. Where do you want my people for the attack?"

"Have them follow me. I may need to use them to take messages to the battalions as we go in. I'm going to divide the force and attack from two directions. We'll come in from the desert and along the bank of the Nile. Now then talk me through this drawing."

McGuire sat next to the commander and pointed at the sheet in his hand. "Right sir, these watchtowers are of stone and they have riflemen in them. All through this area they have made shelter trenches and the houses on this side of the town have been loop holed. The town itself is the usual maze of narrow streets running through between mud brick houses."

"And you're sure the reinforcements have not arrived yet?"

"They may have had some, but the main force is still on the way from Berber."

"Good. We will start the attack at first light. Let your men get what rest they can. I'll be moving the rest of the troops into position in the dark."

McGuire returned to his troop and told them to settle down and wait. With the infantry forming up and the artillery dragging the guns forward around them there was no chance of sleep. They contented themselves with an early breakfast of fried bully beef and flat unleavened bread. With the camels watered they were ready to move when Hunter's runner came looking for them. They mounted and followed the commander out towards their objective.

By five in the morning, just as the sun was turning the landscape into all sorts of fantastic colours, the force on the landward side was ready. No more than a quarter of a mile from Abu Hamed the three battalions of Sudanese troops were concealed in the wadis and folds in the ground. The artillery battery stood alongside them, guarded by a battalion of Fellaheen troops.

Hunter rode forward with his entourage around him to survey the village in the depression before them. There was an eerie silence, it appeared that the enemy had withdrawn during the night, but the scouts had reported no movement.

Hunter turned in his saddle and waved McGuire forward. "Captain, take a few of your men and go forward. Tell me what's going on down there. If the enemy has actually left then fire three shots in the air and we will move in."

McGuire saluted and wheeled his camel round. He called two of his patrols forward and in extended line they rode slowly towards the trenches they could see before the town. At eighty yards from the first trench he reined his camel to a halt and made sure his men stopped as well. He scanned the enemy trenches through his field glasses and could see nothing. The trenches appeared to be empty.

He pulled the notebook out of the pocket of his tunic and called one of the men across to him. He started to write a note for the man to take back up the slope to Hunter. As he did so he felt the shock waves as three bullets whipped past his head. He turned towards the town to see dozens of dark heads emerging from what he had thought were empty trenches. There was a concerted volley of fire and McGuire and his men beat a hasty retreat back towards the army. He thanked God that the bullets were flying high and lashed his camel to make best speed.

A second volley was aimed at the command party on the top of the ridge. Again it flew high, and Hunter wheeled his horse and rode back three hundred yards yelling for the artillery to open fire. The Krupp guns opened fire together and shells pounded into the Dervish trenches sending clouds of dust and sand into the air. The infantry rose to their feet and formed their lines. As they rose they could be seen, by the defenders, silhouetted against the sun on the crest of the ridge.

Despite the noise and fire, the guns were achieving very little except to keep the enemy in their trenches. The shape of the terrain made it difficult for the guns to depress their barrels far enough to be truly effective.

The infantry was given the order to "Fix bayonets" and along the lines the long shining blades clicked into place on their rifles. Then came the order to "Advance" and the men stepped off as if on a parade square. The regimental colours were unfurled and flew in the breeze of the forward movement.

The intention had been to advance the three hundred yards towards the trenches and then launch a bayonet charge. It was not to be. The 11th Sudanese on the right hand end of the line opened up with independent fire and the other two battalions soon followed suit. The Dervish trenches were being pounded by hundreds of rifles being fired into them. Officers struggled to bring the excited Sudanese soldiers back into control and as they did so the Dervishes stood up and fired two huge volleys. Dozens of men were hit and fell to the ground.

The enraged soldiers roared their hatred and launched a charge at the Dervish trenches. The Dervish defenders panicked and seconds later they were leaping from the cover of their defences and running for the cover of the town. Moments later the Sudanese were into the town, going from house to house and street to street, using their bayonets. The Dervishes were never given the chance to rally and form a defence within the town. The Sudanese ran into the houses, climbed on the roofs and in very short order had passed completely through. Here they reformed and fired volleys at the Dervish Cavalry who were the only ones able to make their escape from the slaughterhouse that was Abu Hamed.

Less than an hour after the attack started the town was in the hands of the Egyptian army. McGuire rode through the town close behind Hunter. Bodies lay everywhere, many with multiple bayonet wounds. Some four hundred and fifty Dervishes had died and only twenty were taken prisoner, among them was the Dervish commander Mohammad az-Zayn.

One man though refused to give up and hid himself in a small house, down by the river, then started to snipe at the Egyptian forces. Six men were sent to finish him off and he killed them all. Two Krupp guns were brought forward and reduced the house to rubble. An Egyptian soldier went forward to find the body and was shot down when the sniper reappeared. The Krupps opened fire again and totally destroyed what remained of the house. The sniper's body was never found.

Hunter had Mohammad az-Zayn brought forward to question him. He asked him why he had fought against such overwhelming odds and the young Mahdist explained that since his men were worth four of the cowardly Egyptians he had thought he had an even chance. He also told Hunter that in five days the force from Metemma would be there and Hunter's bones would bleach in the sun.

The reinforcements from Berber turned back when they met the cavalry that had escaped from Abu Hamed. The force from Metemma never even started out to the aid of their comrades, refusing even to cross the Nile. Within days of the victory, armed steamers arrived on the river to provide artillery protection and the threat was over.

Hunter called McGuire to him as he rested after the battle. "Captain that was sound work by you and your men. However, the price of being useful is that you don't get much rest."

McGuire smiled wearily. "We're used to it, sir. What can I do for you?"

"I need you to ride forward towards Berber. I need all the usual details. How big is the garrison? What defences are in place? Water shouldn't be a problem this time as we will be marching by the side of the Nile. When can you start?"

"First thing in the morning if that would do sir?

Hunter looked at the tired and dirty officer in front of him. "No I think you and your men deserve a short respite. Take a day to gather your strength. Let the men sleep and bathe in the river. The next day will do just as well."

McGuire and his men accepted the day of rest gratefully. They washed in the river, mended their clothes and saddles and ensured that the camels had drunk their fill and eaten well. Then they settled down by the riverside for a meal cooked by Yussuf and Asif. The next morning, an hour before dawn, they left their encampment, heading south towards Berber.

The ride across the open desert accompanied by a dozen of the Ababda passed without incident. Not once did they see a Dervish patrol. The small villages they passed were deserted. Riding beside the river kept the camels in good shape with plenty of water, whenever they needed it, and, despite the intense heat, the men could keep their water skins full.

Away to the west, the rest of the Ababda and the Egyptian Camel Corps advanced towards Metemma to discover the situation there. The promised reinforcements from there had never approached Abu Hamed and when the scouts arrived at the town they found the Baggara still there. The town had everything a nomad from the goz could wish for. Houses to live in, abundant food from the stores the Ja'aliyyin had laid in and captive women to abuse. They had refused to obey their orders to move to support Abu Hamed and were on the verge of mutiny.

As McGuire's troop reached Berber they were in time to see the last of the Dervishes leaving the town. They waited until nightfall before venturing into the silent streets to confirm what they had seen. They walked into the town with their rifles at the ready spreading out as they moved. Parks found an old man sitting in the doorway of his empty shop and brought him gently to McGuire.

McGuire sat down cross legged and indicated the old man should sit as well. "Greetings grandfather. Your health is good?"

"My health is good for my years and you?"

"My men and I are tired from crossing the desert. We thought to find the Dervishes here, but there are none."

The old man nodded. "It is true. They were here waiting for Mahmud to bring his Baggara from Metemma, then they were to move north and destroy the invaders. The ones from Metemma never came and soon the Emir Zaki 'Osman tired of waiting and left."

"Do you know where they went?"

The old man spread his hands and shrugged. "There was talk of going to Omdurman to join with the army that the Khalifa is assembling there. They say he will fulfil the prophecy and destroy the Egyptians, and their infidel masters, on the plains of Omdurman. The last thing they will see is the gleaming dome on the tomb of the Mahdi."

"It may be so, but I think not. Tell me old one, where are the people of Berber?"

"A few hide in their houses, others went to the villages around to keep away from the Dervishes. They will return now our town is free of them."

McGuire leaned forward and took the old man's hand. "Thank you grandfather, it is good to know the news. My friend here will take you back to your house. Go in peace."

They stood up and Parks started to lead the old man away, until McGuire called after him. "Parks, once you've delivered the old boy, round up the men and meet me by the gate."

McGuire turned and walked across to where Donnelly and Macklin stood waiting with their patrols. "Find the men and get them back to the gate. We're done here."

On the 5th September Hunter arrived on the river with four gunboats and half of the 11th Sudanese battalion. In 1884 this town had been a major problem, this time he was able to just walk in with no opposition. Kitchener arrived days later having ridden across the Bayuda desert. In the Sirdar's mind Berber was the key to the Sudan and now it was in his hand. He was conscious that his force there was vulnerable if the Dervishes attacked in force but the railway was moving towards them and that could rapidly bring him reinforcements.

Chapter 56.
The British Arrive

At Christmas 1897 the British Prime Minister had given Kitchener permission to call for British troops if he needed them. On the 1st January Kitchener called forward a four battalion infantry division made up of units of the British garrison in Cairo. Reinforcements also started out from Britain.

McGuire and his weary troop, still wearing their desert *jibbas* and riding their camels were in Berber as the British troops marched in and began setting up their camps. The men of the Cairo garrison were suntanned and their uniforms were faded. In amongst them were other soldiers with paler faces and new desert uniforms.

As McGuire led his men through the lines of neat white tents he saw a face he knew. He reined in the camel and dropped to the ground to wait for the soldier who was walking towards him. The man passed him with a casual glance and McGuire turned.

"Is that any way to greet and old friend Tom?"

The soldier turned and McGuire saw the three stripes of a Sergeant on his sleeve. The man glanced at the dirty Arab by him and then looked to see who had spoken to him.

McGuire smiled and raised a hand. "Sergeant Tom Drabble of the Grenadier Guards and you don't remember an old comrade?"

Tom Drabble stared at the dark skinned man in his jibba and shook his head. "Who the hell are you and how do you know me?"

McGuire was enjoying himself now. "Tom, we stood at the rail of a troop ship in Alexandria taking our first look at Egypt."

Drabble's mouth dropped open. "Michael? Is it you? Did you leave the army?"

"No Tom I'm still serving. I dress like this for doing patrols deep behind enemy lines. Those are my boys riding down to the river."

Tom stepped forward with his hand out and McGuire gripped it. "I never imagined I would see you again and certainly not here in the middle of the desert."

"We've been down here a long time. Since this all started in fact, but what are you doing here?"

"Hang on. I thought they made you an officer?"

"They did Tom. I'm a Captain now and I command that reconnaissance troop."

Sergeant Drabble rapidly came to attention and saluted. "Sorry sir. I didn't realise."

McGuire shook his head sadly. "Don't bother with all that Tom. Now come on, why are you here?"

"The battalion is on the way out from England and we are the advance party. We've come ahead to sort things out for when the rest get here."

"Is there anybody left that I would know from the old days?"

Drabble looked around quickly. "Just one. The hero of Abu Klea, Captain Storr-Lessing."

"Hero? Him?"

"That's the way it gets told. Colonel Latham told us all how he made a brave circuit to the north to see where the Dervish cavalry was before rejoining the square. Then he stepped into the firing line with a rifle when a man went down."

"He didn't mention Sergeant Major Lewis pushing the bugger into the line?"

Drabble smiled and shook his head. "Turns out his Daddy is a General and Latham and Lewis owe him their lives. They spun that story so the regiment would not be disgraced. Lewis made sure we told the same tale when we got home."

McGuire paused. "With a General in the family I'm surprised he's only a Captain."

"So is he. Latham wouldn't promote him it seems, so that slowed him down a lot and the battalion officers know the truth. Once Latham left on promotion, Daddy put pressure on the new Colonel and he got his steps up, but very slowly."

McGuire was about to reply when he heard the voice from behind him. "Sergeant what are you doing lollygagging about talking to that filthy native. I've told you before; the thieving bastards will have the shirt off your back if you give them half a chance."

McGuire turned slowly to see Storr–Lessing strutting towards him, slapping his high boot with his leather riding crop. "And you! Bugger off before I thrash you. Imshi! Yaller!"

McGuire smiled slowly. "I see you're still an accomplished linguist then?"

"What? You speak English! A performing monkey eh?"

McGuire's smile faded. "A little respect for a fellow officer if you don't mind Captain. Name calling in front of the Sergeant really won't do."

Storr-Lessing stopped and peered at the Arab in front of him. With his dark skin, unkempt beard and native dress he certainly looked like an Arab.

"Sergeant on about your duties. Now, who the hell are you to talk to me like that?"

McGuire unwound the Shemagh from his head and looked coolly at the nonplussed man before him. "Captain Michael McGuire, Royal Irish Fusiliers, at your service Captain Storr-Lessing."

"Should I know you?"

McGuire smiled again just slightly. "That depends if you remember a hilltop at Abu Klea where you ran to save your skin and left two men behind to die."

The blood drained from Storr-Lessing's face as he stared at the man from his past. "McGuire. My God!"

"That's right, McGuire. By the way, a little advice for you. Don't treat the natives, as you call them, that way again. The Sudanese in particular are very prickly and you could end up in trouble."

"I don't need advice from a jumped up guttersnipe like you."

McGuire shrugged and put his Shemagh back on. "Maybe you don't, but you're a long way from your London club and your Daddy's influence down here. You might remember that."

Chapter 57.
Mahmud Advances and Enemies Arise

Donnelly leaned across and tapped the sleeping McGuire on the arm. "Wake up sir. Things are starting to happen."

McGuire rolled over, for a second or two he was befuddled by sleep then he shook his head clear and took the field glasses that the Sergeant held out to him. "I hope so. I'm sick to death of lying here watching these bloody people loaf around the place."

The place he was talking about was Metemma and the reconnaissance troop had been hiding and observing it for three weeks now. They had penetrated the town in the first few days of their observation and were horrified to find that the dead bodies left after the massacre were still lying in the streets. The stench was revolting. They had heard the screams of the captive women carried in the clear night air, but could do nothing for them. They had seen the commander Mahmud arguing with his emirs and then stamping back to the Sheikh's house having failed to get them to move.

"So what's going on? The town looks the same."

Donnelly grinned. "Not in the town. Take a look on the river. We've got company."

McGuire rolled to one side and looked to where the sergeant was pointing. He didn't need the glasses to see the three gunboats approaching along the Nile. He looked back at the town and could now see horsemen galloping out towards the six forts that Mahmud had built down by the riverside.

"Looks like Mahmud is going to try and give them a warm reception."

"Could be, sir, unless the Navy wants to give the town a plastering."

McGuire scanned the approaching boats through the glasses. "They've got the guns manned. I wonder how effective they'll be. The town is about half a mile from the river and they'll have to stay out in the deep channel."

"Either way, we should have a front row seat to watch whatever happens."

Before they came abreast of the town the gunboats opened fire, the flat crack of the Krupp guns echoing across the desert. The first shell smashed into one of the forts and from then on the first two forts were pounded to rubble by high explosive and shrapnel shells. As the defenders ran from their collapsing defences the maxim guns opened up and cut them down. As the first two forts fell, the second and third boats came into range and now all three pounded the four remaining forts until their walls crumbled under the onslaught.

With no visible damage to the boats, McGuire watched them withdraw back down the river, their objectives apparently complete. In the town, Mahmud had been stung into action. This was his chance to get his mutinous troops to move to attack the enemy that had just disgraced them. He gave his orders and this time the Baggara obeyed.

Mahmud's timing was lucky as the warlord Osman Digna had been ordered by the Khalifa to move north and support him with his Beja warriors. He arrived on the 16th February with five thousand of his troops. This was not a marriage made in heaven, as both tribes despised the other and spoke different languages.

In a council of war, Mahmud was advised, by experienced commanders, to pull back to the Sabaluka cataract, further up the Nile. Here they could establish gun positions and sniper nests that would make it difficult if not impossible for the gunboats to pass. Mahmud would have none of it. Pulling back would seem like a retreat and already some of his men had saddled up and ridden home. Like many other Dervishes, who had not yet met the retrained Egyptian army in battle, he believed them to be cowards. He would advance and defeat them in open battle. He refused to take advice from Osman Digna and even hinted that the Beja were as cowardly as the Egyptians.

His simple plan was to take his twelve thousand men along the banks of the Nile and to destroy the Sirdar's army at Atbara. Osman advised against this as they would be vulnerable to the fire of the gunboats, he suggested they should strike across the desert away from the river. Mahmud ignored the advice of his senior commanders and ordered the advance.

Once it was clear which direction the Dervishes were taking, McGuire left Donnelley in charge of an observation screen while he rode back to the army, with Yussuf and Asif as an escort, to brief Kitchener. They rode hard and left the Dervish army far behind them.

As the sun rose over Kitchener's camp McGuire and his two men rode in towards the *zariba* with the sun at their backs. They had seen no sign of any of the cavalry screen who could lead them in and their information was too vital to delay.

In front of them a sentry called to the officer of the day. "Riders coming in sir!"

Captain Storr-Lessing pushed open the tent flaps and walked forwards to the sentry. He raised his field glasses and studied the approaching camel riders. A small smile played around his lips.

"Stand the guard to."

The sentry turned and yelled to where the rest of the guard detail lay. "Guard! Stand to!"

The rest of the guard detail grabbed their rifles and ran to form a line by the *zariba*. Storr-Lessing continued to watch the riders come closer. He smiled again and lowered the field glasses.

"Prepare to fire! At three hundred yards, volley fire present!"

The men cocked their rifles and raised them to the aim. "Fire!"

Firing into the sunrise made aiming difficult, but still one of the men was knocked from his saddle. The other two jumped down and lay flat. Storr-Lessing heard the pounding footsteps behind him and turned to see Sergeant Drabble running towards him.

"For the love of God, sir. That's Captain McGuire. Cease fire! Stand down!"

The men of the guard detail looked around confused. Storr-Lessing looked at his Sergeant. "Are you sure? Oh dear, well, accidents do happen in war. Most unfortunate."

Drabble stood for a moment, looking at his officer. He could hardly believe what had just happened. He turned and strode to the line of riflemen.

"Open the zariba. Hurry up there's a man down."

With the thorn hedge pulled back Drabble took four men and ran forward to where the camels stood calmly and the two men were climbing to their feet. They walked across to the body that lay on the ground and one of them fell to his knees.

Drabble stopped. "Who is it?"

McGuire turned to look at him. "It's Yussuf. He's been hit high in the chest. Get your men to pick him up and get him to the surgeons. Tom, move him gently."

The four soldiers slung their rifles across their backs and picked the young Arab off the ground. They started back towards the zariba with Drabble alongside them.

"Just a minute Tom."

The Sergeant stopped and turned back. "Who gave the order to fire?"

Drabble paused and looked at McGuire. "Captain Storr-Lessing sir."

"Could he not see who we were?"

Drabble looked down at the ground and then looked up again. "He watched you through his field glasses. I could see who you were so he should have been able to."

McGuire drew himself up. "Thank you Sergeant. Please make sure the boy is treated well. Asif you go with him and I will go to the General. I'll be with you soon."

He stood and watched as Asif followed his son into the camp. He could see Storr-Lessing now, walking away back to his tent. He nodded to himself slightly then mounted his camel and rode in to the headquarters area of the camp. He dropped down from the camel's back and hobbled it before walking in to speak with the Sirdar and his senior officers.

Having explained in detail what he had seen, McGuire walked out of the tent and looked around. Wingate walked out beside him.

"I hear your young man, Yussuf, has been hit. Is it serious?"

"I don't know yet I'm going to the surgeons now to see what's happening."

"I'll walk with you. So, how did it happen?"

"The officer of the day had the guard open fire."

"Just an accident then eh?"

McGuire stopped and looked at Wingate. "No sir I don't think so. Captain Storr-Lessing could see us clearly through the field glasses he was using. I think he knew damn fine who we were."

Wingate shook his head. "Surely not? Why the hell would he do such a thing?"

McGuire thought for a moment before he spoke. "Just between you and me sir, that officer has built himself a reputation as a bit of a hero at Abu Klea. The only man who could bring that fable crashing down is me."

"Dear God! I hope you're wrong. That's the surgeon's tent. Let me know how our man is will you?"

McGuire walked to the tent. Asif squatted outside with Sergeant Drabble sitting in a camp chair beside him. They both looked up as he approached.

"How is he?"

"We don't know yet sir. They're dealing with another case first."

"Are they indeed?"

McGuire flipped open the flaps of the tent and walked in. Yussuf lay on a low cot with no one near him. Across at the other side of the tent three surgeons clustered around another cot.

"Who is in charge here?"

The doctors looked around and one stepped forward. "I am what do you want?"

"I want you to save the life of my soldier."

"Soldier? Where is he?"

"On that cot being ignored by everyone in here."

"The tribesman?"

"That tribesman is a soldier in the Reconnaissance Troop, and if someone doesn't treat him in the next two minutes, you'll have another casualty on your hands."

"Are you threatening me?"

"Put simply, yes I am."

"Who the hell do you think you are ordering me about in my own hospital?"

McGuire felt the anger rising again, he paused for only a second, then drew the Webley revolver from his waist sash and rested the barrel on the doctor's forehead. He thumbed the hammer back and heard the satisfying metallic click.

"You may have heard of this pistol. It used to belong to General Gordon. And you are running out of time before I use it."

"You're McGuire, I've heard of you." A bead of sweat ran down the surgeon's temple and he blinked quickly. "We'll get right on to your man, now would you mind moving that gun please'"

McGuire withdrew the revolver and put it away. Without another word he walked back outside the tent to where the two men still sat.

"Tom, stay here with Asif. Make sure those bloody surgeons are working on Yussuf."

"Where are you going sir?"

"I'm going to find Colonel Wingate and get myself put under arrest."

Colonel Wingate sat by his map table and listened to McGuire's story. "You're a bloody fool Captain. That temper of yours is a bloody nuisance and you're just damned lucky Kitchener's here."

"Why is that sir?"

"Because the Sirdar is very keen to have his soldiers treated properly and the surgeon ignoring our man will irritate him mightily. Then of course he needs your eyes out in the desert. So when the surgeon goes bleating to him he will end up with a flea in his ear. I will square that away, but don't do anything like it again."

"I can't promise that sir."

"Oh and why not pray?"

"I need a word with the Officer of the Day about the incident this morning."

"You can't let that pass?"

"No sir."

"Don't kill him. I can't sweep that under the table."

"I won't kill him. I'm just going to tell him his fortune."

Captain Storr-Lessing stood outside his tent smoking a cigar and wondering how he could deal with that upstart McGuire. If his carefully constructed reputation was to be protected, McGuire had to be silenced. He stiffened and went rigid as he felt the metal touch his throat.

"What you are feeling against your neck, Captain, is a curved Arab dagger that I took off an emir I had just killed. Have you killed anybody personally yet Captain? Don't shake your head the blade is very sharp."

Storr-Lessing felt the warm liquid run down his leg and he stifled the need to scream. "What do you want? Who are you?"

"I'm the soldier you abandoned on that hilltop when you ran away like the coward you are."

"McGuire."

"That's right. The man you tried to murder this morning. I've come to tell you your fortune.

360

Do you believe in foretelling the future? Don't shake your head remember."

Storr-Lessing stood there trembling and feeling the knife at his throat. He could feel the slight trickle of blood running down into his shirt.

"That Arab boy is one of mine you see and I don't abandon my men, unlike some others. If he dies so do you. It may not be me who sees to it. The other Arab in my party is his father and they are both Bedouin. The Bedouin have a simple code of honour. They believe in an eye for an eye. So here is some advice for you. Learn to sleep with one eye open and watch for me."

Then the blade was gone and the trembling officer turned around. McGuire was gone as if he had never been there.

Chapter 58.
Atbara

To the south, the Dervishes were advancing. Mahmud and his men marched north beside the Nile. They carried no provisions, relying instead on the nuts of the palm trees that grew by the river and could be ground up to make bread. Osman Digna and the other commanders had predicted that the steamers would reappear and harass them if they stayed near the river. They were proved right and eventually Mahmud decided to take their advice and advance directly across the desert. He knew it would be difficult, but the Baggara were hardened to that.

Mahmud had relied on the food his troops could gather on the river bank and carried no provisions and little water. Hundreds of his men deserted during the march and rode away to their homes. By the time the rest reached the Atbara River they were in no condition to fight.

Osman advised that they should move up the river to Adarama where the Sirdar could not ignore them, but would not be able to use his gunboats for support. Mahmud once again ignored the old warrior and moved his force down river towards the Anglo-Egyptian camp. Then, instead of pressing on to the attack, he stopped at the village of Nukhayla about thirty five miles from where the Atbara river flowed into the Nile. Here he ordered his men to build a defensive position by the river.

Mahmud stood outside the *zariba* that was being built and surveyed the area. Osman walked across the flat flood plain and stood next to him.

Mahmud turned and looked at the older man. "And what advice do you bring me today old one?"

"This is a bad place to build your camp. You should move to a place better suited for defence."

Mahmud sighed. "Again you tell me I am wrong. Share your immense wisdom with me."

Osman pointed to the bluffs above them. "From there the infidels can fire down at us with their Krupp guns." He pointed then towards the river. "Those palm groves can be set on fire and we are too near to the Sirdar's camp. He can be on us in one night's march. That *zariba* and those trenches will not be enough. There will be slaughter."

Mahmud nodded. "You are right. There will be slaughter. When the Egyptians reach here we will slaughter them and their bones will whiten the desert. You are too nervous of these cowards we face."

Osman held his tongue. He had faced the new Egyptian army and knew they were not cowards. His scouts had told him that they were now reinforced by British troops. Together they would make a formidable force. As he looked at the trenches being dug he thought they would soon be the graves of the defenders.

"Tell me Osman, are they your men who sit on that ridge and do not help with the defences?"

Osman looked to where the younger man was pointing. He saw five men wearing the patched jibbas of the Dervish and sitting on camels, watching the activity below them.

"They are not my scouts. I have seen them before in the desert and I think they are the eyes of Kitchener."

Mahmud shrugged. "No matter, let them see that we are ready for them."

Osman looked again at the position they were in and looked up at the men watching them. He knew in his bones that this was to be a disaster and he knew too that he would not leave his Beja warriors here to die for nothing.

McGuire and his men pulled back from the ridgeline having seen all they needed to. Connolly had drawn a detailed map of the position, as they sat on the ridge, and was adding detail as they rode away. They reached Kitchener within the day and briefed him on what they had seen.

Kitchener immediately moved his force of fourteen thousand up to Ras al-Hudi on the Atbara and only thirteen miles from Mahmud. He stayed there for a week hoping that the Dervishes would attack. He knew the enemy were short of food as every day deserters entered his camp, hungry and suffering from diarrhoea from eating the palm nuts. Starvation was wearing Mahmud's force down, but Kitchener did not want them to pull out, as that would leave an enemy force on his flank as he advanced on Omdurman.

McGuire and his men had discovered that Mahmud had left what food supplies he had at Shandi, along with the women and children and a small Baggara garrison. Three gunboats steamed up the Atbara and landed the 15th Egyptian battalion and 150 Ja'aliyyan who had now joined Kitchener as irregulars. They stormed the town and the garrison fled. The Ja'aliyyan pursued them, killing one hundred and sixty of them as well as capturing six hundred and fifty women and children. It was a first revenge for the massacre of Metemma.

Brigadier General Hunter was sent forward with six squadrons of cavalry and two squadrons of the camel Corps to make a close reconnaissance of Mahmud's *zariba*. McGuire and one of his patrols rode with them as guides. Hunter sat on the ridge with McGuire and stared down at the position through his field glasses.

He lowered the glasses and turned to McGuire. "With the troop numbers we have that is as close to impregnable as makes no difference."

McGuire paused and thought before he spoke. "Are you sure sir? We have damned fine soldiers and the Baggara are not in good shape."

"You haven't been to the war college have you Captain? For us to attack a defended position we would need another ten thousand men, if not more. Without them the losses would be intolerable."

McGuire nodded. "If they were a properly trained army you would of course be correct sir, but these are tribesmen with poorly maintained weapons and poor leadership."

"They are also damned brave warriors young man. My mind is made up. We should not attack here."

The reconnaissance force withdrew without casualties and Hunter reported to Kitchener. He insisted the attack was unwise and Kitchener reluctantly agreed with him. McGuire did not want to contradict Hunter in front of Kitchener and so gave his opinion to Wingate alone. After the senior officer's meeting Wingate sat down by the map table with the Sirdar and passed on McGuire's opinions.

Kitchener sipped his evening whisky and soda and looked at the map Connolly had drawn. "Wingate, your man is a damned fine scout, but he does not have Hunter's experience and knowledge. I have to take the advice of my senior officers."

Kitchener, Hunter and Gateacre continued to discuss the issue over the next few days. Further reconnaissance was carried out by Hunter and he eventually came round to agree that the attack could be viable. Kitchener gave the order and the army moved forward to Umm Dabiyya from where it could march into battle in a very few hours.

Chapter 59.
The Battle of Atbara.

Kitchener stood on the rocky bluff above the flat plain where Mahmud's defences stood. Behind him, the troops were deploying from their marching squares into line and moving forward to get their first view of the enemy compound. The zariba beneath them was a rough oval in shape about a thousand yards in diameter. They could see the complex of trenches but no movement. Initially they thought the Dervishes must have pulled out during the night, but then cooking fires started to flicker into life all around the camp. Through his field glasses, Kitchener could see the seven artillery pieces that McGuire pointed out to him. They were in gun pits around the perimeter with embrasures built to protect them.

The Anglo Egyptian troops were now arranged in the buffalo horn formation the British had learned from the Zulus in a previous war. Troops from the Sudanese brigades held the right and centre while the British had the left horn. The Egyptian brigade was held back as a reserve with the Egyptian cavalry out to the left. A maxim battery was also located to the left with a rocket battery, commanded by Lieutenant David Beatty of the Royal Navy, that had been placed behind Kitchener's command post in the centre.

McGuire watched as the army deployed and then saw Sergeant Donnelly riding towards him. "What's the matter, Sergeant?"

"It's the lads, sir. They feel they are being left out of the fight again. They want me to ask you if they can join one of the battalions."

"It's a bit late in the day for that. The battalions are just about formed and the men might get in the way."

"Begging your pardon sir, but I've had a word with the RSM of the Lincolns, and he's happy for us to go in behind his men and fill in any gaps as they move forward."

"And all the men want to go in?"

"Yes sir they do."

"Wait here." With that McGuire wheeled his camel and rode over to where Kitchener stood watching the attack prepare. He made the camel kneel and dismounted. He marched up to the Sirdar and saluted.

"What do you need Captain?"

"Sir, with your permission, my men and I would like to join the Lincolns for the attack."

Kitchener lowered his binoculars and turned to McGuire. "It's liable to get bloody down there."

"Yes sir, but the men are getting restive at being held back from the battle. We think we might be able to help."

Kitchener nodded. "I don't need you today. Join the Lincolns if they will have you. And Captain, good luck."

McGuire saluted and ran back to his camel. He rode back to where Donnelley waited and waved him to move with him to the rest of the troop. As he reached them he reined in and dismounted drawing his rifle from its saddle boot as he did so.

"Right then, all of you, don't hang around we're off to do some proper soldiering. Follow me."

The men grinned and grabbed their rifles before following McGuire, down the slope after the Lincolnshire Regiment, at the double. McGuire saw the Colonel of the regiment speaking with the RSM just behind the regiment that had drawn up prior to making their advance.

As he reached the Colonel he saluted. "Captain McGuire sir, with a few reinforcements for you, if you'll have us?"

"McGuire? I thought you were part of the Sirdar's staff?"

"Some of the time sir, but he doesn't need us today and my men would like to join in the battle properly."

"I have no objection. RSM would you place these men where you need them? Better be quick, I think we are about to open the batting."

At exactly a quarter past six the first Krupp gun fired sending a shrapnel shell into the defensive oval nine hundred yards away. That was the signal for the Maxim gun battery to open intensive fire across the compound. The rocket battery fired from behind Kitchener and the rockets arched over into the Dervish defences screaming as they flew. The roofs of a number of huts burst into flame and then the rest of the twenty four Krupp guns opened fire. Dirt, stones, tree fragments as well as human and animal body parts were being blown up into the air all over the enemy compound.

Initially there was no response from the enemy then the first of their captured Krupp guns fired. The shell howled over a Sudanese battalion and landed almost half a mile behind them. The Sudanese soldiers roared with laughter and yelled insults down at the Dervish gunners. More and more shells were fired at the massed ranks on the ridge and all of them flew high and exploded well behind the troops.

Below the ridge, inside the *zariba* Dervish banners were unfurled and waved in defiance. The storm of shot and shell blasted them to the ground in moments. Baggara cavalry were seen forming up with some of their men wearing antique steel helmets and chainmail. The Egyptian cavalry trotted forward escorting two maxim guns and as the Baggara formed up to charge they were cut to ribbons by the intensive fire of these two modern weapons.

Kitchener gave the order for the barrage to be lifted to allow the infantry to move forward. At ten minutes past eight his personal bugler sounded a long eerie note that was copied by buglers along the line. The infantry stiffened ready for action. The bands of the Sudanese, the pipes of the Scots regiments and the fifes and drums of the English regiments all burst into life. The colours were unfurled and Major General Gateacre marched to the head of the Cameron Highlanders with his sword drawn.

The British brigade moved forward as if they were on a parade square. They stopped only to fire a volley and then moved forward again. As they reached an area where they could spread out, the Camerons moved to the right and two companies of the Warwicks moved up to fill the gap. The Sudanese were trotting forward, eager to come to grips with their sworn enemies. The British stopped again and fired more volleys. The Sudanese were firing their Martini Henrys too, but in more ragged volleys. As they crested a low ridge the British halted and the front rank dropped into the kneeling position, before the leading two ranks opened fire.

As the infantry advanced to within three hundred yards of the *zariba* the Dervishes returned fire all along the defences. Men dropped all along the line and the ranks quickly closed the gaps. McGuire and his men moved forward into the firing line and, along with the rest of the brigade, started independent fire. The Lincolns and the Seaforths dropped down into two dry watercourses that led them towards the enemy compound. They were under intense fire, but most of the rounds flew high over their heads. Nevertheless the casualties were mounting rapidly.

Over to their left, McGuire could see a section of three Maxim guns being brought forward to a ridge. The mules panicked and kicked out at the gunners, terrified by the roar of musketry. The gunners released the animals and dragged the guns forward by hand, before opening fire into the Dervish compound. A large troop of

Baggara horse formed up to charge the attackers and the Maxims were in place in time to mow them down.

The Lincolns continued their steady, controlled march forward with McGuire's troop now holding places in the line where other men had fallen. As they marched on a man in front of McGuire stopped and spun round to face him. The front of his tunic was soaked in blood and he said. "They've done for me, sir." before falling to the ground, dead.

Thirty of the Dervish infantry rushed out from behind the *zariba* and formed up to charge. Before they could do so they were cut down by Maxims and rifle fire. Two men remained standing and they turned and walked casually back into the compound. A burst from a Maxim changed the mind of the first one and he started to run. The second was cut down in a welter of blood.

The Sudanese had had enough of the steady advance and broke into a screaming charge. Major General Gateacre was the first to reach the zariba and started to pull at it with his bare hands. A Dervish jumped from his trench and ran forward to stab the General with his broad bladed spear. He was stopped by a bayonet thrust from a private standing beside Gateacre.

The troops found that the *zariba* was not as difficult as they had anticipated. The Highlanders were able to cross it by flinging blankets over the thorns. The long legged Sudanese simply vaulted over it and dashed onward. Once inside they found themselves in a charnel house of dismembered body parts and disembowelled animals that had been ripped apart by the shellfire. They found men in the trenches both dead and alive who had been shackled to heavy logs to prevent them from retreating. All around them tents and palm trees were on fire smothering the area in black smoke that stank of burning flesh.

The place was a maze of trenches and then they came upon the inner *zariba* fence. Pressed on by the men behind them the soldiers threw themselves at the thorn wall and started to rip it apart. Then it was sword and spear against the long sword bayonets. The troops pushed forward stabbing gouging and slashing, but giving no quarter in the blood rage of hand to hand combat.

McGuire tripped over a fallen body and fell flat on his face. As he struggled to rise he saw a large Dervish warrior, his face contorted by anger, rushing at him with his long straight sword raised for the killing stroke. A shadow stepped past him and Donnelly's treasured scimitar whistled in the air as it ripped through the stomach of the charging warrior. He felt Donnelly's hand under his arm as the Sergeant lifted him up of the ground. As he turned to thank him, he saw another Dervish charging at Donnelly's back with a bloodied spear. He pushed the Sergeant to one side and fired the large Webley revolver he had in his left hand. The heavy round smashed into the man's face and pulverised his head.

"Well Sergeant, getting enough excitement today?"

Donnelly grinned. "Yes thank you, sir, most enjoyable."

Together they turned forward and, side by side, pressed on to where they could see a group of Dervishes standing shoulder to shoulder armed only with spears. As they approached, a section from the Warwicks opened fire at short rage and cut them down. To McGuire's left he registered a Dervish rising from a trench and aiming a rifle at him. He took a snap shot at him with the Webley and knocked the man back into the trench with a gout of blood from his chest.

Ahead of them they saw that Corporal Macklin was struggling with a Dervish who had grabbed his bayonet. The two of them spun round in a mad dance until Macklin squeezed the trigger of his rifle and blew the man backwards. One of the Lincolns had been brought to the ground by a defender who was about to slash his throat with a curved dagger when Connolly slammed his bayonet through the man on top, then helped the Lincoln Private to his feet.

The Dervish defenders, ravaged by artillery and now overwhelmed by the savagery of the infantry attack began to give ground. In the centre, the 11th Sudanese battalion came to Mahmud's final redoubt manned by the Emir's bodyguard. They opened rapid fire and the bodyguards were decimated. Those that survived the rifle fire were bayonetted. The Sudanese dashed forward and found Mahmud himself hiding under a bed. They dragged him out and stabbed him in the leg. They would have executed him on the spot, but McGuire saw Corporal Parks run forward and stop them.

The attackers chased the remaining Dervishes towards the river. As they passed trenches, warriors who had been playing dead jumped up and fired at their backs. The enraged soldiers fell on the Dervishes who remained in the trenches in a frenzy of bayonets and swords. None were given the chance to surrender.

The surviving Dervishes had now reached the river bank and were forcing their way across the dry river bed. Many were shot by their own side as deserters and cowards. The British joined in, firing carefully aimed shots and bringing down the majority of the escaping warriors. The Egyptian cavalry pounded past, pursuing a force of Baggara horse who were attempting to flee. Others were caught by the friendlies of the Ja'aliyyan who killed around three hundred and fifty and took more than six hundred prisoners.

Kitchener gave the command and the bugles blew the ceasefire command across the battlefield. Men stopped and started to look for their companies and battalions. Once they were reformed the search for the wounded began. The intense action had taken just fifteen minutes from the first artillery shell. Five hundred and fifty eight of the Anglo-Egyptian force were casualties, both wounded and dead. The Dervish casualties were above eight thousand.

The tired men fell silent as Kitchener rode down from the ridge and passed through them. Then the cheering started and soon every man on the field was cheering their commander. It went on for a full five minutes and the tears were streaming down Kitchener's face.

He paused as he saw a group of Sudanese troops approaching him with a prisoner, flanked by four British soldiers. As they reached the Sirdar, Corporal Parks saluted.

"The enemy commander sir."

Kitchener looked down at the tired and dirty soldier. "My staff tell me you rescued this man from the vengeance of the Sudanese. Is that right?"

"Yes sir. Sorry sir."

"Don't be sorry. They have good reason to hate him, but you did well. I see by the diamond badge on your sleeve you are one of McGuire's pirates, is he still alive?"

"Yes sir. He's assembling the troop now."

"Good. Tell him I want to speak to him and tell him you are now a Sergeant. Well done."

The Sirdar turned to Mahmud. "Why have you come into my country to burn and pillage?"

Mahmud looked up with defiance in his eyes. "I must obey the Khalifa as you obey the Khedive."

"Yet now you are defeated."

Mahmud forced a smile. "It matters not. At Omdurman you will be destroyed. The Khalifa has had a vision and has foretold this."

Chapter 60.
Preparation

Kitchener stood watching the wounded being picked up and evacuated around him. Casualties from both sides were evacuated to where the surgeons had set up their tents and both were treated. Burial parties were working to deal with the Anglo-Egyptian dead, but the Dervishes would be left until later. He turned as Captain McGuire reached him.

"You look tired Captain. Is that your blood on your tunic?"

"No sir that's Dervish blood, my Sergeant saved my life again but it was a little messy."

"He seems to be making a habit of saving your life. What are you going to do about it?"

McGuire smiled. "Once I get time to draw breath I am going to write a recommendation for a medal for him."

Kitchener nodded. "Good. Send it to me through Colonel Wingate. I will endorse it. Now, to business. My next move is south to Omdurman. That's no secret to anybody of course. Mahmud has effectively told me that the Khalifa is assembling his army there to destroy us. What they don't know is that there is a fourth Egyptian brigade on its way down here and a second British brigade, with troops from England not too far behind it."

"That's good to hear sir."

"I'm sure it is, but it means no rest for you and your reconnaissance troop. I need to know what I am going to face when I get to Omdurman and I need to know what the country is like so I can start to plan my dispositions. Wingate tells me that Khartoum itself has been evacuated and that Omdurman is now far bigger than the village it was, when we tried to rescue Gordon."

"Very good sir. With your permission I will rest my men tonight and leave in the early hours of the morning."

Kitchener nodded. "Good man. Be careful as you travel. The Dervishes who escaped from here will be heading the same way and they won't be too pleased to see British troops."

"We'll be wearing the Dervish *jibbas* again and we'll stay clear of any parties of the enemy."

"Good, good. Now how's that man of yours that fool Storr-Lessing shot?"

"Recovered thank you, sir. He's a tough little bugger and he will ride with me in the morning."

"Did your Corporal tell you I've promoted him?"

"He did sir. Very kind of you."

"Not kind at all, he deserved it. Now you get some rest and thank your men for me. They all did good work today."

McGuire saluted and walked slowly away through the carnage of the battle. The flies had arrived and were everywhere, swarming across the eyes of the dead and drinking from the pools of blood. Above him the vultures were wheeling and waiting for the live soldiers to leave, so they could feast.

He found his way to where his troop had set up their small camp away from the slaughter house around the zariba. Asif and Yussuf had arrived and were cooking a meal while the rest of the troop lay in whatever shade they could find and cleaned their weapons. Parks had cut the Sergeant's stripes off the sleeve of a dead Cameron Highlander and was quietly sewing them on to his own tunic. McGuire sat down heavily amongst them and sighed.

Donnelly looked across the cooking fire at him. "What did the Sirdar want then sir?"

McGuire looked up. "What he always wants, information. We head south in the morning to get it for him."

"How far south?"

"Omdurman itself. It seems we are fated to meet the main Dervish army there according to some daft prophecy."

"Do we know how many of them there are?"

"According to Mahmud there's a hundred and seventy five thousand of the beggars, but Kitchener thinks he was trying to scare him. We have to count them and draw a map of the lie of the land."

Donnelly nodded and smiled. "If Mahmud is telling the truth a hundred and seventy five thousand of these people would scare me right enough."

"I'm pretty sure there will be a lot less than that."

"From your mouth to God's ears, sir."

Far to the south, the Khalifa called a council of war in his palace at Omdurman. He had assembled his most experienced commanders and had even let one out of prison to be there. One claimed that the Mahdi had come to him in a vision and told him they should advance and fortify the Sabaluka gorge. The rest of the commanders supported the idea that this would make a good place for a stand. The Khalifa was unconvinced, but agreed to let forts be constructed there.

Secretly he was convinced that the final battle should be on the plain of Kerrari just to the north of Omdurman. Here he believed his warriors could meet the infidels in open battle and wipe them out, as they had done with the Hicks column all those years ago. He had not considered the differences between the old battle and the one he envisaged. Hicks had been short of water yet Kitchener would be by the Nile. The dense forest that had hidden the ambush did not exist at Kerrari and his people would be seen moving into position. Most of all he had failed to realise the immense difference in the Egyptian army that was now a confident, experienced and effective force. Even so, if his warriors could bring the enemy to hand to hand combat there was a real possibility the Dervish army could win.

In the base at Atbara, Kitchener was aware of the danger of letting the Dervishes get in amongst his army and was preparing to prevent that. The railway brought him the fourth Egyptian brigade and then the second British brigade including McGuire's old regiment the Grenadier Guards. Along with them they brought artillery in the form of howitzers, nine pounder field guns and two forty pounder guns. There were also two batteries of maxim guns and a regiment of British cavalry, the 21st Lancers.

As with the earlier Gordon Relief Expedition, socially well connected officers had clamoured to be included in the campaign. Among them were the Queen's grandson and a young Second Lieutenant named Winston Churchill. Kitchener had refused to have Churchill in his command, as he despised what he saw as 'medal hunters'. He had eventually been overruled by London and Churchill was attached to the Lancers as a supernumerary officer.

The railway also brought three new gunboats in sections that were assembled at the riverside. This brought Kitchener's navy to ten gunboats and five armed steamers, all of which could provide mobile artillery support to troops within range of the river.

As this build up was happening McGuire and the reconnaissance troop were riding in small parties across the desert. They saw the retreating Dervishes from Atbara and in their patched robes they looked like them from a distance. They avoided contact with the fleeing groups and at night ate cold rations to avoid the need for a fire. Eventually, they came in sight of the sprawling town of Omdurman. They could see the six forts that had been built on the banks of the Nile facing Tuti Island and the forts on the island itself. From here any steamer could be bombarded from both sides if it came to shell the town. Connolly sat on the ridge drawing his detailed map while the others scouted forward and brought him information to fill in the details.

With Asif and Yussuf beside him, McGuire rode forward into Omdurman itself. The dome of the Mahdi's tomb showed over the mud brick wall of the town as they approached. They rode through the gate without being questioned their dark, sun burned skin and the dirty, patched *jibbas* were enough of a passport. The streets were thronged with the warriors of the Dervish army, shouting, arguing and bargaining in the market places. The three quiet men riding slowly on their camels passed unnoticed. They rode past the palace of the Khalifa and saw the bodyguards who glowered at everyone in the street. As evening came on, they rode slowly out through the gates again and across the Kerrari plain to where the troop was now assembled.

McGuire dismounted and dropped down next to Connolly. "Have you got enough information yet?"

Connolly passed the paper map folder across. "I think so. The lads have been scouting around for me and we have all the features on there, which Kitchener might need."

McGuire admired the skill that had gone into the map. "Good work. Now let's go home and get some warm food in us for a change."

Connolly got to his feet. "I'll drink to that sir. Did you manage to count the Dervishes?"

McGuire smiled. "Not every last one, but my best guess is that there are about fifty thousand of them."

"No problem then, Donnelly could handle that many on his own."

McGuire chuckled. "I think he probably could. Now mount up and we'll get the hell out of here."

Chapter 61.
The Plain Before Omdurman.

By midday on the 1st September 1898, Kitchener was on the Kerrari plain. He sat on his horse and compared what he was seeing to the hand drawn map he had in his hands. McGuire's information was accurate again so his orders about deployment of his forces did not need to be changed. Behind him, five of his brigades were throwing up a zariba to protect the artillery and the transport parks. They would then form a wide protective semi-circle around the village of al-Ijayja that they had occupied an hour earlier. The sixth brigade was positioned in the centre as a reserve.

On the Nile the gunboats were pounding the forts around Tuti Island and reducing them to rubble as well as blowing gaps in the wall around Omdurman itself. The heavy howitzers were being winched ashore by sweating artillery men, ready to lob their new fifty pound Lyddite shells into the town. Kitchener knew he could sit back and level the town with his heavy guns, but that would cause the massive civilian casualties that he wished to avoid. He also knew that the Mahdi's tomb was of special significance to the Dervishes and that would certainly be one of his targets.

Kitchener turned in his saddle and called Wingate and McGuire forward. "Damned good work on this map Captain. I don't need to change my initial plans at all. Compliment your men for me. I just hope your estimate of enemy numbers is as accurate."

"Judging by the numbers the cavalry saw issuing out of the town yesterday evening; McGuire's estimate seems good sir."

"Yes Wingate, I know that. Now the Lancers are forward observing the enemy. They are inexperienced in the desert so McGuire take your troop forward and advise them. Cavalry officers can be a little over confident so be circumspect."

"Very good, sir." McGuire saluted and turned his camel away to collect his troop.

Wingate waited until McGuire was out of earshot them turned to the Sirdar. "I think McGuire has been invaluable to this campaign sir. Might I suggest he is due some recognition of his efforts?"

Kitchener did not turn his head, but lifted his field glasses to survey the plain before him. "I am not unconscious of the work he has done and the load we have put on him. I have put him forward for a decoration already. Will that suffice?"

Wingate paused. "I had thought of suggesting a brevet promotion, but if you think a decoration more appropriate …"

"Put in the paperwork and I will consider it this evening. I'm not sure both a decoration and a promotion are appropriate."

The Dervishes had decided against street fighting and as the Reconnaissance Troop rode forward they could see the warriors pouring out of the town. The 21st Lancers who were located on a ridge overlooking the plain had seen the enemy army on the move as well. Originally they had taken the dark lines in front of the town for a heavy zariba, but then the line started to move and banners were raised above it. As the line moved forward, more and more men poured out of the town behind them until the whole plain seemed black with them.

The Dervish infantry were advancing at a trot waving their banners above them and yelling their repetitive war cry. Horsemen in chain mail rode about among them, urging them on. The Lancers listened nervously to the increasing noise from the war cries and the drums that rattled a steady tattoo.

McGuire reined in alongside the Commanding Officer of the Lancers. "Good morning sir. General Kitchener has sent me forward to see if I can be of any assistance." He looked across the plain. "Impressive beggars aren't they?"

The Colonel turned and looked at the Captain beside him in his dirty uniform. "I take it you've seen these people in action before?"

"I have sir. I was with the Grenadiers during the Gordon Rescue Expedition and I've been commanding the Reconnaissance Troop during this advance."

"I think I've heard of you. McGuire isn't it?"

"That's right sir. Michael McGuire at your service."

"Is it true you were there when Gordon died and that you carry his revolver?"

"It's true sir, but I'm surprised you know about it."

The Colonel smiled. "You shouldn't be surprised. Your adventure in Khartoum is something of a legend in the army at home. Her

Majesty delights in telling the story, I am told. However, tell me what you think the fuzzy wuzzies are going to do next."

McGuire didn't like the nickname the British had given to the Mahdists; he had too much respect for their courage. "The Dervish army are fairly predictable. When they attack it will almost certainly be head on. They believe that a man should show courage in the face of his enemies. Whether they will rush straight into the attack now, I can't predict."

"Hmm, so what would you advise me to tell Kitchener?"

"Tell him exactly what you see. He will make his own mind up about predicting their actions."

The Colonel nodded and turned to an aide. "Get Churchill here. He can take a message to the Sirdar for me."

Lieutenant Churchill cantered up and slid his horse to stop next to the Colonel then saluted.

The Colonel looked at him coolly. "I don't like theatrics Mr Churchill and neither does Kitchener. Take this message to him and tell him exactly what you see out there. And ride your bloody horse properly I have none to spare if you injure that one. Captain McGuire, would you tell Churchill where to find Kitchener."

McGuire pointed out the landmarks to the young round faced officer and showed him where the Sirdar and his headquarters were located. Churchill saluted and wheeled his horse away, then rode towards the area where Kitchener was establishing his command post.

The Colonel sniffed and turned again to McGuire. "God only knows why Horse Guards saddled me with that man. His mother has influence of course and she got him sent. Bloody medal hunter if anyone asked me."

Churchill rode to the Sirdar and handed him the note. Kitchener read it and then asked, "How long do you think I've got?"

"An hour sir, maybe an hour and a half if they continue forward at their present rate."

"Return to your unit and make sure you keep me informed. Dismiss."

Kitchener rode forward to the ridge of Surkab and looked long and hard at the advancing army. At two in the afternoon he ordered the Anglo-Egyptian brigades to begin to advance. Minutes later the pickets of the 21st Lancers saw the whole Dervish army come to a halt. They screamed "Allahu Akbar" and fired their rifles into the air. Then the whole army sat down and began to start their cooking fires. There would be no battle that day.

The worry for Kitchener was that the Dervishes might attempt a night attack. If they managed it and the warriors got in amongst the troops there would be a massive slaughter even if they were beaten. The soldiers were instructed to lie down to sleep that night in their two rank firing lines with their rifles next to them.

During the afternoon the howitzers came into action and began to lob their heavy shells high into the air then down into Omdurman. Their target was the Mahdi's tomb. Their intention was to demoralise the Dervish army. Seven shells were fired with remarkable accuracy and the tomb was badly damaged with its dome cut off like the top of a boiled egg.

As darkness fell the Khalifa was unnerved by the searchlights from the gunboats that swept backwards and forwards across the plain. Asif and Yussuf had been walking through the army stopping at the cooking fires and spreading the word that Kitchener was intending to attack that night. They also spread the rumour that the searchlights were looking for the Khalifa himself. The Khalifa decided against a night attack and gave the order to his commanders.

"Let us attack in the morning after dawn prayers. Let us not be like mice or foxes, slinking into the holes by day and peeping out at night."

Chapter 62.
The Battle of Omdurman (First Attack)

At half past four in the morning the bugles sounded the 'stand to' and the infantry checked the load on their rifles as they formed up in their two ranks. It had rained in the night and they were cold and wet, most had not slept. The cavalry stood by their horses to eat a hasty breakfast and wait for the word to move. Kitchener expected the Dervishes to attack with the dawn and the men knew that an army of savage warriors, intent on their destruction, would be coming for them soon.

As the cavalry were ordered to move forward the Dervish army hidden behind Jabal Surkab were already on the move. Armed with their out dated, but still deadly blades and their poorly maintained rifles they were a force to be reckoned with as they jogged forward. They chanted their war cry in unison as fifty thousand men moved forward like the tide coming in. The front they occupied was just over five miles long with the divisions organised under their different coloured banners. The men of the Black Standard, twelve thousand strong, were held back in reserve to allow them to sweep forward and butcher the enemy as they inevitably fled the battlefield in disarray.

They advanced, fully convinced that the victory prophesied by the Mahdi was about to take place. Despite the defeat at Atbara they remained blissfully unaware of the power of the modern weapons they faced. They were secure in the knowledge of their own undoubted bravery and still believed the army they faced was made up of timid and cowardly people. They were utterly convinced this would be another victory like the massacre of the Hicks column all those years before.

The forward patrols of the 21st Lancers initially reported that the Dervish army was in place behind Jabal Surkab. It was only as the light strengthened they realised that they were actually on the move. They rapidly approached the Lancer's positions and Churchill, who commanded one of these forward posts, ordered his four men to open fire. They were the first shots of the battle that day. They mounted and rapidly rode back to the main army with the cavalry of the White Standard only three hundred yards away.

As the Dervishes crested the ridge that hid them from the *zariba* the first artillery opened fire. To Kitchener's surprise it was the Dervish guns that fired the first artillery rounds and two shells landed a little short of the waiting troops. The Anglo-Egyptian artillery returned fire and soon the shrapnel shells were bursting over the advancing tribesmen flinging ripped and broken bodies here and there. There was a moment of chaos as twenty shells burst among the Dervishes in less than sixty seconds.

Now the infantry could see the mass of advancing warriors the time for nervousness passed, as they could now concentrate on their work. The British troops stood silently in their two ranks and then the front rank dropped to the kneeling position. They watched as the enemy were pounded by the artillery, but never seemed to pause. They just kept on moving forward waving their banners and screaming defiance.

For the British 2nd Brigade, made up of the Rifle Regiment, the Lancashire and Northumberland Fusiliers plus the Grenadier Guards, it was their first sobering sight of the Dervish army in action. They braced themselves for the onslaught and then the gunboats out on the Nile joined in, sending shells plunging and crashing into the enemy ranks. For most of the troops the unbelievable bravery of the advancing men was a source of admiration. The advance never wavered as they were hammered by the artillery.

The Grenadier Guards were the first to open volley fire and the rounds sliced into the Dervishes with machine like precision. They were hand loading their rounds, saving the bullets in the magazine for closer quarters. The rest of the Brigade joined in and their line became a furnace of effective rifle fire. The soldiers could see that their fire was hitting the enemy as they saw them drop, but still nothing slowed the mad advance.

The Maxim guns joined in, tracking their fire backwards and forwards across the front of the Dervish army, until the cooling water around their barrels boiled dry. The infantry were firing twelve rounds a minute until their rifles became too hot to hold and replacement weapons had to be passed forward from the reserves.

The losses in the Dervish ranks were horrendous as whole families and tribal groups were wiped out. No European army would have dreamed of facing such a wall of fire, but still they came on. The soldiers began to believe that their enemy was invulnerable, but it was a false assumption. Lashed by shot and shell they never came closer than eight hundred yards before being slaughtered. Eventually they slowed, then started to try and move across to where the Sudanese were firing the slower Martini Henry rifles, but it was too late, the heart of the army had been destroyed and it began breaking up into smaller groups who recoiled into the desert behind them.

Realising that all was lost Osman Azraq assembled a mass of Baggara horsemen and leading from the front charged directly at a maxim battery. The whole brigade of riflemen as well as the maxims opened fire on the charging men. They were mown down in droves but not a man turned back and they died in front of the men they thought cowardly.

As the Dervish army retired one man refused to retreat. He remained alone firing at the British until a volley from the longer range Lee Metfords took him down. The battle was not yet over, but the smashing victory over the infidels that had been foretold was now a fading dream in the nightmare of slaughter.

Chapter 63.
The 21st Lancers

The Black Standard warriors held in reserve had still not come into action, but they remained a significant threat. A pursuit of the enemy would almost certainly provoke a confrontation with these fresh troops and the army would be on the move rather than in its prepared positions. Kitchener needed to know which way the enemy was retreating and the best way to move forward to Omdurman. He sent the 21st Lancers forward to find him the answers to both questions.

The Lancers, led by Lieutenant Colonel Rowland Martin, advanced at the walk in column of troops. Two patrols were scouting ahead of them. Lieutenant Grenfell rode out to the west to try and locate the enemy reserve while Lieutenant Pirie rode south beside the Omdurman road. After a little over a mile Pirie spotted a force of around a thousand Dervishes blocking his path. He did not know it, but these were the Beja tribesmen led by the old warrior Osman Digna. They had been sent out to deal with exactly the threat that the Lancers now posed.

Pirie's patrol returned to the main body to report. He was not aware that hidden behind the slight rise, where the Beja stood, was a deep wadi. His report stated that the enemy were standing on open ground. The Lancers numbered around four hundred and forty men so were outnumbered by two to one. For a cavalry attack in open country against infantry this was an acceptable ratio.

Martin ordered the regiment to trot and headed towards the waiting Beja.

When Martin came in sight of the Beja he estimated that there were no more than three hundred of them and assumed that the rest had dropped into hiding behind the rise. He was not to know that Osman Digna had used the small elapse of time to bring forward around two thousand Baggara spearmen and these were concealed in the wadi. The Lancers were now outnumbered by around six to one by men they would not see until the last moment. The trap had been well laid.

Martin wheeled the column to the East, riding across the face of the enemy as if to outflank them. As he did so the riflemen among the Beja opened fire. At a range of only three hundred yards the bullets started to find targets. Some horses bolted and a few men were knocked from their saddles. The order was given and the bugler sounded the command to 'wheel into line'. The sixteen troops turned rapidly into line with practised ease and were now facing the tribesmen. Martin looked along the ranks of his men and gave the order to gallop. As they spurred their horses forward, the gleaming lance tips came down and officers drew their sabres as they began what was to be the last ever regimental cavalry charge by British troops.

As they galloped forward across the red sand, Churchill sheathed his sabre and drew the Mauser pistol he had bought in London. His right shoulder had been dislocated, during his service in India, and was always slightly weak. When he looked up again the tribesmen were just one hundred yards away firing their Remington rifles as quickly as they were able. All along the line the long lances were dropping lower into the 'engage infantry' position.

At fifty yards, everything changed as the wadi came into view, filled with a dense mass of spear waving Dervish soldiers, who were rising from the ground and raising their banners. The trap became obvious to every man, but they were committed and could not turn back in time. Realising their danger the troopers spurred their horse to increase speed so that they could get through the mass of the enemy in the shortest time.

The four hundred and forty riders smashed into the Dervish line and the Beja who had stayed on the low rise were sent flying backwards into the wadi. The horses leapt from the lip of the wadi and dropped the four or five feet to the ground. Some horses stumbled and threw their riders who were instantly surrounded by screaming, hacking, stabbing warriors. A man that was unhorsed was doomed from that second.

Lances shattered as they were plunged into enemies and the troopers then drew their sabres to hack at the men who swarmed around them. Men were grabbed and dragged from the saddle to be slaughtered on the sand. Others rode through without a scratch. Churchill managed to force his way through to the far side of the wadi when he saw a warrior fall to the floor ready to hamstring his horse as it went over him. He leaned forward and fired two shots into the man before starting to struggle up the far bank. A warrior with a raised sword ran at him and Churchill shot him in the forehead, the range was so close that the barrel of the pistol actually struck the man's face.

The remains of the regiment began to assemble at the far side of the wadi. Dervishes leapt out of the low ground to pursue them and were met with a rattle of carbine fire as the troopers dismounted to cover the escape of their comrades. The action in the Wadi had taken less than two minutes during which the regiment had been badly mauled. Seventy one men had been killed, and three Victoria Crosses had been won.

Chapter 64.
The Attack of the Black Standard.

The 1st Egyptian Brigade marched away from the remaining five brigades, around to the west of Jabal Surkab. Somewhere behind that hill the Black Standard division of the Dervish army was still being held back in reserve. The Khalifa had held them back to deliver the final killing blow to the enemy, but now they were the last defence of Omdurman. The Black Standard outnumbered the Egyptian Brigade by five to one although they were mostly armed with swords and broad bladed spears. The three thousand men of the 2nd Egyptian, 9th, 10th and 11th Sudanese battalions were armed with the hard hitting Martini Henry rifle and had artillery and Maxim guns to support them.

Abdallahi, the Khalifa, was indecisive and wasted time considering whether to commit the Black Standard or to wait for the return of his son with his ten thousand riflemen. The riflemen of the Green Standard had been diverted and led a merry dance by the Egyptian cavalry that they had pursued away from the main battle. Ya'gub the commander of the Black Standard had his men drawn up ready to move and was waiting with mounting impatience. He saw the flags of the Green Standard away to the north, but knew they were too far away to be of immediate use to him.

Eventually Ya'gub snapped at the sight of his cousin's torn body being carried from the field. He leapt into the saddle and rode along the front of his division screaming his defiance. He gave the order to advance and, with a roar from his men, the Black Standard division moved forward to wreak its revenge.

MacDonald, in command of the Egyptian Brigade saw the banners before he saw the tribesmen. His lookouts had already spotted the Green Standard division behind him and although he knew they were tired they would soon become a problem. He sent a despatch rider to the 3rd Egyptian Division requesting reinforcements, but they had other problems and were unable to help. Knowing that he was in danger of being caught between the two Dervish divisions he decided to attack and defeat each one in turn. He ordered his eighteen field guns and eight Maxim guns to be run out to the front of the division.

The Dervishes were advancing at a walk with Ya'gub leading from the front on his horse. The Egyptian division waited calmly until the enemy were only eleven hundred yards away before MacDonald gave the order for the guns to open fire. The high explosive and shrapnel shells and the rapid fire from the Maxim guns decimated the Dervish lines. The noise was horrendous and men were falling all along the line, but still they came on. As they neared, the infantry stepped forward in line with the guns and opened disciplined volley fire.

Kitchener rode forward to the top of Jabal Surkab and looked down on the battle that was developing below. He urgently sent for the 1st British and 3rd Egyptian brigades to move across to form a continuous line to prevent MacDonald being outflanked. McGuire, sitting his camel behind Kitchener, could see that there would be a time before the two brigades could be in position and MacDonald risked being swamped. Without waiting for orders he waved his troop to follow him and they trotted down the slope of the hill to MacDonald's flank.

They dismounted and formed a ragged firing line on the lower slopes. The thin line of twenty three men could not hope to stop the vast array of warriors moving forward, but the sudden torrent of fire from an unexpected direction did slow them for a few precious moments. McGuire had his men concentrate their accurate fire on the Emirs and banner men, to spread as much confusion as possible.

Broadwood's Camel Corps rode in as fast as they could to take position on MacDonald's right flank and the guns of the 32nd Royal Artillery Battery were dragged up at the gallop to take position alongside McGuire's small troop. They rapidly positioned their fifteen pounder field guns and Maxims before unleashing a hail of fire on the Dervish flank. The flank of the Black Standard recoiled under the onslaught and began to retreat.

The rest of the Black Standard pressed forward towards MacDonald's steady line until they were close enough for the guns to load case shot. The case shot turned the guns into huge shot guns and sprayed a mass of high speed metal balls into the Dervishes. With the intensity of the fire it was impossible for men to stand and take it, yet they did. Ya'gub himself was thrown from his saddle by a burst of fire from a Maxim gun. He was probably dead before he hit the ground. His men tried to pick him up, but they too were mown down. Incredibly, some of the Dervishes managed to get within range to throw their spears before being slaughtered by the intense fire.

As the attack of the Black Standard division slowed and started to collapse MacDonald realised he was now coming under fire from behind. The Green Standard had arrived. Realising the danger MacDonald wheeled one of his battalion out of the line to face the new threat and deployed his reserve alongside them. Once he was convinced that the original enemy division had lost momentum he redeployed some of his guns. The riflemen of the Green Standard had the range now and their Remington's were doing significant damage to the Egyptian troops.

McGuire and his men left their position on the hillside and ran across the rear of MacDonald's division to take a position to the left of the 9th Sudanese. They took a kneeling position and opened fire. The fire from the Remingtons intensified and McGuire saw two of his men go down. As he looked behind him he could see the first of the British battalions moving towards him at the double and recognised the Lincolns. The Dervishes were only a hundred yards away as the Lincolns arrived winded from their long run across the desert floor. They took a moment to control their laboured breathing before opening rapid fire.

McGuire watched as the accurate fire of the Lincolns took effect and the attack of the Green Standard faltered, then ground to a halt. The riflemen began to retreat stopping every few yards to fire back at the British. It was one of these final rounds that smashed into McGuire's shoulder and flung him to the ground. For a moment he felt nothing, then the pain burned into him like a red hot branding iron. In seconds, Jones was at his side placing a crude dressing into the wound.

"Thank you, Jones. You know, I was beginning think I was going to get away with it after all."

"Never fuss sir. It's gone right through and missed the bones. It's going to hurt like hell, but it will heal."

"That's good. Do you have any water? My throat is as dry as the desert."

Jones turned to remove the water bottle from his belt and then grunted as he fell forward onto his face. McGuire leaned forward and rolled the man over. His face was a mass of blood and tissue where the round had passed through the back of his head and out of his forehead. He felt sick, looking down at one of his original few men

McGuire looked around to see Macklin coming towards him. The Corporal paused and looked down at Jones before lifting McGuire to his feet.

"Look at this sir. You wouldn't want to miss it."

McGuire leaned on Macklin's shoulder and looked to where the man was pointing. Around four hundred of the Baggara horse had broken from the retreating mob and were forming up to charge. They raised their swords and spears then gave a screaming war cry as they kicked their horses into a gallop. The Sudanese battalions and the Lincolns fired a massive volley and the charge was over. Not a single horseman made it to the lines they had been charging.

"You know sir. When we get home nobody is going to believe this. How the hell could anybody be that brave? It makes no sense."

"You're right, but we'll know. Everybody who has stood and watched a Dervish charge is never going to forget it."

Chapter 65.
Omdurman.

Even before the Black Standard had moved forward to their doom, the Khalifa had realised that the battle was lost and his regime was effectively over. He was shocked when he heard of the death of Ya'gub and went into his tent to sit on his saddle fleece and await his death, in the traditional Sudanese way. Osman Digna arrived at his tent and persuaded him this was not the way to die. He mounted his white donkey and rode back into Omdurman with others of his defeated army.

The Khalifa was praying in the wreckage of the Mahdi's tomb when he heard that Kitchener was entering the city. Stunned as he was, he pulled himself together and ordered a general evacuation before he too rode away.

Kitchener rode into the city flanked by the men of one of the Fellaheen battalions and accompanied by his staff. McGuire with his left arm in a sling rode behind him at the head of the remaining Reconnaissance Troop. A shrapnel shell from one of the gunboats on the Nile burst overhead, raining metal fragments down and killing the correspondent of the Times newspaper. A second and third shell ploughed into the city and Kitchener beat a hasty retreat after first ordering McGuire to secure the Khalifa's palace and the Dervish Treasury.

Guided by Asif, the troop rode through the empty streets to the palace and rode their camels into the courtyard. They dismounted and walked through the large open front door. They were all amazed by the opulence inside the building when compared to the scruffy buildings that surrounded it. McGuire put guards on the entrance with orders that nobody was to enter without his express permission. Then he and Donnelly's and Park's patrols, accompanied by Yussuf and Asif walked in to clear the building of any remaining Dervishes.

They worked their way through the warren of connected rooms until they came to the inner courtyard. Here a garden with tinkling water had been built to provide a cool place in the cruel summer heat of the Sudan. They crossed the courtyard and came to the inner sanctum where only the Khalifa and his brother Ya'gub had been allowed to enter. Donnelly booted open the door and it crashed back on its hinges. Inside they found the Khalifa's harem with his wives and concubines cowering back against the walls.

McGuire stood and stared at the terrified women, then looked round at his men. He could see why these tough, dirty men would frighten women who had been cloistered here for years.

"Sergeant Parks."

"Yes sir."

"Set a guard on these rooms. Make sure these women do not get molested in any way. Is that clear?"

"Yes sir. No funny business."

"Right. Then get them cooking us a decent meal. I need a break from canned bully beef. Yussuf will translate for you."

McGuire turned away from the room where the women were and looked around at other passages that led into the building. "Where's Asif got to, Sergeant Donnelly?"

"He was here a minute ago sir. Should I go and find him?"

"No, he can look after himself. Start looking for somewhere the men can sleep. Try and find somewhere without bed bugs."

As the Sergeant and his patrol left, McGuire stood looking around the garden and compared it to the Dublin slum he had grown up in. It was another world, yet Europeans looked down on the Arabs. He shook his head and turned to find Asif walking towards him with his rifle slung across his back.

"English, you should come with me."

"Lead on my friend. What have you found?"

"You will see. This way."

Asif led the way through a dark winding corridor to a wooden door studded with heavy iron bolts. He pushed the door open and ushered McGuire inside. A wooden torch burned in a wall mounting to one side of the room, casting a flickering light across the boxes and tables that were scattered around. Asif walked to where one of the boxes rested on heavy wooden table and turned to look at McGuire.

"What have you found my keen eyed friend?"

Asif flipped the box lid open and stepped back. "We have found the treasury of the Dervishes, English. These boxes have gold coins.

Those against the wall have jewels of every type and the big ones at the back are filled with precious silks. There are weapons with jewels in the hilt and other precious things."

McGuire looked down at the box and ran his fingers through the gold coins. He watched as Asif opened three more boxes of coins and then started to open the jewel boxes.

"We are rich men English."

McGuire shook his head. "This is more than an honest man needs my friend."

"Then what do we do?"

McGuire ran his hand across his head and then looked at Asif who stood waiting patiently. "When we have killed a man it is honourable to take his gold, but this is different. We have been told to come here and to secure the treasury for the Sirdar. To take the gold for ourselves would be dishonourable. Tell each of the men they can take one small thing as a souvenir to show their grandchildren, when they tell their stories around the fire. Then we send word to the Sirdar to come and take the treasure of the Khalifa."

Asif nodded slowly. "It shall be as you say, English."

They heard boots in the corridor and Donnelly came in through the door. "Trouble outside sir. Corporal Macklin asks if you can come to the front door please."

"Why? What's happening?"

"There's an officer trying to get in and he's upset with the bayonets pointing at his chest."

"Right I'll go and see what's happening. Sergeant, stay here and help Asif, I've told him what to do."

McGuire left the room and walked briskly through the corridor and out into the garden. He crossed into the first part of the building and found Macklin and two of his men standing in the doorway.

"Corporal Macklin, what's the problem?"

"Sir, we had an officer turn up at the door and demand to come in. I told him about my orders and he told me to get out of his way. When he tried to go by I had the men stop him and now he says he's going to have all three of us shot."

"Well done Corporal. Nobody is getting shot for obeying orders today. Where is he now?"

"He's in the outer courtyard pacing about and waiting for you."

"Thank you. I'll go and see him and explain things."

McGuire walked out into the sunshine and for a couple of seconds was dazzled by the brightness. He turned to see the officer walking towards him and then recognized who it was.

"Captain Storr-Lessing. I might have known it would be you threatening my men."

"McGuire! Get your bloody men out of my way."

"Why would I do that?"

"We've taken the city. The plunder is ours for the taking and I am going to have my share of the spoils of war."

McGuire shook his head. "Not here, you're not. We are here guarding the treasury for the Sirdar. Go and look somewhere else for your plunder."

"Don't you dare speak to me like that you guttersnipe! Get out of my way. I will have my due."

McGuire sighed and called to Macklin. "Corporal, are your men loaded?"

"Yes sir, always."

"Then if this officer attempts to enter the building you have my authority to shoot him." He turned back to Storr-Lessing. "You heard that? Well I was entirely serious. Now leave before your dignity suffers more, when I have them throw you into the street."

Storr-Lessing flushed a deep red. "You scum from a Dublin sewer. You haven't heard the last of this. I'll pay you back. You see if I don't."

Two hours later every man of the Reconnaissance Troop could feel the weight of the souvenirs in his pocket and had a smile on his face. They had been sworn to secrecy and none of them was going to speak a word about the items McGuire had let them take. They presented arms as Kitchener rode in through the gate and then McGuire gave him a guided tour of the palace.

The Sirdar was quiet as he stood in the doorway of the harem and saw the food being prepared there. When McGuire led him into the treasury he was delighted at the booty that would now swell the depleted coffers of the army.

As he was about to leave, he turned to McGuire. "You've done well Captain. Now I have a small favour to ask of you."

"Anything sir."

"I'm going to go across the river to Khartoum now and I would like you to come with me. We are about to have a remembrance service for Gordon, but before that I'd like you to walk me through where he was killed."

"What about my men sir?"

"They can come along as well, they have earned it throughout the campaign. The Paymaster and the Commissary Officers will take over the treasury, the Provost will guard it. Then Engineers are going to demolish the Mahdi's tomb."

"What will you do with the Mahdi's remains sir?"

"I'm going to have his bones thrown into the Nile as a lesson to the Mahdists and for causing us all this trouble."

"Good. That's what they did to Gordon all those years ago. However, sir, before we go the men would be honoured if you would eat with us."

Kitchener gave one his rare smiles. "Thank you Captain, I would be delighted to eat with you. It will make a pleasant change from damned bully beef."

Chapter 66.
To Cairo

Later in the day, Kitchener stood, with McGuire, in silence by the stairs where Gordon had died. He scanned around him and took in the ruination of what had once been a fine building. He walked through Gordon's rooms and picked over a few items, but there was nothing left from the man they had tried to rescue all those years before.

The next day there was a moving memorial service for Gordon that took place in the grounds of the ruined governor's residence. Detachments from all the contingents of the army took part and at the end the Egyptian and British flags were raised alongside each other.

As the service ended Kitchener called McGuire to him. "Captain, you and your troop have given sterling service to this campaign and I want to thank you for it. You have been committed without a break since we started, so now I would like you to be the first element that goes back up north. Transport has been arranged to get you all the way to Cairo as quickly as possible."

"That's very good of you sir. The men will appreciate it."

"One thing though. When you get there get yourself a new uniform. I would hate to have you sew the ribbon of the DSO on such a disgraceful article as that jacket."

"I beg your pardon sir?"

"The confirmation came through by wire this morning. You have been awarded the

411

Distinguished Service Order and your Sergeant Donnelly has been given the Distinguished Conduct Medal, on your recommendation."

"Thank you sir, he deserves it."

The journey north to Cairo was long and uncomfortable in the sweltering heat, but Kitchener had given orders that the troop were to be given every assistance and, at every halt, there was a transport officer waiting to move them on as rapidly as possible.

They arrived in Cairo, in the middle of October 1898, and unloaded their camels from the train. They rode through the thronging streets to the barracks and let the animals drink their fill, then fed them on the sweet grass they had growing behind the building. Once his men were settled McGuire walked to the barrack gate and summoned a gharry to take him home. As he neared the white villa on the side of the Nile he could hear children playing in the garden. They must be almost twelve by now he thought, it had been almost three years since he had seen them. He opened the gate and stepped in. The children looked up from their game and before he could speak they beat a hasty retreat round to the terrace. He walked down the path after them and Emma met him at the top of the stairs.

"Michael?"

She ran down the stone steps and flung herself into his arms. He held her close and whispered in her ear. She snuggled closer then pulled back and looked him up and down.

"No wonder the children were startled, you look awful and by the way you smell of camels. I'll get Achmed to run you a bath and he can shave that awful beard off as well. Then maybe the children will recognise you."

McGuire nodded and walked wearily to one of the chairs that overlooked the river. Now, with the war over, he would have time to spend with his small family and maybe get to know his children again. He and his men had been promised a decent leave before they started to bring the troop back up to strength, to replace the men they had lost in the Sudan.

Emma came back out of the house and shook his shoulder to wake him. "Your bath is ready and I've told Achmed to get some clean clothes for you. I don't really want those filthy things in my house."

He smiled and nodded obediently. Here his authority meant nothing, this was Emma's domain. He lay in the bath and watched the grime float off his body. Then he drained the bath and waited as Achmed cleaned and refilled it. It took three times before he felt clean enough to walk back out to the terrace. His face looked strange, with pale skin where his beard had been, contrasting with the dark sunburned area that had been exposed to the sun for so long.

He settled back in his chair and sighed as he looked out over the peaceful Nile with its native boats sailing serenely past. He was looking forward to the ordered rhythms of peacetime soldiering after all the excitement and tension of

413

war. Most of all he was looking forward to time with his family.

No Road To Khartoum – Factual Content

As with all my books I like to give the reader a chapter on the actual facts I have used, to allow you to make a judgement on whether my story is credible. This book is no exception and so some of the facts about this remarkable campaign are laid out below.

In my 'Jim Wilson' series of books I decided to use the more logical American spellings. Given the time and place of this book I decided to stay with the Queen's English. I hope my American readers will understand and forgive me.

The Sudan campaign breaks down into two major elements spread over a number of years. The British were dragged into Egypt initially to secure their access to the Suez Canal and the all-important trade route to India. This 'protection' mission expanded until the British were effectively running Egypt and its colony in the Sudan. The first campaign involved sending General Gordon to Khartoum as the Governor General of the Sudan, in response to the Dervish uprising led by the Mahdi. He was intended to evacuate the Egyptians and the Europeans; this did not go well and a British Army relief force was, eventually, despatched to rescue him. After appreciable delays, the relief force was ready to make its final advance on Khartoum when the news arrived that the city had fallen to the Mahdi and Gordon was dead.

Years later a second campaign to end the rebellion in the Sudan was mounted and this was successful. This time the lessons had been learned about desert warfare and the remarkable fighting prowess and courage of the Dervishes. The British and Egyptian armies were well prepared and well supplied. The Egyptian army in particular had been reformed and retrained in the years between the campaigns. The soldiers were properly treated, equipped and paid. The corrupt officers who had done so much damage had been replaced with competent men and the Egyptian army of 1898 was now a force to be reckoned with. The Grenadier Guards were involved in both campaigns and were effective in both.

There are misconceptions about the reason for the rebellion. It has been portrayed as an Islamic uprising and possibly a Jihad. This is only partially true. The people of the Sudan had been mistreated for years by their Egyptian masters. They had been hugely over taxed. They had been robbed, dispossessed and their women had been ravished. There was understandably huge discontent in the country and the Mahdi brought this into focus. He had a couple of small victories that proved to the Sudanese people that he was in fact "The Expected One" and a true successor to the prophet. The warlike tribes flocked to his banner and made him a force to be reckoned with. Once his power was more certain he imposed strict Islamic discipline on his people. Some of his followers used the modern weapons they captured; others scorned these and retained the swords and spears of their heritage. In both cases they were formidable warriors.

There are many misconceptions about the British Army at the end of the 19th Century and I have tried to highlight some more accurate facts in my story. Many officers at the time were from the upper reaches of society, particularly in the Guards and Cavalry regiments. They were not the amateurs of earlier years and the more intelligent ones established relationships of mutual respect with their soldiers. Promotion by purchase had been abolished and was now based on seniority and merit, although friends in high places did not hurt. The soldiers were usually less educated, but they were far from being untrained. A soldier was given twelve weeks of training as he joined the Army with at least a week spent concentrating on musketry. Training continued after joining the regiment with battle drills and field days that were designed to make the British soldier among the best in the world.

It is true that Garnet Wolseley raised a force of picked men for the Gordon Relief Force rather than taking whole battalions as had been the practice in the past. He knew the conditions would be harsh and difficult, so needed men who could withstand those conditions, for a prolonged period, and still fight at the end of it. He formed these men into four Camel Regiments and these formed the Camel Corps. Men from the Heavy Cavalry regiments formed the Heavy Camel Regiment, the Light Cavalry formed the Light Camel Regiment and men from Line Infantry battalions formed the Mounted Infantry Camel Regiment. The Guards, with a detachment from the Marines, formed the

Guards Camel Regiment. The Corps when fully formed had 1700 men and 94 officers.

It was possible then for a gifted soldier to rise from the ranks and become an officer, much as it is today. Major General Sir Hector MacDonald, for instance, began his career as a private soldier in the ranks of the Gordon Highlanders and later commanded the Highland Brigade. In these days, before the awarding of gallantry medals to non-commissioned ranks became common, the reward for courage and significant acts was often promotion and battlefield commissions could be awarded by senior officers.

As in all nations, the backbone of the army is the Non Commissioned Officer (NCO). These men would train and drill the soldiers and control them in detail during battle. They would also bring good men to the attention of their superiors, for the good of the regiment.

A couple of points to clarify about ranks. In the British Army a Lance Corporal is normally addressed as Corporal when speaking directly to him. Likewise a Lieutenant Colonel is addressed as Colonel. Brevet rank for officers is nowadays known as 'acting' rank and can be removed at any time. An officer granted a brevet rank would have to wait for his promotion to be confirmed from London before he was secure in his new grade. It was possible at the time to have a brevet rank two or even three steps above the permanent rank held.

To try and place my story as historically accurately as possible I have drawn on a number of sources, some written by people who were actually there. The most notable of these sources are:-

"With The Camel Corps Up The Nile" by Edward Gleichen. Gleichen was a junior Grenadier Guards officer and served in the Guards' Camel Regiment. He wrote a first rate personal account of his experiences during the campaign to rescue General Gordon from Khartoum. He made a point of only writing about what he actually saw and did, so avoiding opinions about the politics and strategy involved. He ended his military career some years later with the rank of Major General.

"Khartoum – The Ultimate Imperial Adventure" by Michael Asher. An ex-member of the Parachute Regiment who lived in the Sudan for ten years, he has a real feel for his subject and has written a well-researched, detailed and very readable account of both major campaigns. The bibliography list of sources he has drawn on is impressive. He does cover the political issues that decided the campaigns should be mounted so has a wider perspective than the Gleichen book.

"Kitchener" by John Pollock. Herbert Kitchener was a key player in the Gordon Relief Expedition as an intelligence officer and advanced scout. Years later he became the Sirdar of the Egyptian Army and as such was in command of the second campaign.

"The River War" by Winston Churchill. The future Prime Minister managed to get himself attached to the 21st Lancers as a supernumerary officer for the second campaign, despite the objection of Kitchener. While with the 21st, he took part in the last full charge ever completed by a British cavalry regiment, at the battle of Omdurman.

"Khartoum Campaign 1898" by Bennet Burleigh. Burleigh was a reporter for the Daily Telegraph and travelled forward with the troops during the second campaign. He endured many of the privations and difficulties faced by the troops and witnessed their actions first hand. In later years he strongly defended the troops against false accusations of war crimes by politically motivated people. A pity an honest person like him is not around today to defend our military personnel from such vultures.

The Martini Henry rifle was a single shot breech loading weapon and a major improvement on previous muzzle loading rifles. The bullet was a .477 and so delivered a massive wound to any enemy. It was possible for a skilled soldier to hit targets out to 600 yards although most men would have struggled with this.

The Nordenfelt machine gun was a magazine fed, multi barrelled weapon that was fired by working a lever backwards and forwards. It came in a number of configurations with varying numbers of barrels. The version most likely to have been used during the early campaigns in the Sudan was the five barrel version. Other, larger, versions were mounted on ships and some were intended to intercept torpedo attacks.

The Krupp Mountain Gun was a small light weight cannon that could be broken down rapidly and carried on one or two mules. To save weight it had no recoil mechanism, so the whole gun would run backwards on firing and need to be repositioned for each shot.

The Lee Metford rifle was the first magazine rifle issued to British troops. With an eight round magazine it was designed to be fired and loaded by hand as the Martini Henry had been. The magazine was used as a reserve for close quarter battle. Since the magazine was slow to load, this method ensured that a steady fire could be maintained. This was also the first rifle, used by the British army, which used smokeless ammunition. The absence of dense clouds of white smoke allowed the soldiers to fire far more accurately.

The Maxim gun was a more advanced machine gun that had replaced the Nordenfelt, in British service, by the time of the re-conquest of the Sudan in 1898. The mechanism of the Maxim gun employed one of the earliest recoil-operated firing systems in history. The idea is that the energy from recoil acting on the breech block is used to eject each spent cartridge and insert the next one, instead of a hand-operated mechanism. It was found to be particularly effective at the battle of Omdurman.

The Gardner gun was an early type of mechanical machine gun. It saw action in the Mahdist War, in the Sudan, notably at the Battle of Abu Klea, where its mechanism proved vulnerable to the environmental conditions of loose sand and dust.

The Webley Revolver was, in various marks, a standard issue service pistol for the armed forces of the United Kingdom, and the British Empire and Commonwealth, from 1887 until 1963. Firing large .455 Webley cartridges, Webley service revolvers are among the most powerful top-break revolvers ever produced. The W.G. or Webley-Government models produced from 1885 through to the early 1900s, were the most popular of the commercial top break revolvers and many were the private purchase choice of British military officers and target shooters in the period.

The Kaskara was a type of sword characteristic of Sudan, Chad, and Eritrea and was probably the type most commonly carried by the Dervish soldiers of the Mahdi. The blade of the kaskara was usually about a yard long, double edged and with a spatula like tip.

The Distinguished Conduct Medal was instituted by Royal Warrant on 4 December 1854, during the Crimean War, as an award to Warrant Officers, Non-Commissioned Officers and men for "distinguished, gallant and good conduct in the field". For all ranks below commissioned officers, it was the second highest award for gallantry in action after the Victoria Cross, and the other ranks' equivalent of the Distinguished Service Order, which was awarded to commissioned officers for bravery. Prior to the institution of this decoration, there had been no medal awarded by the British government in recognition of individual acts of gallantry in the Army.

The Distinguished Service Order was instituted on 6 September 1886 by Queen Victoria in a Royal Warrant published in *The London*

Gazette on 9 November, the first DSOs awarded were dated 25 November 1886. It is usually awarded to officers ranked Major or above, but the honour has sometimes been awarded to especially valorous junior officers.

The mantra quoted for the Drill Sergeant such as - "Today I am going to teach you the right wheel. The purpose of the Right Wheel is to allow a single soldier or body of men to wheel to the right in a smart, soldier like and uniform manner." – may sound strange, but these are exactly the words that were used by my Drill Sergeant during basic training at Poperinghe Barracks, near Reading in Berkshire.

The Nile crocodile is known to be aggressive and daring, even when compared to other crocodiles. Since the completion of the Aswan Dam the number of these animals in the lower Nile has declined, but they are still a danger. The one actually shot by officers of the Camel Corps during their voyage south measured thirteen feet, so I know they grew to this size during this time. The largest one I have seen was not quite this size.

At the battle of Abu Klea I have described a lone horseman charging against the Grenadier detachment and being shot down by McGuire. The incident did actually take place and a single horseman did charge the square. Whatever his reasons for making such a hopeless charge, his actions were admired as hugely courageous by the British troops who saw it. In fact, while having no love for their enemies, the British had now formed a grudging respect for the remarkable courage of these desert warriors, which was to stay with them through the first campaign and into the second.

Casualties on the British side in this engagement were as I have described them. The losses to the Dervish side were horrendous. Modern rifles and early Gardner and Nordenfelt machine guns slaughtered the men armed mostly with swords and spears. Some of the Mahdi's troops had rifles taken from the Egyptian column they had massacred, but they were in poor condition and the ammunition they had was also poor, some of it being homemade. There is no doubt about the incredible courage of the Dervish army, but their complete lack of tactical understanding of modern warfare cost them dear.

The saddles issued to the British were of two types, neither of them were very good. If improperly adjusted they caused large sores on the camel that festered if not treated. Initially the troops tried grooming their mounts like horses. The camels did not appreciate this and often kicked or bit their groomer. The more knowledgeable Arabs smeared mud on their animals, since this kept some of the biting insects at bay and may have protected them somewhat from the heat. The water skins were also a problem. They are intended to leak a little to keep the water inside at a drinkable temperature. The British struggled to maintain them to stop all the water running out. Again the Arabs were more knowledgeable and used their own methods, including the use of camel dung, to patch the leaks.

In the action at Abu Kru, I have described a bullet passing through a man's beard and another being stopped by a brass button. Both of these may sound fanciful, but both actually occurred and were reported on by Gleichen. The commander of the column, Sir Herbert Stewart, was indeed shot in the groin and command did pass to Sir Charles Wilson, who decided on the advance to the river.

I do not know if Khartoum had cisterns that were filled by the river although it does seem likely. Further north, around Luxor, I have seen massive cisterns that were filled in the way I describe, so it would make sense for a walled city to be equipped in the same way. Just before the final assault on the city it is known that food supplies were running very short and there was starvation. Even the defending soldiers were weakened by being on short rations.

It is true that Gordon sent his aide, Colonel Stewart, and various Europeans and Egyptians down river on the last steamer, the *Abbas*, out of Khartoum. With him he sent his code book and despatches. It is rumoured that he also gave him a ruby encrusted ring. The steamer fought its way through the Dervishes until it ran aground on a rock near the island of *Umm Dwermat*. Stewart and three others were invited ashore by people from the *Manasir* tribe who professed loyalty. There, in the house of a holy man who was a fervent Dervish supporter, they were attacked by forty or fifty *Manasir* who hacked them to death with swords and daggers. One of the party, Hassan Bey, begged for his life and was spared because he was a

425

Muslim. The rest of the people from the steamer were then attacked and slaughtered. The *Manasir* then boarded the steamer itself, but found only the wife of one of the Greeks aboard. She managed to shoot three of them before she was speared to death and her body thrown into the Nile.

In my story Haroun says he has seen a steamer on the Nile that came close to Khartoum then turned around. This did actually happen. Two days after the fall of the city the British sent a small advance detachment of troops from the Royal Sussex Regiment on a steamer to give the people of Khartoum confidence. They arrived just too late and when they saw that no flags flew in the city they turned back. To make sure they were recognised as British, this small detachment wore red jackets for the only time during the Relief campaign.

There are a number of accounts of how General Gordon died. I have chosen the version that allowed Michael McGuire to see it and which was used in the movie "Khartoum". However, I cannot guarantee that this is accurate

The Royal Irish Fusiliers were a part of the British Garrison of Egypt in the period of the Gordon Relief Expedition. They were there as part of the British force that was to ensure that the Suez Canal, a vital shipping link to India and the Far East, stayed open to British ships. Their presence also allowed Britain to exercise direct influence over the government of Egypt.

Osborne House is a former royal residence in East Cowes, Isle of Wight, United Kingdom. The house was built between 1845 and 1851 for Queen Victoria and Prince Albert as a summer home and rural retreat. Prince Albert designed the house himself in the style of an Italian Renaissance palazzo. The builder was Thomas Cubitt, the London architect and builder whose company built the main façade of Buckingham Palace for the royal couple in 1847.

Major Reginald Wingate of the Royal Artillery was in fact a very successful and effective Intelligence officer in Egypt at this time. He later became a General and Sirdar of the Egyptian army.

It is true that the Mahdi died shortly after Gordon. It may have been disease although there are strong suggestions that he was poisoned. Abdallahi wad Torshayn was the first person to recognise Mohammad Ahmad as the Mahdi or "Expected One". He took over on the death of his leader and took the title of Khalifa. His leadership was not unchallenged and he imposed his will by using savage tribesmen from the Baggara. This was much resented by the tribes who in the past had looked down on the Baggara as mere nomads.

Osman Digna was one of the few successful Mahdist generals. He escaped after the Battle of Omdurman and returned to the Red Sea hills where he stayed at large until 1900 when he was captured. He was imprisoned at Rosetta and Tura but released in 1924 to make the hajj. He died in 1926 at Wadi Haifa.

Lieutenant Edward Cator did exist and he did carry out the survey of the desert that later allowed Kitchener to have a railway built across that inhospitable region. He also found water that would make it possible for the steam trains to run, carrying less of their own. Sadly he contracted typhoid and died, bringing a halt to a promising career.

It is perhaps understandable that the British give more attention to the few British troops involved in the conquest of the Sudan, but this gives a distorted view. It can be argued that the conquest of the Sudan was a British victory, for the designers of the military and political strategy were British. The Egyptian army was remodelled by British officers and British infantry and artillery did play a significant part at Atbara and Omdurman. Yet, in my view, it is unfair to say that the re-conquest was a British victory, it was the Egyptian army that bore the brunt of the fighting and won the battles.

The Battle of Adowa took place in early March 1896 during which the Italians were soundly beaten by Ethiopian forces. Some reports claim that Italians, taken prisoner at this battle, were castrated, others deny this and claim they were well treated. The Askari troops fighting for the Italians who were captured were regarded by the Ethiopians as traitors and many had their right hand and left foot cut off as punishment. Appreciable numbers did not survive this punishment. It is also true that the Italians asked the British for aid in deflecting the attention of the Mahdists in the Sudan and on the 12th March, Lord

Salisbury, the Prime Minister issued orders to move into northern Sudan. Kitchener received these orders in the early hours of the 13th March and apparently was so overjoyed to be proved right he danced a jig with Captain Watson of the 60th Rifles, who brought him the message.

As with many places in the Sudan at this time spellings of place names vary, Firka can also be found spelled as Ferkeh or Firket. It was the first significant engagement of the reconquest and the battle took place on the 7th June 1896. It held between 3000 and 4000 Mahdist soldiers and was protected by a mud brick wall. The Egyptian army approached in two columns, the infantry following the Nile and the cavalry, horse artillery and Camel Corps crossing the desert and swinging in from the south east. Losses were disproportionate. The Dervishes lost between 800 and 1500 killed, including 44 emirs with some 500 wounded and around 600 taken prisoner. The Egyptian army had some 20 soldiers killed and a little over 80 wounded.

The short sharp action led by Major Burns-Murdoch did take place, much as I have described it, although I have taken the liberty of moving it in time a little and involving the Reconnaissance Troop. The courage of the Egyptian cavalry, in the face of such numbers, is remarkable and reflects considerable credit on them. The number of dead and injured on the Egyptian side is accurate.

The battle of Hafir happened much as I have described it and once again proved the courage of the Dervish troops as well as the skill and daring of the Egyptians. The gunboats on the Nile at the battle were commanded by Commander Stanley Colville RN, who was wounded with a bullet to the wrist. One of those boats was commanded by Lieutenant David Beatty who rose in later years to become the First Sea Lord, the head of the Royal Navy.

The advance to Dongola, and the taking of the town, completed the capture of the northern province of the Sudan. This was the extent of the instructions that Kitchener had been given. He realised that if the Dervish army counter attacked in full force he did not have sufficient men to hold what he had gained. He therefore left shortly after taking Dongola and travelled to London. With the support of Queen Victoria he managed to persuade the British government to grant him funds to continue the campaign and to continue the desert railway that had been so ably planned by Lieutenant Cator. He was also given permission to call for British troops if he felt they were required to reinforce the Egyptians.

It is true that Sheikh 'Abdallah wad Sa'ad sent a letter to the Egyptian army asking for support. It is also true that Major General Rundle sent a caravan of weapons and ammunition that arrived too late. Why the Sheikh also wrote to the Khalifa will never be known, but it certainly resulted in the attack and massacre of Metemma by around twelve thousand Baggara tribesmen.

The battle at Abu Hamed took place much as I have described it. However the officer who rode forward, rather bravely, to reconnoitre the trenches was actually a Major Kincaid.

It is true that the Baggara in Metemma refused to move when called on to reinforce Abu Hamed and it is also true that Emir Zaki 'Osman grew tired of waiting for them and abandoned Berber. The Egyptian forces under Hunter did just walk into the town without a shot being fired. In 1885 Wolseley had been unable to take the town, but now things were moving in a different way.

The lead up to the battle of Atbara was marked by bad decisions made by Mahmud, despite advice from the more experienced leaders under his command. His choice of a place to stop and defend was very poor and the experienced warlord Osman Digna did withdraw his troops when it became clear to him that there would be a massacre. It is unclear why the Khalifa appointed such a young and inexperienced man to this command, but it may well have been because of his loyalty, at a time when others were beginning to seem doubtful. The battle itself was short and intense with much courage and slaughter. I have described it as accurately as possible, though I have taken a liberty by having Corporal Parks save the life of Mahmud. This was actually done by

Major Franks of the Royal Artillery and took considerable courage, in the face of the enraged Sudanese troops.

The Khalifa did decide not to mount a night attack during the battle of Omdurman, but this was not from fear. Although he was confident of victory he was also aware that it is difficult to maintain control of an army attacking in the dark. Even the highly disciplined British army of the time avoided night attacks for the same reason. Kitchener did send spies into the Dervish lines to spread rumours that he was about to attack and about the searchlights looking for the Khalifa. This served to put the Dervishes on edge and indeed the Khalifa's distinctive tent was taken down for this reason.

The charge of the 21st Lancers at Omdurman was indeed the last full charge by a British cavalry regiment and happened as I have described it. Michael Asher in his book 'Khartoum' gives far more detail about the action of individuals who rode in the charge. Churchill did use a Mauser pistol instead of a sabre, due to an old shoulder injury that made his sword arm weaker, and he believed that this saved his life that day.

The main battle of Omdurman took place as I have described it, with incredibly courageous charges by the various parts of the Dervish army. They continued to advance into extremely heavy fire when any European army would have retreated long ago. Most of these soldiers came from a warrior ethic that prized courage and honour above such mere trifles as money or possessions. They looked down on the Egyptian army as cowards and in that they were entirely wrong. The final attack on MacDonald's division came very close to succeeding and MacDonald himself must take a major share of the credit for holding his nerve and manoeuvring his battalions so well.

As Kitchener rode into the city of Omdurman he came closer to death than he had through the whole campaign when a shell from a British gunboat exploded above him. Hubert Howard the Times correspondent was in the Sirdar's party and was killed. The group beat a rapid retreat out of the city until word could be sent to the boats on the Nile that the city had fallen.

Kitchener did order the Mahdi's bones to be thrown into the Nile just as had happened to General Gordon's body, years before. There was debate about what to do with his skull which was eventually buried in a Muslim cemetery in an unmarked grave. The memorial service for Gordon did take place in the ruins of the governor's residence and was attended by elements from all parts of the army.

Three days after McGuire departed Khartoum, Kitchener was obliged to travel south to Fashoda to deal with a French expedition attempting to establish a claim on the White Nile.

The Fashoda Incident, as it became known, almost led to war between France and England and was prevented by careful diplomacy between the two commanders on the ground. McGuire was not involved so I have given no details.

Almost exactly a year after McGuire returned to Emma, on the 11th October 1899, the Boers of South Africa declared war on Britain. The British expected it to be a short sharp conflict that would be over by Christmas. Despite the lesson that had been taught by the Dervish army they were still underestimating colonial enemies and were to be taught another savage lesson by the Boer Commandoes. Troops were drawn from all parts of the army to sail south, to try and win the war, including units that were serving in Egypt. Command of the army was initially given to Sir Redvers Buller. The early weeks did not go well and he was replaced by Field Marshal Roberts with Major General Kitchener as his second in command. Kitchener naturally wanted people with him that he could rely on, so McGuire and the Reconnaissance Troop will ride again.

"I'll Take You Home Again, Kathleen" is well-known for being one of the most popular songs in the traditional Irish music ballad repertoire, but as it turns out, the song was not originally Irish. It was, in fact, written in 1875 by one Thomas Paine Westendorf, an American of German descent, for his wife, Jenny. The song was written as a "response" to (and thus in a similar style as) the song "Barney, Take Me Home Again," a popular song of the era.

Despite its origins, Westendorf struck a romantic chord in the hearts of some Irish music-lovers with his use of the popular Irish feminine name "Kathleen" as well as his use of poetic Irish-ish (for lack of a better term) language, all describing the wistful thoughts of home shared by so many immigrants, and the song quickly entered the repertoire of Irish folk singers on both sides of the Atlantic, as well as plenty of pop singers, including Elvis Presley. Nowadays, it's a Public Domain folk song.

Lyrics for I'll Take You Home Again Kathleen

I'll take you home again Kathleen across the ocean
wild and wide
To where your heart has ever been since first you
were my bonny bride
The roses all have left your cheek, I've watched
them fade away and die
Your voice is sad when e'er you speak and tears
bedim your loving eyes.

And I will take you back, Kathleen, to where your
heart will feel no pain
And when the fields are fresh and green, I will take
you to your home Kathleen.

I know you love me, Kathleen dear, your heart was
ever fond and true
I always fear when you are near, that life holds
nothing dear but you
The smiles that once you gave to me, I scarcely
ever see them now
Though many, many times I see, a darkening
shadow on your brow.

And I will take you back, Kathleen, to where your
heart will feel no pain
And when the fields are fresh and green, I will take
you to your home Kathleen.

To that dear home beyond the sea, my Kathleen
shall again return
And when thy old friends welcome thee, thy loving

heart will cease to yearn
Where laughs the little silver stream, beside your mother's humble cot
And brighter rays of sunshine gleam, there all your grief will be forgot.

And I will take you back, Kathleen, to where your heart will feel no pain
And when the fields are fresh and green, I will take you to your home Kathleen

Although probably not completely acceptable today, Rudyard Kipling expressed the respect that British troops gained for their enemies in the Sudan in the poem below. The tribes of the Sudan had been underestimated and they taught the British and Egyptian armies a salutary lesson. They were defeated eventually, but proved that even a modern well trained army needs to be careful when opposing people with a warrior ethic and considerable courage.

"Fuzzy Wuzzy"

Rudyard Kipling (1865 – 1936)

Soudan Expeditionary Force
WE 'VE fought with many men acrost the seas,
An' some of 'em was brave an' some was not,
The Paythan an' the Zulu an' Burmese;
But the Fuzzy was the finest o' the lot.
We never got a ha'porth's change of 'im:
'E squatted in the scrub an' 'ocked our 'orses,
'E cut our sentries up at Sua*kim,*
An' 'e played the cat an' banjo with our forces.
So 'ere 's *to* you, Fuzzy-Wuzzy,
at your 'ome in the Soudan;
You 're a pore benighted 'eathen
but a first-class fightin' man;
We gives you your certificate, an' if you want it signed
We 'll come an' 'ave a romp with you
whenever you 're inclined.
We took our chanst among the Kyber 'ills,
The Boers knocked us silly at a mile,

The Burman give us Irriwaddy chills,
An' a Zulu *impi* dished us up in style:
But all we ever got from such as they
Was pop to what the Fuzzy made us swaller;
We 'eld our bloomin' own, the papers say,
But man for man the Fuzzy knocked us 'oller.
    Then 'ere 's *to* you, Fuzzy-Wuzzy,
      an' the missis and the kid;
      Our orders was to break you,
      an' of course we went an' did.
    We sloshed you with Martinis,
      an' it was n't 'ardly fair;
      But for all the odds agin' you,
      Fuzzy-Wuz, you broke the square.
'E 'as n't got no papers of 'is own,
'E 'as n't got no medals nor rewards,
So we must certify the skill 'e 's shown
In usin' of 'is long two-'anded swords:
When 'e 's 'oppin' in an' out among the bush
With 'is coffin-'eaded shield an' shovel-spear,
    An 'appy day with Fuzzy on the rush
    Will last an 'ealthy Tommy for a year.
    So 'ere 's *to* you, Fuzzy-Wuzzy,
      an' your friends which are no more,
      If we 'ad n't lost some messmates we
      would 'elp you to deplore;
      But give an' take 's the gospel,
      an' we 'll call the bargain fair,
      For if you 'ave lost more than us,
      you crumpled up the square!
'E rushes at the smoke when we let drive,
An', before we know, 'e 's 'ackin' at our 'ead;
'E 's all 'ot sand an' ginger when alive,

An' 'e 's generally shammin' when 'e 's dead.
'E 's a daisy, 'e 's a ducky, 'e 's a lamb!
'E 's a injia-rubber idiot on the spree,
'E 's the on'y thing that does n't give a damn
For a Regiment o' British Infantree!
So 'ere 's *to* you, Fuzzy-Wuzzy,
at your 'ome in the Soudan;
You 're a pore benighted 'eathen
but a first-class fightin' man;
An' 'ere 's *to* you, Fuzzy-Wuzzy,
with your 'ayrick 'ead of 'air—
You big black boundin' beggar
for you broke a British square!

Other Books by this author

Drummer's Call
Revenge of a Lone Wolf

Simon Drummer is on loan to a bio-warfare protection unit in the USA when the terror they fear becomes real. A brilliant Arabic bio-chemist is driven to bring an end to the suffering of his countrymen. He believes that the regime that oppresses them could not exist without the support of the US government and the weapons they furnish. He needs to bring the truth to the American people in a way that will grab their attention. So begins his journey to bring brutal death and understanding to the USA. And now Simon must help to find him and stop him.

Also available as an Audiobook

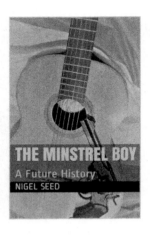

The Minstrel Boy
A Future History

Billy Murphy minds his own business and sings his songs in the pubs around Belfast. Then the IRA decides that he can be useful to them in preparing to restart the armed struggle for Irish unity. He finds himself caught up in their plots and learns the truth about the Troubles that he had never been told. But there are others who watch and take revenge for past atrocities. Billy must be careful not to come under suspicion and find his own life at risk from the terrorist killers he is working for.

The Jim Wilson Series

V4 – Vengeance
Hitler's Last Vengeance Weapons Are Going To War

Major Jim Wilson, late of the Royal Engineers, has been obliged to leave the rapidly shrinking British Army. He needs a job but they are thin on the ground even for a highly capable Army Officer. Then he is offered the chance to go to Northern Germany to search for the last great secret of World War 2, a hidden U Boat base. Once he unravels the mystery he is asked to help to spirit two submarines away from under the noses of the German government, to be the central exhibits in a Russian museum. But then the betrayal begins and a seventy year old horror unfolds.

Also available as an Audiobook

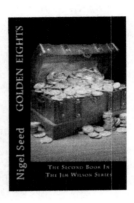

Golden Eights
The Search For Churchill's Lost Gold Begins
Again

In 1940, with the British army in disarray after the evacuation from Dunkirk, invasion seemed a very real possibility. As a precaution, the Government decided to protect the national gold reserves by sending most of the bullion to Canada on fast ships that ran the gauntlet of the U boat fleets. But a lot of gold bars and other treasures were hidden in England. In the fog of war, this treasure was lost. Now, finally, a clue has emerged that might lead to the hiding place. The Government needs the gold back if the country is not to plunge into a huge financial crisis. Major Jim Wilson has been tasked to find it. He and his small team start the search, unaware that there is a traitor watching their every move and intent on acquiring the gold, at any cost.

Also available as an Audiobook

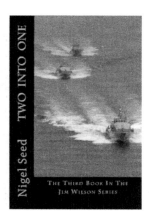

Two Into One
*A Prime Minister Acting Strangely and World
Peace in the Balance*

Following his return from Washington the Prime Minister's behaviour has changed. Based on his previous relationship with the PM, Major Jim Wilson is called in to investigate. What he finds is shocking and threatens the peace of the world. But now he must find a way to put things right and there is very little time to do it. His small team sets out on a dangerous quest that takes them from the hills of Cumbria to the Cayman Islands and Dubai, but others are watching and playing for high stakes.

Also available as an Audiobook

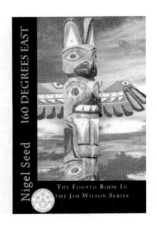

160 Degrees East

A fight for survival and the need to right a terrible wrong.

Major Jim Wilson and his two men are summoned at short notice to Downing Street. The US Government has a problem and they have asked for help from Wilson and his small team. Reluctantly Jim agrees, but he is unaware of the deceit and betrayal awaiting him from people he thought of as friends. From the wild hills of Wales to the frozen shores of Russia and on to the mountains of British Columbia Jim and his men have to fight to survive, to complete their mission and to right a terrible wrong.

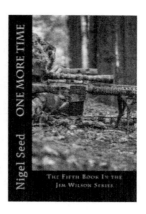

One More Time
A Nuclear Disaster Threatened By Criminals Must Be Prevented At All Costs

Jim and Ivan have retired from the Army and are making their way in civilian life when they are summoned back to the military by the new Prime Minister. Control of two hidden nuclear weapons has failed and they have been lost. Jim must find them before havoc is wreaked upon the world by whoever now controls them. It is soon apparent the problem is far bigger than originally envisaged, and there is a race against time to stop further weapons falling into the hands of an unscrupulous arms dealer and his beautiful daughter. The search moves from Zimbabwe to Belize and on to Norway and Spain, becoming ever more urgent and dangerous as the trail is followed.

Twelve Lives
A Threat to Millions But This Time It's Personal

During a highly classified mission for the British Government, Jim Wilson and his two companions make a dangerous enemy. A contract has been put on their lives and on those of their families. Jim moves the intended victims to safety and sets about trying to have the contract cancelled. However, his efforts to save his family uncover a horrendous plot to mount a nuclear terror attack on the United States and the race is on to save millions of lives.

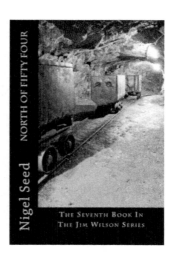

North of Fifty Four
A Crime Must Be Committed To Prevent A War

Jim Wilson is forced to work for a Chinese criminal gang or his wife and child will be murdered. While he is away in the north of Canada, his wife manages to contact Ivan and Geordie for help. The two friends set out to save all three of them, but then the threat to many more people emerges and things become important enough to involve governments in committing a serious crime to prevent a new war in the Middle East.

Short Stories

Backpack 19

Nigel Seed

A Lost Backpack and a World of Possibilities.

Backpack 19

A Lost Backpack and a World of Possibilities.

An anonymous backpack lying by the side of the road. Who picks it up and what do they find inside? There are many possibilities and lives may be changed for the better or worse. Here are just nineteen of those stories.

The Michael McGuire Trilogy

No Road to Khartoum

From the filthy back streets of Dublin to the deserts of the Sudan to fight and die for the British Empire.

Found guilty of stealing bread to feed his starving family, Michael McGuire is offered the "Queen's Hard Bargain", go to prison or join the Army. He chooses the Army and, after training in Dublin Castle, his life is changed forever as he is selected to join the 'Gordon Relief Expedition' that is being sent south of Egypt to Khartoum, in the Sudan.

Also available as an Audiobook

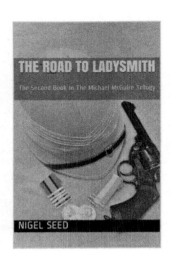

The Road to Ladysmith
*Only just recovered from his wounds Captain
McGuire must now sail south to the confusion and
error of the Boer War.*

After his return from the war in the Sudan,
McGuire had expected to spend time recovering
with his family. It was not to be, and his regiment
is called urgently to South Africa to counter the
threat from the Boers. Disparaged as mere farmers
the Boers were to administer a savage lesson to the
British Army.

Also available as an Audiobook

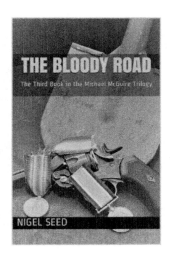

The Bloody Road

Michael McGuire has left the army, but as the First World War breaks out his country calls him again.

At the start of the war the British expand their army rapidly, but there is a shortage of experienced officers and McGuire is needed. He is sent to Gallipoli in command of an Australian battalion that suffers badly in that debacle. He stays with them when their bloody road takes them to the mud and carnage of the western front.

Also available as an Audiobook

The Thomas Mason Trilogy

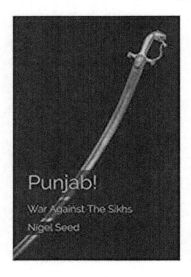

Punjab!

War Against the Sikhs

It is 1843 and to avoid the hangman's noose two brothers flee from England. The first available ship out of Liverpool takes them to India where they join the army of the East India Company. Even before they have finished basic training they are marched north to the Punjab to face the most professional native army in India – the Sikhs. The British will now face their most severe test in the sub-continent and the brothers must stand in the firing lines to survive.

Crimea!

War Against the Russians

1854. Thomas Mason has returned from India where he served in the East India Company Army throughout the First and Second Anglo-Sikh wars. He and three companions returned to England as the guard detail for the Koh-i-Nor diamond and were then offered the chance to join the Rifle Brigade with their officer Lieutenant Warren. All of them have agreed, but had to return to basic training to learn the ways of their new regiment. In India, Thomas rose to Corporal, but must now return to the bottom of the rank ladder. It remains to be seen whether their wartime experience in India will serve them well in the Regular Army in Britain. Their lives are suddenly turned exciting when Britain and France declare war on Russia and the Brigade is sent to the blood and confusion of the Crimea. Here he will see a very different war to the one he saw in India with the massive incompetence of British senior, aristocratic officers and the weakness of the army's support system that led to massive neglect and suffering for the troops.

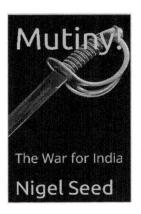

Mutiny!
The War for India

The Rifle Brigade has returned to England from the Crimea to lick its wounds and to be brought back up to strength. Now the Sepoys of the East India Company, loyal for so long, have mutinied and the regular British army is sent south to save the jewel of the empire from chaos and slaughter and to restore British rule.

Photograph "Courtesy of Grupo Bernabé" of Pontevedra.

<u>Nigel Seed</u>

Born in Morecambe, England, into a military family, Nigel Seed grew up hearing his father's tales of adventure during the Second World War which kindled his interest in military history and storytelling.

He received a patchy education, as he and his family followed service postings from one base to another. Perhaps this and the need to constantly change schools contributed to his odd ability to link unconnected facts and events to weave his stories.

Nigel later joined the Army, serving with the Royal Electrical and Mechanical Engineers in many parts of the world. Upon leaving he joined the Ministry of Defence during which time he formed strong links with overseas armed forces, including the USAF, and cooperated with them, particularly in support of the AWACS aircraft.

He is married and lives in Spain; half way up a mountain with views across orange groves to the Mediterranean. The warmer weather helps him to cope with frostbite injuries he sustained in Canada, when taking part in the rescue effort for a downed helicopter on a frozen lake.

His early books are inspired by places he has been to and true events he has either experienced or heard about on his travels. He makes a point of including family jokes and stories in his books to raise a secret smile or two. Family dogs make appearances in some of his stories. Nigel's hobbies include sailing and when sailing in the Baltic he first heard the legend of the hidden U-Boat base that formed the basis of his first book (V4 Vengeance) some thirty eight years later.

If you have enjoyed this book a review on Amazon.com
would be very welcome.

Please visit my website at www.nigelseedauthor.com for
information about upcoming books.

Printed in Great Britain
by Amazon

84131550R00261